PENNYBLADE

PENNYBLADE

EXILE. MERCENARY. LOVER. MONSTER.

J. L. WORRAD

TITAN BOOKS

Pennyblade
Print edition ISBN: 9781789097610
E-book edition ISBN: 9781789097627

Published by Titan Books
A division of Titan Publishing Group Ltd
144 Southwark Street, London SE1 0UP
www.titanbooks.com

First edition: March 2022
10 9 8 7 6 5 4 3 2 1

A CIP catalogue record for this title is available from
the British Library.

Printed and bound by CPI Group (UK) Ltd, Croydon, CR0 4YY

For Matt, who bears some responsibility.

PART ONE

1

I stumbled along the dirt path with a bag over my head. I thought of you, Shen; strange that I should think of you.

'Easy, girl,' the innkeep said, hands tight on my shoulders.

April-sharp air in my nostrils. Boots sinking, slipping in the mud.

I thought I'd see more through the hessian blindfold, but the light that bled through only dazzled my eyes. The long dress they'd made me wear hindered my stride.

'Easy now…'

'Shut up,' I hissed.

'Easy.'

'I said put a cock in it.'

The innkeep shut up. Peasant.

Clearly, I was drunker than I thought. Not *drunk* drunk, but subject to that weathering of sobriety that only three whole days spent in an inn can procure. By the second night none of us thought this Rossley arse would ever show up.

Awful plan. Awful.

I smelled rain-soaked wood. Fresh-cut. We'd entered the

timber yard.

'What's that?' a man ahead of us shouted. Rossley, I assumed.

'I can explain!' the innkeep shouted next to me.

I tensed, half expecting an arrow in the belly. None came.

'That's not the girl.' The voice was more refined than I'd expected.

An ox lowed nearby.

'Girl ran,' the innkeep said. I knew we were close now.

'Bloody find her then,' the voice said.

We halted.

'She ran, sir,' the innkeep replied. 'Swear.'

'Then I'll have my money, eh?'

Rossley was right before me. I smelled perfume, lavender and spikenard, heard the fabric of his clothes as he made some gesture.

The innkeep sniffed. His fingers tightened on my shoulders.

'Thought this might do.'

The bag came off. Noon blinded me. A man's silhouette loomed, its head shaped like a mushroom. Presumably a bad haircut. My eyes watered and I pretended to sob.

'Pilgrim's mercy,' the man muttered. 'This is…'

'Real beauty, in't she?' the innkeep said.

'She's—'

'But see the comely olive skin, sir. Her hair like raven's wi—'

'End the sonnet, you arse. She's a fucking sprite!'

Awful plan. Awful.

Ah, but, Shen, I get ahead of myself, to the tune of an hour or more. Forever rash, you and I, do you recall? Our shared fault.

She smelled of violets and yeast, the innkeep's wife, and in the cellar's gloom I seized my chance. I pressed against her back as she stood over a barrel, slipped my arms around her waist. My face was in her blonde hair, my lips upon her neck.

'Turn around,' I told her. Blood pulsed in me, as it did whenever I drove steel into flesh. 'Taste my lips.'

She shivered. 'Wouldn't be… right.'

'I'll tell you what isn't right,' I said, licking her neck, sucking her earlobe. 'Your boredom.' I reached up, seized her tits and rubbed them. Classic human dugs: formidable and heaving. Way I like them. 'I want to wake you. I want you to *bloom*…'

She pressed her wide arse into my crotch.

'Devilry,' she muttered. 'Pure devilry.' Oh, I had her now. The sky-madness was always their last defence. 'Perverse. Uh, twice perverse.'

'Surely we can beat twice,' I whispered. 'If we really try…'

She turned around. The afternoon light, peering in from the half-open coal scuttle – the only light in the cellar – caught her face like a pale mask. She was good for her years, with a plumpness to her cheeks that lent youth. Wide brown eyes. She placed her hand against my face, and I kissed her palm, made passionate eyes. She stroked the sharp of my ear, the pointed tip. Humans always do for some reason.

I feigned ecstasy.

'One kiss,' I whispered. 'One.' I leaned in.

My lips pressed to hers. So gentle. I lashed the tip of my tongue over her upper lip, then left one little secondary kiss and pulled back.

'How was that?' I asked her.

'Tastes like strawberry.' She touched her lips. 'An' it *tingles*…'

I raised an eyebrow. 'And merely your mouth.'

Her face fell blank. She stared at me.

'Alright, fae-wench,' she said. She sat down on the barrel and lifted her skirts. 'Stoop.'

'Well, since you insist.'

I got down on my knees.

Someone banged on the door to the cellar.

'Kyra!' Young Ned's voice behind the thick – and locked – timber door. 'Kyra! It's on!'

I screwed up my eyes.

'Me husband's back,' the innkeep's wife said. She stood up and stroked down her skirts.

I got to my feet. 'Alright, Ned!' I shouted at the door. I looked at my intended. 'Tonight then? I *need* you.'

'No,' she said. ''Tis devilry, woman.'

She barged past me and was already up the stairs to the inn. She opened the door and barged right past Ned too.

'She alright?' he asked me.

'What is it?' I strode to the bottom of the stairs and gazed up at the young man. All lank hair and pimples, Ned. Wet puppy eyes above a donkey nose.

'Rossley's arrived at the timber yard,' he answered. 'He's waiting.'

I shook my head and sighed. Three nights in this bleak shithole, and this Rossley arse elects to shamble into the village just as I'm promised a helping of tongue purse. He was more than another mark now. Oh, he was my nemesis – at least for today.

Ned headed back to the barroom. I stretched, shook my head, then noticed an earthenware bottle of wine sat in a nook below the stone stairs. I brightened. A drop of that would see me right, lend me some moral fibre for the coming fiasco.

Frankly, the inn had been irresponsible not to offer me a preparatory nip.

The nook reeked of a hundred dead candles and possessed a dusty layer of melted tallow speckled with blackened wicks. I had to prise the bottle free of the wax with a deft twist. I pulled out the cork and a stink – half sour milk and half piss – assaulted my nostrils. I popped the cork back before I retched and spat on the floor. What a shithole village.

Something else on the ledge caught my eye: a fist-sized object I could not discern in the gloom. I picked the thing up and held it up to what light there was.

A human figure, crafted from the same earthenware as the bottle. Crude in aspect, cruder than even the majority of human art. It had two tiny arms that grasped at its own pot belly. Two legs, backward-kneed and hoofed like a goat. The artist had taken great pains with the prick, which was ornate in its rigidity, a veiny spike amid a whirl of pubes. Yet it was the figure's head that drew me – someone had bound it in coarse yarn, tight to the skull. Empty divots gouged out of the yarn were the creature's eyes and mouth. The masked face had a vile grin, as if holding back the punchline of some cruel joke.

I put the bottle and the figurine back. It was the sort of rustic fuckery I'd come to expect from the more inbred enclaves of Hosshire, and experience told me searching for reasons would only procure the most imbecilic, depressing and dribble-flecked answers.

Speaking of which…

I climbed the steps to the barroom to be greeted by Ned and two other faces I'd tired of. First the innkeep, newly returned from the timber yard, grey hair wild as briar and his expression a very lighthouse of ignorance. He clearly had not figured out

I'd tried to swive his wife. They never did.

Shortleg, by the bar, tankard in hand, smiled knowingly. At least his plump whore wasn't about. Likely she was wasting our ever-depleting kitty elsewhere.

'Bad news,' the innkeep said. He was stood by the front door. 'He's three men this time.'

'Three? You said he always has one.'

'He *does* always have one.'

I waved a finger at him. 'That's another forty pips, right there. Twenty a head.'

'We ain't got forty pip'strells,' he said.

'You have or we walk.'

'Kyra, love,' Shortleg said, putting his tankard down and waving a gloved hand. Big ugly fat bastard, Shortleg, top of his skull like dying scrubland. 'C'mon. For me. For, you know, the public good and that.'

Shortleg hailed from Tettleby, or thereabouts. Probably knew the girls' parents. Frankly, my public spirit was weak as the innkeep's fucking beer. But Shortleg's loyalty was... useful, I suppose.

'Thirty,' I uttered with finality. Last night I'd noticed the hook-shaped patch above the bar. These God-fearing rustics had even sold their symbols of the Church. You can't squeeze them for much more after that.

'If three men's too much...' the innkeep's wife said from behind the bar.

'I said I'll do it.' By the Blood, she was shaming my valour already. The nerve of the woman.

Coward! Fucking coward. The memory came, sudden and clear as shattering glass. Your words, Shen, barked at me in a wrecked market square, four years past. The fresh morning, the onyx towers of the city, the way I'd turned and laughed in your face. Your blood-stained forehead and wild red hair. The moon follows the sun, Shen, and a memory of you as assuredly follows whenever I try to fuck a woman. Sooner or later.

I was staring at the tiled floor. A silence had filled the barroom. An uncertainty.

'What were you doing downstairs?' I heard the innkeep ask his wife.

'Shifting a barrel,' I told him, looking up.

Shortleg drank from his tankard to hide his grin.

'Ned,' I said. 'Where's that dress?'

He brought it over as I unbuckled my long jacket and threw it on a table. The dress was white, long-sleeved and muslin. Humans have a custom for their men in one kind of finery, their women in another. Why is anyone's guess. I'd gained a taste for dresses on a girl in my four years on the Main, but not for wearing them.

'Awful plan,' I said. 'Should have let me plan.'

'It'll work,' Shortleg, our gambit's originator, insisted. 'You'll have a bag on your head.'

'I'm pretty tall for a ten-year-old, don't you think?'

'I've seen ten-year-olds your height,' Ned said, still holding the dress.

'Aye,' Shortleg said. 'But it dun't matter because you're not—'

'Shortleg,' I said. 'I've tits, you bollock.'

'You're not *meant* to be ten,' Shortleg said, like I was the idiot. 'That's not the plan. We *tell* him Tettleby's outta sprogs.'

'Shortleg—'

'Every man wants to fuck an elf slag, Kyra. Ain't a man on the Main ain't pulled his plank over that notion.' He nodded, sipped his beer. 'Well, 'cept arse-bandits…'

'They'd think about elf cock,' the innkeep added helpfully.

Shortleg gave him a look of disgust and disappointment, a common reaction to such things on the mainland. 'Cheers for clarifying.' He turned and casually gestured for me to get a move on.

I glared at him, snatched the dress off Ned and worked it over my vest and trousers. 'Most humans haven't even seen my kind.'

Shortleg laughed. 'You're pretty, Kyra, elf-pretty. Nice face. Nice body. He'll take.'

'Shouldn't say "elf",' Ned told the room. 'Sprite neither. They don't like it. She's a come-rat.'

'Commrach,' I corrected him. I took a deep breath. 'Sorry, Ned. And... thank you.'

'S'alright.'

'Right,' I said, trying to muster what remained of the de facto command I usually enjoyed, despite the dress. 'Ned. Short. Get going.'

'Me beer...' Shortleg said.

'Take it with you. Circle the timber yard on either side, one left, one right. Stay hidden.'

'Don't tell me me plan,' Shortleg said.

'You know the exact shed right?' I asked.

'Course,' Shortleg said.

'Course,' Ned said.

'Because it's a big timber yard. More than one shed.' I stared at them both. 'Right?'

'Course,' they replied in unison.

Such allies. How I'd come down in the world.

My eyes had adjusted to the daylight. Rossley's bellend head was, indeed, a centre parting of blond that clutched tight to his crown and sprung up at the ends. His eyes were classic piggy-squinters, his moustache a piss-soaked string: yellow and foetid. Behind him and all about rose dark piles of felled trees.

'We ain't got no gold, sir,' the innkeep said. 'And, as I say, the girl ran. So I thought this might show Tettleby's good faith like.'

'Can you believe this, gentlemen?' Rossley said.

I sneaked a look around. Rossley was well turned out: yellow jacket, quality dye. No blade. A pleasing eccentricity.

At his right stood a man with a tattoo on either cheek: goat's eyes below his actual pair. A falchion at his belt; a human weapon, half-sword, half-cleaver. To Rossley's left stood an ox and cart. Nothing on it save a lump under a tarpaulin. Two shitkickers – straw-haired like most humans of the Main – stood before the cart's wheel. They'd homemade longknives in cloth scabbards, the sword choice of scum. All three pennyblades shook their head in answer to Rossley's question.

I'd seen this setup before: the money, the paid iron, the iron's two gormless friends. Remove the first two and your job's done. Likely Ned, with his bow, had figured that too.

'You think this is what I like, yes?' Rossley asked the innkeep.

'Different,' the innkeep said. 'You're…'

'I'm what? A degenerate?'

'Refined.'

'Wetting my length in a soulless abomination? You call that refinement?' Oh, he would definitely have me stabbed, if only for emphasis. 'This is respect in Tettleby, hmm? Throw your guests a bloody caliban?'

'I'm not a caliban,' I muttered, before I could stop myself. Pixie I'd take. Elf even. Not that.

He slapped me. I bent over with the stinging pain. My eyes watered and I moaned. I drew it out into the most pitiful mewl.

'Please…' I begged.

I saw Rossley's stance change, hiding a growing root. Probably. I mean, fuck, I'm no expert.

He grabbed my chin and looked in my eyes.

'I suppose there is something,' he said. 'A fine face, youthful complexion.'

'Pale bronze like summer's honey,' the innkeep added, ever the fucking poet. 'And those eyes like polished amethyst…'

Evidently Shortleg had been right about all men's imp fetish.

'Please don't hurt me,' I said, trying to sound my most pitiful. An ugly sort of bait, but they're like that, the human men.

'Come along,' Rossley said.

The innkeep let go and I followed.

Rossley stopped. 'Binds,' he said to Goat-Eyes.

Goat-Eyes pulled out thin cord handcuffs and bound my wrists. We had not planned for this. He grinned and his breath smelled of onions. At least he hadn't bound my wrists behind my back.

'If she isn't pure,' Rossley said to the innkeep, 'I'll know.'

The shed lay atop a small muddy rise forty feet behind where Rossley stood. Where he took those girls. Where he fucked them, threw them aside like old fruit and plucked the next. Because he had money. Because money bought blades. Pennyblades.

Piles of logs rose either side of us, thirty feet high. Ned up on one pile, Shortleg behind the other, in theory. I couldn't see them. I didn't dare look up.

Rossley didn't hold me as we walked. He followed, steps behind, like a servant wary of his mistress's appointments, urging her on politely. He hadn't checked me over, the fool.

Blood, I could have carried a dagger all the way.

I'd still do my part, despite bound wrists. He was large, but only his money lent him iron, as the Hosshire folk say. Whereas I…

Well, the commrach word for youth meant 'blade', for we are taught to wield one the moment we can walk. I was twenty-three now. Count the days.

But were my boys ready? I didn't put it past them to have got lost in this yard and its labyrinth of dead wood. The innkeep had said the forests around Tettleby had bear traps. For all I knew they might be screaming their balls off betwixt iron jaws.

Five steps led up the rise to the shed.

'Punishment awaits,' Rossley said.

I thought that very perceptive.

Not even a door, just a length of sackcloth that hung from hooks. He pushed it back and ushered me in.

I knew the layout of the shed, the position of my weapons. A stiletto under the stained and sheetless bed by the wall: for the gutting. My rapier, that love of my life, sat in the tool pantry next to the doorway. That would be for sweeping the last of the scum outside, should my colleagues be tardy.

The little man lying on the bed was new though. He looked up, a wide-brimmed hat obscuring his features so I could only make out his beard. An empty goatskin sat atop his pot belly. He reeked of cider.

'Who the hell are you?' Rossley demanded.

'Work here,' the man said, high-pitched and slurred. 'Who the—'

'Robert Rossley.'

The man had clearly heard of him. He stumbled to his feet, goatskin in hand.

'Soz, pal,' he said in a high croaky voice. 'I were having a clean-up…'

'Commendable,' Rossley said. 'Now fuck off.'

'Soz.' The man stumbled past us, head bowed and face obscured.

Rossley breathed out. 'Despicable.'

I pretended to break down. I fell to my knees then dropped on my left side. I flailed my arms up and down in feigned terror, my hands searching under the bed.

My stiletto was gone.

Rossley grabbed my shoulders and lifted me up. Stronger than he looked, and I was nothing without a blade. That damned drunk: he really *had* cleaned up. Hocked my knife for cider.

Rossley threw me face-down on the bed. My tied hands lay under my collarbone, my knees on the dirty floor. My arse in the air, albeit beneath skirt and trousers. I heard Rossley groan low.

Fear hadn't kicked in. I wouldn't let this sad sack of shit humiliate me, couldn't think like that. Had to buy time till the boys turned up.

'Show me your prick,' I said.

'What?'

I started humping the bed. I made scandalous faces.

'Stop it,' Rossley said, his chin quivering and his brow furrowed. 'That's… stop it.'

I ceased my humping and looked him in the eyes. 'I'm experienced, Rossley. I'll *teach* you things.' I licked my incisors. 'Pixie things.'

Face of a child, Rossley. A terrified boy behind a ridiculous moustache.

'Liar,' he barked. 'Liar! You're a virgin, you whore. You bloody fairy-maiden-witch!'

'Show us your broomstick.' I giggled. 'I'll ride through the night!'

That did for him. He looked around the room.

'Beat you,' he said. 'B-beat…'

He turned to look in the tool pantry. I pushed myself off the bed and leapt at him. We commrach are fast, nimble as hares. I slipped my leather bind over his head, pulled my wrists back tight. He gurgled, groaned, his hands clawing at me. I drove my boot into his spine and held it there.

Not my skill set. I'd never strangled anyone in my life.

It showed. Rossley grabbed my fists and it took all my strength to keep them there. He lumbered sideways, threw himself at the wall before the pantry doorway. My shoulder hit timber and I yelled.

No great mind, Rossley. I'd have lurched for the tool pantry, found something sharp, but he chose instead to run out of the shed. He stumbled through sackcloth and into daylight, me on his back. He tripped, fell face first on the steps and I fell atop him. Something cracked. Rossley stopped moving.

I looked up. His men were forty yards away, all of them alive, untouched by Ned or Shortleg. Staring at the virginal faerie maiden with a garrotte around their dead boss's neck.

I stared back.

Goat-Eyes drew his sword.

I lifted Rossley's big head and worked the leather cord over it, freeing myself if not my hands.

Goat-Eyes was strutting over.

I ran, back into the shed and into the pantry.

There: the swept hilt and the black blade, the patterns of silver. All of it a-piece, beauty made metal, elegance forged.

My rapier. Forty inches of death.

I pulled it out from behind a crate. Hilt in my right hand, left hand tethered to right, I ran out again.

Goat-Eyes made to grab me.

I leapt away, then retreated three paces along the rise and pointed my blade at him.

'Shh, hen,' he said, no anger on his tattooed face. He had a thick Ralbride accent. 'Wha's tha' ye got, hen?' He laughed. His ugly blade waited in his hand. 'Knitting needle, is it?'

Like most humans, he'd never seen a rapier before. Savage.

His two blond friends waited at the bottom of the rise, their longknives drawn, ready to gut me if I made to run.

'Put it doon, hen,' he said, smiling. He stepped forward, soft as a panther. 'Won't warn ya twi—'

Three jabs to his heart. He didn't even lift his blade. Goat-Eyes looked at me like I'd tumbled his sister, then he fell forward.

I drove my rapier's point into his spine. He shuddered. I dropped to my knees, threw my wrists over the freestanding hilt and sliced the leather binds on the eight inches of sharp at the point. I stood up and pulled the rapier out. Blood pooled in the rain-turned mud, I could smell it.

I looked down on the two shitkickers waiting at the bottom of the rise. I swung my rapier through the air and the steel sang. It sprayed red droplets, the silver glyphs along its length stretching and warping and dancing as I worked the hilt. Commrach steel. Sorcerous alloy.

I bared my teeth – such dainty razors – and hissed. I'd make a pretty monster in their tales to their grandkids, I thought.

They ran.

They made thirty yards before an arrow hit the rearmost one in the neck. From the opposite direction came Shortleg,

barrelling along. He lifted his axe high and brought it down on
the fallen man. The other man kept running.

I leaped down from the muddy rise and strutted toward
Shortleg.

'Nice work, love,' he told me. He grinned.

I swung my rapier at him like I was swinging a club. Not to
kill, yet more than enough to scare.

'Donkeyfucker!' I yelled. I swung again and again. 'Feckless
bull-buggering arsehole!'

'Oi!' He stumbled back.

'Where were you? Where fucking were you? Have you *any*
idea, I...'

The anger went out of me. I was breathing too fast and I
began to shake.

'Sorry,' he said with a shamefaced smile. 'Wrong shed.'

I wiped my brow, took deep breaths. I'd only been on the
Main four years and, despite one close call in the first week, I still
hadn't absorbed the powerful danger of human men, that they
could do what Rossley did. I wouldn't have partaken in such a
remorselessly stupid plan if I had.

I heard a scuffle behind me, and turned to see the innkeep
kicking the shit out of Rossley's corpse and swearing. I looked
back at Shortleg.

Shortleg shrugged. 'He's paying. Can do what he likes.'

I nodded, my hands shaking. I tried to sheathe my sword and
remembered the scabbard was back in the shed.

Ned came around some timber with his bow in hand. He
took one look at me and knew not to say anything. Wise for
his years.

'Time to divvy up,' Shortleg told him. He was already bent
over, checking the nearest corpse.

'Rossley and his big bastard are mine,' I said. 'No arguments.'

'What about the cart?' Ned asked.

I'd forgotten about that.

The three of us walked over to it. The ox ignored us, blithe to the slaughter of its owners. We walked around the back of the cart. The tarpaulin, with its head-sized lump, lay on the cart's flatbed. Ned looked at me and, when I nodded, pulled the tarpaulin off.

A square lump of dried clay, ripples all down its sides.

'What's that?' Ned said.

'Aww fuck,' Shortleg said.

'Look at the top, Ned,' I said. I shuddered.

'There's a seal,' Ned said. 'A crown.'

'Tax money, Ned,' I told him. 'Sealed in clay.'

His mouth fell wide. 'We'll hang...'

'Hey!' Shortleg shouted at the innkeep. 'Whyn't you tell us he were a tax man?'

Apparently satisfied with kicking cadavers, the innkeep walked toward us.

'Thought you knew,' he said.

'What?'

'You're from round here, Shortleg. Everyone round here knows Rossley.'

'I ain't been here for years,' Shortleg said. 'I hadn't a frigging clue, pal.'

The innkeep shook his head. 'No wonder you lot were cheap.'

'Twat!' Shortleg snapped. 'Dun't *believe* this.'

The point of my rapier went under the innkeep's chin.

'You're with us in this,' I told him. 'Don't think we won't point the finger. You're the ringleader.' I spat at the ground. 'The brains.'

'I know,' he said, terrified. 'I'm ready for that.' He winced. 'I couldn't take that bastard no more. None of us could. Whole village.' He collected himself. 'Go get your stuff from mine. Get moving. I'll clean up here.'

I lowered my blade. No one said anything.

'What about the one that run?' Ned said eventually.

No one spoke.

'What do we do?' Ned said. 'Kyra? What do we do?'

'We take the money.'

'But it's the *Crown's*.'

I shrugged.

'We'll hang for Rossley. Can the rope bite worse for taking his gold?'

2

'We'll miss the parade, Kyran,' I said to my brother as I watched the less-than-heaving crowds sixteen floors below my open window. They were being made to split either side of the street in readiness for the Shame Parade. The evening was warm and my own freshly dabbed perfume filled my nostrils: jasmine and lily. I was eager to get out there. To be seen.

'Kyra my dear,' he replied, 'one cannot rush the fucking immaculate.'

I didn't look back at him. He'd only be gawping in his long mirror on the other side of his boudoir, all fuss and eyeliner and combs. I straightened my black longjacket and checked my nails. Satisfied, I gazed down upon the basalt paved street once more.

The crowd wore their festival masks, all identical in shape if not material, and from this height – and beneath the silver glow of a hundred hanging moontiles – the face of every citizen was a shining blank. The many roofs of our district rose above them, and beyond those roofs, right out to the horizon, stood the towers of the other families, lithe columns of onyx and wrought iron terminating in bulbous spires. From our tower, I had a perfect view.

'You'll be wearing a mask,' I told Kyran. 'Why dally over rouge and powder? It'll be a mask beneath a mask.'

'Good,' he replied, his lips half-still as he applied something. 'One can never have too many.'

'Sirs,' came a familiar voice from the boudoir's doorway.

I turned to see 'Slow' Thezda Sil'Thezda, her twin silver monocles glinting beneath the light of the moontile chandelier above. A year older than us, Thezda was a bondswoman to the Cal'Adras. Her family had protected ours for generations.

'Thezda?' I said.

Thezda made a languid gesture to the corridor behind her.

'Masks,' she explained. Thezda had a certain way, eschewing all unnecessary words or movements. Her rapier style was infamously as lean.

I nodded, and Thezda ushered in a lowblood servant holding a tray with mine and my brother's masks upon it. The servant boy wore a rabbit mask of lacquered pine. All the lowblood castes wore animal masks during the Festival of Youth. Rabbits, deer, fish: all the hunted creatures.

I permitted the boy to approach and took my mask from his platter. It was an abstract rendition of the ideal commrach face, as predicted by our natural philosophers, the Explainers, and strived toward by their breeding programme.

The Final Countenance: perfectly symmetrical, androgynous, beautiful in that way that's hard to recall once you cease looking at it. I'd seen that face all my life. In truth, I was more intrigued by my own reflection caught in the mask's silver leaf surface. *By the Blood*, I thought, *I'm so pretty it's a scandal.*

As was my twin brother Kyran, his face as close to mine as to be almost identical. He was away from his standing mirror now, his ritual of fuss complete. He stood beside me and took his own mask from the platter. It was exactly the same as mine. As all the highbloods'. He hung it around his neck.

'I see no difference,' I said to him, pointing at the cosmetics on his face. He'd done his thing of adding and removing to no good end. I knew his ways.

'Of course not,' Kyran replied. 'You've no eye for the sublime.' He laughed and rubbed my mop of black hair, the same style as his own. 'Now *do* come along, Ra-ra. We'll miss the parade.'

We made our way down our tower's wide and curling stairwell of onyx, Thezda two steps behind us. We passed black-and-white frescoes recalling our family's greatest deeds, sinuous figures moving through landscapes of brushwork and pattern, languid beneath ink-black stars.

'It's not the usual cretin this year,' Kyran said, referring to the parade. 'I suppose he must have died.'

'Good,' I said. 'The fewer Roshos the better.' I rested my palm upon the pommel of my rapier. I would look fine, posed like that. The women in the crowd would love it.

'It's some young man now,' Kyran said. 'They say he's been bawling from the moment he got off the ship.'

'Nice,' I replied. 'Mother would have liked that little detail.'

'Yes.' He looked at me and we both smiled. 'I do believe she would have.'

We passed by slit windows as we descended, the sound of harps and chatter rising as we did so. Odd to think the Roshos once had a tower such as this, similarly daubed with their own family's triumphs, all forgotten now. They had been Cal'Rosho back then. An act of incompetence had torn the 'Cal' from their name and brought them exile. It had also, in a roundabout way, taken our mother.

'Why do we let them live?' I said, surprising myself. 'Each year they send someone to be humiliated and we send them back.' I shook my head. 'By the Blood, why didn't we just kill them all from the first?'

Kyran descended more quickly, though only a touch. 'We do not have a say in the matter.'

'Not *us*, Ran-ran,' I replied. 'I mean all the tower-families and the Explainers and, well, our entire Isle.' When my brother made no answer, I looked over my shoulder at Thezda. 'Do you know? Answer me, Thezda.'

Requests for opinion always discomforted our bondswoman. I got a mean sort of joy from making them.

'Explainers,' she answered with a shrug. 'Their decree.'

'Then they were too soft,' I said, more to Kyran than Thezda. 'We all are. The Rosho's high breeding shouldn't protect them. We should have slain them all, from cot to cane.'

'That's anger talking,' Kyran said.

'Common sense,' I replied.

Kyran snorted. 'How often the former masquerades as the latter.' He shook a pointed finger. 'I'll tell you both why we send their offering back home each year: death would be a release. An honour even. Humiliation is the greater punishment. Rather obvious when one thinks of it.' He looked at me and grinned. 'Do try and catch up, eh?'

His smugness vanished when he saw Grandmother stood on the chequered floor of the entrance hall, her guards flanking her. She glared at us hawkishly, an image only enriched by her hands, with their talon jewellery, resting on her walking cane like a bird of prey's feet.

The three of us stopped upon the stairs, uncertain.

'Don't just stand there,' Grandmother rasped. 'You're late enough as it is.' She sneered. 'Dissolute toads.'

Kyran coughed, then waved a hand and carried on walking down the black stone stairs, me in tow.

'Our apologies, Grandmother,' Kyran said. 'We're—'

'Late,' Grandmother said, finishing his sentence.

If only you *were*, I thought. I did not voice it. She had had me caned for less.

The three of us crossed the hall. Along the walls the pewter statues gleamed in their alcoves. They had been freshly imbued, and even now a few servants were caressing the figurines, drawing out the pewter's vitality and the sculptor's passion.

I glanced at the sculptures so as not to meet Grandmother's eyes. Maudlin youths and dancing maidens, all bright and alive though never moving, at least not when one looked at them directly. Yet I could not ignore my fate forever. Grandmother awaited me on the other side of the onyx and marble floor like some particularly mean-faced cliff. All confidence and joy would dash against her rock.

Age had not enfeebled our grandmother like others of her years, though it had sucked the flesh from her skeleton and hunched her shoulders and spine. Her cheekbones were knives beneath leather, her eyes embers in sunken pits. Her hair – currently up in a dated style resembling a stunted peacock tail – was black save for a vicious streak of white to one side of her crown.

'Stand up straight, the pair of you,' she said.

You first, Grandmother, I thought.

Her cane moved, swift and sudden, and I flinched – for a second, I genuinely panicked that she could read my mind – yet it did not hit me; it tapped Slow Thezda's right monocle. A tap, yes, but it must have pained the piercings that held the silver lens in place.

'You're a dullard as well as half-blind,' Grandmother told her. 'Make sure the twins don't dally in future.'

'I will, sir,' Thezda said. 'Apologies, sir.'

'You had better be more astute when you guard me tomorrow.'

'Yes, sir.'

Grandmother turned her attention to Kyran and me.

'Comport yourself when you step outside,' she told Kyran. 'None of your gesticulations.' She turned to me. 'Try not to molest every female creature in the street. At least until the parade has passed, eh?'

I said nothing, my face a rigid blank like the mask hanging from my neck.

With brass-clawed fingers she lifted Kyran's from his chest and inspected it.

'The Final Countenance,' she said. The flint vanished from her eyes and a softness, of a kind, replaced it. No: an awe. 'The Blood passes through us, children. It has passed through me and it has passed through your parents.' Her breeding talk. Neither I nor my brother had enthusiasm for breeding, indeed we feared our birth-ordained purpose. No mate selected for us could ever please our tastes. 'This is your generation's time,' Grandmother reminded us. 'A tiny increment on the climb to perfection, but vital. The Festival of Youth is for you, so that you might appreciate these truths.'

'A highblood must reach for perfection in all things,' Kyran said, repeating the old adage, 'or fall.'

'Good, good,' Grandmother purred, and she let the mask rest on Kyran's chest once more. 'Let the family Rosho be a lesson.' She gestured at the threshold to the street behind her with her cane.

'We will savour this particular Rosho's humiliation,' Kyran said. 'When he passes before us.' He grinned.

'Idiot,' Grandmother said. 'Savouring humiliation is for the masses. Fodder for stunted tastes.'

'We were just talking about that,' I said. Grandmother didn't look at me, but I continued regardless. 'Kyran believes the Roshos are continually spared because humiliation is crueller than death whereas I...' I searched for the words that would gain her approval or, failing that, lessen her scorn.

'Dear sister believes,' Kyran cut in, 'we spare the Roshos because we're all too soft.'

'In this modern age,' I added quickly, hoping to assuage Grandmother's traditionalism. I always hated the way I tried to please her, yet there it was again. A survival instinct perhaps.

'You're both wrong,' Grandmother said. Surprisingly, there was no venom in her words. 'But the day you finally comprehend why we let the Roshos live will be the day you're fit to rule the family Cal'Adra.' She leaned in a little. 'It is a truth best not dangled before the lower-blooded mob. And the charade of public humiliation does much to hide it.'

'Yet another mask,' I noted.

Grandmother glared at me and for a moment I thought I would meet her cane. Instead, she turned around and headed for the double doors that led to the street.

'The Shame Parade approaches,' she said aloud to the hall. 'Take up your countenance.'

We stepped out onto the stairs of our tower and were instantly noticed. The modest crowd were young and of the higher castes, Cals and Sils and Marns, those of a blood permitted to wear masks of the Final Countenance. They waved at us, each a perfect metallic face, silver and brass and bereft of expression.

My vision limited by the eyeholes, I turned to look at my brother. He was waving a hand high in the air, languid as a willow branch, his mask sparkling from the lunar glare of the many moontiles festooning the tops of posts along the street. Corso city turned silver and black at night, illuminated by those tiny clay replicas of the moon.

Grandmother's bejewelled hand was upon Kyran's shoulder. I felt nothing on mine. I supposed her other hand had to grip her cane. Well, I gave it no mind. I didn't want that bitch's claws on me anyway.

'Go on, children,' I heard her say. 'This is your evening.'

We made our way down the shallow stairs toward the crowd, which by now had turned its attentions back on itself and the street. Two servants in animal masks approached carrying platters, a pincer movement of refreshments and unctuous bowing. To Kyran's left came a trout mask with drinks, to my right a fawn holding a plate of wild olives. I popped a few in my mouth and took a bowl of wine.

I turned to my brother. 'You've memorised your poem?' I asked. After the Shame Parade would come the purification of several poetry contests and Kyran had entered the elegy.

'Yes,' he said over the crowd's chatter. 'And should I forget a line tonight I dare say I'll spin something better in the moment.'

I dared say he would. The trait I most admired in my brother was his confidence, though I never told him so. Whenever Kyran set out to accomplish something in life, life would step back and demur.

'You'll win the prize,' I told him. I patted his forearm. 'This is your year, Ran-ran.'

His head tilted in such a way I knew it to be one of his smiles. No mask could ever hide it.

The fawn-faced servant still lingered at my right, her platter at my disposal. Her hair was in a single tight braid that ran down her back and did nothing to hide the fact it was as red as autumn leaves. One of the hinterforest folk, then, or a very recent descendent. Even the lowbloods of my city had bred out scarlet locks.

'Enough,' I said to her and waved her away. For a second she remained and I almost slapped her. But she turned and left.

What terrible service. The knave should have known to scuttle off as soon as I'd taken from her platter. But I didn't let it bruise my evening.

I studied the women in our crowd, their smooth shoulders and elegant backs, their necks exposed by the fashion for high hair. One noticed me notice. She caught her friend's attention – a delicate waif with unusual and much-prized silver locks – and the two of them looked me up and down. A pity I could not see their faces beneath their masks. I rested my hand upon my pommel once more, inclined my head toward them and then looked elsewhere among the crowd. They knew who I was. Plenty of time tonight. Kyran had his pursuits, and I had mine.

Drums echoed across the walls of the tower and the buildings along the curving street. The crowd settled into a silence peppered with hushed words.

We saw the Obsidians first, the Explainers' lowblood guards with their greatclubs and frightening skull masks, marching in three lines. Behind them were drummers with pennants strapped to their backs, black flags with white glyphs upon them: 'sickness', 'ugliness', 'deformity', 'weakness'.

The crowd booed. We booed louder when the troupe of acrogoyles danced and cavorted and somersaulted past us. These dancers portrayed the chaos our species had risen from and would fall back into if we ever diverted from the path to final perfection. It felt good to yell at their clay faces, their warty and lumpen masks full of cowardice and idiocy. The parade was a once-in-a-year release, something you felt in your chest that was all the more vital because everybody around you felt it too. We were one, a new generation: the new blood, proud and together.

Last came the palanquin, carried by sixteen condemned criminals, and our screaming filled the street to the stars above. Atop the palanquin's cushions sat a thing like a gigantic scaly pear with legs and arms. It was a suit of armour, composed of hundreds of pieces of painted wood in horizontal segments that encased a padding fashioned to resemble obesity. The armour had a porcelain face of repellent aspect, a face that could glean no pity in this world save the strangling hands of any mother that bore it. Inside this armour was the young Rosho, offered up by his family for the yearly abuse.

The abomination suit. It, the palanquin it squatted on, and the criminals who carried it were already smeared with rotten fruit and shit, for they had already passed through several public squares full of Corso's lowbloods. The mob never missed their once-a-year opportunity to curse and defile a highblood.

Now he passed a tower of his once-contemporaries, the Rosho inside that armour would soon know a vitriol far more personal. He was no longer Cal, no longer highblood – today he wasn't even commrach. He was nothing but a portrait of abomination, that monstrous result of commrach and human congress. A *caliban*, to use the human word, for even those beasts upon the mainland understood the wrongness of it.

I threw my wine bowl, no care for where it landed, and screeched; I was too focused on that plump and callow porcelain face. Rosho idiocy had led to my mother's death and human thuggery had supplied it. This blend of commrach and human was a fetish of both my mother's killers. And my hatred was *right*. The Explainers and my city and everything our Isle's civilisation stood for made it so.

My brother screamed with me. I saw the silver-haired girl I'd just admired scream too. She swore and threw stones, cursed Rosho through her elegant mask of silver. More drums, more marching, more yells, our screaming the howl of some vast and unseen creature.

I don't know why I stopped. The loathing just went out of me or, at least, out of me swifter than any of my contemporaries. I'd even less reason to turn around. Yet I did.

The fawn-girl, that red-haired servant, was looking at me. Stood there some fifteen feet away, her plate of olives still in hand.

I stared open-mouthed, though I imagine my mask obscured the fact. The sheer temerity...

The servant took an olive from her plate and, slipping her fingers beneath her mask, popped it in her mouth. She stared at me a second longer and then, quite casually, walked away. To wherever servants of my family's tower went.

I laughed. I could do nothing else. Bemused, I returned to the crowd and its abuse.

3

The barn stank of cowshit. We were all sat in the hayloft so as to avoid the stink's origins below. I ran my finger along the flat of my rapier, felt myself pouring into its steel. One has to feel what the blade wants, sense its potential, its dream of sharpness. The moonlight from a hole in the roof caught each silver glyph along its yard of sleek black metal.

'That's a kind of prayer, in't it?' Ned, sitting and shivering beside me, said. 'Touching it like that.'

'Practicality, not prayer,' I told him. I kept my eye to my work. 'My people's touch brings vitality, improves all made things.'

'Craft magic.'

'I suppose. We call it imbuing.' I snorted. 'Prayer? We have no god upon our Isle. Does that scare you, Ned?' I rather enjoyed scaring him, the poor boy. He knew nothing of the world.

He looked about the barn, his breath misting in the April night.

'No. Just... dun't make sense.'

I was tempted to mention the devil, to see the fright in Ned's eyes. The humans' church insisted the devil was the defiant enemy of their omnipotent lord of all creation, a premise that made no sense even on its own terms. But the devil of peasant folk like Ned was different to that of altar carvings and dusty parchment. More visceral, primeval, a half-beast lurking in nature's shadows: forests, barrows. Old barns. I recalled the fertility doll back in the inn. It had possessed goat legs, had it not? Perhaps I should have taken it and left it in Ned's bag or some such sport. Fools like him saw the 'Dark One' in just about anything. Cruel, but it might have passed an hour.

'Better have penny,' Illsa the roadwoman was saying to Shortleg. He was mounting her like a sow somewhere behind Ned, hard against a boarded-up window at the rear of the hayloft. Mercifully in the gloom.

'I got penny,' Shortleg said. He grumbled as he penetrated her. 'Two hundred fucking pip'strells today, love.'

'Show some.'

'Fucking *now*? Buried under cowshit downstairs yer daft twat.' He grunted. 'Saw us bury it.'

Shortleg's idea, that – a good one for once. Hide the loot, return some time thereafter. Six hundred pipistrells. Another good idea would be to split up and meet in Hoxham later. Yet no one had suggested it. No one trusted anyone else not to run back within minutes and start digging. None of us were in a rush to sleep either. We were pennyblades; we knew our kind.

'Pull out 'fore yer spill,' fat Illsa told Shortleg. 'I mean it this time.'

I looked down at my sword again. I hated Illsa, she me. If not for the boys she'd joyfully report my carnal 'devilry' to the Church, quick as hares. My own fault. I'd got shit-faced under the stars when we first met, offered tuppenny for her hand,

and not in the matrimonial sense. She'd screamed til' Shortleg slapped her.

'Never known a point sharper,' Ned said. I hoped he meant my sword. 'Can it pierce mail, Kyra?'

'As through loaf,' I answered. 'Well... tough loaf. All Isle blades can.'

'Why'd you leave? Wish you'd tell us.'

I gritted my teeth, sniffed. I put my rapier back in its scabbard and lifted my blanket around my shoulders.

'Why'd *you* leave *your* home?' I asked Ned.

'Mottlesthorpe? Dunno. Got sick of threshing hay.'

'Then my reason is exactly your reason. Minus the hay.'

He laughed and it became a shiver. I looked at him and chuckled too.

'You're a... good man, Ned. A fine bow.'

Shortleg and Illsa shuffled in the dark, finding their rhythm, shambling and snorting like the placid cattle below us. A handful of them, wretchedly thin.

'What'll you do with your share, Ned?' I asked.

He looked at me. A strange look, as if he were readying to shoot a man.

'Dunno,' he said.

'The finest tailor for me. Then a finer whore to tear it all off.' I wiggled my eyebrows and grinned my sharp grin. 'Eh?'

He didn't smile. He looked about the barn again. Something was scaring him. The rope, likely. Thoughts of the gibbet.

'Ooh, that's it,' Shortleg muttered. 'Fuckin' magic.'

Illsa didn't moan. Roadwomen weren't expected to; they just lived off the pennyblades and the pennyblades lived off everyone's misery. Hard times here on the Main. A whole generation of men who knew no trade save death. Forty years of war had seen to that. The Church had brought peace some four years before I arrived on the mainland. Yet a swift peace leaves folk with swords and no work. A pennyblade summer.

'Kyra,' Ned said.

'What?'

'Got summat. To give you.'

'Another cold?' I joked. When I saw his face was serious as plague, I ceased smiling. 'What?'

He pulled something acorn-sized out of his jacket. I hoped it was an acorn because I was famished and we'd only bread, and bread gives our kind the shits. But no: a tiny oak circle. A ring. He passed it me.

'Hmm,' I said. 'Is this what you've been carving?'

'Yeah,' he said. He stroked his hair.

I studied it under the moonlight. I could make out patterns, the same as the glyphs on my rapier.

'This is beautiful, Ned,' I said. It really was.

'Ain't finished yet,' he said. 'But… now we've money I thought…'

'You'd make a few? Sell them?'

'No.' He met my eyes. 'Kyra Cal'Adra… please, be me wife. I beg yer.'

Silence. Nothing but the *schmeck-schmeck-schmeck* of Shortleg's accelerating enthusiasm.

Illsa grunted. 'I'm not a bloody anvil,' she told him.

I laughed. The idea of it, the whole moment, everything – the absurdity of this new low I'd reached. The daughter of Cal'Adra, the twelfth family, encircled by rutting morons, an illiterate boy her suitor. I'd become everything Grandmother predicted and I laughed to elude a stirring fury.

'Well?' Ned asked.

I shook my head. 'Oh, Edward. I chase the girls, remember? I'd have thought I'd made that clear.'

'Yeah, but… that's just playing, havin' fun and that. Everyone settles. And I wouldn't mind. You could keep chasing. I wouldn't mind, Kyra. I wouldn't.'

Idiot. 'I'm touched, Ned. But we're not even the same beasts.'

'Hearts are the same. I love you, Kyra.' The last part came out a squeak.

'You don't. It's just—'

'Got it planned. There's this pub back home, just outside Mottlesthorpe. We could buy it with our share. Stop the penny-life. I'd make you a daisy chain every day o' spring. Winters by hearth, children beside—'

I threw his ring across the barn. It landed in the darkness. In the shit.

'Don't say it,' I barked. I must have looked a monster, but I couldn't hold back. 'I don't birth calibans, peasant. If you knew anything about me, about commrach, you'd know that.'

Ned's puppy eyes watered. His lips shook.

I wouldn't weaken. 'And I *certainly* won't pour ales in fucking Mottlesthorpe.'

Ned whimpered, tears falling.

Best like this, I told myself; the kindest blade is the swiftest. One stab. Over. Besides, he'd slurred my blood. The Blood entire.

Shortleg groaned.

'Bastard!' Illsa shouted. 'I said dun't spill in me!'

Shortleg laughed. 'Guess you're just too pretty, eh?'

'Bastard!'

Shortleg chuckled. Like an idiot, I looked over to see him pulling his trousers up. I got an eyeful of the base of his still-engorged cock, the outline of its tip pushing against his trousers. Shortleg saw that I saw. He grinned and winked at me.

'I need a shit,' he announced to the barn. He buckled up and walked by me and Ned.

'Twat,' Illsa muttered. She started looking through her satchel for her vinegar and cloth.

Ordinarily I would have laughed at her, but shame was clawing at me, demanding payment for anger's excess.

'I'm sorry, Ned.'

He kept sobbing.

'I'll search for the ring come morning,' I said. 'You can give it… You'll find a nice girl. You're a… you're a handsome lad, Ned.'

'Y'broke me heart,' he said, between squeaks and snot.

I heard Shortleg unlock the barn door and leave. Uncharacteristically polite, I thought, taking his shit outside.

'Don't hate yourself, Edward,' I said. 'It's just me.'

Illsa laughed. 'Lovebiiiiirds.'

'Shut it, twat,' I snapped.

Illsa gave me a filthy look.

'She hurt you, Ned?' she said.

Ned put his head in his hands and his shoulders juddered.

'Shouldn't chase pixie arse, Ned,' she said. 'They've no soul. Plain evil they are.'

I scowled at her.

She grinned at me. 'Ned, want me to suck it better? Gi'yit free.'

Ned roared with tears.

'Here, Neddy,' she cooed, still looking at me. 'Close your eyes and you can pretend I'm *her*.'

I leapt up. Oh, I'd give Illsa the back of my hand, like human men did.

Smoke. I smelled smoke.

I grabbed my belt with my sword and buckled myself.

'I'm going out,' I said.

'Yeah, fuck off,' Illsa said. 'Mardy twat.'

I clambered down the ladder, stepped over cow pats. The gap between the barn's doors shone orange. I ran at the doors and kicked. Barricaded. I felt an oven's heat against my face, heard flames snap and crackle.

Terror filled me. Not like this – a blade, an arrow. Not this.

Fingers of smoke poured in under the barn door. I turned and clambered up the ladder as fast as water runs down.

'Barn's on fire,' I said. 'Doors locked.'

'Y'what?' Illsa said.

Ned looked at me dumbly, his mouth an O.

There was a hand-thin window to the front of the hayloft, same side as the doors. I ran to it, climbing over straw.

The flames beneath the window blinded me with their glow. I squinted, trying to see past the rising embers. I could see figures, twenty or more.

Monsters. Dead men. Bodies with rotting faces, lit by the burning hay surrounding our barn.

I blinked. No – they wore masks. Masks just like the little figurine back in the cellar. But not yarn, rope. Rope bound tightly to their faces, with ragged holes for their eyes and mouths.

One of the ropefaces wore the innkeep's breeches. Blood, what *was* this?

I ducked from the window before any could see me.

Ned and Illsa were already on their feet.

'Men out there,' I said. 'It's their fire.'

'Fuck,' Ned said. In the moonlight his eyes were red and wide. There was the hole in the roof above, a cool blackness peppered with stars. I was nimble, could leap high. It wasn't that high. I'd just fall, break my ankles in the cowshit below.

'Over there,' I told the others. I pointed at the boarded-up window where Illsa and Shortleg had swived, the opposite side of the barn to our murderers. 'Get Shortleg's axe.'

'S'not here,' Illsa said. She looked as if her heart had broken like Ned's. 'Bastard took it with him. Planned it! He told us to sleep here. Burn us! Take the pip'strells his self.'

I couldn't process that. They must have killed Shortleg, had to have. Shortleg was loyal.

'A lever then,' I said, words ahead of my thoughts. 'Ned, your sword!'

Ned nodded, speechless.

We set to pulling planks from the window, Ned levering with his blade, me pulling back the wood. The cold night outside beckoned.

My arms ached and I had splinters in my palm. The smoke was rising, tainting the air. Down below, the slumbering cows stirred.

'Fucking bastard,' I heard Illsa say. 'Spilled in me and killed me, he has. Spilled and killed.'

We prised three boards off.

'Enough,' I said. There was hay below, smouldering, though nothing like the fire on the other side of the barn. A soft landing at least, and there was no one out there that side of the building. I grabbed Ned's and my bags and threw them out the window, into the darkness beyond the flames, the burning stink in my nostrils.

'Go, Ned.'

'Shit,' he muttered. He pushed himself up by his arms and fell through. Brave, Ned, once he'd set himself to something.

He hit the hay, rolled and got up. He didn't catch fire. He picked up the bags and waited.

'Illsa, jump,' I said. Behind her, the barn's planks had turned to black silhouettes in an orange glow. It was happening so damned quickly.

She took two steps toward the window, then froze.

'Can't,' she said. She coughed. 'I can't.'

'Illsa, I cannot throw your fat arse.' I spat out acrid phlegm. 'Jump!'

'Please…' Her face began to crease. She hugged me. 'S'fire. I… *Please…*'

For the first time, she looked truly, utterly beautiful. I felt like a hero in some tale, the princess trembling in his arms. But, more than that, profoundly more, I saw Illsa, once so precious. Someone's daughter.

I threw her to the floor and turned toward the window behind me. I grabbed the windowsill, climbed, readied to leap.

A hand grabbed my ankle. Illsa. I tripped, falling forward into the burning night.

The drop and then the flames. A snap of agony in my right hand, my sword hand. My ribs. More pain: the fire. I rolled, got up, stumbled from the burning hay, embers spinning about me in the dark.

Hands on me. Ned, slapping out flames.

'Where's Illsa?' he said.

My hand hummed with pain; my whole right side throbbed. 'Let's go.'

'Illsa!' he shouted at the window above us.

'We've seconds, Ned.'

He knew what I meant. They'd have heard us by now.

'She's looking through the window,' Ned said.

I wouldn't look back. That bitch had broken me. Fuck her. I grabbed Ned's hand and tried to pull him away. He fought, but followed when he heard the shouting. They were coming around the barn.

We ran into darkness. Into the old forest.

I could hear them following us. My ears, nose, eyes, all superior to a human's in darkness.

But they were no idiots, these. Country folk. Knew the land, knew well the forest by night. And there were many. I knew from their stumble, their half-blind wade through wet undergrowth.

Ned and I crashed through bracken; I was hoping to evade our pursuers while their eyes adjusted to midnight beneath a canopy. They had just been staring at a burning barn after all.

Ned seemed to share my thinking. We were keeping a good pace together, but not as fast as I might have alone. Ned's eyes were excellent, but still human. My fears began to whisper of parting ways, of running solitary.

He caught up with me again and we struggled down a decline. I couldn't use my right hand to balance against the gnarled trunks I passed and my third and fourth fingers throbbed, a melody atop the ache all down my right side.

'We lost 'em?' Ned whispered behind me as we reached the bottom.

I couldn't hear anyone.

'Keep going,' I said.

'You alright?'

I didn't answer. I moved on, slower now, stealthy. Our pursuers' eyes would surely have quickened to the gloom. Minutes passed. I could feel the fire cooling in me, the pain rising in its place. My hand felt like a club of flesh and snapped bone.

'You think she made it?' Ned's voice behind me. I heard him stumble.

'No,' I replied.

'You dun't care, do you?' he said. 'I'd've got her out.'

I didn't answer.

I heard a stream's burble ahead. We got closer, and its ripples glinted, moonlight blades dancing beneath a hole in the forest's canopy. Our side of it was a muddy bank, the other a tangle of bracken.

'We can jump that,' I said. 'Throw your bow over.'

'It's wrong,' Ned said. 'Wrong to be so cold as you.'

'Fall out of love, Ned?' I laughed but it became a wince. Laughing hurt.

I didn't like the look on Ned's face, either. I turned away, ran and leaped. I landed on my left side, scuffled with wet bracken. My right side took it like a punch and I spasmed, managing to get my foot in the stream. I didn't shriek. I refused to.

'Throw me your bow,' I said, louder than I'd hoped. I looked around. No one but Ned.

The bow landed in the bracken next to me.

Ned leaped. He made the stream better than I had.

'C'mon,' I said. 'Leave the bow. It's slowing you down.'

He didn't look at me, just went to get his bow. I turned to walk.

Ned screamed.

For a moment I thought he was betraying me, then I turned and saw him face down in bracken, arms flailing, his left leg frozen, shaking.

He'd trodden on a bear trap.

Ned kept screaming. I ran over, crouched.

'Ned, quiet.'

He wouldn't stop. I held his shoulder with my undamaged hand and looked back where we had come. I couldn't hear for Ned's incessant yelping. I placed my bad hand over Ned's mouth. Took the pain. His yelps sank to sobbing.

What now? *The innkeep*, I thought. If it was the innkeep behind all this then he couldn't allow us to live. I'd already told him we'd point the finger. Couldn't hate him, in a way. Helping his village, cleaning up a long and ugly mess. Blame it on pennyblades.

Ned's foot was at a right angle to his ankle. The trap's jaw ran black; the smell of his blood excited my nostrils.

'Duh't lehme,' Ned whimpered against my palm.

'No,' I said. Could I hear movement from the ridge we'd clambered down? Or was it the wind? It was impossible to think.

I leaned down toward Ned, my face inches from his own.

'I won't leave you, Ned.'

I held his gaze with mine and drew the knife on his belt with my good hand.

I nestled my cheek against his and kissed his ear. He whimpered. His teeth chattered.

'I do, Ned, you hear me?' I whispered, sweet as I could. 'My love. I do.'

I drove the point into his jugular, twisted. The heat on my knuckles. The scent.

Best this way. The kindest blade the swiftest.

He gargled, coughed. Ceased.

I wiped the knife on bracken and took it with me.

Dawn saw me negotiating mire. The trees were thinning out, lone beeches all ghostly upon islands of dry earth. Shoe-sucking mud everywhere else. Mists rolling in.

I tried to keep to the trees, avoiding the mire and murk wherever I could, which was far from always. My teeth chattered, but I felt hot. My arms shook as I walked. Sweat ran down from my scalp over drying mud. I'd broken a rib, two fingers. Sword fingers. I was fucking ruined.

I slipped on a muddy rise, slipped up to my thighs. Agony. I wanted to sob.

I stopped moving, took deep breaths. There was little to see in such mist. Devil's ground, the locals likely deemed it, to be avoided by man. The sort of place, commrach saga tells us, where the fomorg slumber. Where their evil might arise one cursed and distant eve. I kept picturing the figurine in the cellar, its yarn-bound grin widening. I'd no idea why.

Monsters. Oh, but my monsters were real. Rossley, the innkeep and his friends. The Crown. Shortleg.

Had he betrayed us? He'd left before the fire, and after the fire he could dig up the six hundred pipistrells we'd buried in the cold wet mud. Perhaps he'd been working with all of Tettleby, finding them likely pennyblades the world wouldn't miss. Corpses to scrub away their crime.

If Shortleg hadn't betrayed us, he'd been cut down on his way to emptying his bowels. No way of telling. The man existed simultaneously in two states within my thoughts: an object of loss, an object of hate.

I wouldn't dwell on Ned; I might stop moving.

The mists ahead parted and, in that moment, the beeches resembled pillars in Corso, the slender columns that ran along the twelfth tower's colonnades. I laughed, pictured acquaintances passing, saluting them with a mud-caked hand. Perhaps my brother, perhaps…

Illusion. Sucking me down like the mud all about. I set myself to action, struggled to my feet.

Do not expect a tale of revenge. This isn't one, not exactly. A pennyblade's life is such you'd be a fool not to expect this manner of betrayal. Betrayal is life.

No, revenge did not spur me on. Nothing so banal. Rather, my delirium, the increasing visions of my island home, my past.

For I feared I might see you, Shen.

You.

4

A gull shrieked and I awoke on my bed in our family's tower. Sunlight warmed my bare skin. I could hear shouts from the market far below my bedroom's window, hawkers trying to catch those who still revelled after yesterday's festivities.

I felt sticky. My fingers were glued together. My belly felt tight with dried… *something.*

I lifted my fingers to my nose and sniffed: honey. I frowned, which cracked more dry honey on my jaw and nose.

I moved to get up and felt warmth either side of my arms. Blinking, I looked, pain lancing through my wine-lashed skull. A woman either side, both naked as I. They slept on.

My head hurt.

I levered myself upright. My bedroom was a wide marble crescent, the outer side of which looked down upon the streets and canals of Corso.

My dagger rack had broken and fallen from the wall by the door. How had that happened? I rubbed my eyes and only got more honey in my face. The sun baked on my back, judgemental. I needed to piss.

I slid myself forward and off the bed. The women made no sound but their breath. I'd honey in my grove's grass. It made for an unpleasant walk as I stumbled over papers strewn across the pinewood floor: a lexicon of Mainer, the language of humans. Like I'd ever bloody need it.

I pulled out the long chamber pot from the recess in the wall and removed the lid. Grabbing a leaf from the bowl I turned about, squatted and began making water. I gazed at the two women upon my bed.

Yes, yes: the Festival of Youth. My brother had won the silver lily at the recital, after the Shame Parade. I'd been immensely supportive, to the tune of several wine bowls.

The two girls? I had admired them at the parade, they me. We'd got to talking once the screaming was over. The rest was mist. I suppose they had seen my long boots, that symbol of a female twin, and set their hearts upon a practised girl-pleasurer. It happened quite a bit.

I grinned. Their tan bodies were striped with honey too. The left, face down, silver-haired, had a red-raw buttock. My. I'd been an *animal*. Neither would be waking too soon. Their silver masks lay beside the bed. I'd not the faintest idea what had happened to mine.

I recalled a servant too. Red hair. Insolent, in a mute sort of way.

'They should cast a statue of you like that,' came a voice to my right. 'For the ages.'

My brother.

Kyran lay naked and spreadeagled on the floor, his head resting upon another man's bare stomach. The other man lay upon my pillow pile. Both men were smeared with honey. A broken honey pot lay next to Kyran's ankle, its contents half-dried, half-flies. One of the tower's many cats sniffed at it.

I scowled at Kyran, pissed my last and wiped.

Kyran staggered to his feet and made his way over, livelier than he'd any right to be. He'd male's morning-serpent, bouncing along at half-mast, as irritatingly jaunty as its owner.

'Bop,' he said as he poked my stomach. With his finger. I took a step back and let him stand before the pot.

He strained, stopped, then slouched his gaze toward me.

'I thought last night was good,' he said. He nodded, as if to second himself.

'I can barely stand,' I said. I slipped behind him, rested my chin on his shoulder, crossing my arms about his stomach. We were the same height, had the same hair. The same face.

'Don't put me off,' he muttered. I felt him tense and try again. He'd never learn to wait.

'Need help?' I said.

He ignored me.

'Pshh-psh-psh,' I said, 'Psshhh.'

'Fuck off. Stop teasing.'

'You'd always let me help when we were kits.'

'Only because Mother told me off if I didn't.' He jabbed me with an elbow, and I stepped away chuckling. 'You didn't get one and you've never got over the fact,' Kyran told me, focusing on his work.

'My efforts were selfless and noble, brother,' I said. 'See? You've shrivelled.'

His piss ran and he moaned. 'Point taken.'

I found a half-drunk bowl of wine and sipped. Practically vinegar. I grimaced.

'Mother would be proud,' I told Kyran. 'She always knew you'd take the lily.'

'Where *is* my lily?'

'Beside that man's arse over there.'

'Oh. Well… *good*.' Kyran pushed out his last jets: one, two. He shook himself freely.

'Leaf, Kyran.' Beast. It was my room, for Blood's sake.

He took a leaf and wiped, before dropping it in the pot and turning to face me. His face shone smug.

'What?' I said.

'Are you primed?'

'Whatever for?'

'To hunt panther, of course!'

'You're kidding me,' I said.

'I have earned the right, Kyra!' Kyran declared, his eyes full-wide. 'I won the lily-of-the-festival, the city's gardens are mine to stalk. Think on it – a beast pads therein, now, as we speak; unknowing Kyran Cal'Adra shall soon chew upon its heart. I shall take it, sister! Take it with javelin and blade and, above all mark you, with winter-sharp wit.'

I looked his honey-smattered slouch up and down.

'I think this panther has little to worry about.'

'It's *flesh*, sister,' he said. 'Murder-fresh and steaming in our mouths. Don't pretend that does not quicken you. I see your nose twitch.' It hadn't. 'Its essences firing our own.' He closed his eyes, placed his palms above his heart. 'Oh, and its hide. Its silken hide! My very own panther cloak! How many citizens shall whisper my glory as I stroll the byways of Corso, how many men esteem the feline mystery of my sublime and fur-clad form?' He pretended to wipe a tear. '*Fabulous.*'

'You want me to stab a panther so you can have a new coat?'

'And try not to damage the pattern, dear.'

'What's in it for me?'

He opened his eyes and shrugged. 'You may walk beside me when I wear it.'

'I'd rather point and jeer with everyone else.'

He smacked his chest against mine. 'Coward.'

I grinned and growled. I smacked my chest against his, harder. We rammed a third time and then began to grapple. We were rolling on the pine floor in seconds.

'Do you yield, shit-breath?' I said as he struggled under me. 'Yieeeld?'

Softly, he clamped his jaw on my shoulder and growled. I did the same to him. Our sign for truce since childhood. Our lives were something that occurred between an intermittent yet endless play-fight. We relaxed, cuddled a while, the June sun baking our young skin.

'Alright,' I said eventually. 'I'll help.' I looked around at the unconscious guests. 'Nothing else to do here.'

We washed in the tower's baths, dried one another and dressed ourselves fine: matching black trouservests that left our pretty shoulders bare. We applied each other's make-up, strapped our sword belts, then hit the streets of Corso for all to see. We were the Cal'Adra twins.

We'd a notoriety to uphold.

All twins have, or should. Always a boy and a girl, commrach twins, the boy growing to desire only men, the girl women, whereas all other commrach desired both and, indeed, everything in between. We dressed as custom required, Kyran wearing silk shoes, I tall leather boots. We were no traditionalists, we merely wished all Corso to know us an exquisite fuck and we were rarely, if ever, short of applicants to test that very claim.

Oh come now. I'm not one for false modesty. But you know that, Shen.

We sashayed and traipsed and trolled along the curving streets with their black spires, crossed bridges of granite and ancient ivory. We took lavender vials from a market vendor so as to nullify the summer-stink from the canals. They did little.

We crossed Victory Square – its chequered cobblestone still festooned with festival garbage – and climbed the steps to the Great Aqueduct. We loved it up there: the trinket stalls lining the canal, the pretty footbridges, the folks promenading, dressed to their best. Oh, and the fresh-made moontiles, dainty lunar portraits, their clay drying, drinking in the sun so that they might shine at night. In the near distance, either side of the Great Aqueduct, rose the houses of the ten inner families, great towers of deathless wrought iron, their walls twisting up, up into spires. The spears of titans, baked by the sun.

And beyond these towers, beyond the landward edge of Corso, lay the city's hunting gardens. The gardens were a carved mountain a half-mile high, a nine-tiered ziggurat hewn from raw granite in an age forgotten. There were forests upon each level, black spires of pine and deciduous canopies in white blossom, while waterfalls snaked down into mist-veiled ravines below, all of it ordered in such a manner as to appear wild.

Halfway along the aqueduct, a crowd loitered. They surrounded a tidings banner; the latest news daubed on deer hide stretched over bronze. We strode closer, and what we couldn't read we heard from murmurs of fellow citizens. The rebellion in the Jade colonies had been suppressed, its lowblood instigator executed, his heart torn out and thrown into the sea.

'Fucker deserved it,' Kyran said loudly, and with a shrug. 'A bloody-handed puppet of Rosho ambition.'

Those around us, citizens of all tower-loyalties, muttered in agreement, especially on seeing it was a child of Elinda Cal'Adra, Lady of the Jades, who spoke. Our mother had given her life while protecting the colonies after all.

'Hardly,' I muttered.

Kyran nudged my shoulder as if to say, *Don't start.*

'Oh, come on,' I said to him, only half-whispering. 'I despise the Roshos as much as you, but it's not they who are fomenting rebellion. The folk on those islands were having a shit time of things back when *we* were living there.'

'You jest,' Kyran said. He said, louder, 'Mother would weep to hear of such conspiracies upon the islands she governed.'

Maybe it was the last traces of my hangover, but I couldn't take this. 'Mother? Mother was forever asking Corso for aid and resources. The only reason rebellion never happened before was because she was there to speak for them.'

Kyran laughed and, ruffling my mop of hair, drew me in.

'We're in public,' he whispered. 'Say the lies all want to hear, yes? He ruffled my hair again, harder this time. 'Your fondness for candour is not the asset you think it is.'

Patronising shithead. But I checked my irritation. We both knew ourselves sensitive on the subject of Mother, especially as our enemies whispered she died a coward, and our slightest differences of opinion could get magnified.

I sighed. 'Come along. We've a cat to molest.'

The crowds thinned out as we reached the end of the aqueduct, where its granite blocks merged with the rocky face of the hunting gardens.

'I sent servants ahead,' Kyran said, pointing at the two figures waiting by the spring that rushed from the mountain's chiselled wall and into the aqueduct's channel below. Either side of the spring, six rock-cut pathways took different routes into the hanging forests, disappearing into the gloom beneath their canopies. 'I ordered them to bring javelins and snacks and suchlike.'

'That's very nearly forethought, Kyran,' I told him. 'You disturb me.'

Kyran grinned as we walked over to the servants.

The two servants wore regulation peacock headdresses that covered their scalps and hair entire, lacing unflatteringly at the chin. Something about that always struck me as cruel, given peacocks were amongst the game to be found in the gardens. Hopefully these two rustic lowbloods had developed a keen instinct for dodging javelins.

'Sir,' the first said to my brother. A young male with wide nervous eyes and pouting lips. Kyran's uncharacteristic bout of forethought became suddenly explicable.

'Good work,' Kyran said to him, gesturing at the satchel of short javelins the youth held. 'We've ferocious work ahead. I trust you know how to wield a javelin, yes?'

The youth looked askance. 'I'm familiar, sir.'

'With all lengths?'

He giggled. 'I can learn.'

Kyran touched the youth's chin. 'Exemplary attitude.'

Well, if it was that kind of hunting party...

I stepped over to the other servant. I'd never seen her before. Female, the same age as me, expression serious.

You, Shen. Though of course I did not know you. Not yet.

You stared ahead as if I were no more than a canal fly darting about in your vision. I was struck by the beauty and violence of your eyes, bright as emerald, cool as glass, shining out from beneath two black and dagger-sharp eyebrows. But your lips and chin? Too thin for my tastes. Your flesh too pale, milk enough to be a mainland human. Still, needs must in the wild…

'And what's your name?'

'Shen,' you said. 'Sir.'

'Greetings, Shen. You've a family name?'

'Patently.'

'Yes,' I said after a pause. 'Stupid question.' I thought of referring to you as Lady Patently, or some japery, but already you had a way of making me feel a bore. 'And I don't suppose I really need to know it so—'

'No,' you said. 'Sir.'

I let out a breath through pursed lips. 'Nice, er… nice javelins. Shen.'

You made no reply. I could have been talking to a statue. I looked over to my brother, busy making his feather-headed doxy-boy titter.

'Shall we get a move on?' I asked him.

He smiled and nodded.

We made our way downhill, into the deciduous levels. You and the youth led the way.

'Thank you, brother,' I said to Kyran. 'I wasn't enthusiastic before, but now I'm committed to this hunt.'

'Good, good.'

'I'm determined to come down from this fucking hillside with at least *some* pussy fur…'

Kyran laughed and squeezed my shoulder. We strode on.

'I do believe you splendid.'

'I believe you splendid, sir.'

'Oh, but you are splendidest. You shame the very sun.'

The pair of them had been carrying on like this for some time, lying on their sides in the grass and facing each other, putting bluebells in one another's hair. We were 'taking a break' in a glade beside a delicate waterfall. We'd only been an hour at the prowl, the boys making enough chatter to guarantee an absence of panther, when Kyran suggested we rest. He was bored with this hunt already. A sister could tell.

'I'd write you a poem when we return,' Kyran told the youth, 'yet it would be a stain upon your beauteous wings, butterfly.'

'Oh, sir.'

'I *adore* how you blush.'

'Sir.'

'Oh, my butterfly boy…'

They kissed.

I was sat some feet behind them, bored and frustrated.

You, Shen, were cross-legged beside me, staring at nothing in your ridiculous peacock headdress, taking bites from a streak of dried venison.

Seduction was a long-vanished, nay, mythical concept, small talk an absurdity chasing seduction's heels over the horizon. I had hoped for a glade-orgy. Now, sat there, I simply abhorred you. Your cow-placid face, your loud chewing. You were just… *there*. Life-numbingly existent. Cuntishly present. You tore off another piece of dried meat and began chewing again. I grimaced.

Kyran and his lover's pricks had already broken free of their leather confines. Surely a record. Their fists began working each other with a fury even they seemed startled by. The sight just made me depressed and envious. I looked away, over to the waterfall.

'Faces carved into the rocks over there,' I observed, the final do-or-die charge of conversation's shattered legion. 'Ancient heroes, I think.' How I longed to join them in death.

You didn't look. You made a loud swallowing sound.

'You're a shitty fucking servant,' I told you. 'You know that, right?'

You seemed to consider the statement a while. 'I could carry your satchel on my *left* shoulder, sir. Would that be preferable to the right?'

'What? No. No, being a servant isn't all about carrying stuff. You're supposed to be... I don't know. Impressed.'

'Impressed.'

'With everything I say.'

You wiped your lips. 'Congratulations on spotting those carvings,' you said, deadpan.

I could have had you flogged when we got back. *I could run you through here and now*, I thought, *as long as I pay your family reparations.* Shit, they'd probably pay *me*. But that would be to admit defeat. I knew that already. You'd probably yawn at my rapier through your sternum, shrug like I was the most boring arse. I hated you thinking I was boring. I wasn't boring.

'Look at me,' I said. 'Look me in the fucking eye.'

The undergrowth rustled ahead of us. Six figures stepped out, blades in hand.

I leapt up and drew my sword, stepping two paces forward. Kyran's servant ceased fellatio and ran off into the trees, screaming for help. My brother stuffed his parts back in his trousers, drew his two palm-wide daggers and prowled backwards to my side. You remained sitting, watching with bored eyes.

Our visitors had come downwind of us, had used the waterfall's burble to cover the sound of their approach. An effective gambit, if a crude one. They must have been trailing us since we'd entered the city gardens.

I knew who it was before they even entered the light of the glade. Three men, three women, their leader a leering embarrassment in pigtails and too much eyeshadow. Urse Cal'Dain: my worst enemy.

'The Cal'Adra twins,' he said. His assorted arse-whelks chuckled as if he'd told some fresh anecdote, something he was entirely incapable of. 'Fortunate we spotted you. Terrible accidents can occur on hunts.'

'Explains your hairstyle,' I said. 'Tell me, Urse, if I pull on those plaits does more shit come from your lips?'

'Amusing,' Urse replied. 'Love the sound of your own voice don't you?'

'Especially when I say something adroit and witty.' I studied my rapier's steel. 'And cutting.'

I wasn't scared; I knew they'd not the nerve to kill us. That would mean Urse having to answer to my grandmother. Urse simply liked to intimidate, to outnumber. I'd had to share a tutorial with him at the Explainers' observatory earlier that month. The dullard had gazed out the window for most of the hour, but his interest had been piqued when our tutor mentioned the males of the human species were physically stronger than their female counterparts. He'd have loved that, I realised, sat there. Petty power over half those he met.

Urse waved his sabre casually. He hailed from Darrad, the Isle's foremost city state. All those spoiled inbreds favoured the sabre over there. Pricks.

'It strikes me,' he said, 'that our duels get broken up back in the city. Your grandmother is always there to save you. But, oh, look.' He eyed the trees. 'No city.'

His cronies chuckled. I noticed two of them wore the sigil of Cal'Valtah, the family one tower below us in prestige. They were always up for Urse's latest farce.

I stepped forward, but Kyran stayed my hand.

'Don't flatter this fool, sister,' he told me. Loudly.

'Are *you* protecting her now?' Urse said to him. 'If your blade-work's anything like your poetry you'll tumble onto your own sword.'

His cronies guffawed.

'And if your banter doesn't improve I'll gladly throw myself on it.' Kyran spat on the grass.

Urse fingered one of his plaits and frowned.

'Tell me,' he said, turning his gaze upon me. 'How did your dear mother die again? A lowly human's arrow in her back, yes? Her *back*.' He cocked his head. 'Cowards breed cowards.'

I stepped forward, and this time Kyran didn't stop me.

'Hush your poisons, Urse,' I said. 'Let a sliced face be the last word.'

'A sliced face,' Urse agreed.

Everyone else stepped back.

Urse and I circled one another. He wore a grin, but I spied anger in his eyes. I thought that odd; I was never truly happy save for these moments.

I tested with a jab that he parried. Another, then a third. He lunged and I parried then countered, a swipe that near-butchered his shirt sleeve. He stumbled back and away. The silver glyphs on our black blades danced.

My sword had length, his weight. He knew enough to beat my rapier off-point: all its bite lay in its end and the eight-inch of sharp either side. His sabre was deadly all down one edge, ideal for our game of face-slice. But the danger lay in more than that. With a curved sword one loses reach yet gains unpredictability. A twist of the wrist and a sabre's end can be wherever the opponent least expects it, often the flesh. Urse knew this, yet he'd no instinct for it. But he believed he had. I'd use that.

I turned and fled up the rocks beside the waterfall's misty downpour. I span around, my back to it, droplets tickling my neck. I had height *and* length now. I gazed down upon him.

'You run away,' Urse declared.

'I make this ground my friend,' I shouted over the chatter of the waterfall. 'Really, Urse. This stuff's *basic*. Slice your own face now so we may all go home.'

He hissed and ran up the rise. I lunged downwards repeatedly; he stopped, blocking again and again.

'Bored now,' I yelled. 'Are you to beat my blade all day? It's not your cock, dear boy.'

'You'll suck mine soon enough, longboot! And sob as you do!'

I hissed. He'd suffer for that.

He struck my blade and twisted his wrist. His sabre turned and scraped my left shoulder. I shuffled back, into the waterfall, heaving breaths: the weight of the water, the cold. The world all noise and blur. The rock beneath my soles smooth, slimy. I retreated in a careful shuffle.

A fang-like shadow came at me – Urse's sabre. My rapier met its downswing. His sabre's edge changed position, just as I'd hoped. I shoved my weight sideways and drove his blade up against the fall's rocky wall, holding it there with the swept hilt of my own sword. His sabre had twisted upwards now; his wrist must have been agony.

I swung my spare fist blindly, a backhander that met his neck. Urse fell sideways into the pool below. His sabre stayed against the wall and I released it.

I leaped into the waters after him, only a five-foot drop. My feet touched the pool's bed but I felt no pain. I floated up. I barely had to swim. I saw Urse, crawling up the bank of the little stream. Weaponless. I waded over and slashed his buttocks.

He howled.

My brother cheered.

'Where you going, you rancid shit?' I booted him in his side, and he rolled on his back.

'I yield!' he said, covering his face.

Worthless fuck. I leant forward, pulled his pigtail and sliced it off with my sword. I did the same with the other and threw them on the bank. I drove my heel into his hips. He folded up and I grabbed him, forced him back into the stream's shallows, head first. I threw my rapier onto the bank near Kyran.

'This ends with a sliced face, yes?' I said to him. 'Oh, you'll be begging for that!' I shoved his head under the water. I looked up and grinned at his cronies. They stared back, uncertain whether to step in and stain his honour.

I released his head, and he came up spitting water, gagging for breath. I yanked his trousers and pants down. I'd left a goodly wound across his arse, the blood still running. Under the shade of a leafy branch, it glittered with those motes of silver peculiar to commrach life-fluids.

'Are you watching this?' I shouted at Urse's friends. 'Tell all Corso!'

I grabbed a pigtail from the bank, prised Urse's cheeks wide and, laughing, tried to thumb its severed end into his wet arsehole. He screamed and struggled and splashed.

'I came to hunt panther!' I yelled. I hated him more than life. *Hated* him. 'Wag your tail!'

'Kyra,' my brother said. 'That's enough!'

'Shut up and find the other pigtail.'

'Slay her!' Urse wailed to his peers. 'My family will shield you, *please*!'

They wavered, then one of their number – a Cal'Valtah male – charged. The others followed. Only Kyran was armed. Why had I thrown my sword aside?

The man stopped. He screamed. He had a javelin through his thigh.

The others' charges faltered. One of the women ran over to him. She looked to where the javelin had come from, held a hand up in truce, and was rewarded with a javelin through her palm. No scream. She gawped at its sudden appearance.

'Swords down!' a woman shouted.

The cronies dropped their weapons. So did Kyran.

You, Shen. I had forgotten about you. You had a javelin in your right hand, level with your head. A bag of four more at your feet. Your peacock headdress leaning at an angle, a lock of red hair loose from beneath it. The colour reminded me of someone. Your eyes, green and aglow like sunlight through a leaf.

Of course. You had been the servant in the wooden fawn mask, the one who had served olives at the parade. Who had watched me.

'Listen,' you said, your voice quieter now, assured. 'Their mother did not die a coward. Elinda Cal'Adra perished at the Jade siege with an arrow in her back – no one denies this. But she had her back to the enemy as she tended a wounded warrior. If you think me a liar, please step forward. But I warn you: that warrior was my father.'

My blood cooled instantly. A feathery joy moved in me, so faint I feared it might dissolve in the acknowledgement. The slanders of our enemies, whispered in alleys and salons, were as baseless as I'd always suspected.

Kyran broke the tense atmosphere. 'No more,' he said to the cronies. 'Let us be done with this.'

He picked up his daggers, sheathed one and strode over to Urse, now weeping on the bank, his arse still bare and quivering.

'Urse,' Kyran said. He held out a hand and, gently, turned Urse on to his back. 'Let a sliced face be the last word.' With that he made a tiny slice upon Urse's cheekbone.

Urse clutched his face with one hand, pulled his trousers up with the other and stumbled toward his bleeding lackeys.

'No more duels,' Kyran called to him. 'You hear? I can't be doing this every week when we're brothers-in-law.'

I cringed at that. The roots of Urse's and my enmity did not need exposing.

I looked at you, Shen. Even at such a distance your eyes were bright, like sun through emerald.

Go, I mouthed.

You held your ground. You shook your head.

Go. I gestured toward the woods this time. *Go*.

And you were gone. A shadow beneath the leaves, a memory.

5

'Go,' a voice said. Mine.

Stale sweat. Bed-stink. In a bed.

A hard bed. I opened my eyes. The ceiling was white plaster in candlelight. To my left a small table. To my right a woman in a chair. She wore a uniform. A leather helmet thing with the white hook of the Church painted on it. She was rooting around her right nostril with a finger. When she saw I was awake, she pulled her finger out and wiped it on her gambeson jacket.

'Can you get up?' she said.

'Think so.' I was thankful she didn't wear the uniform of the Crown. With any luck I wouldn't have to answer tricky questions about missing tax money.

'Wait there.'

She stood up and opened a door behind her. More candlelight beyond.

'Tell Mother she's on her way!' she bellowed through the doorway. She looked back at me. 'Come on.'

I had to climb out on the left side, had to use my left hand. My right hand hummed with pain, my ribs a pounding ache.

The uniformed woman never offered help, but I was glad of that. There's a saying: pennyblades roam with roadwomen or clergy, never both. I preferred the former; they only want your things.

'Where are my things?' I asked the woman.

'Mother's got them. Come along.'

I was wearing some rough white tunic. A fucking dress again. Roughest unders beneath.

I followed her into the corridor. Brickwork, no windows, just lamps above. The air had that underground tang. Damp. Mildew. We turned a corner and there were five stairs up. Painful.

I recalled a blonde girl's face as I climbed the stairs: pretty, her left eye entirely white. Had I dreamed that? Surely. But other things weren't dream: a day and night, perhaps more, shivering hot and cold under endless trees, stumbling on, drinking from puddles to survive. Eating a worm.

We reached a door. The uniformed woman knocked.

I remembered staring up at the sun, lying in a ditch by a road. Shadows over me. Men. *That's her*, one had said. *That's her. Look at the ears…*

'Come through,' a woman said from behind the door.

The room was small. Daylight fell through a grille near the ceiling. A plump woman in grey robes sat behind a varnished table. Her face peered from out of a plain wimple. A mother of the True Church.

Shit.

She smiled. Her eyes studied me. 'Please, sit.'

She gestured at a wooden seat across the table from her and, groaning, I sat.

'How are you feeling, my girl?' she said.

I looked around the room. Behind her hung a tapestry of a near-naked man hanging upside-down from a tree, a hook through his feet, arrows in his torso. The Pilgrim, they called him.

'Where am I?'

I saw the uniformed woman had a leather truncheon on her belt.

'I'll be outside,' she said to the Mother, and left.

'You're in the Lower Bath,' the Mother said. 'St Waleran's Home for Wayward Girls. In Hoxham. You know of it?'

I nodded. Where the well-to-do had their clothes washed.

'What do you want with me?'

'My girl, we found you on the road. We helped you. We've nursed you better.'

'No.' I'd a sudden pain behind the eyes. I rubbed my lids. 'You were looking for me. Your men.'

'No, my child.' When she smiled, she resembled a pink frog, her rolls of flesh fighting to burst out of her headdress. 'Our journeymen happened upon you. This ministration helps fallen women.'

'No. No, woman. I heard them talk. They were looking for me.'

'You're dehydrated,' she said. She poured ale-water from a jug into a cup and offered it to me. I took it; she was right. 'And I'll ask you to call me "Mother".'

'You didn't birth me.' I took another sip.

'But I'll look after you,' she replied. 'Despite your origins. Despite the fact—' and she frowned here, a physician delivering bad news, '—you've no soul to save. Indeed, perhaps because of that it behoves me to look after you only more.' She shrugged and made her frog-smile, but something told me she wasn't entirely pleased with the arrangement. As if she were trying to convince herself. 'God offers redemption in many forms.'

Lunatic. I had to handle this carefully. The Church had hanged a woman for girl-love during the siege of Hoxham, so Esme and the other Orton Street girls had told me. A human woman. Extreme times, but still. A 'sprite' like me? What chance would I have?

'Could I leave, please?' I said. If I got out now, I might even be able to make use of Esme's particular… services. It was important to keep positive in times like this.

'You have yet to give thankfulness.'

'Thanks.' I smiled. 'Thank you.'

She said nothing.

'Thank you… Mother?' I tried.

'Here at St Waleran's, thankfulness comes with work.'

I knew it. 'You're holding me prisoner…'

'No, no, Isle-child,' she said. 'You can leave whenever you like.'

'Thanks. I'll—'

'But the Church would keep your clothes and blades.'

'Oh, fuck you.'

The Mother didn't look shocked, but she made the hook gesture over her chest. I noticed that upside-down Pilgrim prick was there too, in pendant form upon her breasts. He was fucking welcome to them.

'Our journeymen need to be paid, my girl,' she said. 'They saved your life. You've no money, so you can either give thankfulness with your possessions or in kind.'

I squinted at her. 'How d'you mean?'

'Washing clothes. You've washed clothes, yes?'

I looked down. 'Since I came to the mainland.'

'Do you wish to confess your story?'

'Not remotely.'

'You know, St Samulis tells us—'

'Religious talk between a holy person and a "soulless elf"? Please. No one needs that.' She was lying to me, holding back.

'Three weeks' thankfulness. Is that really so much to ask for your life? Besides, a Perfecti arrives tomorrow. She'll heal your hand. Your ribs.'

I'd no idea what a Perfecti was, but I'd have fellated a lobster if I thought it'd help my sword-hand.

I grunted. I nodded.

'Welcome to St Waleran's,' she said. 'Your name?'

'Shen.' It felt strange, saying your name aloud.

'Welcome, Shen. You will find this a kindly home. I would ask you not to be troublesome while you stay. Trouble would necessitate further thankfulness. And remember the other girls are not used to… your kind. In a moment Gilbertia will take you to the baths and then you can meet the others.' Her lips trembled. 'There's just a small matter: I've questions about your satchel's contents. I may let you keep some.'

She lifted my satchel onto the table and opened it. She lifted out a delicate box of patterned mahogany and placed it upon the table.

'Mascara and pencil,' I explained. 'Cosmetics.'

'Well,' she said. 'I think we can keep that with your blades. Now, erm, this intrigues me…'

She pulled out Cuchulin and popped him upright on the table. I'd have thought a person in charge of so many cloistered women would have seen the purpose of his nine-inch onyx length. But of course, human penises are different, more club-like, than commrach's. Besides, Cuchulin was very… abstract. A trusty companion. And given our people's touch, our effect on crafted objects, Cuchulin only improved with use.

'Mother, your worship, I'll definitely need that,' I said.

'What is it?'

'Gift from my mother.' Which was true. 'Religious significance.'

'Your people are godless.'

'Ancestor worship then.' It wasn't working. 'Haemomancy?'

'Haemomancy?'

'Well, I find it bloody magic.'

'No,' she uttered with finality. 'It could be used as a weapon.'

True. Cuchulin doubled as a fine crown-basher.

'Finally, this.' She held up a bundled cloth, a hole-stricken burgundy rag.

'Remains of a shirt. My brother's. We... used to swap garments. The smell of each other would help us sleep. It still helps me sleep.' I shrugged. 'That's ridiculous, isn't it?'

She smiled, shook her head.

There were black stains on the cloth: ink. I pulled the rag flat. Someone had daubed a shape on it, a circle.

'What's this?' I said. 'Why would you people do this?'

'It was already like that, my girl.'

'No. No it wasn't.' A circle. Crude triangles jutted out from its edge, like spikes upon a ring. 'What is this? One of your sky things?'

'I was hoping you could tell me.'

'Your people must have done it when they found me. They must have.' I grunted. 'This is an awful thing to do, awful.'

'Where is your brother?'

I said nothing. I closed my eyes.

The Mother smiled. 'You may keep that.'

It occurred to me, as the uniformed woman, Gilbertia, ushered me along a sandstone corridor, that this establishment had no idea what jeopardy approached. My three-week sentence would include late March and its vernal equinox. I'd come into season here. My, I thought, they'd thrown a fox into a rabbit hutch.

'The Mother is very forgiving,' Gilbertia said behind me as we walked. 'We journeywomen are less so. Remember that, sprite.'

'Noted,' I said. 'Henchman.'

I would have to escape. Best for all, that. Liberate my things, break out, visit Esme's boudoir before I had my equinox. She understood commrach girls, Esme. Hopefully she'd be understanding enough to put it on the tab till I found a little penny-work.

We walked into a vestibule. There were tunics and underwear hanging from hooks. I could hear talking beyond, running water.

'Clothes off,' Gilbertia ordered.

I pulled my tunic over my head and hung it up. Slipped off my unders. Gilbertia made no pretence of averting her gaze.

I feigned surprise, threw coy eyes. I stroked back my hair.

'Do you like your job?' I asked her. 'I must say, I feel protected with you ab—'

'Move,' she said, and she nodded at the threshold. Savvy then. Liked her job too much to lose it. But she hadn't met me yet. I'd break her.

I walked through to a warm square sandstone room with a wet floor, ready to get my own eyeful of all these infamous 'wayward girls'.

I got one, but it was bruised, pock-marked and hairy. These wayward girls were only so in the sense they'd steered clear of leg-razors. There were five of them by two wall fountains, cackling to each other. They'd horrendous Hoxham accents, the kind that made groups of women sound like barking terriers. One of them froze upon seeing me. Her grin ceased.

"Ere, Liz,' she muttered.

'Liz' turned to face me. Big-boned, chisel-faced, her skull mottled with patches of dark hair. The other women looked to her.

'You can stand over there, caliban,' Liz said. She pointed at the fountain nearest me. The others moved closer to Liz and her friend.

I tensed at the caliban slander, but I was in no condition to fight. I didn't even want to *touch* these feral harpies.

I checked myself over. A great bruise on my ribcage. I didn't think there were any breakages. I'd got lucky.

My hand though…

My knuckles were scabbed. My little finger was curled, and I could not move it. It was red, with a red line running from it into my palm. Less painful than it looked, but whether it might ever hold a sword again was another matter. By the Blood. Please no.

I put my hand in the fountain's basin. Well, this was something at least. I hadn't bathed like this since Corso.

'We should smack her around, Liz,' one of them announced, broomstick-thin with dark rings about her eyes. 'Say it were an accident.'

'Slippy floor 'ere,' Liz said. 'Could break 'er ratty fucking face.'

I soaked my hair, ignored them.

"Ere, Liz… shit in 'er gob like yer did wi' Poppi.'

They laughed.

'Still my kiss would be sweeter than yours,' I remarked.

'I'll shit in yer fucking eye sockets,' Liz said, turning to glare at me, 'time I'm done. Shit on your feet. Mek yer lick it off.'

'Exactly how much shit have you got?' I asked. I pointed at her belly. 'Ah, who am I kidding? You could bury all Hosshire.'

She stepped toward me. A foot taller, twice my weight.

Me and Liz glared at one another. She could break me, I knew. I'd no blade, a ruined hand. But my stare wouldn't tell her that. It was inhuman, an unknown thing. Unguessable. She owned brute power here, and I fear.

'What you need to learn, sprite,' Liz said, quieter than before, 'is I'm queen in these halls. They're mine.'

'Keep them,' I said. 'I won't be staying long.'

'Don't like that attitude,' she said. 'Keep chatting shit and I'll smash yer good hand.'

I blinked but held my stance. She could sniff out vulnerability, this one.

'You don't want to touch me, Liz,' I told her. 'See, my kind, we stain people. Sink into your bones. Your very dreams.'

'What's she mean?' the skinny one asked Liz.

I gazed at Skinny and smiled, let her take in my almost human features. None of these women had seen a commrach before. Had never expected to. I hailed from a place beyond the horizon of their daily conversation, from a strange and shadowed isle. The devil's work in flesh: that's how this skinny one saw me. She couldn't meet my eyes for long, looked to her Queen Liz.

If Liz feared my otherness, she made no show of it. She had the look of someone who'd spotted a ruse and wished her trickster to know it.

I kept my smile, my gaze. Whatever happened, I told myself, would happen very soon. Me and Liz. Right here.

The door at the opposite end of the room swung open.

''Ere,' said one of the whores. 'Look 'oo it is.'

Liz looked. Her scowl broke to a grin. 'Fucking Poppi.'

A young woman had come in carrying towels. She had two blonde plaits, wore the regulation tunic. Her left eye was entirely white. I was stunned. I recognised her from my dream. From my fever…

''Ello,' she said to the whores. 'Got towels fer yer.'

'Can see that,' Liz said. 'Pilgrim's arse, yer stupid.'

Poppi looked frightened. 'Shouldn't say that. Pilgrim hears all.'

'Yer giving me mouth, Poppi? Think you're queen here now?'

Poppi squeezed the towels in her arms. She looked at the floor and shook her head.

'Keep an eye out,' Liz muttered to one of her acquaintances.

She strode toward Poppi and the others followed. She pulled the towels out of Poppi's arms and they tumbled to the wet floor. Poppi yelped. She didn't move. She hugged her own shoulders.

Liz wrestled Poppi to the floor and pushed her head against the tiles.

I watched, still washing myself.

Liz, her face above her victim's, let drool run from her mouth. Then she said, 'I'll shit in your gob again, cow. Yer want that?'

'No…' Poppi said. She sounded like a dying cat.

'Mek yer do things. Eh?'

Poppi said nothing.

'I could take yer good eye, Poppi,' Liz said. 'Mother'd throw yer out then, wun't she? Do yer want that?'

'No.'

Liz hovered her hand over Poppi's good eye.

Funny, I thought of Urse Cal'Dain then. Even now, I don't know which woman made me think of him.

I made a howling noise, but backwards, drawing the air into my lungs.

The whores all looked at me.

I bit the inside of my mouth, spat blood on the wet floor.

'I'll chew your souls,' I announced in a demonic voice.

A silence.

'Shurrup,' Liz said, her face blank.

I made devil eyes at her, bared my dainty fangs. I stretched my left hand out and made some gesture with my fingers that meant absolutely nothing. Blood trickled down my chin.

'Leave her be.'

'Bollocks,' Liz said. 'Daft twat.'

Her skinny friend held her shoulder. 'Let's go, Lizbet.'

Liz stood up. 'Troll's a fucking bullshitter, Sally.'

Sally slapped her arm. 'Lizbet, please.' Her eyes watered, panicked. '*Please.*'

Liz looked at her. 'Fuck it, let's go. Be dinner soon anyhow.'

They traipsed toward the changing room and were soon gone.

I sighed with relief, chuckling to myself. I looked at Poppi on the floor. 'Are you OK?'

'Please dun't chew me soul.' She looked pathetic. I felt a pang of pity. Strange.

'It was a joke,' I said. 'A lie. To save you.'

'Shouldn't joke about that.' She rubbed her shoulders. 'Was clever though.' She stood up. 'I'm Poppi.'

'I know.'

'Thank you.' A peg-toothed grin broke out on her face, as if she'd thought of some wicked ploy herself. ''Ere, you don't recall me, duhyer? I looked after yer when you were poorly.'

'I thought so.'

'The Mother told me to look after yer.' She suddenly looked guilty, as if she'd insulted me. 'But I would have anyway. Nice to be nice.' She raised her chin and rocked her torso. 'You were me special pixeh.'

'Pixie?'

'Yeah.' She laughed at me. 'Pixeh.'

'I just saved you, bitch.'

'Sorreh,' she said. 'Not bein' funny. Mum used to call me Pixeh. Meant it nice.'

I stepped closer, pushed my wet hair back to reveal a sharp ear. 'You know I'm from the commrach Isle, right?'

She thought about this. 'That near Tiddleton?'

Poppi had no clue. No clue that she should have a clue.

Blood, she was like a child. A child-mind; one sees them about the Main. Unlike we commrach, the humans have never learned to put them to sleep. I felt revulsion, horror almost. I'd never talked to one before. Pitiful beast.

'Yer still feel poorly?' Poppi asked.

'I'm fine.' The water on my body was getting cold. My hand throbbed. 'Pass me a towel.'

She picked one up that was still mostly dry and passed it to me.

''Ere,' she said. 'Mother says yer can have bunk under mine. I'll show you round.' She faltered, looked askance. 'Be yer friend if yer like.'

My stomach reeled at the thought, but a notion struck me.

'The Mother likes you then?' I asked, drying myself.

'Yeah. Cuz I work. Pilgrim loves a worker, Mother says.'

'Well, isn't that nice?' I said and I forced a smile. I tried to dry my back. 'She lets you walk around the place?'

'Carrying stuff, moppin'. Not bright for much else. Dry yer back if yer like, erm…?'

'Shen,' I said. 'My name is Shen.' I turned around.

'Ooh, loveleh name.'

'So's Poppi.'

She took my towel and started drying my back. I shivered.

'Poppi, where do they keep things? The girls' things when they first come here?'

'There's this cage,' she said. 'Back of main hall.'

'They let you go in there?'

'Yeah. Help carry stuff.'

'My,' I said. 'The Mother must think you a *very* special pixie to let you in there. Do you think you could show me? I'll bet you know everything in there.'

'Finished,' Poppi said. 'There's fresh unders in that basket over there. Shifts too.'

I turned. 'Poppi, I'd like to look in that cage. You see… I left some sweetmeats in there.' I shrugged. 'But I don't suppose you like sweeties, do you?'

She looked fascinated, then a fright sad. Her small chin trembled.

'They don't gimme key.' She walked over to the basket and brought me fresh clothes. 'Guards have it. You better ask the Mother about them sweeties.' She grinned. 'Now come on, Shenny, you'll look a right silly puddin' if you go out of here like that.'

I took the clothes off her, feigned a laugh. I climbed into the underwear and put on the tunic.

'Poppi?'

'Yeah?'

'I think I'd *like* to be your friend. Would you like that, Poppi?'

She clapped her palms and giggled. Her good eye watered. For a second, I actually felt like shit.

Poppi seized my healthy hand and squeezed.

'Shenny and Poppi,' she said. She swung our arms back and forth like a child's game.

'Erm… indeed.'

I felt a twinge inside my sternum. A familiar feeling, not my bruise. And, no, not guilt. Vocal cords shifting, readying.

'Poppi… how long was I bedridden?'

'Poorly? Erm…' She thought long and hard. 'Six days.'

Shit. Spring equinox. Tomorrow, the day after, I'd have my yearly season.

'You alright, Shenny?'

I smiled. 'Yes. Yes, Poppi, quite alright.'

I woke up in my bunk, pleased not to have been shivved or beaten. I could hear thunderous snoring down the tunnel to my left, likely that humungous bitch Lizbet. The dormitories lay under St Waleran's. They had once been sewer pipes when humans had managed to get something like a half-respectable civilisation together, before, predictably, allowing it to collapse. Hoxham was laced with these subterranean nooks, sewers and catacombs and such, the infrastructure of a lost and much more populous city. I'd once visited a gambling den with skulls for walls and a water channel you had to step over in order to get to the bar. I never went back there but, in fairness, that wasn't the décor's fault.

The bunks were carved into the cracked brickwork. Poppi, and now I, had a bunk in a bend in the tunnel, rather separate from everyone else, partly because there'd been only enough room to carve two bunks in the walls there, partly because it stunk of damp. The outsiders' corner.

Limes. I could smell limes. I lifted my forearm to my nose and sniffed. That familiar citrus of the season musk. I put my hand under the blanket and checked. My grove's lips had hardened. I'd be in full equinox tomorrow, crazed, mounting St Waleran's altars and making *awow-woo* sounds. The residents of St Waleran's didn't need that, poor darlings.

Escape, Kyra. I had to escape tonight. Earlier if opportunity became my friend.

I let my finger slip onto my grove's stud. A tension went from my limbs, my toes curling. My body's changes had awoken me early. Why, I told myself, it would be the decent, the civilised, thing to placate myself before the others woke.

I found Kyran's old shirt beside my pillow. I tried not to think about the ink scribble upon it. Who had done it? The journeymen who had found me? Or... earlier, in those delirious nights I stumbled through mire and forest? I shivered. Too unnerving to give credence, that.

I shoved the rag in my mouth. A key skill in the travelling adventurer game is stealthy alleviation while companions snooze. The epics never seem to mention that.

You, Shen. I pictured you that time in the midnight forest, the Milky Way above, caught in your eyes, as you, as—

A thud upon the tiles. "'Ello, Shenny.'

Fuck.

I sat up and spat out the shirt. Poppi was stood over me, bent so as to look in on my bunk.

'Poppi,' I said.

'Shenny.'

I coughed.

'Heard you moving,' she said. 'I'm an early-birdy too. That your cuddle blanket?' She pointed at Kyran's shirt. 'Got it stuck in yer mouth, yer did.' She giggled. 'Want to see mine?'

She reached up to her own bunk and brought down two objects. She sat by my legs with no invite. Her hair was out of its plaits and she looked more like the adult she actually was.

'This is meh comb.' She showed me a broken-toothed example, more like a fish's spine in its deterioration. 'And *this* is Lady Coney.' She squeezed a cloth rabbit to her face and grinned. Like its owner, Lady Coney had but one good eye. It seemed to beg for death. 'She's not real, but if you *pretend* she's real then she *loves* to cuddle.' She looked nervous. 'But don't tell other girls. Lady Coney hides under meh pillow, see…'

'I understand.'

Her long hair hid her bad eye. She had beautiful hair.

'Shall I comb your hair, Poppi?' I heard myself say.

Poppi nodded and grinned. 'Mum would do that.' She passed the comb. 'Must do it ten times ten though. Please. Important.'

I manoeuvred myself behind her. I began to comb her yellow locks.

'You've *lovely* hair, Poppi.'

'Thank you. Yours is nice too. Black's nice.'

By the Blood. Her thighs tight together, the arch of her legs. I combed, watched her bite her lip and release as she studied her cuddle-toy. *She must have urges*, I told myself, *trapped in this hole*. Her body was adult. A civilised society would have snuffed her in childhood, inarguably. But, well, while she lived could she not be useful to others?

'Such shoulders,' I whispered in her ear. 'Such… such shiny skin.'

I placed a finger against her shift and, gently, pulled it down, exposing her left shoulder. I leaned in and kissed the smoothness there. A scent like butter.

Poppi tensed. She drew Lady Coney to her chest.

'Thank you for being meh friend,' she said. She winced. She shivered. 'Friends is… Friends is nice…'

I felt something like cold rain in my stomach. I stopped kissing. I replaced the shift. I gazed at the tunnel where Queen Liz slept. *Make you do things* she'd hissed at Poppi yesterday.

'I'm sorry, Poppi,' I said. 'I… I was being a silly pudding.'

Poppi wiped her nose. 'Would yer like to hold Lady Coney?' She passed the cloth rabbit without looking and I took it.

'Thank you,' I said. I fell back on my bed and clutched the awful thing.

Poppi combed her hair. She didn't look at me.

'Why do you stay here?' I asked her. 'Everyone here…'

'S'not their fault. They've 'ad bad lives. We all 'ave. Makes 'em silly puddings sometimes.' She eyed me briefly. 'But Pilgrim and Heaven's Hand love 'em.'

I wanted to snap at her, at this sky-madness, this mass fiction. *Fuck your Pilgrim, Poppi. His earthly cronies make you work for naught and keep you in a hole.* I scratched my chin. Blood, why should I even care?

'Where's your mother, Poppi?' I didn't care. Merely curious, I suppose.

Poppi stopped combing.

'Poppi?'

'Hey,' she said, brightening, 'Sister Benadetta's coming today.' She looked at me. 'Ooh, she's good. She'll fix yer poorly fingers I reckon. She made me funny eye better than it were.'

'The Mother mentioned her, I think. The, er, Perfect, yes?'

'Perfecti. B-but she's like the *bestest* Perfecti. Friendleh. And yer get extra food. Meat.'

I perked up at that. There'd only been soup and bread. I'd had to have soup, which was fine as mainland cuisine went, but a commrach of quality needs her flesh.

'Ooh, Shenny,' Poppi said. 'When Sister Benadetta speaks! It's like you can feel Heaven's High Hand deep inside yer. You know?'

I gritted my teeth. 'Sounds unmissable.'

The stained glass mottled everyone in the chapel, eighty women's bodies fractured by light and colour. I was sat in the rear pew beside Poppi. I could feel dust falling on me from the rafters above. The stink of wood polish pained me, stung at my temples. I wanted out.

'I cannot imagine the hardships you girls have known,' Sister Benadetta, stood upon the low stage, insisted. 'It would be an arrogance, a sin, for one such as I to speak for you. But I say this: I salute you women. The choice each of you has made – to leave your prior lives, to leap into what was unknown – inspires me. You are leaders, my friends. This world may insist otherwise, but I assure you.' She paused. Her act was impressive. 'You are leaders of your own hearts.'

I'd expected another overfed matriarch like the Mother. Not so. Sister Benadetta seemed no older than me. She was tall, statuesque.

Yes, that was what she reminded me of: those sculptures by Attawan the Perverse. We'd had a few stood around in the Jade colonies when I was young. Before Attawan, commrach statues of human women had been ugly, comical things: fat faces and swollen bottoms, spines warped by weighty breasts. Attawan's perversity lay in extracting that unique beauty of human females – their fuller, taller figures, their sublime faces full of strength. He'd even used – horror! – real models. The statues had provoked fancy in my then pubescent mind. I would picture myself sailing to the Main and defeating the Queen of Humans in single combat, taking her home in chains before admiring crowds. Attawan's perversity has long been mine.

Sister Benadetta might have been carved by Attawan, discounting her robes and wimple. Her face was round and healthy, her lips full and sensual, her cheekbones proud. But no way would I have ever wrestled and dragged her across the waves. Her lust had clearly been drained long ago, sucking the misty and ubiquitous cock of the Pilgrim. Frigid as marble.

'This world, all its matter, is evil,' she was saying. Her presence grew the more she spoke. The more one listened the more it filled the hall, turning the very air unreal. 'This world is pain. It will break our bodies.' She scanned the front row. It must have been hard not to be captivated when she did that. 'But not our spirit. Never that. For there shines a pearl of God inside each of us.'

Queen Liz leapt to her feet on the front row.

'Praise the Pilgrim!' she shouted, raising a palm high. 'For God is inside!'

'God is inside!' her crony Sally said. She leapt up on her feet beside Liz. 'Praise Him!'

'Yes!' Sister Benadetta stepped forward and waved her hands. The stained-glass light turned her face to a sky-blue mask. 'God is inside!'

Her words were churning the world into something like a dream, the air and light taking on the quality of a childhood memory, bright and drowsy and barely real. It was uncanny. Only my reason and the pain in my hand kept me from falling into it. Something, I had to keep telling myself, was not right here.

I looked at Poppi beside me. She was like a puppy at a second-storey window who'd spied a squirrel. Desperate to leap, but too scared to. She grinned and quivered in her seat.

'I feel the Pilgrim!' Liz shouted.

More stood, then the whole room. All of them consumed.

Praise the Pilgrim! Heaven's Hand! God! God is inside!

Even Poppi was on her feet now, her eyes closed, her face to the rafters.

My stomach rumbled.

This… whatever this was… reached its crescendo. There followed a weird sort of reverie where they all fell quiet and rocked on their heels. Sister Benadetta gestured for them to sit. In time, they did.

'So, when do we get fed?' I called out.

Everyone looked at me. The room was suddenly itself again, rudely awoken.

'What?' I said.

'Shurrup,' Liz said, scowling over her shoulder at me. 'Monster.'

'Calm,' Sister Benadetta told her. She studied me for a moment, and gave her well-drilled benevolent smile. '*Shoola*.'

'Greetings' in Commrach. Her accent was awful.

Caught out, I nodded.

'I'll level with you, Sister,' I said. 'This?' I waved around. At the audience, at the strange, undefinable ambience still evaporating around us. 'You?' I nodded toward her. 'It's genuinely fucking terrifying.'

There was such a drawing in of breath I fancied the chapel's windows might shatter inward. I was shocked myself. After all, they said Sister Benadetta would heal me; self-interest alone dictated I should remain quiet. But the wood-polish stink, the throb of my hand and above all, the nonsense here: I couldn't. I just couldn't. St Waleran's was a madhouse.

'Blasphemy!' Skinny Sally shouted. She was facing me, kneeling on her pew. 'Soulless beast! She's a devil in her, Sister! A devil! I saw!'

Others shouted. Poppi said nothing beside me. I didn't want to look at her, see the disappointment and confusion on her stupid face.

Sister Benadetta gestured for calm. The guard, Gilbertia, rose lazily from her chair beside the stage. Sister Benadetta indicated to her that, no, a beating wouldn't be necessary, really. In moments the room had acquiesced to the Sister's formidable serenity.

'Hey,' I told the room. 'Just one person's opinion. You shouldn't take things so seriously.'

Much muttering. Though quiet, as the Sister had directed them.

'A commrach,' she said, her face like an ivory cameo within her rough cloth wimple. 'We are honoured. Understand that our ways are different to yours. Yet there is much we both can learn.'

'I'm learning to avoid chapels 'til lunch,' I said.

Sister Benadetta stepped off the stage and walked down the aisle toward me, her sandals clacking against the tiles.

'May I ask your name?' she said.

'Shen.'

Sister Benadetta smiled at that. I didn't see the joke myself.

'Shen. I'm aware your people feel no compulsion towards faith. But God gave each of we humans a test, one for the immortality of our souls. These congregations, the joy they bring, are vital for us. For that spirit we each possess.'

'And which I don't.' I smirked. 'Of course.'

'Your purpose is different.' She frowned the slightest fraction. 'You are here as a test.'

'You're welcome, I'm sure.' The arrogance of this woman. 'My people built cities when you all lived in caves. You know that, right?'

'Might we pursue this discussion after lunch?'

'So, as I understand it, I am without this "soul" mummery of yours? That makes me mere matter, yes?'

'Let's—'

'And *you* just said all matter is evil. So—'

'*Shennn.*'

She raised her little finger before me. The most fascinating thing. She ran it across her own lips.

My mouth fell slack. I could not speak. My hands fell either side of my hips. Keeping my head up became a task. Things took on the dream quality again, but more intense this time, more focused. The world remained visible, but at a remove, like I was watching it all upon a stage, alone in the galleries.

Benadetta smiled. 'Let us pursue this discussion after lunch.'

She turned around and returned to the stage.

'Ha!' I heard that big bitch Liz declare. 'Never mess with a Perfecti!'

The hall roared with laughter. At me. And I could not summon the energy to retaliate. Everyone was so far away.

'Now, ladies,' Sister Benadetta said. 'Let us sing "I March To You, O Pilgrim".'

And they did. Fuck, it was awful.

———

I felt myself again once we'd had lunch. I had been careful to steal a few dried rashers of bacon and now carried them about in my good hand, taking bites as fancy took me. To pass the time I imagined looking Shortleg in the eye, driving my dagger under his chin. Good method that, I'd long found. Intimate.

Sister Benadetta's visit had brought St Waleran's to life. Many of the girls loitered in the main hall, chatting and, surprisingly, the female guards let them. One guard sat nonchalantly by the building's entrance, more concerned with visitors coming in than residents going out.

Frustrating. It would be nothing to belt out of there, even with my injuries. Yet I'd be leaving my blades, those better parts of me.

I looked toward the other end of the hall. There was a doorway and, shaded by gloom, I spied iron bars. They barely hid their cage. And why would they? It contained only the keepsakes of whores.

'That the cage?' I asked Poppi beside me.

Poppi shrugged. She nodded.

'You didn't talk to me at lunch,' I remarked. I hadn't noticed before, in my bizarre docility.

She chewed her lip.

'What's the matter, child?' I said.

'You were horrible to Sister,' Poppi said. 'Sister's nice. Got Pilgrim's power.'

'Is that what a Perfecti is?'

Poppi nodded.

It made sense. I'd suspected as much already. I'd learned in my old tutorials that humans possessed a power unlike our own people's imbuing. It did not affect objects; rather it clouded minds. This power only manifested in a fraction of the population, unlike imbuing's race-wide ubiquity. Fortunate, that; Sister Benadetta's power was immense. Clearly the Church had co-opted these individuals, given their singular nature's context and purpose within a religion. No wonder the Pilgrim's hook hung above every spire and doorway upon the Main. Perfecti. How shrewd.

'We're no longer friends, then?' I said to Poppi.

She shook her head. 'Don't fret: friends forever, Shenny. You just got mardy cuz you hadn't eaten. Happens.' She touched my chin. 'Yer forgiven.' She winked her working eye.

I sighed. 'You know, Poppi, talking to you is like staring right at the sun.'

Poppi thought about this. 'Thank you.'

She closed her eyes and raised her hands, then began wiggling her fingers. She was actually imagining herself radiating light and heat.

I took a bite of dried bacon. She was still impersonating the sun by the time I'd swallowed. If I were a moral person, I told myself, I'd have given her the mercy of my pillow as she'd slept…

Sister Benadetta glided toward us. She nodded at passing staff and residents.

'*Shoola*, Shen,' she said when she'd stopped before me.

'*Shoola*,' I replied, careful to highlight the proper accent.

Poppi opened her eyes and looked at the Sister.

'Hello, Sister. Sorreh, I were just being sun.'

'And a fine impersonation too, Poppi,' the Sister said.

'I loved yer talk today, Sister,' Poppi said. She looked at me as if expecting me to offer the Sister an apology.

She could keep waiting.

'Thank… Thank you, Poppi,' Sister Benadetta replied. She'd made a strange pause between those words, her expression like she was about to nod off. 'Poppi, I've got to help Shen here with her injuries. Do you think you…' She did it again. '…could get one of the guards to open the cage and c-collect my travelling things? Then would you bring them outside the chantry and wait for me and Shen there?'

'Love to help, Sister.'

'Thank you, Poppi.' The Sister touched the child-woman's shoulder.

Poppi beamed at us both, displaying two rows of wide-spaced teeth, and then she was off.

I studied the cage a moment and, when I looked back, Sister Benadetta was smiling.

'Come along,' she said.

The chantry was a small room whose walls were covered in wooden slats that held scrolls. Daylight poured in from a single window above head height. I could hear the noise of Hoxham's markets outside, smell its bakeries. A rectangular table stood at the room's centre with a leather satchel, a cloth and a bowl of water upon its surface. Sister Benadetta closed the door behind her.

Wariness here, I reasoned, would be common sense on my part.

'How did you know I was injured?' I said.

'The Mother informed me.'

'Right.' I thought about those journeymen 'finding' me on the road.

She looked at me. 'I'm sorry,' she said. She dipped her hands in the bowl then dried them. 'I've never met one of your kind. Frankly, I'm perplexed why a commrach would…' That pause again, her face frozen, as if taken by some ecstasy. She raced the rest of the sentence out: '…choose to entertain the crudities of the mainland.'

'Remain perplexed.'

'I should not pry. Let's look at your ribs first. If you, er, could lift your shift.'

I went to remove the whole thing, but she stayed my arm when it got past my bruise.

'Just… hold the shift up,' she said.

I chuckled. 'So amusing.'

'Pardon?'

'Your great Holy Pilgrim, petrified of a pair of perky pippins. Him *and* his followers.'

She had one of her facial moments, then said: 'Brazenness is a shout from an empty hovel.'

'I don't understand,' I said.

'No, I don't imagine you would.' She bent and placed her palm on my bruise. It possessed a curious warmth. 'No… breakages. The work… of moments.' She breathed out. Sighed, barely audible. '*Heal*…'

I can only describe the feeling as a tide of hot water and ice rippling through my torso. More of her powers. I moaned. I slammed my palm on the table, near-spilling the bowl.

She pulled away and the bruise tingled wonderful-nasty.

'You can… lower your garment now.'

'Of course.' I yawned and pretended to stretch, exposing my left nipple to the pious cow.

The Sister coughed and looked up at the ceiling.

'What?' I said. 'Oh. Sorry.' I let my shift go and it fell back in place. I chuckled again. 'Not bad for a hovel, eh, Sister?' I raised my eyebrows. 'If the cold persists I'll get it repointed.'

She looked straight at me, her face blank.

'You'll be on heat soon, yes?'

'Erm…'

'You do rather… stink of limes.'

I stroked my hair. '"On heat" is somewhat crass.'

'You cannot abide crassness? Well, well. Hypocrisy appears more than acceptable.' She studied me. 'They won't abide you here… on heat. You should be careful. I dare say the Mother might turn a blind eye if you weren't… t-t-to wake up one morning.' She shrugged. 'Now for your hand.' She went through her satchel.

Was that a threat? Interesting.

'Hey,' I said. 'What's with your voice?'

'I have an affliction of speech. One I've learned to control with my breathing. It was fear…ful in childhood.'

'Pretty alarming now. I didn't notice it when you were speechifying earlier.'

She pulled out a vial from the bag. 'Yes. Almost as if some deity moves through me in those moments, eh?'

I shook my head and made a show of exasperation. I noticed pins inside the bag, practically on display at the top of the contents, bound by thick thread.

'Hold out your hand, Shen.'

I did so. She sprinkled the vial's contents on my bent finger.

'What's that for?' I said.

'The pain.'

She grabbed my hand and pulled.

'Fuuuuck!' I'd never known such agony. I dropped to my knees. 'Fuckingarrgghhh… fuck!'

'Look at me,' she said. The air shifted, stretched, became laced with drowsiness as it had back in the hall.

I couldn't fight it. I winced. My hand tickled.

Water dripped from the table, slowly. As if time's thread were slowed in its loom.

'*Look at me, Kyra.*'

My name. I looked. Her eyes poured into me. I felt ethereal, hollow, like an outline. Nothing else.

She was you, Shen. It was *you* gazing down on me. Your eyes. Their green ice. Your healing palms upon my wrecked fist.

And then she was Sister Benadetta again.

'All better,' she declared. She smiled perfunctorily.

After a few breaths I got to my feet.

'What just happened?'

'An astonishment, they're called,' she said. 'The strongest feat Perfecti offer.'

'You said Kyra. Then you—'

'Matters from the well of your own conscience,' Benadetta said. 'It often occurs. I knew naught, Shen.'

'Right.' I felt dizzy. 'You've no stammer again.'

'God moves through me.' She washed her hands in what water remained in the bowl. Then she took the cloth and began wiping the spillage.

When she kneeled to wipe the floor, I took my chance. I lifted the bundle of needles out of the bag with my left hand, drew two with my right and popped them in my mouth, between my left cheek and my teeth. I dropped the rest back in the satchel. Only then did I realise my right hand functioned properly – my blade hand. I grinned and felt two needles stab at my gums. I hid the pain.

Benadetta stood up once more and smiled at me.

'I enjoyed our little talk earlier,' she said, 'back in the chapel. It was edifying, truly. Now run along. Poppi will be waiting.'

I grumbled.

'A heart like Poppi Simmuns', Benadetta said, 'could fill this world entire with light. She thinks you her friend, yes?' She dipped her brow a touch when I looked at her. 'How often are women like us called "friend"?'

I pretended to weigh her words, though I didn't really grasp them. I certainly wasn't going to enquire with all that metal in my mouth.

Sister Benadetta, Perfecti, opened the door. I walked out of the chantry.

I must have drifted off right after lights out. I awoke in my bunk in the tunnel's dark, heard moaning.

I jolted upright. Not from the noises – they were too human and pitiful – but from the realisation I'd fallen prey to slumber, had almost let opportunity pass.

Everything was black, everyone asleep, and so it must have been the early hours. But when? One only knew it was dawn when a guard came through and lit the lamps.

I fished out Sister Benadetta's pins from beneath my pillow and got up.

The moaning was Poppi's. I could only hear her in this blackness. Lost in her night-world, chased by her past. Whatever it was.

The soles of my feet were getting cold. I couldn't just stand there all night. This subterranean dormitory was so bereft of light even my kind's nocturnal vision was useless. As memory served, I'd fifty feet of tunnel before I'd come to the stairwell.

I used my ears, my nose. The scent of fresh air my guiding star, I steered by the snores of girls in their bunks either side of me. No human could have traversed this dormitory without waking someone. It seemed St Waleran's guards had long depended on the fact. The wrought-iron gate halfway up the stairwell confirmed as much. I barely needed to use a pin to work the lock. The gate's creak, however, was another matter. I heard a girl stir, but nothing more. I left the gate open and headed upstairs, a dim glow leading me on from somewhere above. Moonlight, I realised.

Ground floor. Corridors, cool air. No sounds. St Waleran's seemed deserted, and I had that sensation one has in these moments that none of this was real, that I was a figure in a sleeping girl's dream. The guards, if there were any, were probably at cards, too dependent on that shabby gate and the compliance of the girls.

I stopped before the main hall. No lamps there, but moonlight fell in from two skylights above, their wooden slats slicing the light, segmenting it.

I ran across, darting between the moon-glows, my bare feet smacking against cold tiles. I ducked into the doorway at the hall's far end, where the caged room lay. There was a space before the cage as one entered, an antechamber. I set to work.

I took a pin and worked the cage's lock. It snapped, but fortunately the part left in the lock still jutted out. I pulled it out with my fingernails then used the final pin.

It bent. I pulled it out, tried to work it back into shape, and the thing broke, leaving a stump between my fingers.

I wanted to scream.

Footsteps in the main hall behind me.

I ran into a corner of the antechamber, fell into a pile face down and pretended to weep.

Lamplight fell on me.

'Oi,' Sergeant Gilbertia's voice. 'The fuck are you doing here?'

I kept the weeping act up.

'Get up,' she said.

I ignored her. The light shifted as she placed the lamp on the floor. I eyed Gilbertia's silhouette on the wall before me: she was taking out her truncheon.

'Cage stop you, did it?' She sounded closer now. 'Won't tell you again, pixie. Get up.'

She grabbed my elbow. I twisted around, embraced her. Close, so she couldn't get leverage with her weapon.

'Poison,' I hissed in her ear.

Gilbertia froze. Her bones shivered against mine. No doubt she felt the bent pin at her throat.

'We call it the Jharrat Siln,' I told her. I'd said 'rabbit' and 'wall' in Commrach. First words that came to my head. 'I break your skin, the agony will be like giving birth through each pore.' I paused. 'Don't make me kill you.'

For a moment Gilbertia did nothing. Then I heard the truncheon hit the floor.

'On your knees, human,' I hissed.

She did so.

'Thanks,' I said. I seized the truncheon from the floor and swiped her across her helmeted crown. Gilbertia dropped.

I bent down and checked: she was alive. Good. I'd no wish to be wanted for murder. Assault on a church guard would be bad enough.

I took her keys and opened the cage. Then I dragged her inside. I panicked briefly when I couldn't see my things, but there they were, under a tarpaulin on a lower shelf. They'd wrapped my sword and Ned's knife in a cloth. I kissed the hilt of my rapier. I took off that hideous St Waleran shift and put on my old garb.

I strapped on my weapons, my bag. Kyra again. No one would stop me leaving this place.

I used the shift to bind Gilbertia's hands and legs. Taking one end of the tarpaulin I filled her gob with it. There'd be no screaming through that. I searched around the cage for money. None, but I found a decorative hook on a neck chain. Symbol of the Church. Silver. Might fetch a price.

I strode up to the double doors of the main hall, the door out, out into Hoxham. I stopped before opening it.

Sister Benadetta had been right. How often did women like us, like me, get called friend? I'd been a sibling, a fight partner, a bed mate. On the mainland I'd been a drinking buddy. But no one had called me...

I shook the sentiment off. I placed my palm against the door.

I'd come back, I told myself. I'd get Poppi out of here. Easy enough, that. I'd use the buried money under that barn in Tettleby, if it was still there. I would. I'd find Poppi employment, I'd...

No, I bloody wouldn't. This was *me*. I'd stabbed a boy who'd professed his love and I'd run. I'd let a woman burn to death. And that was in the last fortnight alone. I'd forget Poppi in a week. One can outrun guilt, despite what they say. I always had, always would. My lone virtue lay in knowing the fact.

Minutes later I was back in the blackness of the dormitory tunnel. I had to work fast. Poppi had fallen silent. I passed her by or must have, for I could see almost nothing. I hadn't the moral fibre, the strength, to wake and persuade her dull mind out of this hole. I scuttled on through the dark.

Easy enough to find her. I homed in on her monstrous snoring. She lay in a lower bunk. Lizbet, Queen Liz of the dorms. By the deep timbre of her wheezing I judged she lay on her back. I opened my bag.

Three years back I'd been on my first penny-tour, scrounging up work in south Ralbride, close to the Spine Mountains. Miserable time. I travelled with three men, bastards all, and one of them kept cracking jokes about raping me. He did so to get a laugh from the others but, when even they groaned to hear it, he carried on. I realised he was really talking to himself, normalising the act in his mind. I was damned if I was going to let him take me. Trouble was, we were tailing a good bounty. I needed the gold. Him or me. I knew there couldn't be any marks. The others would have to suspect nothing.

Plenty die in their sleep.

Liz barely fought. She'd no time to assess what was happening to her in the blackness. The trick is to gently push their heads back so that the oesophagus is straight, then slide Cuchulin in. An empty glove wrapped around its onyx base ensures their teeth do not break. My knees I rest on their upper arms.

She gave one push, but my shoulders hard against the brick of the higher bunk's underside took it. I realised I was coming into full equinox: my muscles stronger, more capable.

I thought to whisper something, some curse to take with her. But, really, where was Liz going? This was no vengeance but a mercy, the only sort I'd ever be capable of. Things would be different in Poppi's world tomorrow. Better. Brighter. Like a sun.

I walked out of St Waleran's soon after. Into the night.

6

The city state of Corso sits around the great crescent bay. Within this crescent the streets, canals and buildings are laid out in thirty-two groups of concentric circles, and, to a soaring gull, probably resemble the expanding ripples of thirty-two stones cast into still water. There are many public squares in the spaces between these circles, which should rightly be called diamonds now I think on it.

At the centre of each one of these thirty-two circular districts stand solitary and looming towers. They are the tallest edifices in the known world, standing between twenty and twenty-eight storeys high.

There are thirty-two towers in all, sleek as they rise and swollen of spire. The outer twelve – six to either horn of the city's crescent – are made of granite. Further in, five-a-side of Corso's centre, stand the onyx towers, and at the city's very heart loom the final ten, tallest of all. Each is cast from a single piece of deathless wrought iron. No one remembers when or how they were made.

Since the Golden Times, the state has awarded these thirty-two towers to the families with the greatest blood. That is to say, those judged by the Explainers (whose local observatory resides within a lush woodland at the city's heart) to have produced individuals with the greatest powers of imbuing.

These thirty-two families play an ages-long game of arranged marriage, timely duels and clandestine plots in order to strengthen their blood and be moved 'up house'. It is always possible to rise; it is always possible to fall.

Cal'Adra, formidable in prestige though embarrassingly mercantile in origin, were at that time of the twelfth tower. An onyx family, two towers from being iron. In the lifetime of Zadrikata, matriarch of Cal'Adra and my grandmother, our family had risen by two towers. Lightning speed in this dance of blood. Whenever we'd moved to a new tower Zadrikata, matriarch of Cal'Adra, had chosen quarters with a view of the next.

Kyran and I, fresh from our incident in the city gardens, were sat in her audience chamber, an austere room of pinewood, glum tapestries and stuffed panther heads. Late afternoon sun poured through the window to our left. Beyond, the eleventh tower cut the clear blue sky in half.

Our small chairs faced Grandmother's: a fan-backed wicker throne resplendent with silk cushions from the Far West. Slow Thezda, grandmother's guard today, stood silent and still just behind her. Thezda looked less our old acquaintance and more our indifferent executioner. Duty's puppet.

Kyran opened his mouth.

'Grandmother, I—'

Grandmother clicked her brass talons and Kyran shut up. The talon jewellery was traditional: a symbol of marriage, of preserved touch. Hers was a marriage of one and had been so for eighteen years. In highblood society even death is no divorce.

Striking features, Grandmother, even in her stately years. The most comely of her generation, they said. Her hair had kept its raven black save for the white stripe all women in our family gained in middle age. A feature, sat there in her chamber, I half-doubted I'd ever attain. Her hair rose up in two buns, wrapped around two sticks that jutted outward.

'I had an invite for tea today,' she said at last, her voice the creak of a recent hanging. 'From the patriarch of the eighth tower.'

The pair of us knew not to reply. Notably, no tea carriage lay before us.

'I had to decline,' she said. 'I had to *decline*, an hour before their patriarch expected me.' She sighed and adjusted the delicate silver chain around her neck. The chain matrimonial. 'I wonder what he read into that.'

Kyran squeaked. Or perhaps I did. I felt dizzy.

Her face fell blank. 'Why do you hate your grandmother?'

I looked at Kyran. He stared at his painted fingernails. I looked to Thezda, but she was a statue, palm on her sword's pommel, silver lenses staring at the wall behind me.

I spoke. 'I-I don't. I—'

She clicked her talons again.

'Have you the slightest idea,' she said, 'the remotest notion, you spoiled delinquents, of the lengths I have gone to to secure the Cal'Dain boy and his sister's hands? Hmm? The sacrifices? The promises made and alliances broken?' She leaned forwards. Her words did not rise above conversational volume, but they dripped with venom. 'Of how the blood of Darrad, the first city, would strengthen our own humble strain? Would proffer us a new home within a generation?' She gestured at the eleventh tower beyond the balcony. She leaned back. 'No. You see nothing beyond the mire of your pleasured little lives.'

I braced myself. 'I...'

She glared.

I spat it out: 'I hate him, Grandmother. Urse is a beast.'

'Why would that be of import, girl?' she said. 'How did you become so uncouth? So *ungrateful*? You are but an object for the Blood to pass through. As are we all. As is all our race in its climb to the final perfection. You are not required to question. A canal does not question the water. You are required to part your thighs when in season, to permit Urse to squirt, then to part your thighs again seven months thereafter. Repeat as required.'

I couldn't help but shudder. 'But I'm a longboot.' I sounded pathetic.

'Longboots have wombs. Why should you be spared?' She shook her head. 'This perpetual stupidity of yours sickens me, girl.'

I felt Kyran look at me. He turned to Grandmother.

'Grandmother,' he said. 'We were foolish. The heat of summer, our youth. Mistakes are—'

'Unforgivable. Urse tells me you set upon him and his friends. They were weaponless save mandatory daggers, intent on a peaceful glade-orgy.'

'Weaponless?' I laughed 'They set upon *us*. He followed us to the gardens intent upon a duel.' I shook my head. 'Glade-orgy? Blood, he's a nerve.'

'He's the one injured,' Grandmother noted. 'I see no wounds on you.'

'I'm the superior blade, clearly.' What a stupid thing for Grandmother to say.

'Cease your cheek, girl. I'll have you hang from my window by your fingers for the common blood to see. Urse says you threw javelins at them, maimed his friends. He says that was the first they knew of you.'

Kyran raised a palm. 'No, Grandmother, in truth—'

I cut him off. 'Don't protect me, brother.' I looked at Grandmother. 'I threw the javelins,' I lied. 'Me. But not before they drew their blades.'

Kyran gave me a look like his sister had been replaced. Yet he said nothing.

'Urse's family look set to break from us,' Grandmother said.

She let the statement hang. My relief was profound. Kyran's probably was too, but he made a good show of shock.

I didn't. Why should I?

Grandmother placed a brass talon against her chin. 'However, they may change their position—' Her talon lifted the silver necklace about her neck. '—if you take the chain upon your wedding day.'

I leaped up.

'No!' I shook. My eyes watered. 'No…'

The chain. The chain matrimonial, the insurance of blood. Unbreakable, unremovable save in death. The wearer lost desire for all save their spouse. But it didn't *ensure* desire for the spouse. No magic could do that. Certainly not in my fucking case.

'You can't,' I muttered. I had to control my breathing. 'I'm a twin. That's guarantee enough.' Twins don't bed the other sex, after all, not willingly. 'Why?' I grimaced, waving a finger. 'Urse. Urse wants to torment me. For *life*, Grandmother.'

'Excellent,' she said. 'You need taming, Kyra Cal'Adra. Anyone—'

'Fuck you.' I couldn't believe I said it.

My brother couldn't either. He gawped at me, mouth like an open tunnel.

'Sister…' he whispered.

'It's fine, my boy,' Grandmother said. A grin had seized her dark red lips. 'She may curse me. I am but another object in time. Used up, in fact.' She stared at me, calm as a panther. 'But I wonder whether she has the nerve to curse our family. To curse the Blood.'

It was as if she'd dared me to draw a blade when she had a loaded crossbow. To slander the Blood, to mock our climb to racial perfection, was the oldest taboo upon the Isle. It was to invite dissection beneath the Explainers' obsidian scalpels.

'Fire inside you, girl,' Grandmother whispered. 'But not that much. Eh?'

I stared at her for what seemed an age. I stomped out of her chamber.

I stepped in front of a passing servant and threw him across the corridor. He mewled an apology and I strode on. At the stairs up to the tower's roof I punched a guard who saluted me.

There was no one on the roof's west balcony, a slash in the great black spire. Servants had left clay moontiles on the floor to catch the sunlight. They cracked and powdered under my feet and I felt their sculptors' imbued energy shiver and evaporate into the air. I leaned against the parapet, looked down upon my monstrous city, and screamed. I screamed again.

I heard shuffling behind me and turned to see my brother.

'Kyra,' he said. 'How could you curse at her?'

'She always saw it in my eyes.'

'Try keeping it there.'

'Well then fuck you too.' I spat on the gritted onyx floor. 'It's not your life that's over, is it? You can keep screwing youths till you're a senile embarrassment.'

'Kyra.'

'They will cauterise my *heart*, dickhead. Her and Urse.' I gestured at him. 'All you fuckers.'

He looked hurt. 'She won't go through with it, sis.' He stepped closer. I let him hold my shoulders. 'Think how bad it'd look on the family. Grandmother just wants you scared. Compliant. Not bridled.'

'She means it.' I growled, held it back. 'Brother, let's run.'

'What?'

'Let's leave. Disappear. Neither of us want this.'

Kyran squinted. 'What? To Darrad? Skarrach? They'd send us back, you fool.'

He was right of course. A childish thought.

'Over this parapet. Why not? Hand in hand.'

'Ra-ra...' He rubbed my shoulders, stroked my cheek. 'We both know you'd never end your life. You love yourself too much.'

I sighed. 'Well, naturally. Have you *seen* me?'

'True,' my twin replied. 'Hmm. Funny how Urse didn't mention the part about the pigtail. Now why would that be I wonder?'

I laughed. 'My sweet Ran-ran.'

We gazed in each other's amethyst eyes.

'Go forth and beat the shit out of something,' he whispered. 'Preferably inanimate. Then drink.'

'Brother, you know me to the hilt.'

I'd been saving the cadaver for a special occasion. I whacked and jabbed its mummified form with a wooden sword as it swung upside-down from its hook. A kick to the face and its upper lip came loose. I stopped to look. Its leathery expression had become a grin. Back and forth.

Alone in the domed gymnasium. Me and a desiccated human corpse.

I panted and gazed at the thing, wiped fresh sweat from my brow.

'Bet you never pictured this to be your tomb,' I told the hanging man. 'I hope it was agony, savage. I hope you writhed on the sands begging – no, what would you call it? – *praying* for death. Whoever you were.'

I grimaced at its rictus grin. They had come for us, the humans, a whole fleet. Sent by some mad dictator of one of their cities in hope of swift victory, in hope of wiping the stains of defeat against their own species in some absurd and prolonged war. Not the Isle of course; they'd attacked our colonies. The Jades. They'd thought my childhood home soft quarry. Indeed, at first it was. The Jades' co-governing family, the Cal'Roshos, had neglected to spot the human fleet despite having several maritime patrols in the area. An incompetence that had reduced them to the Roshos of infamy. That, at least, was the charitable take. During the hearing my grandmother had been quick to point out the Roshos had often had dealings with the mainland. She'd added no more. There was really no need.

'What?' I asked the cadaver. 'Is that a smile? Are you *laughing*?'

I raised the wooden blade and swung, a downward stroke to the head. A bend of the knees and the blade flew level to its husk of an ear. The ear tore, pissed a trail of sand across the gymnasium floor. I stepped back and watched the sand make lines on the dark pine as the cadaver swung back and forth. A pattern of no plan, no ultimate goal.

I flexed my shoulders, my neck. My padded body stocking chafed my throat. I had sworn at Mother before she'd walked out of our home. Demanded to fight beside her. I'd been thirteen.

She'd left two guards to watch me and Kyran. We had held each other as arrows fell like rain upon the roof. Our army had no answer to their longbows. Imbuing cannot strengthen metal, merely hone it to a sharpness that had made shields obsolete millenniums past. Amongst ourselves. A volley of human arrows, near-impossible to dodge in their sheer mass of numbers, were another matter entirely.

'Animal,' I told the cadaver. 'Not one of you made it home.' I grinned. 'I hope your children *weep*.'

I swung with all my strength before I realised I'd even meant to. The collision raced up my forearms. An explosion of sand. It hit the floor and snaked up in plumes. Into my eyes.

I dropped my sword and spluttered. My eyes watered. I'd got stuffed-corpse sand in my hair. A fine day, this.

'Is this a bad time?' came a voice from the gymnasium's threshold. 'I see you two have much to discuss.'

You, Shen. No longer in servant's garb, you wore a body stocking like me. And no more headdress. Hair tumbled from your head in thick scarlet curls. A sign of ill-breeding, that, not enough to be snuffed at birth but sufficient to procure only lowest marriage. Commrach hair should be magpie black or – just occasionally – silver. And yet…

'I should thank you,' I said, wiping what sand I could away. 'For earlier.'

'Please,' you said. 'Don't say you owe me your life.'

'I don't.' I stood straight and crossed my arms. 'But you saved me undue bother.'

'Doubtless.'

We looked at each other awhile and for the first time I registered the sunlight, falling from the hole in the dome above, beating upon my neck.

'You're dressed for practice,' I observed.

'Is that a challenge?'

'If that's assent.' I picked up my training sword. 'Your style? Rapier? Sabre?'

'Kai-bolg.'

I chuckled. 'A traditionalist. Your javelin-play should have told me as much.'

'My family hails from Skarrach,' you said. 'How could we be anything else?'

You walked over to the weapons rack. Skarrach. Explained the hair. A rural 'city' on the south coast, their family towers were of various timber. I'd never been depressed enough to visit. Still, Shen, you had wonderful legs in that body stocking. And I knew you knew I watched.

Taking two wooden and dusty kai-bolg from the rack, you strode toward me. We stood two paces apart.

A new creature, nothing like the ignorant serving girl before. Fierce. Fundamentally ready. Sometimes one sees fascination in a stranger's eyes, recognises it as the mirror of one's own. And neither understands precisely why. Only hate, or want, can possibly follow.

You span the kai-bolg in your left hand and offered me the hilt. Somewhere between sword and spear, its hilt was the length of its two-foot blade.

'You don't know how to use one, do you?' you said.

'Of course I do.'

You smirked. 'You Corso folk. Strutting about with your oh-so-modern rapiers. This isle would be wasteland if not for kai-bolg. What would you do if the fomorg slithered from the earth and sea and air once more, hmm? Think a rapier would help you then?'

I took the weapon from you. 'Hardly fucking likely, is it?'

Say what you will of Corso, we were a city state with at least one eye on the present. The forest folk of the interior were still, mentally speaking, locked in a war that had dissipated ten millennia ago. Which was impressive, for the fomorg incursion was near-impossible to even picture, let alone fixate upon. The fomorg race, if race they were, came in a tumult of forms: headless giants with slavering mouths at their hips; clouds of moths that gnawed flesh to milk; long-haired corpses and shark-faced men; worm-fisted animal-hags and androgynous beings of malicious, glittering beauty. The list of entities went on, only becoming weirder, each nightmare but a handmaiden to King Bolgada, whose face-mask makers cannot imitate without going mad.

That the incursion happened in at least some form was beyond doubt; we do not permit myth and fancy to consume us as the humans do and, besides, there were still places in the north west of the Isle warped by fomorg touch, crags twisted and crystalline where visitors disappeared or simply dropped dead. However, the Explainers are at a loss to this day to, well, *explain* the matter. An imbalance in the world's four humours is their most solid hypothesis, or perhaps some pan-racial psychic event so powerful it achieved flesh (it should be noted the fomorg incursion occurred during the commrach fertility season). My own take? None of it fucking matters because it happened so long ago.

We strode over to a ring, its circumference delineated in dried tar. We faced each other, eight feet apart.

'You've been studying me for some time now,' I said. I began to stalk you, circling, as did you. 'You came here to protect us, I take it? Me and my brother? For the debt your family owes mine?'

'I should think that obvious.'

'You think me worth protecting?'

'I think life should have meaning. I've known little of that. Look at my hair. No one would thank me for womb-work.'

'They might its precursor.' I grinned. 'Doubtless.'

We kept circling. In truth I talked because I'd no wish to strike first. I hated kai-bolg, hadn't handled one since childhood. Even a wooden version felt clumsy and imbalanced.

'You utter bore,' you said. 'Buying time with… "charm".'

'Please; strike first. I need amusement.'

'You're as much use with that as you are a man's fuck-spear, longboot. Your stance says all.'

'You're a fawn before a fire,' I told you. 'You cannot best—'

You fluttered your eyelids, eased out your tongue. Delicate, it curled and quivered at your command. A profound control.

I gulped.

My right hand's knuckles spasmed. Then agony. My kai-bolg's tip hit the floor and the flat of your own hit my stomach. I stumbled back to find your foot behind my heel. My shoulder blades took the impact of the floor.

You were atop me, sat upon my chest, wood blade against my throat.

'Call me a traditionalist,' you said. 'But isn't it custom now for you to say "yield"?'

My stomach burnt with an anger that soon travelled south. I laughed.

'If I'd my rapier…' I ran a palm along your thigh. Tight muscle below the stocking, smooth as polished oak. 'I'd *have* you.'

You leaned down a little. Your long scarlet hair became a curtain all around, blocking the gymnasium from my sight. Your face became the world, Shen. Your rose perfume. Your breath.

'You'd like that, wouldn't you?'

I squeezed your thigh. 'My reputation reaches Skarrach?'

'Don't flatter yourself. Your house staff warned me. They say Kyra Cal'Adra works a girl's body like a harp.'

'I'd pluck a tune from you.'

'And then forgets them. That's what they say.' You leaned closer, inches from my lips. 'I won't be another tale to tire your brother with.'

'Never,' I lied.

'Good. Then, I suppose... you'll just have to court me.'

'Court you?'

You stood up and the sunlight blinded me.

'Court me,' you said. 'Like the humans do. You've heard of human courting?'

'I've heard of human religion too. Doesn't mean I kneel to fictions.'

'I understand, sir.' You had returned to that cold servant once more, she of the fawn mask and the peacock hood. 'I shall return to my quarters.'

You began to walk away.

'I'm a highblood, woman.'

'With a low mind. Sir.'

'Wait...' I couldn't believe this. I couldn't believe what I was doing. 'Fine. I'll do as you request.'

You stopped. You didn't turn around. 'Do what, sir?'

'I'll...' I muttered the next part: 'Court you.'

'Very well. We begin our courtship tomorrow.' You began to walk away once more. 'A promenade along the Great Aqueduct perhaps. You can decide the details.'

'You're crazy,' I called to you. I got up onto my knees. You were gone.

But, oh, who was crazier? You? Or I, frittering my time on your eccentricities before the necklace bound my life like a noose about a thief's throat?

7

'Awoo-woo-woo.'

The noise bubbled up from my ribcage and raced out my mouth. Pathetic, the long, drawn-out sound of the season, like a cat who had its tail stamped on hours ago and won't stop moaning about it.

Fucking equinox. This was a bad one. Citrus-stink, muscles burning, thoughts tiny, obsessed. I hid in rat-fat alleys till noon and struggled not to frig myself indolent. No easy task. Blood, I was *on*.

Noon. She'd be working by noon.

Hood up, I stumbled toward old Orton Road, home to artists, gangsters and slum lords, fakers, fakirs, fuckers. And whores. Understanding whores, from the lowest Orton Road goose to… specialists. A very special specialist. Sweet, sweet Esme Damaris.

'Awoo-woo.'

I put a hand to my mouth. This damned mount-me song; nothing a woman in season could do about it, like a little animal in one's chest. In the unlikely event a commrach male was within two hundred feet, I'd soon know about him.

Sweating, the stink of musky limes in my nostrils, I snaked through Orton Road's crowds. Ordinarily I felt at home here, or as near as I might anywhere. Hoxham was more relaxed than most human city states. Instead of burning its discontents at the stake it gave them a slum and looked the other way. Sodomites and dykes held court here, as did men born as women and women born men. Foreigners too, people of the Far West or Antardes blood, their skins saffron and brown. A commrach was marginally less remarkable along rotten and rickety old Orton.

Two Crownsmen were talking with an apple trader. Armed keepers of the Crown of Hosshire's peace, their profession was essentially the opposite of mine. It didn't do for any pennyblade to dally in a Crownsman's presence for long. Never was this truer than for an easily recognisable commrach woman who'd squirreled away six hundred pips in Crown revenue.

I opted to turn into a backstreet, thoughts of the Crown's noose weighing upon me and ultimately only making me hornier. Life, after all, is apt to be cut short at any moment.

At the alley before Esme's, I stopped. At the other end stood two men in servants' garb, leaning against a box palanquin. Whoever they were charged to carry was no longer inside.

I looked toward the back stairs of Esme's boudoir and spied a chubby handmaiden disappearing up them. Competition.

I growled. I'd no intention of waiting.

I ran down the alley and bolted up the wooden stairs. The handmaiden turned to face me, her expression scandalised. Just ahead of her on the stairs was her lady, comically dainty next to her servant. At the first hint of someone approaching she'd pulled her heavy skirt over her head, her soft underskirt remaining to hide her dignity. I never saw her face.

The chubby handmaiden stared at me, eyes wide, waiting for me to speak.

'*Awoo-woo-wooo…*' I said. I hadn't meant to, obviously.

I bent at the knees, my spine arching. A wave of heat spread out from my groin.

'Ooooh…' I said.

My hips began thrusting, a most formidable attack of glitter-gusset. I collected myself, glared at the handmaiden.

'I'm from the Church,' I informed her. I wiped sweat from my brow.

She looked terrified. Her lady shook.

I stumbled up to their level. I fished the pilfered silver hook pendant from my bag and waved it at the handmaiden.

'Perverts, eh?' I said. 'Sickening.'

Under her lifted skirt the lady – a merchant's wife by the look of her garish dress and the acrid stink of far too much perfume – mewled. The handmaiden shook her head violently.

'The whore's to hang,' I told them, nodding toward Esme's door atop the stairs. 'There's spare hemp for both your necks, sinners.'

They started to cry.

'Go!'

They did so, the lady nearly tumbling over her help. She kept her skirt over her head the whole way.

I didn't stop to watch. I reached Esme's door and, finding it unlocked, barged through.

A single lantern lit the small room. The place smelled wonderfully of sandalwood and old candles. There, next to a sumptuous deep bed, stood Esme in a red silk nightdress, her back to me as she brushed her dark hair. Six foot of luscious fancy, Esme, her arse a pear I'd proffer all Corso's towers to chew upon.

'Lie on the bed, me lovers,' she said in her buttery Talonshire accent. 'I be with thee in moments.'

'Please, continue brushing,' I said, unbuckling my weapons and throwing them on the floor. 'I'll tup you where you stand.'

Esme turned and frowned. Her lips were beautiful when she did that.

'Kyra? If I'd known it were you I'd have told you to scram. I got a client coming, you galley-beggar.' She waved her brush at the door I'd come through. 'Off with thee! Go!'

I hadn't the wit to deceive again, not in my state.

'Change of plan,' I said, strutting closer. 'We had a talk on the stairs.'

I'd braced myself for her rage but instead she looked perplexed, even fascinated.

'You and her? About what?'

'About telling them both to fuck off, what do you think?' I'd never known her this slow. I ignored it. All my focus was upon her fulsome, heaving bosom. The pride of the Main. Nothing quite like it existed back home.

'Thought you were up country,' Esme said. 'Shoulda booked a—'

I was on her. Face in her hair, palms working her back and bottom. My burning grove hard against her thigh.

'Oi!'

My right ear pulsed with agony. I yelped. She whacked it again with her brush.

'You bad'un!' she said. 'Filthy girl! Down!'

I stepped back and she took the opportunity to whack the other ear. They're sensitive during equinox. When I said Esme knew how to treat a commrach girl, I meant in all respects.

I fell on the bed and whimpered, clutching my head.

'Traipsing in here all puggle-headed and stinking!' She yelled. 'The nerve!' She looked down and scowled at me. 'Tryin' to rape me or summat? That it?'

I looked up coyly. 'Only if you *wanted* me to, Esme.'

She whacked my ear again and I yelped.

'I'm sorry.'

'Better fucking be, eh? What a way to talk! Know what? I reckons I should hire security. Only I've no money coz some sprite bitch keeps scaring me clientele!'

'You could always try locking your door,' I suggested.

I got another whack. The fight went out of me.

'*Awoooo…*'

'This ain't how I reckonsed life in the city.' Esme turned from me and began combing her hair again. 'I know that much.'

'*Awoo-ooo.*' Fuck, my howling was like hiccups this year, as incessant as it was incurable. A pleading mewl laced with something that bordered on anger.

'Better than this,' Esme continued. 'Got dreams. So much I could do if I just…' She worked a particularly resistant lock. 'Had some *fucking* money…' She stopped brushing and massaged her brow.

I thought of the six hundred pips we'd buried under the barn, me and Ned and Shortleg. Shortleg and his village pals had all that now, most likely. I dreaded to think what dreams he'd spend it on. Blood, I dreaded my own.

'Where's your coin then?' Esme said, never looking.

For a moment I thought she meant the hidden stash. But she was making the best of a ruinous afternoon.

'I've got silver,' I told her. I held up the hook pendant.

She took it off me, inspected it. Bit it.

'Found religion all of a sudden?' she asked.

'I bow before your altar alone, dear Esme.'

She sighed. 'Alright lover. Two hours. Mount and pound?'

'Well, it is the season,' I said. 'Oh, and the hand mirror.'

She opened her bedside drawer and passed her mirror.

'Bloody narcissist,' she said. 'Which number?'

'Five, I think.'

She walked over to the cupboard beside the door and opened it.

'Awoo-woo-woo…'

'There-there, me kit-kit.'

She undid her nightdress and took a strap from the cupboard, began to clamber into it, her bottom sheer against the dress's red silk.

'What would you do if you had money?' I asked. I liked to let her undress me, she being an artist at that. The wait was near-unbearable. I had to roll about the bed, draw my knees to my belly.

'Private club,' Esme said, adjusting the strap. 'For all us sisters, see?' Her back still to me as she took number five down from its place on the shelf and began to screw it on. 'Maybe the queer boys too, if it thrived. Private. Safe. For all our sort.'

The beauty of it halted my writhing. I'd never considered the like.

'Pleasant dream,' I said, running a palm down the length of my thigh. 'How much would it cost?'

'More than you could afford, kit-kit. More than any of us.'

Don't be so sure, I thought. Perhaps, if…

Esme turned around and let her nightdress fall. Naked, save for the varnished phallus strapped to her sex. Eight inches of island dark-oak, carved in imitation of a commrach's erection. One of several imports. She walked towards the bed.

'You're on the brink of starting without me,' she said with eyebrows arched. Her business demeanour had vanished. All creamy warmth.

She seemed to pour onto the bed beside me. She kissed my forehead and, gently, put her lips over my sword-hand's fingers and sucked. She pulled her mouth away and closed her eyes with bliss.

I began to purr. She drew my head in and let me nuzzle at her tan bosom.

'Good girl,' she whispered. 'Who's a *good* kit-kit? Eh? Ooohh... have a suckle on Mummy...'

About that. That was just a name Esme used. I never asked her to or anything. I fucking *swear*.

The door swung open and Esme jolted. I looked up.

A handsome blond youth in a long red jacket barged in. Behind him was a man in grey uniform like Sergeant Gilbertia had worn. A church man or journeyman or whatever they were called, mace in hand. And behind him, stomping into the room came—

'Shortleg!'

That big bastard looked at me and Esme on the bed.

'Fuckin' 'eck,' he said.

The man in journeyman uniform picked up my weapons belt. I cursed my stupidity, yet who could have predicted?

Shortleg held up a piece of vellum with a hook stitched to it.

'By the one and only Church's authority I place you, Kyra Cal'Adra, under arrest.' He looked at the uniformed man. 'I get that right?'

Esme was up and off the bed.

'What is this?' she thundered. 'I'll have you all in stocks before the night's out! This woman—' She pointed at me. '—is under *my* protection, and I have the protection of nobles, merchants and masters! You'll see! I've had bigger men than all three o' you broken!'

Shortleg stared at Esme, this vision of a woman: furious, naked, oaken-cocked. He waved his parchment at her strap-on.

'Reckon you're a bigger man than all of us, love.'

'Oh bet on it, shithead,' Esme yelled. 'You men are all as useless as a fucking—'

The handsome young man punched her cheek and she dropped. He shrugged, then gestured at Shortleg to continue.

'Sorry it has to be this way, Kyra,' Shortleg said to me.

'Arsehole,' I told him. 'What's even going on here?' I moved my hand toward the hand mirror. I'd bludgeon the journeyman who held my rapier, improvise from there on. 'You're not pious, Shortleg. You're just some paunchy twat.'

'People change.'

'Not paunchy twats.' I had the mirror's handle now. I could hear Esme sob. 'You betrayed us all. Killed Illsa. Killed Ned.'

Shortleg frowned at that.

I moved to strike.

A cracking sound, and the hand mirror was impaled to the bed. A thin six-inch spike had pierced its surface without shattering it. Only imbued blade points could do that.

'Inadvisable,' a polished male voice said, 'commrach.'

I looked up to see the handsome young man, another spike in hand. Blond spiked hair, a broken nose that lent him a feline quality. A torc around his neck. There was something about him.

His ears. His ears were pointed. A commrach, with the power to imbue. But his blond hair made no sense. And why was he not in season's grip?

My stomach turned. I recalled the deformity parades of old. Sterile abomination, violation of the Blood. Sick alloy of commrach and humanity.

The blond thing was a caliban.

I smelled that underground smell again. Tunnels. Perhaps St Waleran's.

I'd hang. Hang for that petty sadist Lizbet. I struggled. Trouble was, my wrists were tied behind my back and I'd a sackcloth over my head. At some point Shortleg and his caliban had exchanged me, passed me on to silent hands, never replying to my taunts. The equinox was stronger in me now and my curses were scant more than growls.

I was led along somewhere that echoed. Two pairs of hands gripped me at first but, as my body strengthened, another pair joined in. A leather truncheon slapped my belly. I snarled. *Bite the fuckers*, I thought, *tear them*.

Onward.

I wanted to kill Shortleg. Not for his old betrayal, nor for his arrest now, but for the mystery he'd left me with. Why had the Church seen fit to make that whoring, guzzling oaf their puppet? I didn't want to die without knowing. I didn't want to die.

A metal door opened. I was jostled forward, likely into a cage. They untied my wrists and truncheoned my shoulder before I even fought. They stripped me down to my underwear and chest bindings. They threw water on me and pulled off the bag.

Women, all of them, in the grey robes and wimples of the Church. Surrounding me in a cobble-walled cell. Grabbing my arms and shoulders, forcing me toward a high-backed metal chair. An iron band with padding for the neck. For the wrists, the thighs.

'Relax,' a woman said. 'This chair's a sprite-seat. For when you're in slut.'

I struggled, but there were more on me now. Compelling, heaving me toward that thing.

'No.' I said. 'I *don't*... *awoo-woo-woo*... nuh... *awoo-ooo*...'

'Devil's in her.'

'Pilgrim preserve.'

'Fuh...'

'Push her down.'

'*Awoo-woooo*... no... hgh...'

'Devil's strength she has!'

'Trust in Heaven's Hand, Sister. She'll give—'

'*Awoo*...'

I felt the iron on my arse and back. They pulled my hair back and locked the neck band. I was so focused on struggling with my arms that I didn't notice them brace my thighs. Wide, those thigh bands, diagonal. They kept my thighs from touching each other. I comprehended the chair's function now. Purity, their sky-mad purity. To stop a commrach woman in equinox from alleviating herself. From satisfaction. From nature's law.

'Please!' I screamed. 'You don't know what you're doing! *Ple-awoo-woo-woo*...'

I wasn't ready for this. One needed training for this. One needed, one—

'Dangerous!' I yelled. 'You don't know.'

One woman prayed. Another kissed my forehead, hot and sticky.

'The Pilgrim is with you, girl,' she said. 'Always.' She smiled.

'*Please*...' As I spoke she shoved something soft yet solid between my teeth. I couldn't spit it out.

They left. They locked the cage.

The bands were unbreakable. I heard myself sob. My muscles burnt.

They put out the lamp.

'Arur-rur-ruuur...'

I forgot my name. My past. I struggled and hissed. I tried to jut and rake my groin. Rub against the seat. Nothing. No relief.

I spasmed. My muscles locked. Shivered. Burnt. I—

My sex. My sex, an animal biting into me, chewing into hot guts. Dirty teeth, infecting, raw.

I whined. My eyes watered.

Visions came. I knew they would. The Explainers experiment with such. A river runs below the rational mind, it is said, a subterranean stream only encountered in sleep, cushioned by dream. An abstinent woman could visit in her equinox. Reach some peak and encounter whatever the rational mind ignored. It wasn't something that had ever appealed. Right now it terrified me.

Strange women brushed by me, blue-skinned with hooks for teeth. I couldn't touch them, and when I tried to touch myself they grinned and sighed in strange caverns; they moaned and melded into one another, became new forms. Now red-eyed, many-eyed, black spines for pubic hair. They swirled around me, some becoming quadrupeds, others growing fins. I didn't want to touch them anymore. My thighs struggled against iron, bled. This was the realm of the fomorg, chaos made flesh.

I shook against the iron bands, horrified, pain-wracked, screeching. The women were a blur now, all one, a spinning wall of wet blue skin, a hurricane of bleeding eyes and tongues like seaweed, of hysterical laughter.

The cell floor had given way to a black void and a low moan rose beneath me. The moan below wanted to *touch* me, I knew it did. I knew if the moan touched me I'd…

It emerged from the blackness, floating up the eye of the flesh-hurricane to meet me. The figurine, the clay figurine from the cellar in the inn, the rustic devil I had held to the light for inspection. But far larger now, larger than any man, large as a cathedral, a city, a world. His pot belly was a dome, his goat hooves ramparts, his pinched clay prick rising up like the towers of home, its bulbous spire wet and twitching.

But it was his mask, that coarse twine bound to the head, I feared most. The twine, far larger than any rope, was snapping, fragmenting. Coming loose. The moaning grew louder. My limbs spasmed against the hot iron of the chair. My sweat poured. I screeched through foamed lips.

By the Blood. Here the devil. Here the King of Nothing, the un-life. Rising closer. Lord of all fomorg. Him.

King Bolgada. His face. Soon I'd see his…

I screamed into the void and the void consumed me.

Candlelight. I lay in our cot. Me and Kyran. Babes. My scream had become a child's cries.

Warm hands lifted me to a soft embrace. Eyes gazed at me, eyes I only saw in dream. Mother. Her soft body my world.

'Oh, oh, oh,' she whispered. 'Hush my child.' Her kind face. Her smile.

She touched my nose.

'Why be always so, sweet Kyra?' she said. 'Pouring out snakes and digging hearts from the ground…'

I didn't understand. She had never said those words, not ever.

Yet I stopped crying.

I let the holy women clean me: my hair, my skin, my grove's blood. They dressed me in my own clothes. My wrists and thighs were bruised.

My season had passed. I didn't struggle. They had my weapons. And so they had me.

For now.

I was led down a candlelit hallway. We stopped at a small timber door and I was urged through. Garlic wafted to my nostrils as the door opened, and my stomach growled.

The room's long ceiling was arched, with a round window on either incline. The windows cast daylight at an angle, forming a bright V whose point met on a wide table's surface. A plate of food steamed there, on the side closer to me. On the other side sat an indiscernible figure. Someone wearing a pale wimple of the Church.

I walked over and sat before the plate of food. Chicken wings with a white sauce. Boiled acorns. Carrots. I dug in before whoever it was behind the table offered the food to me. Deny them power, however small. Always.

'I trust you feel better?'

I recognised the voice. Sister Benadetta.

I looked up.

'Bitch,' I said. I shoved a chicken wing in my mouth and chewed. 'Bitff.'

She took a breath.

'I quite understand,' she said.

The food was amazing. Fuck her.

'You could hardly ask the Church to placate your carnality,' she observed.

'Indeed.' I didn't look up. 'I wouldn't even ask it to kidnap me.' I chomped on a carrot. 'Cunt.'

'You're not…' She paused, that speech impediment of hers. 'Interested in how we tracked you down?'

'Not really. I presume your church has a tab with every whorehouse in Hoxham. Orphanages too, I'd wager. Give me my weapons.'

'In time, Kyra Cal'Adra.'

I stopped chewing.

'I see that's got your…' Benadetta was having a bad stammer attack. She looked like she had one of those sneezes that brews but never comes.

'Attention,' I said, finishing her sentence off. 'Kyra Cal'Adra is merely my cover name.' I gave her a sarcastic smile. 'Thought I'd say that now and save you a half hour of getting to the point.'

'I'm in your blood, Cal'Adra. I know where you are at all times. You gave… me that power, recall? You let me heal you.' She shrugged. 'Now I can track you whenever I please. That's how we found you.'

'Arsewater.'

'You're here, are you not?'

I spat out some gristle. 'My name's not Cal'Adra.'

'Weapons registry.' She pushed a piece of paper across the table. 'Room lease.' Another paper. 'Bank account.' She casually threw this last on the table. 'Nothing in it.'

'I spend as I please.'

'I meant in identifying you,' Benadetta said. 'If you were planning to start a new life your highblood arrogance negated it.' She looked me up and down. 'I'd have… thought a Cal would have better t-table manners.'

'We delegate all that to the lower orders.'

I farted. It was funny and it bought time. She knew my name but that would be it. No commrach would deign to tell her lunatic establishment the details of my disappearance. Not that that would stop Sister Benadetta feigning she knew.

I had, however, to take Sister Benadetta on her word about being able to track me. No one saw me leave St Waleran's and Esme hadn't expected my arrival. This Church bitch had some human magic over me. It would explain Shortleg's behaviour, too. Church property the pair of us. Yet why?

I waved a chicken bone at her. 'You meant me to take those pins from your bag, didn't you?'

'I did?'

'A test. To see if I could get out of the place. Otherwise, you'd have just brought me here soon as your journeymen found me unconscious in that ditch.' Of course. 'They were waiting for me, yes? Our dear, mutual fiend Shortleg pointed the direction I stumbled off in and your cronies waited the other side of the forest.'

Benadetta smiled. 'There was a vial of sleeping agent too. In the buh-bag buhh-beside the pins.' She looked annoyed with herself, before her smile returned. 'Thought I'd give you options.'

'And learn my skill set. Very clever. I suppose Poppi kept you informed.'

'Unknowingly, yes. Dear heart.' She raised an eyebrow. 'Pity about the dead girl. The bully.'

'No idea what you mean.' I shrugged. 'And the pattern on my shirt rag? The circle with the spikes.' The thought still made me angry. My last connection to Kyran. 'That was your people, yes? Why?'

'No,' Benadetta said. Her expression became sombre. Contemplative. 'Assuredly not.'

Her sudden lack of explanation made me uncomfortable. If not her church, then who? The innkeep and his wife, with their clay figurines and rope-faced secrets?

The visions. I had visions of that figurine. The hoofed and hard-cocked devil, large as a landscape, its mask giving way to, well, what exactly? My mother, with her nonsense about hearts in the ground. Blood, I missed Mother. I had kept those feelings at bay for half a decade or more. There was a softness to her I'd forgotten, beneath the cold command, reserved for me and my brother. How had I forgotten?

'Wine?' Benadetta lifted a jug and chalice from somewhere behind the table.

I reminded myself this was no time for tender memories. The world was clawed, especially right now.

Benadetta stood up and walked around the table. She placed the chalice before me and poured. 'You've absolutely... no redeeming features, Cal'Adra,' she said.

'Making me ideal for whatever this conspiracy is that you're hatching, no doubt.' I lifted the chalice, toasted her. 'You're a real piece of work, Sister.' I sipped. Wonderful bouquet. 'Let me guess: I'll quietly disappear if I refuse?'

'Oh no,' she reassured me. 'Quite the opposite. Hoxham's never seen a commrach staked and burnt before. It would draw quite the crowd.'

PART TWO

8

Corso marched to war. Which, in truth, meant five hundred and sixty-four unmarried highblood combatants, plus a personal servant for each, as well as all thirty-two tower archons, with lowbloods to carry their fine-pillowed palanquins. A hundred musicians, a hundred cooks and an unspecified number of courtiers and assorted feckless layabouts followed, the train snaking back for more than a mile.

The rest of Corso, the vast majority in fact, remained at home. No doubt they enjoyed the break.

My war-pride, twelve in all plus attendants, climbed a hill of dry grass and jutting granite. We talked loudly, spat, passed wine. High to our left, the war-prides of Cal'Fokzon and Cal'Eals raced one another under the blazing sun. They leapt from rock to rock, scurried uphill, made playful feints and chased each other off. Swearing, hooting, singing old fight rhymes.

We had no fear of attack. It wasn't that kind of war. Indeed it was hardly war at all, more an elaborate and highly ritual fracas. The agreed battlefield – where, admittedly, *some* deaths would occur – lay ten miles ahead, deep in the hinterwoods. The oldest forest on all the Isle, perhaps the world.

'I fucking hate war,' Kyran said beside me. 'Too many hills for starters. Dirt. The only baths slick with reeds and fish.'

'There's fighting,' Slow Thezda said, offering the suggestion with that lazy swagger of hers. Her silver-lensed monocles were two tiny moons in the bright day.

'How pleasant for you,' Kyran said. 'For masochists like you and sis, this yearly travesty is a delight. But *some* of us have standards. It'll take hours polishing my new boots free of dirt. My heart weeps for the lad.' He pointed at his servant, the same one from the gardens months earlier. The youth struggled under a bulging rucksack, the feathers of his peacock headdress crushed. Kyran shook his head. 'Where's that fucking wine?'

'Shen's got it,' I replied.

I gestured to you, Shen, and you caught up. You passed its uncorked skin to my brother. A look passed between you both, respectful yet awkward. I'd permitted you freedom from wearing a servant's headdress, something no one in my war-pride had brought attention to. To them you were a foible, a favourite-of-the-moment, something for Kyra Cal'Adra to set aside in time.

You had fought bitterly not to come. Had argued every servant of Cal'Adra would seethe at a new arrival lifted to the kind of honours old favoured families had struggled for for generations. You fretted your father back in Skarrach would be notified and vetted. That matter truly discomforted you, and the more I enquired the more you met me with a strange and mannered silence, to the point where I actually had to promise he would not be contacted.

But I would not hear no. I never had to, being of a Cal family. I merely had to give the word, pass instruction to my bondswoman Thezda, who was of a Sil family, who, I assume, passed the order down to someone of a Marn family who, in turn, trickled the iron law down through a hierarchy of lowblood castes my kind never dirtied themselves with the details of. So what if those masses would hate you, Shen? They could not act upon it. You were marching to war with me and that was the end of the matter.

'Fucking war,' Kyran muttered. He gulped down a glass's worth then returned the skin to you.

'Wait-o!' came a voice from behind us. Cousin Zymo.

Kyran grumbled. I frowned. Neither of us had wanted her in our pride, let alone our four-person pack. Grandmother's orders.

I turned to look back down the hill. I'd long stopped putting on the pretence of a smile, but cousin Zymo didn't seem to notice. Her mind was a fortress against the entire world's insinuations that she was a prick.

'Blood, I love the march to violence!' she exclaimed to the sky. She bounded up to us all, her hair – wrapped and bound to resemble two ram's horns curling around her ears – bouncing comically.

'Please don't feel obliged to keep up,' Kyran said. 'We won't be distressed if you travel at your own leisure.'

'And let my pack down?' Cousin Zymo said. 'I don't think so! Ha!' She stepped up to Kyran and slapped his shoulder. 'Eh, couz?'

Kyran forced a smile, which was more than I did. Yet we could never be seen to outright insult her in front of the lower-blooded. Worse luck.

Zymo gestured at you for the wine. She didn't even look. You were but a wineskin on legs.

She seized the skin as you offered it. A little spilled.

'Careful, Ruddylocks,' she warned, eyeing your hair. 'Nearly stained my sleeve.'

I looked at you, Shen, and you smiled back. As if to say, *Forgive your cousin, Kyra*.

I have kissed those lips, I thought. That was all you had permitted me this last month. Courtship? Sweetest sadism, I thought it. A blade in honey, thorns on a rose.

I was no longer myself, though I hid it. I had become your secret hound, Shen. I had become… free.

Cousin Zymo swallowed. She wiped her mouth.

'You know what?' When no one responded she continued: 'I mean to cross paths with Urse Cal'Dain. I mean to ride his infamous snake. Before you snare him, eh, Kyra couz?' She saluted me with the wineskin. 'You're such a lucky thing, you know that?'

She took another sip. The depths of her social ignorance were plumbless.

I decided to change the subject. 'Let's push on and—'

'Know what my plan is?' Zymo asked the group. She stroked her left hair horn. 'I'm going to slice him, again and again, come battle. Little cuts. Then, when he lies in his tent, recuperating, defenceless…' Her eyebrows danced. 'I'm going to steal in. No words. Just…'

She gyrated her hips, expecting us to fucking well cheer.

'Your ambition is a lesson to us all,' Kyran said.

We heard commotion down the hill to our right, on the path.

Grandmother's box palanquin had stopped, its bearers trying not to let it topple. And a good thing they hadn't, for she would have had them all skinned for such humiliation, especially since other matriarchs and patriarchs sat in palanquins behind her own.

The trail was almost entirely free of rock. I couldn't imagine how they'd tripped.

I saw a shape soaring high above. A great kite, a rhombus of burgundy material. A black glyph upon it: the symbol of Cal'Waid. One of Darrad city's tower families.

'A jape,' Slow Thezda said, sounding as underwhelmed as she always did.

She was right of course. Japes such as this were commonplace before any battle. Harmless, audacious. Irritating.

Personally, I'd always wished we had a proper war against Darrad, like those the humans had against one another. Kill and take; unfussy, over. This ritualised nonsense over forestry rights we'd indulged in for millennia suffocated. But one took what action one could.

A high wind pushed the kite nose-up. It hung there a moment before toppling. Within seconds it had crashed into a bush some way off.

'Ha!' Cousin Zymo exclaimed. 'Clever. But we'll show 'em a jape or two, eh?'

Sit on a catapult, I thought. *Give both armies a hoot.*

Bored with the wine, Zymo practically shoved the skin at your chest, Shen. Your patience was remarkable. I'd never noticed servants' patience before.

I returned my gaze to the trail on the side of the hill. Grandmother's box palanquin was on the move once more, as were the rest of the archons' litters. Grandmother, I'd long suspected, was as frustrated by the summer war ritual as I, though for different reasons. These ancient and yearly conflicts existed for two ancient rationales. Firstly, for neighbouring city states to decide boundaries and resource rights in a non-internecine manner and – on a more subtle, long-term level – to allow the Explainers to assess highblood youth, and thus current vitality at the racial pinnacle. My grandmother had a reputation in archon tea circles for suggesting that maybe, just perhaps, the war ritual could be streamlined and simplified, and that the energy might be better spent in forming an Isle-wide defensive army, given the events in the colonies only years before.

Thanks to you, Shen, I had acquired a little insight into these tea circles, given that you had gleaned talk that dripped down from the tower's upper floor to the servants' levels. Grandmother's suggestions were typically met with a swift change of subject. The other archons were even more hidebound than Grandmother, and the very idea of people below Sil family status being given weapons and training en masse seemed distinctly un-commrach, foolhardy and prone to manipulation by a single highblood family, with our infamously hungry Cal'Adra clan seen as likely suspects in that regard.

The more charitable matriarchs and patriarchs put Grandmother's penchant down to her daughter's death at the hands of the human invaders, and perhaps that was even true. Then again, she may just have been using her daughter's sacrifice as a wedge to siphon in her army idea. To me the latter seemed more likely.

I continued up the rocky hill. I was nothing like Grandmother. Nothing. Yet all her moves were legible to me. They made sense.

Shouting came from the summit ahead. Members of Cal'Fokzon's war-pride were beckoning to us.

'Oh, what fresh hen shit is this?' Kyran said.

We made our way up.

'A jape!' One of Cal'Fokzon shouted down to us as we neared. 'For Cal'Adra!'

'You better not be playing tricks!' I called back.

They weren't.

I heard the flies' buzz before we mounted the hill's summit. Ten feet below us, on the hill's decline, stood a naked figure, slouching, its head down. Pale skin, black hair, belly distended. Large breasts.

I stepped closer. The stink from her was heavy and acrid. We were gazing at a corpse. Too big for any commrach.

A human woman. I'd never seen one before. She'd been pregnant. Someone had painted my family's glyph on her roundness. They had staked her through the anus. Dark blood had dried down the wood's length. A halo of offal and shit surrounded the base. The stink reminded me of the bodies after the siege of my childhood home. Peculiar stink, human shit. Unforgettable.

None of us spoke.

The human's hair had been painted black. Yellow streaks were discernible: her original colour. Someone had used a dagger to chop the hair into a mockery of my own. A chain matrimonial hung around her neck, a copy.

I heard vomiting. I turned to see you, Shen, bent and retching to my right. I knew better than to console you. Knew your pride.

I looked back at the corpse.

'Urse,' I said.

My brother stood by my side.

'Cal'Dain humour leaves me cold,' he muttered eventually.

'Should I,' Slow Thezda said to us both, 'inform the matriarch?'

'No,' I snapped. 'No. Let's… we'll march on.'

'Ha!' Cousin Zymo's voice approaching behind us, last as always. 'Now *there's* a jape!'

'Shut up,' I said. I glared at her.

Zymo stared back in bewilderment, more shocked by this break in public protocol than my anger.

'Apologies,' she said. 'I should have known, couz. It cannot be pleasant to be impersonated by such an animal. I wonder where they got her—'

You were upon her. You dived around her back, got your arm around her neck, the other over her chest.

'Look!' you yelled in Zymo's ear. 'Look at her! Imagine her pain! Fear! What's fucking—'

Slow Thezda was quicker than anyone in moments like this, her family famously loyal to ours.

You yelped as she pulled you off Zymo, grunted as you hit the grass. That Thezda did not smash your sternum when she put a boot on your chest said more about her regard for Cal'Adra property than anything.

You struggled, your scarlet locks in your eyes and mouth.

'Appreciated,' Cousin Zymo said to Thezda. She pulled out her rapier. 'A little practice, methinks.'

I drew my rapier, placed its edge against Zymo's cheek.

'Leave her be,' I snarled.

Zymo eyed me over her shoulder. She didn't dare move her face.

'Cousin,' she said. 'You're absurd.'

'Touch her and I'll get positively ludicrous,' I hissed. 'Fucker.'

My brother stepped between Zymo and you.

'Sister,' he said to me. 'A servant cannot behave so.'

'Shen's not a servant, she's a bondswoman. Like Thezda there.' I nodded at her.

'Bondswoman?' Zymo said. 'When did that happen?'

'Moment she assaulted you,' I said. 'I value good taste.'

For the first time, Zymo actually picked up on a hint.

'How dare you,' she said.

'With a blade to your face,' I replied. 'Clearly.'

'Friends, friends,' Kyran said. 'Come now. We're on the march, yes? High spirits and so forth. Let's save our blade arms for our enemies.' He looked at Zymo. 'Come, couz. Surely you've had a servant you've felt sentimental over? Indulge my sister that.'

Zymo relaxed. She sheathed her rapier.

'Bondswoman.' She said it like she'd heard a lame joke. 'Fine. Whatever.'

I lowered my rapier, sheathed it.

Zymo took that opportunity to storm off down the hill.

'Fire-mane's bred scant better than that beast on the stick!' she shouted over her shoulder.

Slow Thezda had taken her boot off of you. Face blank, eyes behind silver glass, she offered you her hand. A fellow bondswoman now.

You studied her palm a moment. Your scowl softened. You took it and got to your feet.

Kyran put his arm on my shoulder and walked me away from the scene.

'You lied to me,' he whispered, his voice ringed faintly with mirth. 'You haven't fucked her yet.'

Made me scowl, that. But I nodded.

'She's blackmailing you? That it?' he said.

'No.'

'Fine, fine.' He stroked my hair. 'Never known you like this.'

'You've been like this,' I said.

'I'm a poet. We're allowed.' We stopped. He met my eyes. 'Whatever this is, get it out of your blood, Kyra. And quick.'

I sighed.

Kyran looked away from me, out to the hinterwoods beyond the valley below.

'He'll be watching,' he said. 'Urse, I mean. He wouldn't have missed this for all the towers in Darrad.'

Kyran was right. I glared at the mist-laced forest. I felt suddenly naked.

I stepped forward and held my arms out wide, made of my face a wide, grinning theatre mask.

Here I am, Urse. Right here.

Grandmother planted the dreadmask helm upon the table and we jolted.

We really should have expected that.

Just the three of us in her yurt-grand, a hundred muffled calls outside, far-off drums beating like hearts. Four moontiles hung above the small table we stood around, their lunar glow filling the tent.

'Same reaction since childhood,' Grandmother said. 'I always told your mother she should have put a dreadmask in your cot. Toughen you up.'

I looked directly at the thing so as to spite her. The initial shock had passed but within the curves and lines of the mask's design, carved and treated so as to capture the darker energies of our family's touch over centuries, lay the essence of primeval fear. A panther's countenance, fangs bared. The predator of our race's forebears.

It sat upon a map of the elected battlefield. Fear emanated like heat waves from the helm, rippling the map's illustrations of trees and units in a way as much felt as seen.

'I wonder which of my two grandchildren has earned the right to wear this?' She studied us awhile. Neither of us replied. 'Be shameful to give it to that idiot Zymo, eh?'

I'd no desire for Grandmother's games. I pretended to take interest in the yurt's walls.

'Come, Kyra,' my brother said. 'We both know it's you. It's always you.'

'Put a mask on me, put a chain on me.' I shrugged. 'Does it matter what I think? Has it ever?'

Kyran sighed. 'You're no follower, so you may as well lead.' He looked directly at me. 'What about Urse? You want to hurt him, yes?'

I glanced at Grandmother. Her expression had not changed. She must have assumed Kyran meant the fight in the city gardens, the chain matrimonial doomed to bind me, not the staked human.

Grandmother tapped her brass talons upon the table.

'Kyran, my boy,' she said. 'Leave us.'

'Yes, Grandmother.' He brushed my arm. 'I'll be outside.' He said the last part as if he meant to say, *Fucking war.*

He left the tent, the sound of drums and laughter briefly pouring in as he did so.

She moved closer to me. I didn't flinch. I wouldn't give her the pleasure.

'So like your mother,' she noted. 'The same crease in your brow when you feign disinterest.'

I feigned boredom instead. I wished Kyran had remained.

'If you knew what our city plans for tomorrow,' she said, 'you wouldn't sulk so.'

Something in my face must have betrayed me for Grandmother smiled. A scalpel's slit before the bleed.

'Lead well on the morrow,' she said, 'and you can forget a chain about your neck. The chain limited Elinda.' She sighed almost imperceptibly. My mother's name was a spell upon both of us. 'The governess of our colonies needs to be a free animal, a wild panther.'

I stared at her.

'Now I have you,' she said. 'You have heard the reports: rebellions, anti-Blood demagogues. All caressed by the unseen hand of Rosho, of course.'

She paused, waiting for me to comment, I realised, to voice my opinion of the Rosho family. There was some facet to them, some obscure reason why they still lived. Grandmother had intimated as much at the festival two months past. So much hung before me in this moment, a sudden future, mine to take. It would be prudent, then, to agree.

'We both know only Mother could hold those islands together,' I said. 'She was their hero.' I looked down at my boots and steeled myself. 'The Roshos are not fermenting rebellion on the Jades. The most they could ever do is fan a fire that began with Mother's death.'

I felt the back of a cold talon rest upon my cheek.

'And her martyrdom becomes a path for her daughter.'

Lady of the Jades. Me.

'The other families,' I muttered.

'They see it our way. They've really no choice, have they? Corso has no wish to lose its hard-fought-for property. My girl, you even look like her.'

'I'm not your—'

'Property?' She brushed her jewellery through my hair. 'Perhaps now, but not soon, eh? Our interests converge.' She brought her hand away suddenly. Her smile had vanished, her face pale in the false lunar light. 'No chain matrimonial, no binding to Urse Cal'Dain. Just a legal marriage.' She shrugged. 'Provide, say, two children, and you can throw that wretch into the deep sea for all I care. Urse's use will be over, and your children will inherit. You can chase however many women would finally placate you. Assuming such is possible.'

Shen. I thought of you, somewhere outside.

'Well?' Grandmother said. 'It's not perfect. But you'll be freer than any commrach has right to expect.'

I looked at the map beneath the dreadmask.

'Tell me this battle plan,' I said.

Kyran was waiting outside the yurt, far away enough not to listen in.

'Please tell me I'm not leading this farce,' he said.

'You'll be delighted to learn I'm farce-mistress.'

'Like it could be any other way.'

One side of his face was in darkness, the other flickering red and silver from the campfires all about and the silvery glow of moontiles, now that night had drawn in. Drums rumbled on the edge of camp, a challenge to Darrad's drums far out in the darkness. Shrieks closer by, male and female. A play-fight perhaps, or foreplay.

'You were very compliant in there,' I told him.

'Somebody had to be.'

'She called you in before me.' I nodded at the yurt-grand. 'What did she want?'

'Compliance,' Kyran answered. He chewed on his lower lip. 'My marriage date is set. Eight days after next year's equinox.' He looked at me and tried to smile. 'I'll be living in Darrad. With her family.'

'Oh…' I embraced him, kissed his temple. He'd found a way to clean his hair out here. It smelled of jasmine.

'It's fine, fine,' he whispered. 'We'll visit. Who knows? Perhaps you'll live in Darrad too.'

'Not if I can help it,' I said. I thought I'd not mention the Jade colonies there and then. I pulled away a little. 'We always knew this would happen. A relief to have it confirmed. And, and anyway: you're a twin. No chain matrimonial for you, eh?'

He looked down. 'Yet one for my wife. A cauterised heart; that's what you called it, yes? All her desire reduced to a man who desires men. Poor creature.'

'It's not your problem. That's just marriage. Marriage for most men and women on the Isle.'

He shook his head.

I held his jaw and made him meet my eyes.

'Do not make it your problem, Kyran. Don't.'

'We're just conduits for the Blood, eh?'

'Ultimately.' I sounded convinced. Perhaps I was.

We made our way to our campfire. A pack of drunk warriors jigged past us, a panther skin raised between them.

A silhouette approached us from the direction of our campfire, the motion of its limbs possessing a familiar laziness. Slow Thezda.

I nodded at Thezda. We had a hesitant relationship, awkward yet amicable. She was considered the most promising young blade in all Corso, I… a fraction beneath. She was without her eyepieces tonight. She only needed them in daylight; a weakness common in our people and frequent in her family. She looked a stranger without them.

'Sirs,' Thezda said. 'A problem.' She made a languid search

for the words. 'Your cousin… has taken ill.'

'Zymo?' Kyran said. 'How so?'

Thezda barely shrugged. 'Stomach…'

We strode over to the campfire. You were there, Shen, staring into the fire. Kyran's servant, the lad, was sat beside you on the log. He sung some old rhyme, almost whispering it.

'Where's Zymo?' I asked you and him.

'In the herbalist's tent,' you replied. You smiled at the fire. 'Clutching a bucket and cursing this world. Something she ate.' You looked at me. 'She'll be fine.'

'We ate what she ate,' the lad mumbled.

'It's fine,' you told him. 'We'd know if we were ill by now.'

'You seem very sure, Shen,' I said.

'I picked the mushrooms. It was hard to see in the increasing gloom.' You watched a spark rise from the fire and up into the night. 'I've seen her illness before. Loamcap. Far from fatal.'

'But incapacitating,' Kyran said.

He looked at me and gave a knowing smile.

'I should have been more careful, my lords,' you said. You shrugged, stroked your loose red hair.

'Doubtless,' I replied. 'But what's done is done, eh?'

'I suppose we'll have to choose a replacement,' Kyran said.

'Think you're ready for war, bondswoman?' I asked you.

'For a moment there,' you said, 'I thought you'd want me and the lad here to duel for the honour.'

Kyran's servant froze. His eyes went wide.

'She jests,' Kyran told him. He walked over and ruffled the young man's hair.

'Lad,' I told the servant. 'Fetch two wooden blades.'

He got up and did so.

You looked at me. The first time since I'd returned to the fire.

'We cannot just send you in without knowing your rapier skills,' I explained. 'I have to see.'

You stood up slowly. 'Here?'

The lad passed you a wooden blade. He passed me another.

'I wouldn't embarrass you,' I said. I winked. 'There's a quiet glade in the trees over there.'

You looked into the dark beyond our fire. Toward the night-hidden boughs.

'Fine,' you said.

I led the way into the trees, into the dark. Perhaps you studied me as I strode ahead of you, Shen, as I had studied you in the gymnasium, walking toward the ring. The arch of my back, the rim of my tall, tall boots as they pushed against my backside with each step. Perhaps you lusted for me. I know you did. I knew you. I strode accordingly.

We stepped into a grove, moon's silver catching ancient branch and silent grass, lending import to each winged insect's dance. The hinterwood. Forest old as Isle. Untamed.

I turned to face you.

You stopped. Gazed at your wooden sword.

'So,' you said. 'This practice. What is it to be?'

'A beating,' I replied.

I struck your hand and your sword fell to the dew-soaked blades. Another to your red locks and you screamed and clutched your face. A third, your shoulder, and you dropped.

You struggled onto your knees. You moaned.

'The term's "yield",' I said. I whipped your side with the thin wood. 'Come on, you're a stickler for tradition, remember. Say it.'

'*Why?*'

I began to circle you. 'This is how we fight nowadays. Rapier, sabre. Modern weapons. None of your kai-bolg, your romance, your maudlin…'

I struck your spine. You fell onto all fours. No lasting injuries, but you weren't to know that.

'You do *want* to fight, yes?' I said. 'Enough to poison my cousin? Enough to presume you could?' I leaned in. 'Enough to lie your way into…' I faltered.

You stared at me, eyes green lightning in the moonlight.

'What?' you said. 'Lie my way into what?'

'Who is it you serve?' I said. 'Grandmother? Hmm? Urse Cal'Dain?'

'No.'

'Then you're just some… fucking jape?'

'This life is a jape.' You wiped your mouth of spittle. 'All our lives.'

I waited.

'I ran from Skarrach,' you said. 'I'm wanted there. They would kill me, throw my heart into the sea.'

'What do you mean?' The anger left me.

'I cursed the Blood. I cursed our people's ways.' You shrugged, a gesture to say, *There, it is what it is.* 'My family helped me run.'

A criminal. An enemy of the way.

'I do not hate our race,' you said. 'I hate what our race has become. I hate the chain of matrimony. I hate the pressure never to think but only to fuck. The mindless acceptance of moronic law. I believe the breeding programme pure folly. I believe the final perfection a lie. I want it all burnt. I want it gone.'

My legs were trembling.

'If you've any mercy,' you said, 'you'd get your real sword and end me now.'

'Why…' I couldn't find the words. 'Why come here? To me?'

'To hide within the storm's heart.' You shook your head. 'I had nowhere else to go. Your mother saved my father. I used that. No one back home would think to look for me in the tower of a highblood. I run from death as long as I can. What else is there?'

I chuckled bitterly.

'For the first time,' I said, 'I've no idea what I'm supposed to do.'

'Strangle me,' you said. 'It is the custom. For lack of a good knife and the sea.'

I threw my wooden blade to the ground. You couldn't be lying. No one would lie like this.

I kneeled before you, the mirror of your stance. I placed my hands around your throat and you didn't fight.

I didn't squeeze. I waited.

'I only ever wanted the things denied me in this life,' you said. 'To bear a child and to love freely.' Your eyes watered. 'I should thank you for the second, Kyra Cal'Adra.' You closed your eyes.

I watched my hands slip from your neck and up to your face.

'Teach me this hate of yours,' I whispered. I kissed you, once, upon the lips. 'Teach me this love.'

Your eyes opened. Your lips shook.

My face, so used to irony, held its smile.

We kissed. Away from the laws, the japes and fools. Ourselves, soon naked in a forest that had stood long before cities had risen. The only true commrach in existence. An isle within an isle.

But why describe? It was between me and you, Shen. And I tell this to you.

—

Mist drifted across the forest floor. Isle fog.

Where the morning fell upon it the mist was mundane as any. In the shadow of bowers, however, beneath the canopies of ancient dark-oak, the mist rolled grey-blue. Motes of silver tumbled and glittered within it. Like our blood, our fluids. The Explainers hold Isle fog to be connected to our origin, perhaps the very essence of our kind.

Our army – each pride, pack and warrior – waited on all fours, silent as the forest itself. My muscles trembled with the waiting, the watching. I wore no dreadmask, no sword. Not yet. But I'd three screamdarts, foot-long javelins: one smooth in my fist, two hanging from hoops upon my right thigh.

The army of Darrad were out there, beyond the fog. Waiting for the signal too.

Kyran, by my left shoulder, spat upon the ruddy soil. *Fucking war*, it seemed to say, though he enjoyed all this more then he'd ever care to admit. You were just behind me, Shen, beside Slow Thezda. I tried not to think of your words last night. Not to—

The horn, the signal.

We were up, sprinting into fog. I leaped over a dead log and heard Kyran step upon it and leap. Black trunk ahead, ancient and fat. We split around it, regrouped the other side.

Screamdarts, ahead and left.

I ducked and a scream raced over me, slammed into the trunk. Other screamdarts flew past. I heard you hit the ground, saw Kyran swerve.

'Strike!' I yelled.

They had thrown too early; this enemy pack had jumped at shadows.

You ran past me and I felt relief. Forest girl, raised with javelins, you needed no orders.

I followed. The fog rolled back and there were the enemy: two reaching for another dart, two unsure.

We threw as one, all four of us.

One dropped her screamdart and belted away. Another followed her. The other two ran in the opposite direction.

We'd split them.

I howled.

The forest howled with me. The air was alive with screamdarts now, a caterwaul with no conductor, a piping chaos.

We didn't pursue the broken pack. An amateur's gambit, that. We drove hard through the space they had left, fast as deer, then curved in the direction of our battle line. With luck we'd get behind some unwitting Darrad pack.

We burst through low branches, the rattle and slice of hard leaves against my skin. Luck met us the other side.

A Darrad pack, their backs to us, punishing our comrades with whistling death. Thinking themselves winners.

I made hand gestures: hold fire, get closer. We ran forward, intent on the sure kill.

'Right!' Slow Thezda yelled.

I twitched with idiot anger, believing she'd given us away. I turned to see her cartwheel, her silver monocles flashing, a dart screaming past her legs.

Two Darrads, of the pack we'd just broken. Braver than they'd seemed. One yelled, tried to get the other pack's attention.

You ran out before me, Shen. Stopped, stood your ground.

A lock of your hair flew off. You barely flinched.

A screamdart inches from my ear, loud then quiet then gone.

You threw a javelin underarm. I'd never seen the like. It had no time to catch the air in its scream-hole, never made a sound. It embedded itself in our attacker's flank.

They yelled and dropped into bracken. Their friend ran away into the blue fog.

I span back to face the pack we had intended to set upon.

Our darts were ready. So were theirs. Ten yards from each other.

The second horn sounded. The Whittling had finished.

Only then did I see the other pack we had nearly ambushed. Urse. Urse Cal'Dain. My betrothed. My enemy.

He recognised me too. He stared, the rest of his face blank as a youth night-mask. His hair cut to a tight crop.

And then both packs belted back toward our respective lines. No one had to be ordered. Anyone who didn't make it back within the minute would either have to hide in the mist or be chopped down by the longaxes of the Obsidians.

We ran back, all four of us. I was glad of that at least. The Whittling was by far the most lethal round of the war. I saw one of our own side, prone and splayed, a screamdart in the back of their skull. Likely the work of Urse's pack.

'We made it,' Kyran said as we crossed the line. 'Fine work.'

'Blood!' I cursed. 'I could have *killed* him.' The realisation set a fire in me a-sudden. Urse had had his back to my throw. 'Chance will never offer such treasure again.'

Kyran looked set to say something, but thought better of it. He could counter that I was alive and should be thankful, but what life awaited me? No chain matrimonial, yes, but still Urse, still his body upon me.

I felt your palm upon my back, Shen.

I kissed you, fierce and long. I cared not who saw. And when we broke apart your eyes were a picture of shock and delight.

Kyran's servant – I'd never caught his name – ran over to his master and hugged him.

'There, there,' Kyran said to the youth. 'All's fine.' He looked over at me with an expression I'd long understood. He was tiring of this lad's affection.

'Good work,' you said to Slow Thezda. 'Bondswoman.'

'Bondswoman,' Thezda replied, the canopy reflected in her eyes' silver discs. She half-smiled. A grin by her standards.

Moans rose from the mist. The wounded, the dying. One, a male, cried for help.

'You mewling baby!' a woman cried out from our side. 'You shouldn't've let yourself be hit!'

Our battle line cheered at that. Many joined her jeers. Those wounded who hadn't made it back were the weak, had failed their family and the Blood entire. Not for nothing did they call it the Whittling. One simply had to clutch one's wound and keep silent till the battle finished. Then, maybe, someone might bring a healstone.

'Please…' the distant voice begged.

'You better be Darrad or a squirrel!' Kyran yelled, suddenly vexed. 'Because you sure aren't fucking Corso!'

Our line laughed.

I chuckled too. But when I looked at you, Shen, I stopped.

'Good javelin work,' I said to you. But my eyes said, *Please, you have to play along.*

Our line's mood changed as an Obsidian strode along the front. His stone axe was high and ready, keen to slaughter any wounded who might crawl back to the line. Lowblood muscle of the Explainers, the Obsidians wore naught but leather trews and a dreadmask fashioned like a living skull.

That mask. It seemed the totality of everything you had cursed last night, Shen: the breeding programmes, the refinement of blood. That rationally prophesied 'final perfection'. And it knew. It knew our sins. Or soon would.

I couldn't look at it. I couldn't look at you.

A horn gave signal for us to take our allotted positions.

We were on the right flank of the line, at the very end. The Explainers had already placed their special rapiers for us: hilts upright, points buried in the soil.

We took our places beside each sword. To our left and right came the other two packs of our pride: eight ready warriors, clan and bonds all.

'Be true to our tower,' I told them all. I wasn't much for speeches.

Another was doing as much anyway, one of the iron families, the highest towers. Strutting up and down and barking platitudes. Of how today would decide which city owned what acre of forest, determined marriage rights, foreign policy; of how our actions would serve our subjects' hopes and dreams, such as they were. When she said to hold to the plan, she gave me a look.

'Dreadmask,' I muttered to Kyran's servant.

Nervous, the lad opened his satchel and removed the helm, safely wrapped in sackcloth. He handed it to me.

Bracing myself, I unwrapped the thing and, eyes screwed, placed it over my head.

The others stepped back a little. I could not look around now for fear of catching my comrades' eyes. I'd become the panther's aspect, the rage and bite.

I gazed ahead into the blue mist and its silhouette trees, my world ringed with darkness – the rim of either eyehole. I pulled the points of my ears out of the holes provided and I could hear again.

Shouting beyond the fog. Someone called from the Darrad side.

'Kyraaa,' it came. 'Kyraaaa...'

'How's your arse, Urse?' I shouted back.

Laughter broke out along our own line. What can I say? Good stories spread. Especially when I ensure they do.

Silence, then: 'Did you like my gift, Kyra?'

'I'm going to hurt you, Urse Cal'Dain!' I shouted. 'Hear me?'

'Oh, I'll hurt *you*!' he called back. 'When I make your belly round!'

A chorus of cackles from his harpies, his arseholes.

'Laugh now, prick!' I spat. 'Prick!'

A hand squeezed my shoulder. You, Shen.

I remembered not to look.

The first horn blew. I readied to sprint. My hand hovered over the silver rapier's hilt.

The second horn blew. I prised the sword from the ground and we were off.

A-la-la-la-laiiiii! Our battle line yelled, a fierce ululation that spiked to a shriek. Corso's war-scream.

We raced over rock and stump, through bracken and branch. One could not rest with these swords: they were imbued so as to burn the palm if one ceased moving.

One could not run a man through with one either, the tip being blunt. These rapiers possessed only the eight inches of sharp either side of the end. Few fatalities. I'd have to make do with slashing the very shit out of Urse Cal'Dain.

I ran. The pride followed. A dwarf elm lay ahead, its trunk obese and its boughs sagging. I'd take the chance. Trust in audacity.

'Leap!' I yelled to my pack.

I pressed all my strength into my legs and jumped up, into the tree's boughs. I heard most of the others do the same behind me. Twigs rattled against my helm.

We poured down from the dwarf elm like a waterfall. The risk paid off: we fell upon a Darrad pride sweeping around the trunk. I slashed downwards upon a woman's scalp. She screamed and toppled. Screams everywhere. I slashed her back and buttocks. The scent of fresh blood.

Someone ran at me. I looked up and my dreadmask broke their charge. Not Urse: some other man. He clutched his face.

Slow Thezda slashed his chest twice and warmth sprayed upon my bare shoulder.

My palm began to burn. I growled. I ran again, toward the Darrad line.

'Hooool!' I shouted. The pride-leader's call to break and follow.

My rapier had already darkened. I noticed Thezda's was darker: one slash more. Likely neither of us would mention the fact.

We reached what had been the Darrad line and was now ours. We jabbed our rapiers into the ground.

I bent over and removed the dreadmask helm, hid its mask against my chest.

'Everyone here? Fine?' I heard Kyran say. He drew breath and whistled. 'Not a cut on us! Ha!'

'Whose pride did we get?' I asked around. 'Was that Cal'Dain? Anyone see Urse?'

Everyone around me shook their heads.

I looked at you, Shen. 'Any luck?'

You pointed at your rapier on the floor. Pure silver. Not a slash.

Most of the prides had reached this side of the battlefield, though there were still shouts of *hoool* in the glittering fog. The Darrad servants eyed us fearfully. One pride-leader, of Cal'Rhudmun I think, taunted a few with his dreadmask. He stopped when an Obsidian threatened him with her longaxe.

'Ready yourselves,' I told everyone.

The minutes passed and our army was lined up again, hands ready to grip rapiers. *This time,* I thought, my dreadmask back on. *This time.*

The second horn blasted, and we belted into the fighting ground, the hilt warm in my hand.

A-la-la-la-laiii!

Shouts of *'Dain!'* ahead. Urse and his cronies were as eager to make contact with us as we were them.

'Adra!' I bellowed.

'Adra!' my war-pride repeated.

Shadows ahead to my left, then forms. The war-pride of Cal'Dain. I tilted left and charged.

So did they.

Between our prides lay a wild glade. Gold poured through a hole in the canopy above. In the long grass there, beneath that sun, we met.

Yells, blades biting through air, the snap-snap of clashing metal. I dived under a blade's swing, ran on, hunting for Urse.

He was sprinting at me. His face was death: a moa skull, silver-beaked and black-eyed. The dreadmask of his city. He held his rapier wide and low.

I struggled to look at him. All my muscles fought to run, to break. *You're running into death,* they told me. My hate saw me through. The pleasure of knowing my mask terrified him also.

We struck simultaneously. Neither of us tried to dodge the

other's swing. Neither of us blocked. Fear evaporated as my arm shuddered with contact. Wild joy, such bliss putting pain in another. In *him*. I ran on.

'*Hoool!*' I cried to my pride. Follow, run.

Pain raked my shoulder. He'd got me. Heat rolled down my skin. My blood.

My rapier's metal was darker. A good strike. The hilt's heat was increasing against my palm. I ran faster. Too hot and I'd drop my blade before I got back to our line. I wouldn't be allowed to fight.

The pain in my palm matched that in my shoulder by the time we crossed the line. I threw my rapier upon the ground and rolled onto my back. I panted.

'Healstones!' I shouted to whatever servant was nearby. When I didn't hear their boots approaching I remembered to take off my dreadmask and put its face against the soil. 'Healstones!'

Kyran's lad fell to his knees and rubbed a stone against my wound. Its sting became a buzz and then numb.

'How are the pride?' I asked him.

'All back,' he said.

'All with swords?'

'Think so.' He looked up. 'All but one. Kalika.'

One down. Disqualified from the next round.

I got up. My shoulder stung, but not as bad as before.

'Fucking sword!' Kyran shouted. He was gripping his palm. 'You lost it?'

He shook his head. 'Fucker's on the floor there. I'm good to go.' He whimpered. 'Fucking hand.'

'You'll have to use your left,' I said.

His cheek was bleeding. A scratch. The lad ran over and worked the healstone on him.

I looked for you, Shen. You were sat on the grass, swinging your sword-hand through the air. I sat before you and ran my left hand through your locks.

'How'd you fare?' I asked.

'Not a hit. Blocked.'

Your sword was still fresh silver, heatwaves rising from its hilt. A servant came over and lifted it up with a pair of callipers. They took it away for the next round.

You sniffed. 'If they let me use a kai-bolg—'

'We'd look hopelessly out of fashion,' I said.

You frowned at me. Then you grinned. You stroked your knuckles across my belly.

'Gather around,' I said to the pride. 'Listen.'

They looked at me, nursing their wounds and hot palms. Servants attended them with healstones and water skins, obsessing like hoverflies.

I didn't know what to say. I looked to Kyran.

He nodded, spoke.

'There is a greater pride here than the pride of self, friends. Yes, our individual blades now show our prowess—' He eyed Slow Thezda's blade still lying on the grass; it was near-black from successful strikes. '—but come day's end each sword shall be thrown in one of two piles: Corso and Darrad. They shall be counted. Our swords' tones shall be added together and measured against the enemy's. Think of *that* and not your own hit count. Since its founding, Corso has—'

'Look,' I said, cutting him off. 'I know this next round will be a slight to all our pride. But this order comes from Matriarch Zadrikata, my grandmother.' Not everyone looked convinced. Many of them had yet to have spouses chosen for them, were depending on this war to improve their blood-standing. 'Please.

Remember we of Cal'Adra think differently. We *fight* differently. That has always been the root of our success, our lightning rise.' I waved a finger. 'Darrad made this game we play today. They defined its rules millennia past. Let's buck that. Let's deny them a little comfort. Eh?'

'Cal'Adra!' you shouted, your fist in the air. You got to your feet. 'Cal'Adra!'

They bellowed back with a fierceness that shocked me.

'Let's prepare,' I said.

We strode toward the starting line.

You looked at me and smiled.

'Let's enjoy this game for itself,' you whispered in my ear. 'Not for what it stands.'

It seemed to me the wisest thought ever uttered. I smiled.

The swords were cooler now, though still warm. Heat rose from their hilts as our hands braced to grab them.

The horn signalled for the final time. We seized our swords and ran.

'*Ah-la-la-la-laiiii!*'

Into the woods, the mist. Thicker now, rolling in from the heart of the deep forests, its whispering blue-grey all about.

'*Dain!*' came the calls, directly ahead, calling us out. Black figures in the mist, racing full-forward, hungry to slice our flesh.

'Now!' I yelled.

We threw our swords at them. We belted left.

Faster, without hot swords, full speed, dodging around trunks and leaping over rock and bracken. I hoped our sword-throwing had confused Urse's war-pride, had broken their charge. That I could hear none of my pride scream lent me hope. We were clearly ahead.

We flew straight into the flank of another enemy pride, making our war-cry. They stumbled to see their enemy run at them from completely the wrong angle, panicked when my dreadmask burst through the mist.

One flinched as I ran at him, never noticing I was unarmed. I jumped and landed one foot upon his shoulder blade, jumped from that height over another, came down in long grass and kept running. Screams rose behind me as the very pride they had intended to charge collided into their broken mob.

We ran out in front of the next Darrad pride, their pace somewhat slower. I'd had enough of my dreadmask helm by now, too constricting. I unbuckled and threw it at them, causing them to falter. They gave chase.

I was at the back of my pride now, the dreadmask's removal having slowed me down. A blade swiped the air behind my neck. I ran faster, heart pumping, expecting pain at my rear any moment. A rumble of boots to my left and I knew my fear was done with: another one of our own packs charging in the traditional direction, no doubt delighted to find their enemy's flank. My pursuer whelped with that sound only a rapier's edge can procure.

I felt elated, alive, on fire. This was incredible; Grandmother's ploy was incredible. Technically we hadn't cheated. We had relinquished our weapons, disqualifying their strikes and putting ourselves at incredible disadvantage. Yet here we were deciding the battle, rolling up the enemy's battle line as if it were a carpet.

Now *this* was a war.

We broke another pride. I saw Kyran slap one soldier around the back of the head before disappearing into fog. I couldn't see anyone. I started shouting, whooping. I could hear others in my pride taking my cue. We were too dispersed to break a pride now, but we could certainly confuse them, surround them with noise.

We'd won this. Us. Me.

A broken pack of Darradians crossed my path, swordless and bleeding.

'Cal'Adra!' I shouted at them. 'Kyra Cal'Adra!'

I kept running, though now there was really no reason to. I could see no one. I whooped. Blood, this day was my lover!

Hands grabbed my right thigh and I toppled. I got up and still they clung.

'Please…' A man with a javelin in his belly, one of my side. Holding onto life after the Whittling took his honour.

'Get off!'

'Please…' He sounded exactly like the wretch who'd begged earlier.

'Kyra!' came a shout. Not this fool below me, a voice behind. Urse Cal'Dain.

I twisted my neck to see.

Urse, running at me, his beaked dreadmask hammering my nerves. I whimpered. He would break me now. He—

He had no weapon. He slowed down, a bank of heaviest fog behind him, a curtain between us and the battle.

He reached up and produced his sword from behind his back. He must have lodged it between his inner and outer doublet, in order to slow its rising heat. In order to give chase. Surely that had to be cheating.

I don't think he cared. He began to circle me, throwing the blade from hand to hand.

I struggled with the man grabbing my thigh. He was a limpet; I couldn't get him off me.

'If I strike an artery,' Urse said, voice muffled behind that terrifying bird mask, 'it'll seem an accident.'

I couldn't look at him.

'Please...' the man at my thigh moaned.

He'd kill us both. I seized the length of his javelin and pushed it deeper. Right in. His hands dropped from me. If I pulled the javelin out, I recalled, if I used it against Urse, our city would forfeit.

'Pull it out,' Urse said, reading my thoughts. 'My city wins.' He threw the sword to his right hand. 'But I'd rather kill you. I'll be free then, Kyra. Free from *you*.'

His hatred was the mirror of mine, our marriage a shared noose. Killing me would end his terror of the chain matrimonial, the one whose cold silver awaited his own neck.

He came at me.

His helm span around. He stumbled and a hand took his sword. You, Shen.

'An artery, eh?' you said. You picked up his rapier and struck his shoulder. He tumbled to one side and you whacked his buttocks. He dropped to his knees.

'You're going to die, Urse,' you said. 'Never think nor feel again. Nothing.' Your face was pained; anger, the rising heat in your sword hand. 'Think about that.' You stepped behind him. 'Think of how there will be nothing.'

I was frozen, caught by this vignette. You enjoyed toying with your prey. You had toyed with me: your 'courtship'. Even true love was a gleeful sadism to Shen Asu.

You sliced his arms once, twice. A third to his shoulder.

'Let me help you, Urse,' you said. You pulled off his helm and threw it deep into the fog.

Urse gawped. He shivered. He looked at me, perhaps pleading. I couldn't stare back. I couldn't.

'We'll tell all you ran, Urse,' you told him. 'You'll be remembered a coward.'

Urse couldn't lift his arms.

'You shouldn't have fucked with my woman.' Your words came out a growl, the scorching hilt in your palm.

It wasn't even a swing. A tap against his throat and it sprayed fine red. So thin a slit it hissed. You dropped the blade.

Urse couldn't lift his hand to his wound. Kneeling, he watched his own lifeblood, wine-dark and glittering, pour onto the old forest's soil.

'Can you feel it, Urse?' you hissed in his ear. 'Awareness dissolving? Everything that was you pissing out to nothing? Hmm?' The grin on your face. 'Is the blackness coming, Urse? Is it—'

He fell forward.

You looked disappointed.

I had to admit, it would pass for a lucky cut.

'We have to run,' I said, striding toward you. 'Get from here… back to the line. We saw nothing.'

When you didn't look up, I grabbed your shoulder. I ran. You followed.

And I loved you.

9

There had to be some way of covering long distances swifter than a donkey and more comfortably than walking. Palanquins, I suppose, like they used back in Corso. Clearly the Church was not that generous.

Sister Benadetta rode side-saddle upon the former and I'd been doing the latter beside her for some hours, all of it uphill. So far the uphillness of this mission, whatever it bloody was, seemed inexcusably excessive. My thighs ached. The bright day mocked me.

'I hate mountains,' I told her.

'We're not crossing the mountains,' Benadetta said. 'We're crossing between them. The Great Southern Pass. There's n-no mountains a mile either side of us.'

'There's this hill. Hill with pretensions of… pinnacleness.' I looked at her. 'When do I get a go on that donkey?'

'It belongs to the Church. I'm certain…' She had one of her pauses. '…you'd never allow that edifice of lies and delusion to aid you, eh?' She smiled. 'Think of your *self-respect*, Cal'Adra.' She smiled again.

'Up yours, Sister.'

She made a gesture over my head.

'What did that mean?' I said.

'I'm absolving your sin.'

'Well don't. You're my kidnapper. Screw you.'

She made the gesture again. 'My forgiveness will forever exceed your profanity, Cal'Adra.'

'Sounds like a wager.' I shook my head. 'Actually, forget it. We'd be a hound chasing its tail.'

'If I infur… iate why not speak to our travelling companions?'

I looked back over my shoulder. Shortleg, axe swinging from his belt, seemed to be struggling with the incline. He heaved and perspired. Good. Fat fucker.

Beside him, the caliban prowled leisurely. The blond abomination had my blade prisoner, held in place by the flap of his satchel. The sight made me queasy.

'No thank you,' I told Benadetta. 'Shortleg betrayed me. At least I think he did. He won't tell me because you've made him all weird.'

'Mr Shortleg has seen the Pilgrim's light.'

'Precisely.'

'Talk to Mr Nail then,' she said. She meant the caliban. 'He's a knowledgeable soul, largely self-taught, which is always to be commended. Don't you think?'

'I won't converse with *that*.'

The Sister chuckled. 'Ah, the purity of the Blood. The final perfection. You cling to your isle's beliefs, if not your isle itself.'

'Some things are just fact,' I said. 'You wouldn't expect a panther and a donkey to produce anything that would exceed them, would you?' I pointed at the specimen the Sister rode, just as it took a large shit. 'Species should not dilute one another. Animals know this, as should we. Nature's first law.'

'So you are judge of all donthers and pankeys? Should not they be given the chance to prove themselves by their actions?' She took a deep breath of mountain air. 'Anything else seems an irrational c-custom to me. Mere…' She smiled. 'Belief.'

'*Fact*,' I said. She was simply annoying now. 'Natural law must be observed.'

Benadetta looked down on me. 'Perhaps someone should have reminded the commrach who raped his mother.'

I elected to look at the landscape. For some moments.

'Why did you have to give it my sword?' I said eventually. 'You could give it to Shortleg. Shortleg I'll talk to.'

'You answer your own question.'

We reached an inn-fort by late afternoon. It sagged atop a ridge that overlooked the pass. The sign said *Quenchpeak*. Inn-forts were a common sight wherever roads impinged on the Spine Mountains – even drinking establishments had to become stunted castles thanks to the raids of Spine men. However, the local tribe, the Cenabosauvi, had mostly been beaten, boozed or evangelised into timidity. At any rate, Quenchpeak seemed peaceable enough these days. They'd taken down a part of the courtyard wall in order to extend a barn.

Within the inn proper the walls loomed grey, the windows were slits, the fittings were cosy, and the barmaid never returned my smile. A quintessential inn-fort. I doubt they'd have let us in had a Perfecti not accompanied us.

The innkeep let us a private lounge, one so thin and cramped I suspected it had once been used for the passing of alcohol rather than its imbibing. A ceiling lamp cast light on the lone table we sat around. The lamp twisted on its chain, stretching our four shadows across the faded red walls.

'High Hand and Pilgrim,' Benadetta spoke to no one, her eyes closed, 'we thank you for the gift of this sustenance and for another day of life.'

I looked at the ale before me, the one before Shortleg, the cup of water-ale before Benadetta and the empty patch of table before the caliban.

'Well. Mission accomplished,' I said. 'We can go home now, I trust?'

I looked to Shortleg for a hint of a smile. I still hated him, but I needed a pinch of that geniality I'd grown accustomed to around drinking tables.

Shortleg didn't even look at me. No easy task considering he faced me across the table. I'd tactically positioned myself before him and beside Sister Benadetta. The caliban I kept at a diagonal. With luck he wouldn't make some bishop's move and try to... I don't know. Whatever sickness such half-breeds entertained. His sharp cheekbones and defined chin unnerved me. That a caliban could be handsome was something I'd never contemplated. It wasn't right. A little hair dye and he might have even passed through the streets of Corso unstabbed.

I shuddered, put the grim thought off and took a sip.

'This ale is worse than the company,' I said.

'You've had worse,' Shortleg said. 'On both counts.'

It was the first time he'd spoken to me since we'd left Hoxham. During the long river trip that had been the first leg of our journey then the slog over the foothills he'd kept surprisingly nimble in avoiding me.

'Yes,' I replied, giving him a look. 'That inn in Tettleby for one. Care to tell us why you ran, Shortdick?'

He sipped and said nothing.

'Our purpose,' Sister Benadetta said. 'Let us speak of our purpose here.'

'Dark, no doubt,' I said. 'Deniable.'

'Evasive,' she said, apparently correcting me. She steepled her fingers as if in prayer. 'You've a fellow commrach, Cal'Adra, somewhere in this mountain pass.'

I put my ale down.

'Commrach?' I mouthed.

'Of course it's possible they're only claim…ing to be commrach. No one has set eyes on this individual. They leave notes overnight, embedded in the cracks along this inn's walls.'

'No one's seen them do so?'

'Your people are cunning,' she said.

'For inbreds,' the caliban muttered, studying his index finger as he traced it along the table's surface.

I tried to pierce him with a quick stare, but he had no interest in looking up.

Sister Benadetta made no reaction. It was clear she and the halfbreed had a little act going on; he twisted a blade she owned but never deigned to handle herself. Pathetic. I let his insult go.

'Well,' I said, 'what do these notes say?'

'They hint of a…' Her stammer again 'Plot. Apparently. That part is rather garbled.' Her face became seized with that beatific look. She allowed it to pass and continued. 'They keep asking for a meeting at night somewhere within the pass, though the places vary and they soon change their mind. At first they asked for a Perfecti. The Church selected me but when I went to the rendezvous no one approached.'

'The Church ever consider this may just be some slippery lunatic?'

'No.'

'Why not?'

'We have our reasons.'

When she didn't give them, I looked at Shortleg. He looked at his pint. A bad liar, Shortleg. This had something to do with the events in Tettleby. The ropefaces. Yes, that would explain his presence well enough. Maybe mine too.

'I found an apology tucked in the wall the next day,' Benadetta said. 'Which was appreciated, I'll admit. Our friend had deci-decided he'd no wish to meet a Perfecti. So the next night I sent two of our journeymen. No luck.' She turned her wimpled head and looked at me. Her brown eyes shone in the lamplight, a wet amber. 'Now this commrach wants to speak with a commrach. The Church hopes your p-presence will alleviate their continued vacillation.'

'I'm an errand girl now, hmm?' I said. 'A skivvy? That's a woman I'd neither be nor touch.'

'You've had worse,' Shortleg replied. He sipped his beer.

I tightened my hair's tail. 'There's an entire library of facts you're not giving me, Sister.'

'Naturally,' Benadetta said. 'I only need you to extract information, not assess it.' She studied my face. 'Or, better yet, persuade the information source down from the pass. Rest assured, when this is over you'll be free to pursue whatever wretched transgressions you prefer to wallow in. And, candidly, I'll be more satisfied for it.'

'Well, if candid satisfaction's your aim I've something in my bag you're clearly in need of, *darling*.'

She slapped my cheek.

I leapt to my feet, glared at her.

The caliban was on his feet too. He pulled back his fur-trimmed coat to reveal a row of iron spikes along his belt, one readied. He'd been prepped to throw this entire time.

I stared at Benadetta. 'No one humiliates me.'

'No one needs to,' she replied.

Shortleg bellowed with laughter. He slapped the table.

I hissed, then pretended to chuckle. *But I'll get you, Sister,* I thought. *You'll pay for it all before we are done. You and your yellow-haired mongrel.*

I sat down. The sting on my cheek lingered, hot and ticklish. The first time she had touched me since the chantry.

Benadetta nodded to the caliban and the beast sat too. I swear he almost smiled.

I thought about this enigmatic commrach, their curious knack for hiding.

'I want a mirror,' I said. 'Small. A hand mirror.'

'Whatever for?' Benadetta asked.

'Because it's unfair you fools get the benefit of my looks and I don't.'

'No,' Benadetta said. 'We don't have one.'

'Find one,' I said. 'I won't leave this inn. I won't entertain whoever this elf prick is unless I've a mirror.'

I made my pout, the one I'd often used on Grandmother.

Benadetta frowned. The bitch couldn't work me out, which delighted me no end.

'Mr Shortleg,' she said eventually, never looking away from me. 'Find Cal'Adra a hand mirror.'

'Sister, your grace,' he replied, 'We're sat on a mountain. Not a barber's chair.'

'There's a large mirror in the front saloon,' Benadetta said.

'Make a hand mirror from it.'

'Sister…'

'Orders of the Church.'

'I'll get my axe.' He got up. He looked at me. 'Weird twat.'

I grinned and blew him a kiss.

I woke early, for me. I found Sister Benadetta out on the inn's wall, gazing toward where the great pass rose to a hump. The morning was already warm but a wind was coming over the mountains, conveying a little of their cold.

'Good morning, Cal'Adra.' She'd heard me approach, much to my disappointment. She didn't look at me.

'Hypothetically speaking, I could push you off of here. It's, what, fifty feet down? Then I could run.'

'Hypothetically speaking, the Church would hunt you down.'

'The Church could try.'

'If you meant murder you wouldn't tell me.' A few strands of hair had escaped her habit and danced about in the wind. I'd never seen her hair before. Deep auburn, spun with gold.

I took a deep breath of mountain air. 'True.'

'I…' She winced suddenly; a muscular attack of her speech affliction. She gripped the wall. 'I think something greater than my machinations holds you now anyway, hmm? How long since you've seen another commrach? What might they have to tell… you of your isle? I'll hazard you've even practised how you will explain your exile – whatever it is – or woven some charming lie.'

I smirked. I wanted her to see that smirk, but she wouldn't take her eyes from the horizon. Her fucking attitude. So self-pleased, as if the dirt of this world could never touch her.

'Barmaid here's a frigid bitch,' I said. I laughed. 'You know that? Some women, some women have these wide hips like one of your church altars. Proud and powerful and you just want to drop to your knees there and then.' I made a gesture of grabbing wide hips before my face. No use; she didn't look at me. 'But last night her altar refused my supplications. I've this problem, see, Sister. All human women crave a woman's touch at least once and, moreover, I'm implausibly pretty and darkly charming. But its these eyes and these sharp teeth and these renowned pointy ears. Your sky-madness makes it so your women leap on me or run. Either way, they call me demon soon after. Always.' I clicked my tongue. 'I found a chalked hook on my door this morn.' I gestured at the hook pendant around Benadetta's neck. 'Only thing that barmaid's good for is my tongue in her love-glove and she presumes she can exorcise me. *Me*. Like some... some bad dream.'

'Quite the soliloquy,' Benadetta said. 'You cannot shock me, Cal'Adra.'

'Another wager?'

'You shock but to evade.'

And somehow ended up depressing myself, I thought.

'How perceptive,' I replied. I spat over the side. 'You want my philosophy, Sister? Everything's fucking. Everything. The root of all endeavours. Empires, war, art. Love.' I shivered in the breeze. 'Pure varnish, all of it. Lechery's many-honeyed glaze. And yet you waste your life on celibacy, yes?'

'Decency aside, ought else would be pointless,' she said. 'We Perfecti are infertile.'

'*Pointless?*' Incredible. 'Now if ever there were proof I'm in your cohort by coercion alone. I'm certainly not here for your company.'

Benadetta reached into her vestments and produced a tiny scroll. She passed it to me.

I unrolled the parchment, careful not to let it fly from my hand in the breeze. A spidery script read:

Midnight. High Redoubt. The commrsch, one other.
No wespons. No Perfecti.

'They know I'm here?' I'd expected to wait days.

'Our friend must have seen us arrive.'

'Where's this redoubt?'

She nodded toward the great hump. I could spy a black shape like a row of broken teeth. Benadetta had been gazing at it when I approached her.

'Midnight,' I said.

'You and Shortleg, I should think. He knows this land.'

I was glad it wouldn't be the caliban. 'Let's get this over with,' I uttered.

'I apologise for raising the matter of your past,' Benadetta said. She turned and our eyes met. Her skin was white as vellum in the morning light, the bridge of her nose delicately freckled. 'I shall not again. I can see it… distracts you.'

With that she walked away.

I thought to shout something vulgar into the pass below, merely to hear it echo back to me. The fancy passed soon enough.

'You know what I think?' I said to Shortleg as we walked up the moon-drenched rise. 'I think you're trying to save yourself.'

'Well, yeah,' the big man replied between wheezing breaths. 'Found God, din't I?'

'Quit the stage act, Shortie,' I said. 'I mean in this world. The only world. Dead taxman, missing money. You've found God in order to lose the chopping block.'

'Shurrup,' he muttered. 'Let's keep this bollocks professional.'

The moon shone ahead of us, full-round and low. The redoubt sat within its silver disc at the top of the hill, a silhouette of ruined battlement and swollen earth. It had once possessed four corner towers. Now only one on the far side remained intact, some four storeys high with a pointed roof. A shadow before the moon, it reminded me of the onyx towers of home.

'Know what I think happened?' I said.

'Couldn't give a toss.'

'I think the good citizens of Tettleby talked you into a deal long before we arrived. They said, "Kill this rich child-fucker and we'll keep the tax money. But just blame your pals after we've burnt them to death in a barn." That it?'

'Ain't nothing like that.'

'Buuuut the Church turned up. The Church turned up and so you betrayed Tettleby too. That right? And then I came in useful again. You pointed the Church in my direction once you'd heard I'd escaped, cried *praise the Pilgrim* and presumed they'd stake and burn me.' I made a surprised sound. 'But you had not figured they'd been scouring for a commrach dolt for a while had you? And ta-dah – now we're lackeys to a frigid sadist.'

He stopped. 'We're husband and wife the way you're going on, yer fang-eared slag,' he snapped. 'It ain't nothing like yer say. Nothing.'

'So how is it?'

'Think you're fucking better than me, dun't yer?' He stepped closer. 'Why's Ned dead, bitch? Riddle me that, fucker. He ran out the barn with yer. Now he's crow food. Curious that. Paint me fucking intrigued.'

'I didn't kill him,' I lied. I realised the smugness had drained from me, so I forced it out again. 'The fool trod on a trap. I couldn't free him.'

'So you stabbed him.'

'I *left* him.'

'Bollocks.'

'Alright, so I killed him. You think I wanted to? A mercy, man. You'd do the same.'

'Bollocks,' he said. 'You've frost for blood, yer bint.'

'Oh yes? *You* walked out into a mob of thirty masked men intent on burning us to death. If you were Ned's friend, how come you're alive now?'

He pulled out a knife.

'We're not supposed to have those,' I mumbled. I'd nothing. I took a step back.

Shortleg glared at me. Then his expression softened. He turned the knife and offered me the hilt.

'I don't meet strangers at midnight with me arse cheeks splayed and a grin on me face,' he explained. 'Don't fret, troll-tits.' He patted his jacket. 'I got one too.'

I took the knife. I hid it in the holster inside my right boot.

We walked on. I swore I'd never understand Shortleg if I lived a thousand centuries.

'Good times here,' he said after a little while. 'Back during war. You'd have been on your isle back then o' course, flouncing around your devil-tower and pissing in servants' gobs.'

'*Hey*. Err, actually that's quite accurate.'

'We came up this hill laughing, thousands of us. Came back down here crying, mere hundreds. Grand Army of Hoxham.'

'You attacked this redoubt?'

He groaned. 'We'd o' took that fucker in an afternoon. This place were just a stopover. Grand Army were marching over the pass to siege Becken. All the Ruperts in their fine cloth said we'd take Becken in a week. Did we bollocks. Month later I were sat shivering in this very redoubt, most o' me pals dead. Just a boy.'

He fell silent. I heard a pebble roll. Ahead and to our right. Shortleg didn't notice.

'Is that when you gave up the army?' I reached for the piece of broken mirror in my pocket.

'Oi. I'll have you know I stuck the whole war.' He sighed. 'And I'm the kinda twat who'll sign up when it kicks off again. Which it will.'

'Interesting,' I said. I'd the mirror readied in-between fingers. I carried on the conversation as if nothing had caught my ear. 'You've a sense of duty then?'

'Yeah,' he said. 'And no. I just sorta do things. Dun't matter what. Have to. Keeps me out me own head, you know? So I do things and knit most o' the reasons later.'

'Very telling,' I observed, 'this philosophy of yours.'

'Mine?' he said. 'It's fucking everybody's, love.'

I aimed the mirror in the direction of the pebble's roll, careful to catch the moon's rays.

A figure clutched its face. Thirty feet away, short and heavy-cloaked.

'Fuck,' Shortleg said. He stumbled back. 'Oh fuck.'

I put the mirror away. 'Isle trickery.' I said it again, louder and in commrach.

The figure's cloak was of leather, a thousand pieces of it cut and fixed to look like leaves. They wore a deer's skull as a mask.

They stood watching us.

'Fucking 'eck,' Shortleg muttered. 'Dressed up like devil.'

'Hinter cloak,' I said. 'You'd see night as day through that mask, everything profoundly brightened. A mirror's glare dazzles like a sun.'

'Devil's work.' Shortleg sounded nervous. Quite unlike him.

'No devil, just quality craftsmanship,' I assured my colleague. 'Have no fear: they can't be invisible now we've seen them.'

The deer-skulled figure beckoned for us to follow. They turned and headed for the redoubt.

We walked through the broken gateway, over the slippery remains of its fallen door and into a wide muddy courtyard surrounded by high crenellated walls. There'd been buildings in there, barracks and such, but someone had taken the pains to level most of them. Bracken grew from their ruins. The far right tower's spire sliced the moon above, a raised black dagger.

'Chapel's still intact,' Shortleg muttered. He jutted his chin at the tower.

'No sense in razing something useless,' I said.

Ahead of us, the cloaked figure climbed stairs that led up to the wall's battlements. The figure seemed familiar with the place, surefooted in the darkness and the wreckage.

We followed along the battlement. The cloaked figure headed toward the tower, the chapel. It stopped at the entrance, looked back at us briefly, then shouldered the door open.

We followed, faltering at the open door. Blackness inside. No windows.

'Come inside,' came a croaky voice. Male.

I let Shortleg go through first.

A tight room, damp-smelling, the walls grey granite.

'Close the door,' the voice said.

I did as he asked, and everything went black. I readied myself, urging my sight to adjust, expecting hands from every angle.

A lantern on the far wall flickered to life, the cloaked man coaxing it. He turned to face us. His mask was indeed a deer skull, swirls and stars carved into its bone.

A cramped archway led to darkness to our left: presumably a stairwell. Bed linens lay before the small stone altar in the corner. A short cupboard the other side of the room had a door behind it. A bookcase stood beside the door we'd entered by and I'd a suspicion it had of late served a similar function to the cupboard. Here was the chamber of a man with nothing left but his fear of the outside world.

'I like what you've done with the place,' I said.

'Which obelisk are you from?' he asked me in Commrach.

He meant the trade obelisks. Our race had built them on small islands and reefs outside human ports centuries past; outposts for our mercantile interests, a way to gain necessities for the isles that weren't found there. A segregated closeness that suited both human and commrach.

'None,' I told him in our language. 'I'm sort of freelance.'

He laughed beneath his skull mask. 'Lost. Good. I'm lost too.'

'Friends in damnation.' I smiled. 'Might you remove the mask?'

He paused, then did as I asked, though he kept his hood up. His was an old face, older than the late middle years he likely was. His eyes were coldest green.

'Your name?' I said.

'If I asked for yours, would you give it?'

I shrugged. 'I've a false one prepared.'

Shortleg laughed.

'What?' I asked him. Could he understand our words?

'That funny language o' yours,' he said to me. 'Sounded like you said "suck-bollock".' He looked down and scratched his chin. 'Carry on…'

'This idiot's here to watch you, yes?' the commrach asked me in our language.

I nodded. 'They want me to bring you down from here.'

The man looked at Shortleg. 'You,' he said in Mainer. 'Move that bookcase there in front of the door. Do it now.'

Shortleg nodded and did as he said.

I pointed at the door with the cupboard tight against it.

'Expecting visitors?' I asked in Mainer.

'We shall be here till dawn,' he said.

'That weren't part o' the plan,' Shortleg said, still moving the bookcase. 'What do we do fer a shit?'

The man ignored him.

'I've seen them about,' he said to me in Commrach. 'The last few nights.'

'Who?'

'His people. His damned.'

He added no more.

'Why are we here?' I asked him. And myself. I was prepared for anticlimax. Secretiveness, I've found, rarely fails to be affectation.

'Could you get word back to the Isle?' he said. 'You and the Church? Could you do that?'

'Depends on the word,' I lied. The Isle had no use for me and vice versa.

'House Rosho aims to own the Isle,' he said. 'To own the very world. Yet Rosho are puppets.'

Rosho. I had not heard the name in years, nor thought of it. That family were the byword for dishonour and trickery back on the Isle. They spent out their days in exile inside a trade obelisk in Becken. This man's opinion of them fitted with the Isle's at its foundations, but his notion that the Roshos grasped for the world entire was a, let's say, singular take. The Roshos had no army to speak of, no warships.

But they did have a sort of power. I recalled Grandmother's words to me after we had ventured into those ancient caves beneath the Explainers' observatory, when she spoke of the Rosho's true and secret purpose.

I shook the thought off. No one had the power to conquer the world, secret purpose or no. Paranoia was a tar pit if you lost your sense of proportion. I had to keep that in mind.

'Continue,' I told him.

'The Roshos took me in. I, a lowly huntsman from Skarrach wood. They take in all the exiled.'

'They do? Huh. Never thought to ask.' I don't suppose they'd have appreciated a Cal'Adra at their door either, now I thought about it.

'I knew of their reputation,' he said. He had ice-green eyes just like yours, Shen. Perhaps you all did in Skarrach. 'I was careful not to mention it, naturally. Their young patriarch, Arlo Rosho, said I'd return to the Isle if I served them, told me my family would be lifted, brought to a height we'd never known.' He grinned ruefully, the face of a man who'd been lied to, who knew himself a fool. 'They'd need us to rule Skarrach, after all.'

'Naturally.'

'I nodded along,' he said, giving me a pointed look. 'I wanted to keep in their graces. Just big talk, I told myself. But I do not doubt their power now.'

Something crossed his face, a tight-jawed expression that unnerved me.

'Arlo took me down by the waves,' he said, 'before the mouth of a cave.'

'Where?'

He didn't look at me. 'By the obelisk. But they said the tunnel went all the way to some caverns up the coast. And to...' He took a deep breath. 'Lower places.'

I noticed Shortleg studying us both. No doubt he understood our body language, if not our tongue.

'They bade me kneel on the sand,' the commrach said. 'They lit braziers. I—'

He looked up suddenly.

'What?' I said.

'Did you hear that?'

I shook my head.

'I apologise. My nerves...' He took down his hood, revealing a shock of red hair. Like yours, Shen. So like yours. 'Men came first. From the caves, some twenty or more. In masks. Hired hands, I assumed. This was surely a game. I looked to Arlo Rosho. He smiled back and for the first time I felt scared. This game's wager might be my very life.

'And then he emerged. From the cave. From the world's heart. Nine feet tall, crowned. Arms wide and I could see he had two thumbs on either hand. *Taloned* hands.'

I squinted at him. But it was as if I wasn't there anymore. He was on that beach of his.

'As he came into the light, I saw his legs were... the wrong way. As a goat's. Then the light caught his face.' The man clutched his own throat. His eyes became wide as coins. Mad, quite mad. 'Like the dreadmasks of home. But alive, *real*.' His jaw shook.

'I hope I never see that face again.'

I stepped forward, raised my palms, exuded sympathy as best my face allowed.

'It's fine,' I said. 'You don't have to say any more. Let's leave this place and go to the inn-fort, where it is warm and welcome and—'

'Don't you understand?' he snapped, and his eyes met mine. 'He's out there. *Him*. His people. I've *seen* them.'

'I have not seen them.'

'They're scared,' he insisted. 'Scared of this chapel. They were humans once and are still bound by their sky-madness. They keep clear. So far.'

Banishment had driven him insane. This wretch was a time-waster. Worse, it was *my* time he wasted.

I looked at Shortleg. 'Let's leave.'

'What? Without him?' He pointed at the man. 'Sister'll have our guts for garters if we let him go.'

'Bolgada!' the man said to me. He spoke in Commrach: 'His Crawling Majesty! King of the fomorg!'

'Absurd.'

Sick of me, he looked at Shortleg.

'The devil,' he told him in Mainer. 'The very devil is out there.'

'See?' I said to Shortleg. I grinned and tapped my temple.

Shortleg did not smile. He did not move. He was like a man who'd had sentence passed over him. I hadn't pegged him for the sort of human scared by devil-talk, bugger his newfound 'piety'.

'Fuck's sake.' I walked over to the bookcase before the door we'd come through and tried to shift it.

'Kyra,' Shortleg said, still static. 'Maybe—'

'Maybe you should help me shift this bookcase.'

'Kyra?' the commrach man said without thinking, a question and a sadness in his words.

I stopped pushing at the heavy weight. I turned to face him.

'You know me,' I said in our language.

Mania had drained from him, leaving only fear. Oh, he knew he'd misspoken. He knew.

'We've never met,' he said. 'I…' He faltered. His jaw tightened.

I stepped closer. 'Tell me who you are.'

Small he seemed now, shrunken, more wary of me than his fanciful daemons outside.

'Red hair. Green eyes.' I stopped, inches from him. 'Skarrach-born.' I smiled. 'You wouldn't happen to know a… Shen Asu… at all?' Slowly, I reached out. I touched his hair. 'Who are you?'

'Her…' He faltered. He took a shaking breath. 'Her father.'

My blade went in his right shoulder. The next stroke drove into his neck and this time he struggled. Downstrokes. As he fell backwards, the point impaled his cheek, his nose, his jaw.

And I saw you, Shen, in my mind. Rising from an ornate chair, turning to face me. Your eyes. That naked and hideous second as I met your eyes, and they told me nothing.

Him. He had been its maker. His compliance. I watched my blade deliver his due.

Someone grabbed me from behind and I screamed. Big arms hooped around my elbows and I could swing my blade no more.

'Gerroff him,' Shortleg barked in my ear.

I yelled, yelled so as to push the last of the fury out. Then I took deep breaths, felt Shortleg's belly rise and fall against my spine.

The man was still alive. Gasping for air, throat rattling, his face a dark and pulpy wetness in the lamp's light.

'You killed such love,' I hissed at him in our shared language. 'Such *love*.'

Your father shuddered, Shen. He went still.

Something like shock was setting in. At my own handiwork, swifter than my rational mind, but also at my words. I'd never used those words. I should have long ago.

'Shit,' I heard Shortleg mutter by my ear. 'What the fuck did he say to yer?' He let go of me. 'Shit...'

'Payback,' I muttered. And it was. The ignorant shit had played his part alright, small though it was, in those final days. My past. My lost and ruined past.

'*Payback*?' Shortleg blew out a long breath. 'Fuck me, I'm never lending you tuppence. And you can tell the Sis—'

A howl outside, close by.

We looked at one another. Mouths wide.

More howls, many. Echoing in the courtyard outside. Human. Humans *howling*, like some twisted pretence of wolves.

Then silence, sudden as a clap.

Boots shuffling on stone.

The door behind us shook. The bookcase before it shuddered. Pounding, again and again. Splinters flew from the door's timber.

'Axes,' Shortleg said. He pulled out his tiny knife. 'Shitty bollocks. Shitty bastard bollocks fuck!'

If I'd had my rapier I could have run it through the door and into their guts, such was its bite. But I didn't. I had a knife, a blood-slicked knife. Blood-slicked hands.

'Stairwell,' I said.

I ran over to find someone had filled the downwards stairs with earth years ago. The stairs up were fine enough but the higher floor would only lead to the spire. Suicide, that, a dead end in the sky.

I shook my head at Shortleg.

'Other door,' he said. His face was white.

We made it to the door with the cupboard before it, Shortleg nearly slipping in your father's blood. We each grabbed one side of the cupboard, he left and I right.

'Push,' he ordered.

We hefted the cupboard and it toppled over onto the corpse. Shortleg pulled the door open.

A ropeface screamed at us. A man in a mask, like the men back in Tettleby. He'd a knife in hand.

I grabbed the ropeface's wrist and Shortleg drove his blade into the man's belly. A red tongue jabbed out from the hole in his tightly bound mask. Yes; one of the rope masks from Tettleby exactly.

I heard the bookcase that blocked the door behind us collapse. I turned my head to look, limbs clambering through the half-gone door, the night sky and the battlements behind them.

Shortleg tried pushing our assailant out of the way but the ropeface held to him, gurgling animal sounds. The pair of them stumbled, both yelling, falling into the courtyard below. I heard a slate roof collapse.

I didn't stay to investigate. I ran along the battlement, the cold air upon my skin. I saw stairs halfway along, leading down.

Two new ropefaces were coming up them. One of them had a shield. No apparent weapons.

I turned and saw another, a huge one, stumbling toward me from where I came. He'd a great axe, larger than the one Shortleg normally carried. He had it raised over his head, wobbling amateurishly. But it was still a fucking great axe.

I'd a knife and no space to dance with it. Hard earth in the courtyard thirty feet below. The drop the other side of the battlement far deeper, falling into darkness.

'Shit.'

I ran at the two with the shield, tried to leap over them. The shield bashed my boots and I dropped onto my back on the battlement walkway. I opened my eyes to see an axe flying down at me. I rolled, face hard against the wall, and the axe crashed into the stone where I'd just lain.

I shuffled and grabbed the axe's haft. I jabbed my knife into his axe hand. I got back on my feet.

He'd dropped it. I tried to grab for the blade but he punched me in the forehead. It didn't have the momentum to stun me, but I stumbled back onto what felt like the other man's shield.

A filthy arm went about my neck, keeping my back tight to the shield. I felt teeth try to bite the back of my head, though they found no purchase.

I jabbed my knife over my shoulder but connected with nothing. I had to watch as the big ropeface picked up his axe again. He raised it high.

'Commrach!' came a voice from below, in the courtyard.

I couldn't turn to look. The shield-man holding me went limp. His arm was a dead weight around my throat.

Big man swung his great axe down upon me.

I threw myself face forwards onto the granite walkway. I'd pulled the limp man down with me, and the great axe went through him and lodged in the shield's wood between us. I shuddered with the force of it, lost all breath. But I was alive, unhurt.

I pushed myself up, found strength in terror, the weight of the corpse atop me. Skull shards and brain rolled into my hair and down my face. Typical. I noticed something jutting out of his side.

The hilt of my rapier. Someone had pushed, or thrown, it

into his side.

I didn't think. I pulled it out and pushed his corpse at the third man behind him, the one who'd tried to bite my head. That bought me space. I took a stance: rapier in my right hand, dagger in my left.

Big man lunged at me, using his axe as a frigging lance.

I jumped onto the battlement wall just before the metal crushed my chest.

He rushed past me, then stumbled to a stop. He tried to spin around but he was slow, imbalanced by a weapon he didn't respect.

My rapier slid through the back of his head. I dropped back down onto the walkway behind him. I pulled out and the weight of his weapon carried him down into the courtyard. I could hear more fighting down there.

The last man stared at me. He drew a shortsword.

'Size *does* matter.' I flicked the blood from my forty-inch rapier and grinned. 'Darling.'

Running footsteps behind me. I held my rapier ready to parry the man before me and glanced over my shoulder.

A ropeface woman with a kitchen knife. Marvellous.

I changed stance, my back against the battlement wall, dagger to the woman, rapier to the man. This was the sort of thing that was better to brag about later than actually do.

The man was careful, tapping my sword point again and again, trying to find a way to get his short blade within stabbing reach. The woman was a flailing maniac.

I had to continually block her kitchen knife, predictable yet ceaseless. The fight on my right side was more a chess game, each of us trying to guess the other's move, find a feint. My brain ached, performing both. I could almost smell smoke rising from my skull.

The woman sliced my knuckle and I hissed. The man took his chance and drove his point.

I thrust my own through his wrist, his sword inches from my belly. I pushed until his wrist had passed the eight inches of sharp edge and was onto the blunt. Still glancing the woman's slashes with my dagger, I lifted the man's skewered sword-arm above his head with my rapier. He screamed. He held to his own blade, but the thing dangled like a pendulum before his face.

The woman booted my thigh. I nearly lost balance, nearly tumbled down to the courtyard. Luckily, my blade through the man's wrist lent me purchase and I righted myself.

'Nice try,' I told her.

The man grabbed his own sword by the blade with his free hand, prising it out of his skewered right.

I pulled my blade from his wrist and plunged it into his heart.

I pulled out again, spun around in time to block the woman, drove my rapier into her belly and jabbed the knife in her eye. Gore poured from her socket and down her rope mask. I withdrew in one flourish and she collapsed.

Fighting in the courtyard below. Shortleg was alive still. He had his axe now. He was back-to-back with someone holding a short spear: the caliban. The pair of them were surrounded by seven ropefaces. Ropeface corpses littered the ground, a halo of meat.

I ran down the stairs. The ropefaces didn't see or hear me coming. I'd run three through the spine before the rest noticed. The others hesitated, bewildered by my attack. Shortleg and the caliban made quick work of them.

We waited, panting, weapons ready. The moonlit night had returned to silence and silver.

'How many was that?' I asked. My own voice made me shiver.

'Fifteen,' Shortleg answered. He lowered his axe. 'Summat like that.' He looked at the blond halfbreed. 'Cheers, pal.'

The caliban barely nodded.

'He were trailing us,' Shortleg told me. 'With our weapons. Sister's orders.'

'Did he bring my sword belt?'

The caliban opened the backpack he was carrying and offered me my belt.

I took the end furthest from his hand.

'Don't bother thanking me, inbred,' the caliban said. It still vexed me his accent was so clear-cut and mannered. I hadn't expected a caliban to talk at all.

I ignored him. I sheathed my blades and put my belt on.

'Let's go,' Shortleg said.

'Wait,' I said. 'I want to take a look at these absolute fuck-ends.'

I bent down before the nearest corpse, took out my knife once more and started slicing the rope mask open.

'Bastard's dressed like a baker,' Shortleg observed. 'He's got a fucking apron on him.'

I pulled the mask off. No one I knew. His eye sockets were painted black, as were his lips. There was some black wax-like substance on his forehead, beaded with sweat and dirt. A circle, a circle with spikes, drawn with a thumb or finger. The same as on Kyran's old shirt, the one I'd kept in my satchel. What was this? Had one of these dead wretches drawn it?

I looked up at Shortleg. He seemed nervous.

'These are your friends, right? From the barn.' I frowned.

'How about you tell us who they are?'

    'Not *here*,' the caliban cut in, shaking his head like he was a tutor and I a disappointing pupil. 'Let's get back.'

    I couldn't fault that logic. Unfortunately.

10

I entered the observatory's grounds on the shoulders of my fellow warriors. They chanted our city's war cry. They threw leaves from the battlefield over me. Men and women beat upright six-foot drums with our house's glyph painted on their skin. I won't lie – I bloody loved it.

Our army filled the observatory's courtyard. Corso uniforms were everywhere, stretching out from beneath my arse to the wall of woven trees that surrounded this most ancient place. I was certain this army was larger than the one that had actually fielded this morning but, really, why let the facts get in the way of my victory procession?

I waved and saluted everyone. I clambered up onto my feet and stepped from shoulder to welcoming shoulder. I'd never seen a side get this excited. Usually, a certain reserve was held for the observatory, the time-shrouded seat of the Explainers. Not now. The radicalism of our tactics had infected even here, the most conservative establishment on all the Isle. Nevertheless, among the throng I could see stern-masked Obsidians with long clubs, waiting for an order from their masters.

I wondered at that. Did they know of Urse's unlawful death? The victory would be void then. Perhaps you and I, Shen, would watch our own hearts cut from our chests. We were bound now, in crime if naught else.

At some point we reached the foot of the observatory's stairs and, as I climbed down, someone placed a leaf crown on my head. There was no greater accolade to be had from one's fellow fighters; I'd never seen anyone receive one before. I made my way up the wide set of stairs, twirling just the once to give the hooting crowd the full benefit of my innate glory.

Grandmother awaited on the plinth, as did the High Explainer, every matriarch and patriarch of Corso and the mandatory minimum of their Darradian opposites. Losers.

I nodded at Grandmother. Her face was placid but there was something in her eyes beyond satisfaction. For the first time, I could truly see we were family.

She placed a taloned hand on my back and presented me to the High Explainer, an old woman with tattooed skin blue-black as magpie feather. Behind her shaved head rose the observatory tower, a coiling edifice of living trees woven into one another, with younger trees grafted atop them and likewise woven. A thing ever-changing, ever the same, its dying components replaced with the living. As old as our philosophy of blood.

The High Explainer said nothing, her face as granite. She passed me a rolled deer hide.

I bowed and took it. I unrolled the hide and showed it to the crowd. A declaration of victory followed by a list of temporary forest rights. The list so long, our victory so utter, they'd had to stitch an extra half of hide on. The army yelled and ululated. Three hundred fists punched the air.

I was careful to savour this moment. It might well be the peak, the summit before a deadly drop.

Grandmother stood beside me and gestured for quiet.

'Let our words be brief,' she said, 'for the truth is plain. Till next war season Corso is pre-eminent across all the Isle.' She placed a taloned hand upon my shoulder. 'Thanks to the tactical planning, the vigour, the unprecedented vision of Kyra Cal'Adra, daughter of Elinda Cal'Adra, that defender of our colonies, now Corso's greatest child.'

The throng chanted my name. I could not believe this. The plan, the unprecedented battle tactic, was not mine. It was Grandmother's.

Oh, but she was making legend of me. Her eyes were upon the next tower, the next marriage, the colonies. She could leave glory to others. I was happy to take it.

'Corso thanks you all,' she told them. 'In all my years I have seen no finer army.'

She gestured for them to cheer themselves. They happily obliged. I would have given anything to have been able to turn around to see the faces of all the other matriarchs and patriarchs, many of them from higher towers than Cal'Adra's present seat. I'd bet Grandmother would have liked that too.

Tradition dictated we could not. Instead, I looked for you in the crowd, my Shen. But I could not find you.

We walked down one of the many underground tunnels of the observatory, Grandmother in the centre, my brother and I flanking either side. A little fleet of privilege and significance. Initially these tunnels – moontile-lit and carved with tales of our people – had been a delight. They offered a coolness the summer outside ceaselessly refused. Now I just felt cold.

'Grandmother,' Kyran said. 'If Darrad should find a way to render our victory illegal, some detail in the statutes, what then?'

Grandmother sighed. But before she might answer him, she noticed movement down the hall.

Another entourage strode toward us, almost a reflection; the one at its centre clearly a patriarch, all high hair and gown, two young blades flanking him.

Tylis Cal'Dain. Urse's father. He would know his son dead, now. Everyone knew.

We stopped before one another. Grandmother greeted her fellow archon in the traditional manner, lifting her chain matrimonial's medallion with her thumb.

Tylis Cal'Dain fumbled with his own. He held his head high, which had the undesired effect of causing his chin to tremble.

'My condolences, patriarch,' Grandmother said. 'Your son was the pride of his city.'

'I thank you, matriarch,' Tylis replied. He tried a smile. He noticed me. 'Kyra.'

I felt suddenly hot in the cool tunnel. I nodded.

Tylis reached a taloned hand out to my own and squeezed gently.

'Urse often told me of the affection between you,' he said. 'He was a stranger in your city, and you welcomed him.'

I hoped the fact I dared not speak seemed to be mourning. I heard sobbing and turned to see Urse's sister, Ousile, being consoled by Kyran. Her betrothed.

'Kyra,' her father said, his eyes still upon me, 'I'm sorry the marriage you waited for has been denied.' He looked at Grandmother. 'Perhaps we could talk on that?'

'My dear Tylis,' Grandmother said. 'You need rest.'

'It's really no—'

'In time,' Grandmother assured him. She placed a brass-taloned hand upon her fellow archon's upper arm. 'Be with your family.'

Tylis sniffed, nodded. He and his party proceeded the way we had come.

We walked on.

My status as bargaining chip had risen. Why give me to a family that already had Kyran? There would be other tower families now, of all Isle's cities, eager for a little Cal'Adra audacity in their blood. After all, I would be governor of the colonies, Lady of the Jades.

'Strange no one has stepped forward to claim Urse's kill,' Kyran said. He looked at me a second.

'I should think that was obvious,' Grandmother said. She let the thought hang. 'Idiot was likely slaughtered by his own side.'

The double doors to the lecture hall lay ahead. A lone moontile above cast stellar light upon the story cycle carved into their wood: the world and the stars and planets forming from chaos, life rising from the drying earth's panblood, variating, coalescing into the earliest species.

Someone waited before them. Cousin Zymo. She scowled.

'Zymo,' Grandmother said to her, coming to a stop. 'Better, I see.'

Cousin Zymo strode forward, as if ready to maul me with her ram's-horn hairstyle.

'Matriarch,' she said to Grandmother. 'I wish to report treachery. I was poisoned, my right to glory most blackguardly stolen.'

'Grandniece,' the old woman said. 'If being matriarch has taught me anything, it's disdain for anyone who lets themselves be poisoned.' She cocked her head to one side. 'Just take pride in our family's unprecedented victory and we'll say no more, eh?'

Zymo shook her head and her ram's-horn hairstyle dashed against her cheekbones.

'I simply *cannot*, Matriarch,' she insisted. '*Will* not.' She pointed at me. 'Your granddaughter's m—'

Grandmother slashed her cheek with a talon.

Zymo yelped. She clutched her face.

'Enough,' Grandmother hissed. She simmered then calmed. 'You're an embarrassment to Cal'Adra. You barely register my attention. If you'd any decency you'd refrain from existing entirely.' She raised a talon. 'Accuse Kyra of anything, *anything*, and I'll toss your skull into the sea.' She gestured to me and Kyran. 'Come along, children.'

We passed cousin Zymo. I made the mistake of looking back.

Zymo glared at me with a hatred I'd have thought her shallow mind could never encompass.

Kyran stepped ahead of Grandmother and pushed the double doors open. Flamboyantly, so that we'd be seen.

Inside the First Lecture Hall every archon of every tower in Corso and Darrad argued. They filled the first two rows of the stone tiers. Explainers stood on the stairs of the aisles trying to solicit calm. The legality of our family's tactics was, it seemed, being hotly debated.

Seeing us enter, the throng fell silent.

'Is this a bad time?' Grandmother said. She smiled.

The hall erupted once more, half in applause, half in shouting.

I'd never been in the First Lecture Hall before, and I took the opportunity of drinking it in. A large subterranean cave carved into a circular theatre, the hall was perhaps the most ancient construction in existence, older even than the cities we had built around those mysterious towers.

The shouting continued. In fact, it only seemed to be getting worse. I made a show of indifference and looked upwards. The ceiling was renowned for displaying the oldest known model of the heavens. The sun hung at the centre, a boulder-sized protrusion belted with dried clay that shone in exactly the same silverish manner as moontiles. All twelve planets – far smaller than their mother sun – were similarly illuminated and were shown in orbit in their midsummer position. The fourth planet, the world itself, I recognised from its doting daughter the moon. Yes, even I had to admit that this ceiling really put things into perspective: the heavens were distant and boring.

A female Explainer halfway up one of the aisles blew a horn, cutting the chatter with an acidic note.

'Thank you, sirs,' she said, cradling her hunting horn like a pet kitten. Youngish for her senior position, the Explainer dressed in the traditional manner of all her brethren, which was however she liked. Her hair was a thorn bush of tangled locks, her clothes a single whelkwool jumper that ran past her knees and entirely obscured her hands. Her spectacles were asymmetrical and devoid of glass, and her chin was tattooed black for reasons that were likely buried in some obscure treatise only she had read. The Explainers were beyond earthly considerations of fashion and caste, yet it always seemed to me their disinterest took great pains to be individual.

'Thank you,' she repeated. She looked distracted a moment, looked to us and then said, 'Ah yes! The Cal'Adras are here! Now...' She skittered down the stairs and came to an abrupt stop one step from the bottom. 'We can begin.'

'Thank you,' Grandmother said.

The Explainer shushed her and smiled. Shocking, to see that. But this was an Explainer on her own ground. There were chuckles from the Darrad archons.

Grandmother would be furious, of course, but her mask of serenity was impeccable, especially as the Explainer might be of low blood. Unlike the tower families, Explainers were picked rather than bred.

'We have a system here,' the Explainer told Grandmother. She repeated the phrase to everyone in the rows. 'Those who have something to say must raise a hand and wait. Old as this very cave that system, oh yes.'

A male Explainer with shaved head and painted eyebrows approached us with delicate bowls of tea. The drink of archons. I hated the taste, but I wasn't so foolish as to decline. This was dangerous ground; I could sense it. A foot wrong and I'd fall down a social crag I could not even see. I smelled the tea's steaming aroma and pretended to sip.

'Now,' the Explainer continued, 'we gather there's rather been some, err, consternation, over the family Cal'Adra's interpretation of the rules of war.'

The patriarch of Cal'Mojaid held his arm aloft. Cal'Mojaid were of the greatest tower in Darrad, which – in an understanding as ancient as it was unspoken – made this patriarch the most highblood figure in all the Isle, Corso included. He certainly looked commanding.

'You, sir,' the Explainer said.

'The rules of the summer war are as explicit as they are ancient,' the patriarch declared to the hall. 'How can the vitality and race-perfection of each participant be measured if a callow minority bring chaos to the whole experiment?' He shook his head and gestured at me and my brother. 'These youths cheated. They dropped their swords, by the Blood!' He looked to the Explainer. 'Aren't you offended? It is an insult to your time-honoured methods of evaluation, surely?'

Much applause.

'It is not within the purview of the Explainers to be offended,' the Explainer said, her sleeve-obscured hands cradling her horn. 'Only to judge.' She looked over to Grandmother. 'Perhaps Cal'Adra wish to explain themselves?

'Thank you, sir,' Grandmother said to the Explainer. 'I must say, I am intrigued by Cal'Mojaid of Darrad's peculiar statement that my grandchildren and their comrades are cheats. I wouldn't have thought anyone who dropped their only weapon could be accused so.' Corso's patriarchs clapped and laughed. Still, there was a cockiness to Grandmother that would surely work against her. 'Worse, he appears to labour under the impression that the summer war exists to measure the race-perfection of each individual who participates.' The brass talons of her right hand fanned back and forth. 'Well, perhaps the Explainers here will put him out of his misery—' Someone in the hall audibly drew breath. '—and inform him an individual is not a race.' She jabbed her index finger in the air, fierce as a spear, and her pleased demeanour flashed into a noble scowl. 'We are perfecting the *species*, sirs. Forging ourselves from the ore of nature into a blood of steel.' Her talon pointed to the replica heavens above. She paused. 'It is the *generation* that must be measured, not its constituent parts.' Her finger pointed to me and Kyran. 'This generation. The generation of a new Corso, a new unity, unflinching in self-sacrifice, capable of fresh stratagems in the face of a dangerous age!'

Cheers from the Corso archons, muted dissent from Darrad. The Explainer blew her horn again and the ensemble quieted, if slowly. They were not used to being marshalled. Not in the slightest.

A patriarch in Corso black lifted his arm in the air. I recognised him: Ezral Cal'Valtah, the tower family directly beneath our own in prestige. He was powerfully built, almost human in mass, and had lost his nose to a sabre decades ago. Cal'Valtah now sported a silver nose modelled from that of the Final Countenance which, sat upon his wide face, evoked a spindly beak.

The Explainer permitted him to speak. He smiled and chose to stand up, his palms upon the onyx rail before him. I heard Grandmother take a deep breath beside me.

'Zadrikata,' he said, using Grandmother's first name among all her peers, 'I wonder if this talk of a new generation with its new rules would be so pronounced if its exponents were not of your own house.'

Darrad's archons chuckled.

'Sit down,' snapped a Corso matriarch before being shushed by the Explainer.

'There are things,' Cal'Valtah continued, 'that come before city and family. I speak for the Blood and future of our Isle. Can no one else see that she—' he pointed at Grandmother with his own taloned finger. '—chases the putrid dream of a standing army – swords in lowblood palms – with herself in charge?'

Silence. I don't think anyone had voiced this publicly before, though doubtless many an archon had thought it.

Grandmother scowled. 'Say it,' she rasped up at Cal'Valtah. She stepped forward. 'Just say it, man.'

Everyone looked at Cal'Valtah. He stared down at we Cal'Adra upon the stage, his silver nose catching the light of the false sun above. He held silent.

'You can't,' Grandmother said, dismissively. 'You can insinuate, you can mutter in small chambers again and again, but you cannot outright say 'Matriarch Cal'Adra means treason. She wishes the Isle her own'. You cannot, dear patriarch—' She spat the greeting. '—because it is absurd.'

'Perhaps I cannot,' Cal'Valtah replied. He slapped the rail before him. 'But by the Blood, *someone* should!' With that he looked to the Explainers and to every archon of greater standing than he.

Chaos. The hall ruptured with cant and caterwaul. *How dare you* I heard Grandmother hiss, but few would have heard.

Damn this talk, this to-and-fro and calcified ritual. I had been promised a future away from the Isle, with you safe in my arms, Shen. It was too good a dream to have it taken from me in this tumult.

I strode over to the Explainer, still standing at the foot of the stairs. I took the horn from her and blew it.

The sound came out so strange and discordant that everyone turned and looked.

'Might I speak?' I said loudly to the Explainer.

'That waif is no archon,' someone shouted but the Explainer dismissed them with a wave of her hand.

'It was she who led the stratagem today,' the Explainer observed. 'Whether legal or not. She may speak.' She looked at me through her glassless spectacles and whispered, 'You have an impressive skull shape, dear.'

'Thanks,' I replied, somewhat taken aback.

I addressed the patriarchs and matriarchs of both cities: 'Archons, I thank you for your time.' I paused, uncertain what to say, aware my grandmother would likely punish me soon enough. 'But if you are afraid of a mere ruse then you are already fucking dead.' Voices drew breath. I persevered. 'Dead as my mother, killed by a human incursion none of you prepared her to face nor even expected. That is inexcusable. Forgive my candour, but I and my brother and all my family will not just sit and drink tea—' I dropped my empty bowl and it cracked upon the granite floor. '—while the outer world readies to eat us whole. I can understand some of you fear my Grandmother's plans for an Isle army. Fair enough.'

I stepped back from the stairs and took my place at the centre of the hall's low stage. This was my future in the balance, doubtless.

'Would it be more comfortable to try it at a remove?' I said. 'What if each of you give me, say, thirty youths, and – in my mother's name – I give you a force to defend our colonies in the Jades? A force that is no threat to you, but will ensure the mainland's beasts will never grasp for our islands again.' I took a breath. Some were warming to my proposal, if not vocally. It was time to give them what they wanted. 'As Lady of the Jades I shall make rebellion less than a dream; I shall crush it beneath my boot.' I grinned. 'And those traitors the Roshos shall think twice before…'

People were laughing. Politely, but still.

I persevered. 'The Rosho family will…'

More laughter. The pitying sort. The archons were looking to one another, giving each other those eyes the old do when they think the young have said something silly. Silly and adorable and beside the point.

I couldn't find the words. I hadn't a clue what was happening. My speech had been going so well. Now… it was over. I was over.

A palm rested on my shoulder. Grandmother. Gently, she took the horn from my grasp and offered it back to the Explainer. She looked up to all the archons in the hall.

'It's been a long day for my grandchildren,' she said, a smile on her face that prised indulgent smiles from all her peers. 'Best we let them play outside.'

Laughter. They were laughing at me. I, who had been held aloft only hours before.

I thought I would vomit once I got outside, but the feeling subsided and I was left hanging my head, arms outstretched with palms against the rough bark of an ancient tree. The cool of the trees' shade felt good at least.

'I'm finished,' I said.

'Don't be dramatic,' Kyran replied. He squeezed my shoulder.

'You don't sound convinced,' I said, standing up straight.

'Well no. I've never seen someone laughed at by the entire establishment before.' Kyran smiled. Regret crossed his face. 'Sorry. I was trying to make light of the matter.'

I took deep breaths and massaged my temples.

You had confessed to me, Shen, beneath trees such as these. Last night. Before we made love. There would be no getting away now, no living in freedom. I had failed you.

'I need to find Shen,' I muttered.

'I'll have someone bring her,' Kyran said.

I ignored him and turned from the edge of the trees to look across Corso's camp. I couldn't see you anywhere amid the milling crowd.

Kyran slapped my shoulder. 'Let her find you, damn it. She's the bondswoman.'

I gave him a stare then made to head into the camp. He got in front of me.

'We spoke about this,' Kyran said. 'Stop being her lackey.'

I glared at him. Curses readied upon my tongue.

'Sirs.'

We both turned to see Slow Thezda at the edge of the tree line. A silhouette save for her two monocles flashing silver, reflecting the sun above.

'Now that's a bondswoman,' Kyran said.

I ignored him. 'What is it?' I asked Thezda.

'The matriarch…' She paused, her head leaning to one side. 'Would see you.' She pointed at me.

I cringed. So this would be it.

'I'll stand with you,' Kyran said.

He reached out and I knocked his hands away.

'It's fine,' I replied.

He had an odd expression, simultaneously annoyed and concerned.

'Fine,' he said.

I left him there and followed Thezda to Grandmother's yurt-grand.

People came up to thank me as I passed through the camp, others cheered and hooted from afar. I was surprised how glory could become tiresome so quickly. I nodded and smiled as best I could and allowed Thezda to push ahead of me.

By the time I reached the yurt I had steeled myself for Grandmother's onslaught. I would, I'd told myself, return to the old way of things: moody defiance as Grandmother tore me apart over the course of decades. And why not? I had been offered glory and responsibility and had lived down to my early lack of promise. On some perverse level, I suspected, she probably even preferred me a failure.

I stepped through.

Grandmother lay on a chaise longue as two young men in loincloths fanned her. She wore a loose silk robe, and her hair was no longer up in some typically fierce style. Her dark locks hung, genuinely *hung*, down past her shoulders.

I stared. I had never seen her as comfortable as this, I'd never even considered such a scene. Any second now she would scream at me for entering, surely.

'Come, child,' Grandmother said, beckoning me with her brass claws. She'd never remove those, it seemed. 'Take a seat.'

The yurt's red cloth gave everything inside a pinkish lacquer, especially on such a bright day. Between that and the heat and my grandmother's leisure, nothing seemed real. I lowered myself onto a stool by her manicured yet calloused feet.

My surly act had already evaporated. I was in unknown territory.

'I'm sorry,' I said. 'My speech was foolish.'

'Yes,' Grandmother affirmed. 'Which, fortuitously, put many a crusty archon mind at ease. Your naivety and lack of subtlety reassure them, just as your mother's did. Congratulations.' She gestured at the servant nearest me, and he began to fan in my direction. It felt good. 'Lady of the Jades.'

'It's official?'

'It would have been anyway,' she said. She stroked her hair back and her long strand of white laced itself behind her ear. 'But your blunder sped the process. My child, not an archon in that room hasn't blundered in their dense-headed youth, and publicly. It's the children who keep circumspect that fail in later life…'

She trailed off and looked a little wistful, for her. She was referring to Kyran of course. Her old favourite.

She was wrong: my brother was capable and wise. But I hadn't the energy to argue. Instead, I asked the question Kyran had been eager to know in the tunnel.

'What happens if Darrad finds a way to render the war's result null and void?'

'They shan't,' she replied. 'Anything they – or that silver-nosed brute Cal'Valtah – say shall be discounted. The Explainers will ensure as much.'

That stumped me. 'How can you even know that?' I looked up at the servants and back to Grandmother again, muttered: 'We haven't… *persuaded* the Explainers? Have we?'

'Fool,' she said, back to her old self. 'The Explainers have had millennia to become truly incorruptible.' Her face softened. 'But they are not without fear. You've inherited a shifting age, child. Dissent in the Jade colonies, aggression from the animals of the mainland. The Explainers know the Blood cannot be seen to stagnate. They've been needing something radical – yet controlled – in order to reassure the lowbloods. Our audacity in the war today provided them with that.'

'That's brilliant, Grandmother,' I said.

'Thank yourself. The battle tactic was yours after all.'

'If you say so,' I muttered.

'*You* will say so,' she chided me. 'Because *we* say so. Cal'Adra. That which defines succeeds.'

Success is being defined for me, I thought. Yet I said nothing; it was what I wanted. This tide Grandmother had set me on would take me to the colonies, after all. I would rule there, as Mother had. Free from the tight air of Corso, from Grandmother's claws, free as any highblood could hope to expect. And I would take my bondswoman. My favourite. I would take you, Shen.

Yet something didn't feel right.

'Why did you invite me here?' I asked.

Grandmother almost smiled. She sat upright. For a moment, in the scarlet gloom of the yurt, I could almost see her as the girl she had been. Comely and dashing and lethal as blades.

'To congratulate you,' she said. 'You have made enemies; now you are a woman.'

'I had enemies already,' I said. I meant Urse, but he was already dead.

'Enemies in love and hate – like the boy Urse and your cousin Zymo – are childish and passing things,' she observed. 'But today you have made a reputation. That is the soil from which the best enemies grow.'

'Ezral Cal'Valtah?' I pictured him back in the cave, his eyes piercing me above his silver nose. 'Well that's plain enough. His family would rise to our tower if they could. We're directly in their way.'

'You made a young fool of yourself with your speech, but foolishness soon passes with youth.' Likely, that was Grandmother's idea of a compliment. 'The Cal'Valtah family have long feared my strength of spirit.' There was no vanity in her words, a statement of fact. 'They've always thought weakness would follow my death. They're not thinking that now.' Her mouth curled. 'Neither are the Cal'Dains.'

'The Cal'Dains were too overwrought to be at the meeting,' I said. I shifted upon my stool. Did Grandmother know you and I had murdered Urse? Had all the archons surmised as much? It was confusing. In truth, Urse's death seemed like years ago now, yet it had only occurred this morning.

'Oh, they were there,' she replied. 'Because the Cal'Valtahs were there.'

'I thought we were the Cal'Dain's allies in Corso.' My left eye was watering from the servant's fan.

'We're their *public* allies in Corso. The Cal'Valtahs are their *private* allies.'

'I can't keep up.' I shook my head.

'You'll learn, girl,' Grandmother said. 'The Cal'Dains have more power and prestige than us, yet they wish to mix their blood and fortunes with our vigour and audacity. Naturally they fear us for the very same reasons. Thus they throw sweetmeats to another family, one neither audacious nor vigorous. Ultimately the Cal'Dains see us as a useful animal, much like a hunter sees his lynx.'

I nodded. 'Marriages are the treats this hunter gives.' I gestured at the servant to stop fanning me. 'And the Cal'Valtahs are the stick.'

'Just so.'

'Don't you ever get insulted, Grandmother,' I said, 'being thought a useful animal?'

'The perception serves us,' she replied. 'And blinds them.'

Blood! It was like gazing down a deep abyss, one that had consumed Grandmother long ago. So much ploy and counterploy. Presumably all the archons thought like her. I'd be happier when I finally got away from the Isle.

'Talking of perception,' I said, getting up. 'I'd better get among the troops so they can admire me.'

'Doubtless you are capable of that,' she said.

I nodded and went to leave.

'Girl.'

I turned back to face her.

'You haven't accepted your gift,' she said. She waved the servants away and they left the scarlet-walled yurt. There was just her and I now, looking at one another in a world of red light and shadow.

'Where is it?' I said. I couldn't think of a time when we had been alone together, certainly not when I was armed. Grandmother *trusted* me.

'Your little speech earlier,' she said. 'When exactly did they begin to laugh?'

I thought about this. 'I was talking about defending the colonies.' It hit me. 'The Roshos. I was talking about the Roshos.' I recalled her words to me and Kyran, just before the Shame Parade. 'You once told me I'd find out the reason we didn't kill the Roshos when I was fit to rule.'

'Yes, Lady of the Jades,' she said. 'I did. But I'm getting hot. Fan me.'

Her little reminder of who held the power. It was as if by vocally permitting me into her confidence she had to physically reduce me to a servant. So be it. As long as I didn't have to walk out of here with her piss-pot.

I walked to the rear of her chaise longue, lifted up one of the silk and wicker fans that lay upon the floor and began wafting the fucker.

Grandmother closed her eyes and smiled. A rare sight.

'Of course,' she said, 'I was chief among those calling for the Roshos' extinction. I owed your mother that, at the very least. But it was pointed out by another archon that no highblood – indeed, no commrach – wants to owe gratitude to another. Well, we all rather delighted at the thought of exiling the Roshos upon hearing that.'

'Humiliation?' I said. 'But Kyran mentioned that and you mocked him.'

'Let me finish, girl,' she hissed, bearing her sharp incisors. 'It did not take us long to realise how jejune and pointless such a punishment was. Would it not be better, more practical, to offer the Roshos an opportunity for redemption?'

I stopped fanning. I stared, open-mouthed, at Grandmother.

She opened her eyes. 'Redemption from their perspective. Utility for everyone else.'

That figured. I returned to fanning her.

'The Roshos allowed the humans to invade our lands,' she continued. 'Thus it becomes Rosho duty to ensure it never occurs again. And so, once a year at festival, they send one of their number to suffer before the mob, publicly satisfying vengeance-lust. That part is a mask to save everyone's standing. The rest of the time House Rosho fights a secret yet noble struggle from their tawdry little obelisk upon the mainland.'

'They've some kind of army?' I asked. I could see Grandmother supporting that, a prototype for the army she desired at home.

'Of course not. How would that even work? A single one of humanity's cities produces more fighters in a year than our whole Isle could in ten. But a human army is little different to a human's body: hulking and brawny, yes, but under all of that brawn reliant on artery and sinew.'

'Sinew?'

'Gold.' She sneered the word. 'That gaudy useless metal the humans reduce into even more useless discs.'

'Coins,' I said. I knew the term, but I'd got rather bored when my Explainer tutor covered them.

'Coins permit human war,' she said. 'Without coin the hulking carcass of their army cannot move. It cannot even coalesce in the first place. Coinage, then, is where we strike.

'The Roshos are the tip of our blade. Half the ships you see in our bay back in Corso are theirs. They load up the holds with any old tat our craftsmen have imbued and sail them to the main. What the humans would deign to call their nobility cannot get enough of it. They shower the Roshos with gold.'

'And the gold is used to—' I couldn't think of the words.

'Curtail military ambition. A human leader is showered with gold here—' She gestured in one direction with her hand. '—an assassin is showered with gold to kill another leader there.' She gestured in the opposite direction. 'The humans' shame of sex we use too: it bends them to our will.'

'And this works?'

'Humanity hasn't retaliated, has it?'

True enough. Not one human had survived their invasion. Surely they should have sought revenge in some manner. But no, not in the slightest.

I grinned. 'And the Roshos will go about their duties with furious resolve because they dream of the day they are redeemed.'

'Quite,' Grandmother said. Her eyes studied me. It was almost as if she took pleasure in her granddaughter's delight. 'Now be off with you. Grandmother needs rest.'

I found you on the wall of woven trees. It was late afternoon and the sun, low and wide, lit up your back as you gazed into the east. It made wildfire of your hair.

I strode along the wall toward you. With each step I felt the spring of living branches beneath the walkway's planks. The battlement's length had recently been pruned, a leafless straight-cut hedge. Beyond it the wall's outer side was a tumult of summer greenery.

'So, there you are,' I said. I smiled. 'You have a gift for vanishing.'

You turned toward me and smiled back. 'I avoid history's turning points wherever possible.'

'Come, come. It wasn't all that.' I brushed my palm against the wall's fresh-cut bristle. 'Frankly, I'm sick of all this manufactured adulation.'

'You can't expect me to believe that.'

'No. No, I'm loving every fucking second.' I did, mostly.

You laughed. 'Come here, fool.'

I did so. We embraced, kissed soft and long, each second a century. I'd yearned for the taste, the scent of you all day. Rose and apple. The turn of your tongue around mine. To kiss you was a small forgetting, a stronghold against the world.

I stopped and gazed at you.

'What?' you said.

'Let's get naked.'

'Here?'

'Wherever,' I said. 'I *want* you.'

'I want *you*. All the time.'

'For all time.'

And there it was. Our play-talk had become intense all a-sudden. It had stalked us, crept up. All the time. For all time.

I kissed your cheek. 'I've never felt… I suppose I…'

'What?'

'That I'm… inclined towards you, you rustic fuckhead.'

'Then you love a pariah,' you whispered. You stroked my back.

'Perhaps it can be no other way.'

'Oh, I saw that in you from the start,' you said. 'I wanted you then.'

'And now?'

'Now I need you more than life.'

You nestled your head on my shoulder. People worked below us, beyond the woven wall. They picked berries from a huddle of slathertrees, harvesting the wild crop. I spotted a spherical basket near-full with the grey berries. A man and a woman were filling it, picking slatherberries from the very tops of the trees. They wore hoof-stilts bound to their feet. Likely these stilts were imbued by their owners' touch, given a preternatural vigour, for they did nothing to hinder their owners. It seemed a pleasant sort of life. I'd never seen slatherberries picked before. I elected not to mention that to you, Shen. You'd think me arrogant, spoiled. And I'd have no reply.

'I've news,' I said. 'Good, I think.'

'You're to exchange that rapier of yours for a genuine weapon?'

'Shut up.' I stroked your bare neck. 'I'm to be Lady of the Jades.'

You looked at me. 'I see logic in that. Your mother, after all. And today's victory.' Your eyes wandered, looking toward the deep hinterwoods on the horizon.

'Don't you see?' I said. 'Shen, we'll be free. Away from the Isle. People are freer in the colonies. And, if not, I'll be in a position to see that they are.'

'You'd stoke rebellion?'

'No. No… but… we'll be away from the eyes of the Explainers and the archons. As long as I keep peace and raise tribute no one here will care.'

'So, you won't be married off?'

'What?' I shook my head. 'Of course I will be. But not Urse now, eh? Thanks to you.' I squeezed your shoulders. 'And I've a greater say now over who I'll get. I'll pick some dullard, Shen, some non-entity.'

'And have his children.'

'Our children.' I held your chin. I made you look at me. 'And any child you birthed would be ours too.'

'That's… remarkably forward,' you said.

'I'm hardly one to be shy.' I couldn't believe I was saying this. Did I mean it? 'Others plot our lives rationally, why can't we? What choice do they leave us?'

'No choice,' you muttered. 'Kyra?'

'What?'

You grinned. You had that feverish look in your bright green eyes.

'Let's away. To the mainland. Live free.'

I laughed. 'And die swiftly.'

'What?'

'You are joking right?'

You were not.

'Shen…'

'Kyra, why not? Your family's tower is rich with silver. Ornate silver. On the mainland one can exchange such for security, good living.' Your lips shuddered. 'Freedom.'

'Humans?' I said. 'They'd hang us and take it for nothing. They're animals.'

'They're free. Don't you want to be free?'

'You've lived a rustic life, Shen. No doubt pleasant tales of the Main reach you. And they're lies. I've seen what humans will do for shiny metals. Seen them slaughter and burn.'

'We've only seen that side of them. They trade with us, do they not? Why wouldn't—'

'Fuck's sake, Shen, they killed my mother.'

You scowled, readied to retaliate, but then the urge left you. You seemed almost to shrink.

'Shen, Shen,' I said. I held you tighter. 'We haven't the luxury of daydreams. There is what there is. My life is bound. But I can make a life for *you*. I want to use my power, all this horrendous prestige, to craft a world all our own. For you, Shen. Why can't you see this?'

'I do.' You rested your chin on my shoulder. 'You risk all for me.' You sniffed. 'The Jades then.'

'A life away.'

'And children, you say.'

'Children.' No. In truth I didn't want that. Not even to raise them with you. But you did. You did.

'I'm an arsehole,' you said.

'Only one I'll ever kiss.'

'I just thought Kyra Cal'Adra would be more audacious.'

'No one's *that* audacious.'

'You're right.' You rubbed my back. 'Fuck, I love you.'

You looked out toward the pickers upon their stilts.

Audacious. You were too polite to say 'brave'.

And you were right.

11

Fifteen corpses, stripped upon stone tables like altars. Black ink around their eyes and lips.

Sister Benadetta, Shortleg and I walked between them in the underground chamber. Candlelight flickered from the many candelabra all around, lending the cadavers' skins a strange sort of vitality, a continual threat of them shivering, twitching.

'This in't right,' Shortleg said. 'Hanging round the dead.'

'You've made enough corpses in your career,' Benadetta said to him. 'Strange a pennyblade… sh-should fear their companionship.'

It was cold in this wide stone cellar. It kept the bodies fresh. A mercy that, for it had taken two nights to bring them all to Nosford Abbey. I was grateful for the stink of candle wax.

'Why has this place got a storage house for the dead?' I asked. 'I haven't seen an apothecary here.'

'This abbey also serves the Church's investigations.'

That did not please me. I thought of the chair. The binding.

The caliban – Nail; after all, I suppose even a useful hound needs a name – observed the three of us from across the chamber. Standing with one leg raised across the other's knee, he rested against the wall, his face catching the light from a nearby candle. It dawned on me he had a view not only of us but of both doorways into here. His casual pose belied a tactical disposition, much like my old bondswoman Thezda. I immediately chastised myself for comparing the two.

'Fuck me ragged,' Shortleg said out of nowhere. He realised Benadetta was looking at him. 'Sorry, Sister.'

'What is it?' she said.

'That's the innkeeper.' He pointed toward one of the cadavers. 'Bloody innkeeper from Tettleby.'

By the Blood, so it was. I recognised his curly briar of hair. The rest of his grey nude form was new to me, fortunately. We walked over.

'What were *he* doing up the pass?' Shortleg said.

'All Tettleby stood des…olate when our journeymen arrived to investigate,' Benadetta said.

'Why didn't you tell me?' Shortleg said.

'You'd no reason to know,' Benadetta answered.

'Oi. I knew these people.'

'Mr Shortleg,' Benadetta said. 'It's high time you regaled our colleague Cal'Adra here with what oc…curred the night you left her to burn in a barn.'

Shortleg looked at the Sister. He scratched his stubbled jaw.

'You told me not to tell her.' He paused. 'Still happy not to.'

A moment's silence, then Benadetta said, 'Continue.'

'Right. Right.' He looked at me. 'Kyra, I weren't gonna kill you.' He shrugged. 'But I was gonna rip you off.' The lamp above gilded his receding crown, left his rough features dark. 'I told 'em I wouldn't do it if they killed you and the others. And I reckoned if they needed us to kill Rossley, they hadn't the guts to kill anyone. Plan was I'd tell you lot to bury money under the barn for later. We'd head off next morning and then the villagers'd dig it up. Bury it somewhere else probably, until the attention vanished. Tell the Crown's men two pennyblades had made off with Rossley's tax money, had killed Rossley for it.'

'Much obliged,' I said. I crossed my arms.

'I knew you could handle it,' Shortleg said. 'They'd never catch the Hellcat if she'd a day's travel ahead of 'em.'

'The who?'

'S'what they call you round Hoxham.'

'Really?' I patted my hair. 'Hmm…'

'So Tettleby gets its gold back and plenty besides. More'n that they get that child-fuh—' He stopped himself, looked at Benadetta. 'That child-ravisher Rossley off their backs. And I, local lad, friend to all Tettleby, get a fatter cut than I woulda done with you lot.' He sniffed, grimaced. 'What could go wrong?'

'You knew they were out there,' I said. 'Outside the barn.'

'Course. Even told me what barn to go to. I were a local lad but I'm still a pennyblade. I couldn't begrudge 'em a little distrust.' He rubbed his brow. 'So I told you lot I were going for a shit and went outside. Let 'em know the plan were still on.'

'You took your axe, dickhead,' I noted. 'Why bother? They're your friends. Perhaps you didn't want it to burn in a barn fire.'

'Ain't like that. Swear.'

'Then why?' Sister Benadetta said. Her words cut through the cool cellar air, startling us both.

'Cuz…' Shortleg stroked his large belly. 'Cuz, I dunno, something wun't right. Me soldier instinct. They weren't being straight. I could tell. And that holy hook missing from the barroom wall… I dunno. No harm in taking me axe. So why not?'

I didn't buy it. I didn't buy a lot of things in his amply stocked bullshit emporium. But I said nothing. Let him speak, let him spill.

'So I step outside and there they are: whole bunch of bastards in those bleeding masks. Good thing I didn't really want a shit because I'd have painted the barn door behind me. And hay everywhere, all up the barn walls. Well, I could guess what that meant.'

He stroked his rough scalp. 'And one of these weird bastards puts a finger to his mouth and hushes me. Beckons me over to the trees. I were shit-scared now. But no one had taken me axe off me, so—'

'So, you did nothing to warn us,' I said.

'What would you a' done? I hoped it were just some joke. I'm stood under the trees and the man pulls his mask off and it's Tooney, Marc Tooney, old pal o'mine. Known him since we were scrats, the both of us, nicking things from the butcher. He likes a joke and so do I, so when he smiled I smiled back like. I say, "You tryna scare us or what? That the plan? Scare 'em off?" "No," says Tooney. "Gonna burn 'em." I say, "Yer fucking what?" and he's like, "Gotta be this way, Short, just has to." Well, I were gonna kick off, no lie, but then I feel two others behind me, hear a knife slide out. "You'll still get your money, Shortie," he says. "More besides. But it's gotta be this way. Only reason you in't in that barn now is cuz the village stood up for yer. Yer a good lad, Shortie." Well, I thought, fuck me. No point getting meself killed too.'

I could hardly berate him there. Hypocrisy isn't a pennyblade's sin.

'So Tooney, right, he looks at me, says, "You wanna meet royalty, pal?" I'm all like, "Yer fucking what?" and I'm thinking you're burning me mates, pal. Do yer think I want fucking around? Tooney grins and he leads me through the trees, his dickheads behind us. Says over his shoulder, "He wants to meet you, Shortleg. You're honoured."

Shortleg paused. He looked at us and then down at his feet, as if meeting our eyes was too much for his pride to bear. He rubbed his temples, an action I'd never seen him perform before. I'd swear he would've liked nothing better than to run out of the room. 'So they bring me into this clearing.'

He crossed his arms, gazed over the rows of dead. He screwed his eyes shut.

'And there he was,' he said. 'The devil. I couldn't see his face, he had his back to me. A long cloak. A crown. Or horns. Bigger than any man. Nearly twice your height, Kyra. Fuck me.' He lifted his hand up before the light of the candles. 'Two thumbs on each hand. One… one on either side o' the palm…' He chewed his lip. 'And a glint of summat. A silver chain around his neck. I don't know why I recall that, I…'

I took a cool breath of cellar air. I'd this childish fear the innkeeper might stir, all the bodies rising up, like how the sky-madness describes the final days. Blood, but I'd been among humans too long.

'Tell her what happened,' Benadetta said.

'Tooney made me kneel,' Shortleg said, his eyes still screwed. 'He says, "You've got to look at him. Look at his face when he turns around." I'm so fucking frightened I can't speak. I mean, there he was. Lord o' hell. "You'll be one of us, then," Tooney says. "No going back after, pal."

'And then he speaks. The devil. Like nails on iron, like a deep-voiced cat, I… I don't fucking know. "Close your eyes," the devil says. I wun't gonna argue. "When I tell you to open them," he says, "you will see my face." I pissed meself. Really did. I'm not proud. I heard Tooney giggle. And I feel this presence, this presence approaching and it's him. Him stood over me. A smell like, I dunno, burning. And, in his voice he says, "Tell the commrach woman we'll meet in a darkness… full of light." And I wait. I wait for him to tell me to open me eyes, to look at that face. And I wait. So long. And when I'm brave enough to open 'em meself…' He opened his eyes and stared at me. 'I were alone.'

I hadn't the strength for mockery. He'd clearly seen what he'd seen. Whatever it had been.

'And so a ribald wretch found religion,' Benadetta said, her face grey in the gloom. 'My people found him by the roadside.'

'And he pointed you to me,' I said, collecting myself.

'It would seem,' she observed, 'we were not the only ones looking for a commrach.'

Blood. Someone out there was hungry for me, Kyra Cal'Adra. Well damn them.

'There's no devil,' I told them both. 'But I'll tell you what there is in abundance: trickery. And a world of fools to swallow such shit.'

'I know what I saw,' Shortleg said.

'You were frightened. The frightened are deceived.'

'Fucker were ten foot tall, Kyra.' He waved his palms. 'Fucked-up hands.'

'That could be done,' I said. 'Two people. One sat atop the other.'

'Then how did he know you wouldn't die?' Shortleg demanded. 'It were certainty you'd burn in that barn. No mortal coulda known that. Prophecy. Black prophecy.'

He had a point. 'Maybe this trickster knows my reputation. Maybe… well what had he to lose? If I lived he was right, and if I died he could say we'd meet in that after-death punishment house you idiots fear. Whatever it's bloody called.'

Benadetta stepped closer to the pair of us. 'You have your devils, Cal'Adra, do you not? The fomorg? Their king?'

'That's different. That actually occurred.' I shook my head. 'And they were a phenomena, not devils.'

'They slaughtered,' Benadetta said. 'In the thousands, so your histories claim. They tempted and…' She had one of her little spasms. 'Corrupted, often in dream. Posed as mortals. How is that any different to my own faith's devil? Perhaps we view the same evil through different eyes.'

I didn't need to be reminded the fomorg were said to visit in dream. I'd hallucinated King Bolgada's roar when Benadetta had had me chained up during my equinox. Bitch.

'"They rose from the sea and the earth",' Benadetta said, quoting some commrach historian I could not remember. '"They slithered through cracks in the very air." Tell me, Cal'Adra, while the Isle was invaded, what occurred here on the mainland?'

I shrugged, tried to recall my tutor's words on the subject. 'We don't really know. Something similar. By the time the incursion retreated and we checked, your people were no longer upon the Main's coast. Your wooden villages had vanished. We found a few of you cowering in the mountains. We weren't interested enough to ask, and you were too keen on shooting arrows at us.' I tutted. 'But who cares? I don't. This was ten thousand years past.'

'Yet my hypothesis stands,' Benadetta said. 'One race's fomorg could be another's devils. Indeed, carvings of the rural folk devil – he of the goat legs and ragged face – appear to predate both the Holy Pilgrim and the Church.'

'Surely a blasphemous opinion, Sister?' I said. I recalled my visions in the chair: the tumult of strange women, the approaching presence of the figurine. 'Someone should report you to your church.'

'My duties do not permit the luxury of closed-mindedness,' she replied.

'What *are* your duties exactly?'

'Well,' she said, ignoring me, 'we procured some information from our contact tonight, if not the contact himself.' She looked at us both. 'You told Mr Nail the assailants killed him. How exactly?'

'He were brave, that commrach, I'll give him that,' Shortleg said. 'Put himself in front of me and the she-elf here when they burst through the door. Rare that, such bravery.'

'Rare,' I replied, looking at him. I mimed raising a tankard. 'Here's to him.'

Shortleg mirrored my toast.

'Almost unheard of,' Benadetta said. She went to speak but her stammer came to her. She let the spasm pass then said, 'We have our trail. The obelisk in Becken, the Rosho family. We'll make our way to that great city.'

'And good fortune to you all,' I said. 'Whereas I shall return to Hoxham now this is all done with. My purse heavier for doing so.'

'Oh, but, Cal'Adra,' Benadetta said. 'How can we possibly cope without you? We've more commrach to infiltrate.'

'Wear false ears and beat servants,' I suggested.

'And the devil intends to meet you. I cannot possibly allow you to fly.'

'Try stopping me, darling.'

'You'll be safer… with us, Cal'Adra,' Benadetta said. She looked across the chamber to her caliban a moment, then back to me. 'Besides, I'm in your blood, remember? Since I fixed your hand. For which you've never thanked me by the way. The Church knows where you are at all times.' She looked at me. 'Outlaw.'

'Liar.'

I wasn't wholly convinced by my words. They'd found me at Esme's after all. And Benadetta unquestionably had powers, I just didn't know their nature. Vexing, that.

'Leave then,' Benadetta said. She pointed at the stone archway we had come from. 'But if we don't procure you first, those rope-masked maniacs will.'

I looked at the door, then at the many corpses of madmen. If their devil wasn't real, their kitchen knives and axes most certainly were.

'I've no wish to meet the Roshos,' I said. 'I've no wish to meet any more commrach.'

'They'd recognise you?'

'Not the Roshos. They've no idea of events on the Isle, save hearsay. They're outsiders.'

More commrach. One had been enough. And yet...

'My fee has risen,' I told Benadetta.

'Fine.'

'Eighty pips.'

'Agreed,' Benadetta said. 'I was going to say a hundred.'

Shortleg laughed.

I scowled at him.

He stopped laughing. 'Here,' he said to Benadetta. 'Do I get any of that action?'

'You're of the Church now, Mr Shortleg,' she replied. 'Your rewards lie in your good works.'

I laughed right back.

Shortleg scowled at me.

Benadetta said nothing. She turned and began walking around the tables with their corpses. Uncertain, we followed.

'Yeah, I know some of these,' Shortleg muttered. 'Not all though.'

'The wife,' I said. 'Innkeeper's wife…'

We stopped beside her. Odd. I'd lusted for this body, near-swived it too. Now she was meat. Off meat. I recognised the pattern of her dry wounds, her pierced eye: she'd been the woman with the kitchen knife. By the Blood.

'She's a good example,' Benadetta noted, 'of the circle pattern.'

She pointed at the body's forehead. Benadetta was right: unlike most of the bodies the black grease on her forehead had kept its pattern, that circle with the spikes. Perhaps it was she who had drawn the spiked circle on Kyran's old shirt. I'd left my satchel at the inn when we'd set about ending Rossley. She'd had ample opportunity.

'You know what it means don't you,' I said to Benadetta.

'Symbolic,' she said. 'The gate of hell.'

Shortleg let out a long breath. He shivered.

'Trust in the Holy Pilgrim to protect you,' Benadetta advised him.

'Sister Perfecti,' a male voice said from across the chamber.

A young man in church robes stood at the threshold. He looked perturbed by all the naked corpses. And me.

'Yes?' Benadetta replied.

'His Grace the Cardinal has arrived. He would speak with you in the upper west library.'

'Very well,' Benadetta said. 'I shall be there shortly.' She took a long breath, then turned to me and Shortleg. 'You may wait, Cal'Adra, preferably not here. A look about the grounds perhaps. Many wonder…ful windows. Mr Shortleg: Mr Nail will probably need help loading supplies.'

'Sister,' he replied. 'Why dun't Kyra bloody help?'

'Oh she could…n't possibly. She keeps from Mr Nail's kind. A requirement of her faith.'

I bared my pointy teeth at her with a tired disdain.

Sister Benadetta turned and left the room. The robed lad followed.

Shortleg checked she was gone, then looked at me. 'So what happened?'

'I don't know what you mean.'

'Up in the fort.'

I placed a finger across his rough lips. 'Careful, friend,' I proclaimed to the chamber. 'The Sister's gone but she's left her little piss-rag.' I looked across to the blond halfbreed. 'A piss-rag with two ears and a nose that sticks itself wherever it's not wanted.'

The caliban placed his raised foot back on the floor and stopped resting against the wall.

'Quite the image,' he said.

'Go on,' I told him, nodding toward the doorway Benadetta had exited through. 'Be a good boy and catch up with your mistress. You're not wanted here, creature, understand?'

He strode toward us, his boots echoing through the chamber. The torc about his collar glinted in the candlelight. He came to a stop mere yards from my presence.

'Shortleg,' he said, ignoring me. 'Perhaps we should get to loading those supplies.'

'Go ahead,' Shortleg said. 'I'll catch up with yer, Nail.'

I stared right at the blond prick. Even if he wasn't a halfbreed I'd have hated him immediately. I would have. The way he'd punched Esme back in Hoxham. A pure thug.

He sighed and stared right back at me, in a bored sort of way.

'Hey,' Shortleg said, putting his meaty forearms in the space between us. 'Let's not make a scene.'

'But it's her one talent,' the caliban said. He walked past me and headed for the archway that led up to the courtyard.

I watched him leave. 'I look forward to putting you down, caliban.'

'Get in line, inbred,' he said, never turning. 'Wait your turn.'

'Whoreson fuck,' I said but I do not suppose he heard me. He had gone.

I felt a hand on my shoulder and Shortleg turned me around.

'What's yer fucking problem with 'im?' he said. 'He's alright once yer get chatting.'

'It's…' I sighed. 'Look, I sense you're not cut from court historian cloth so let's not get started, eh? It's a commrach matter, let's just say that.'

He shook his head and whistled. 'I'd have wagered you two would get on.'

I stared at him. 'How do you mean?'

'Just…' Shortleg shrugged and pointed at my ears. 'Y'know.'

I made a face that permitted no room for doubt he was anything but a pig's cock then said, 'You were asking me about the fort.'

'What happened?' He checked both doorways then made a stabbing motion with his hand. 'With you and our "contact"?'

I studied the corpses all about.

His was a fine enough question. What *had* happened? The man had admitted to being your father, Shen, and I had killed him. I was almost as surprised as he to find him upon my butcher's block. Pure instinct, a vengeance waiting in the muscles like a sword feint long drilled. Days had passed and I still did not know how I felt about the matter: neither joy nor shame. Your father had been complicit in events, of course, but he was rather insignificant, all told. Satisfaction, that's what I felt I suppose. Or something less. A transaction completed. A formality.

'I told you why,' I said to Shortleg, 'back at the fort. Payback. Don't ask anymore, Shortleg. Really.'

'Payback.' He thought about that. 'Where I come from revenge is always over money. That or a woman.'

I should have spat at him, walked out. He was no friend. Fucker had nearly got me killed, had he not? Would have ripped me off. Still might.

I tightened my hairband.

'Where I come from,' I said, 'we don't have money.'

Shortleg nodded. He said nothing.

We headed for the door.

I stopped before the last corpse. A young woman. Familiar.

I couldn't believe it. The handmaiden I'd threatened outside Esme's boudoir back in Hoxham.

'You alright?' Shortleg said.

'Er… yes, fine. Just a dizzy spell.'

We left.

If ever an institution screamed for whores and lutes, Nosford Abbey was it. I sauntered about the gardens, biding my time before I put a little plan into action, the abbey's scant population studiously avoiding my path. I sliced the neck of a daffodil with a dead twig, a textbook stroke. Spring was warming up, the bees emerging from their hives. A hot summer lay ahead. They'd have to bury those corpses soon.

The corpse on the last slab had dumbfounded me. That handmaiden, the one I'd so cruelly teased – along with her lady – on the stairs up to Esme's boudoir back in Hoxham: what in Blood's name had she been doing up on the Great Southern Pass at midnight? However did she know the folk of Tettleby? And she must have, for she'd been comfortable enough in their presence to be an accomplice in murder. It was almost as if people became crazed after meeting me. That my path, random as it ever was, left madness in its wake.

I wandered to the abbey's west side, into a thin and shady yard. A man-high wall of red brick ran along the right, the three-storey-high abbey the left, a carbuncle of carved limestone and gaudy stained glass. A beech with heavy branches hugged the abbey's side. I looked around. I was alone. Perfect. I waited a little longer.

The lady, I thought. *The dead handmaiden's lady. Where might she be now? Possibly on a slab with the rest.* I hadn't seen her face when she'd lived, of course. She'd covered it with her skirts.

Something that seemed peculiar at the time came back to me. Esme wasn't angry when I mentioned I'd talked to her customer, merely taken aback. Bear in mind I never mentioned to Esme the lady had covered her face. Esme had simply been curious as to what we had said to one another. As well she might if…

Perhaps quotidian scandal had not been that lady's reason to obscure her identity. She'd a woman's height, yes, but a typical human woman was the same as a commrach's. Indeed, she did not have to be female. A male-born commrach can pass for female easily enough, given the right apparel. Had the lady not been hiding her face from me but her race? Her sex?

She might have even been a Rosho. Hadn't Grandmother said they'd financial tentacles throughout the Main? If one of their family operated back in Hoxham she – or he – would be in as much need of seasonal comfort as I. Esme had her collection of wooden commrach pricks in her cupboard. I'd always assumed she had them just for me and the occasional curious human, but that made no sense now I actually stopped to think on it. Blood, where *had* Esme got so many luxury commrach goods in the first place? There was really only one vendor. Esme was part of the Rosho enterprise, if only at a remove.

I should tell Sister Benadetta, I thought. And yet... I liked having this knowledge, this power. Benadetta was draining all the choice and decisions from me, was bent on clipping my wings. Time I clipped hers.

I walked under the shade of the beech. Ah, but these thoughts were ridiculous. Surely there had to be better ways of comprehending me than talking to my harlots. Hadn't there?

Talking from an open window, two storeys above: a deep male voice.

I gazed up through the branches, squinting at the afternoon sun. The open window had a balcony. I could just make out a slice of the room's walls through the balcony's threshold. Dark wooden fittings, likely bookshelves.

A library then. My idle little plan was bearing fruit. Sister Benadetta had been called to the *upper west* library and now here I was, standing beside the abbey's west wing and grinning. Was that her superior's voice I could hear now? My, my.

The tree wasn't easy to climb, having plenty of that grey-black lichen stuff. I'd need to wash after. By the time I'd reached the bough by the balcony my palms were entirely green. I dithered awhile there, hidden in foliage, before climbing onto the balcony itself, keeping hard to its threshold's edge. Exposed, certainly, but I'd hear more that way.

'The corpses of sixteen commonfolk,' the male voice said as I got there. Likely this voice had once been booming, yet age had put a rasp on it like the lichen on my palms. 'Necessary was it? To bring them *all* down from the pass? I trust you brought a spade to bury them?'

'It was you that taught me rigour, Father.' Benadetta's voice.

'And the Pilgrim taught us humility,' the man said. 'You seem to have forgotten that.'

'Forgive me, Father.'

He couldn't be her father, and she his sister. Please no. It had to be one of those sky-madness things, church-folk's need to dominate and be dominated.

'I would not have thought,' the man said, 'your inquiries would invoke such a butcher's bill. *Sixteen*, Sister. Including your sprite informer.'

'Father… I-I… Your… Y-y…' Benadetta's stammer had hit a real wall. I'd a knack for setting it off, though I had yet to make a science of it. But this fellow's mere presence invoked it. She was scared of this man. I had never known her scared.

'In your own time.' I heard him shift in his chair.

'Father, in all humility… these attackers killed him. To silence him. Would have killed my journeymen. If that is… not proof of conspiracy—'

'It's proof of a lynching,' he opined, cutting her off. 'Peasants lynch sprites.' I didn't like this man, but I had to concede his point. 'And, by your own report, he was scaring the locals, lurking about.'

'Father, they were not local. They wore masks, had devil symbols upon their foreheads.'

'The degenerate superstitions of the common. Devil worshippers? Huh. You were assigned to root out heresy:

panolics and reformists. Atheists even. And all from the better classes. You've wasted Church resources on drunken rustic fancy.'

'What of the Roshos?' Benadetta said.

'The what?'

'The commrach family in Becken's obelisk. They tr-trade with Becken's merchant classes, aristocrats too. Before he died our contact said the Roshos were behind all of this.'

There followed a pause. I wondered if this 'Father' used his pauses like Grandmother, evaluating the babbler before him with raised chin and knitted eyebrow. Eventually he said, 'Elves. Yes. You've rather polluted this abbey with them, haven't you?'

'Father, my current journeymen have unique skills, skills ideal for this mission. Mr Nail has proved himself already.'

'And the other island-goblin? The female?'

'The female is a professional.' She paused. 'If, er, idiosyncratic. Besides, the heretics have an obsession with her.'

'Naturally. She's a whore.'

'She's no whore,' Benadetta said. Her tone had become authoritative in that flat way she used whenever someone became vulgar. Already I knew it well.

'She wears men's clothes,' he said. 'A whore. You bring her here…' He grumbled. 'In *trousers*.'

'Her people all wear…' She stopped, checking herself. 'Forgive me, Father.'

He must have given her such a look.

I felt exposed, stood against the balcony's rail, like he might step out and see me. That would give Benadetta trouble beyond reckoning. I stepped lightly, pressed my back tight against the wall of the building itself only then wondering why I was giving that phenomenal bitch my slightest consideration.

'An educated mind suits your present duties,' he told her. 'But not your sex. Know when to conceal it.'

Benadetta always had a comeback, but not now. And not for lack of ideas, I'd wager. No doubt she'd her serene expression set, but I wondered what furies hatched behind her eyes.

Ah, fuck her. What was that term Shortleg was fond of? A bollocking? High time Sister Benadetta got one of those. I set my mind to enjoy it.

'Fine,' the man stated finally. 'Proceed to Becken, if only for Nosford Abbey to be free from pennyblades and wyrdfolk. Use only those resources already bestowed.'

'Father—'

'You've three weeks. And do not interfere with these Rosho beasts. Surveillance alone.'

'But F-F-Father—'

'Then scrape your pervert consortium off your shoe and return to the Holy Palace. You can return to your previous ministrations.'

'Please, Father.' It almost came out a squeal. I'd never heard her upset like this. She took a moment to collect herself. 'I must protest. Huh… humbly. What we have stumbled up—'

The bang made my shoulder blades judder against the wall. He'd a dramatic flair when it came to slapping table surfaces.

'Do not forget you are still paying for your sins,' he said, his voice keeping its calm. 'Pride allowed that demon to enter you in the first place.' He sighed. 'Your very presence is a disappointment to me, do you know that? To think where you might be if…' He trailed off.

'F-F-F-Fah…' Benadetta had melted. His words had ripped her apart. 'Please I-I-I…'

'Pilgrim give me strength,' he muttered.

'S-stain on my soul,' she said, her voice cracking. This scene wasn't entertaining me the way I'd hoped. Far from it. 'I pray hourly, F-F—'

Someone made a clicking sound below.

I leaned a little to my side, looked down and saw the caliban, Nail, gazing up at me. His face expressionless.

My game was up. But the worst thing was having to look at him. To be attendant to that beast's next move.

His eyes darted to his left. Toward the yard's entrance.

I scampered along the bough then climbed down the trunk. I got lichen all over me again. My hair was a leafy mess. I stood beside him.

People were coming into the yard, a gaggle of silent young churchmen. I didn't look at them.

The caliban. He'd looked out for me.

I almost met his eyes. I braced myself to nod him thanks, brief as I might.

'Let's not embarrass one another,' he said before I could. 'Eh, inbred?'

I frowned. I thumbed toward the exit of the yard, signifying I had to be somewhere else. I'd decide where when I got there.

Wrapped in a towel, legs fresh-shaved, I sat on a stool beside my still-steaming bath and dried my hair. I wash my hair whenever I can; it gets horrendous if I don't. I used to have servants do it for me. No more. I'd had to learn how. I'd had to learn many things.

My own bathtub, one of three in the bathhouse, was surrounded by waxed brown curtains which hung from a rail. Modesty at all costs with these abbey people. Absurd.

Someone entered the bathhouse. I heard soft steps beyond the curtains.

I'd no weapons with me. I put my hand on an empty bucket beside the bath.

The newcomer closed the door behind them. Gently.

I put my towel down and waved my fingers through the dirty bath water. I made splashes. I hummed a tune. They'd think me relaxed, and get a chin-full of wooden pail.

They jostled the curtain gap next to mine. Another bather then, using the bath adjacent.

I placed the bucket down and carried on drying. By the Blood, I was seeing killers even here. Clearly these last few weeks chewed upon me.

'We set off early morning, Cal'Adra.' The voice was Benadetta's. There was a determination to her words, one quickly adopted I thought. No doubt she had wished to be alone. 'Be ready.'

I grinned. 'How did your meeting go?'

'There's something I want you to understand, Cal'Adra.'

'Yes?'

'I *can* hurt you,' her voice said. 'I can hurt you without touching you. With a word. God gives me… the power to heal your body. He permits me to damage it too.'

'Didn't go well then?'

'I tell you this for your own safety. Step through these curtains, look over the rail… and I'll boil you in your own skin.'

I heard her robes loosen, fall. I wondered what shape stood beyond the curtain and immediately cursed myself for doing so. Old habits.

'You think me a voyeur?' I said. The nerve of the woman. 'The flesh I ogle is only ever offered gladly. Indeed, it only has any quality then.'

'No,' she said. I heard her step in the bath, heard her lower her body into its tender warmth. 'I think you a hater of women.'

'What?' I laughed. 'I bloody *love* women. You're always scowling about that very proclivity.'

'You want their bodies, Cal'Adra. The sickness of a soulless thing.' She paused. 'But women – their minds, their choices – you detest. You fear their power over you. Whenever you talk of women you reduce them to… matter. Fodder.'

'Nonsense.'

'What was it you called that barmaid?'

I didn't answer.

'But it's easy for you, I think,' she continued. 'You hail from a land where women are equal in stature and strength. Now, here, armed with your magic sword and tutored in slaughter, you ally yourself with our men. The winners. But perhaps I sho…uld not judge. Perhaps I'd be similarly as weak. Given the choice.'

I heard her take a flannel, soap it, draw it across her milk-pale skin.

I chewed my lip. 'I never claimed perfection, Perfecti. I can't imagine what's under that veneer you show the world is perfect either.' I twisted the blade. 'You must have some hidden… sin.'

'There's no mortal without sin,' she replied, quick as a dagger. 'Virtue lies in remaining its watchman.'

'Has your vigilance ever faltered, Sister?'

'Yours never began.'

'You're the one with the imaginary judge.' I chuckled. I put my hair towel down. 'Now *there's* a voyeur.'

'For future reference,' she said, 'though I… enjoy our theological debates, they're best not had in places like this. Walls have ears. Ears misunderstand.' I heard water run, perhaps poured over long auburn hair, no doubt drenching it to a dark tail that ran down collarbone and torso. 'And, yes, I have sinned. Daily. The very world is made of iniquity and the world is bigger than you or I. But the nuh-nuh-nature of my sins are between me and my confessor.' More water. 'Not some pennyblade.'

'Tell me just one,' I said. 'Your *dirtiest*.'

'I wonder: do you hate commrach women too?' She stirred in her bath. 'Is that why you left your isle?'

I snatched up my comb and raked my head. You combed my hair once, Shen, washed it too. Laughed to find I'd never washed my own.

'You keep silent.' Benadetta sounded happier now, her weariness cleansed. 'That was an example of me sinning, by the way. I said I'd never raise your past and I w-went ahead and did so anyway. Sin occurs so very easily.' A little splashing behind the curtain, her fingers tapping the water's surface. 'Don't fret. I'll confess later.'

'Where I'm from, one cannot wash away wrongs so readily.' I stopped myself. Too much. 'So what's our plan? The mission?' I already knew from my snooping of course.

'My superior… is impressed.'

'*Really?*'

'Indeed. He sees the value and urgency of our investigation.' Chalk up another sin, Sister B. Such lies!

'So we travel to Becken?' I said. 'Ask around about the Roshos?'

'Deeper,' she answered. 'We find a way into their obelisk. Take a look.'

A laugh flew from me.

'What?' she said.

'Audacious,' I said. 'I like it.'

And I did. She was going to do exactly what her boss stated she shouldn't. Sister Benadetta, once committed, could never be told what to do.

Audacity. I liked that.

12

The stink. Citrus stink, rising from my pores and clinging to the inside of my veil. The outside air, drifting through my veil's eye-slit, was hardly better. Corso city lay wrapped in a miasma of sex, the combined season-scent of near-seventy thousand women.

A fecund year this, I thought as I marched down the empty curving street towards the theatre, my charges shambling behind me, moaning, purring. No southern wind to ventilate the streets and squares. Vile stillness, a muggy heat rare for this season.

'Easier, back in the countryside,' you said beside me. 'Never known it like this.'

You were wrapped from head to toe in a red veil. We led a column of some thirty women of Cal'Adra's house, similarly attired. The only women in regular apparel were the six past fertility, grey-haired and watchful, spears in hand. The Climacteric Guard.

'You have to pace yourself,' I told you. 'Think on the tumult tonight. The chamber will shimmer with lust.'

'Mmm…' You began to bend at the haunches.

'Cease.' I gestured with the club in my hand.

'Use that on me,' you pleaded.

'I'm obligated to see you bitches through the city, violently if needed.'

'That's not how I'm picturing you using it.'

Cooing came from the women just behind us, those who'd overheard.

I slapped the back of your head with my spare hand.

'Ow,' you said. 'You *actually* hit me.'

'I haven't the luxury of favourites.'

'But you're happy to make examples.' You laughed.

I grunted something close to a chuckle, but in truth I could not muster such. It was hard to be polite, my body a twin's in full season, strong and violent and alive. I had to keep an eye on our surroundings. Young males were fools in season, more so than usual. Prone to rashness.

I spied three male adolescents – lowbloods of some kind – gazing down on us from a tavern's spired roof. Squinting and – judging by their hunched gait – palm-fucking with wildest abandon.

I hissed at the boys, waved my club. They knew from my symbolic weapon I was a longboot, a female twin, that I'd ancient right to murder them today.

Their eyes widened with fear. But they didn't stop.

'*Aroo-wooo*,' one of my column howled. The season's song, that broken-tailed cat's plea, full of impatience and pique and hunger.

Others followed, a chain reaction. *Arooo-woo*.

The column stopped. My women started jutting out their rears, touching each other's arms.

'*Aroo-woo…*'

'Keep moving!' I yelled.

One of the boys buckled up and began clambering down the side of the building, accepting this hint of an invite. *Where are their damn parents?* I thought stupidly. Self-quarantined in their sleeping chamber of course, like almost all those married. But at the very least these boys should have been locked up in one of those great breeding-halls of the common citizen.

'Form a rank,' I told the six Climacterics.

They did so, pointing their spears at the descending lad.

I strode to the back of the column and whacked some backs into movement.

'Move!' I yelled '*Moo-awoo-woo…*' I flowed into season-song mid-word; the others had set me off now, with their own scent. Fuck.

The youth fell four storeys. He hit the cobbles with a cracking sound. Everyone winced, this reminder of mortality a bucket of water over us all.

One of the Climacterics pushed her spear into the dying boy's ear, and we marched on.

The street ahead lay empty. The Climacterics as a city-wide body had ensured several pathways to the theatre for the city's younger women to pass through. This journey was the only time any of us had been out in two days. It typically wasn't worth the chaos. And unmarried women, their desires still broad without the chain matrimonial to limit them, were the eye of that chaos. They were inclined to reciprocate.

I could hear an army of male citizens on the other side of the houses, the other side of a canal. The enemy. No doubt my brother was somewhere out there, seeing to the bountiful harvest of tumescent cocks. There's no accounting for taste.

I caught up with you at the front of the column. Your face was red cloth, your green eyes piercing through the slit.

'Cities were a bad idea,' you said. 'Our season only makes sense in small groups, as forest folk. The world stays half-sane where I come from.'

'The price of progress,' I said. Blood, how far was it now? Two streets? Three?

You leaned in. Your proximity stirred me.

'We're being followed,' you said. 'Lone male, I think.'

'I know.'

'Should we send a Climacteric? Shoo him away?'

'It's fine,' I said.

'But—'

'Please, Shen. I'm fully aware. Just leave it.'

You fell silent, perhaps satisfied, perhaps sullen. I couldn't tell in these body veils. I could barely see out of my own.

We turned and made our way down an alley. A painted wooden phallus hung over the entrance. The alley had been used as a reliefery earlier that morning. Dank, waist-high semen stains mottled the walls, a minority still wet, still glittering with energy.

'Quicker,' you said. 'The scent…'

Being a longboot, male smells never had much effect on me, but I could see your point. Setting the path along here had been foolhardy.

'This can't be the way,' I barked to the Climacteric's captain.

'We've been redirected,' she replied. 'We're working with what we have, sir.'

'What?' I said, moving in closer to her.

'Things shift moment to moment,' she said. 'The streets are heaving this year.' She leaned in, muttered: 'Best we keep moving, sir.'

The alley suddenly echoed with boots, coming from behind us.

Eight males in season's clothing. Young, bearing rapiers. A nightmare.

'Line!' I shouted at our guards.

They were already in the process. The six older women formed a phalanx at the rear of our column, facing our attackers. Just in time too as another four assailants dashed into the alley.

Expecting my women to run in the opposite direction into who-knew-what, I turned to order them stay. The opposite was occurring: my charges edged closer to the fight, trying to get a look at the eager males.

'*Arooooo*,' called my foremost girl.

I jabbed the club into her belly using all my season-rich strength. She jack-knifed and collapsed, retching. I hissed at the others. An example to them all. The guards would not be rushed on both sides, not on my watch.

'Control them,' I called to you, Shen. A forlorn hope in your state. And, looking at you, I was little better. Oh, to strip you naked in this stained and savage alley. To pull you down, Shen. Grind upon your thigh.

I turned away, took deep breaths. I'd more control in a real fight.

The Climacterics were losing ground, shuffling back. Their experience and the length of their spears were putting fresh corpses on the floor, but the numbers and frenzy of the young males were irresistible.

A Climacteric dropped on her back, pierced through the shoulder.

I dropped my club and seized her spear before it fell, took her place in the line.

Her opponent came at me, swinging his rapier like it was an axe. He was a thrall of House Cal'Valtah. He wore their sigil: two dolphins with tails entwined. Our rivals, and Cal'Dain's puppets, as Grandmother had explained to me in her tent.

'*Kaiii!*' I screeched, the warning trill of the female in season that pained the male ear. He froze a moment.

Beating his rapier aside I drove the spearpoint at his mouth. It slipped in between his teeth and his left cheek, the point bursting out the side of his face. I yanked the spear sideways and it took his cheek with it.

Still he attacked.

Then he shuddered. His eyes grew wide. A blade's point slid out of his chest. The blade retracted and its victim collapsed backwards onto the seed-encrusted stones. Whoever stabbed him in the back was already moving onto the next male.

The males broke. Lust runs to panic when pressure is applied; the threat of pain, oblivion. Only four of them escaped.

A lone male stood before us, a dagger in each hand. Silver discs for eyes. Mirrored monocles.

The Climacterics trained their spears upon him.

'Hold,' I ordered.

I stepped forward, keeping keeping the spears behind.

'Thank you, loyal bondswoman,' I said.

Slow Thezda didn't nod back. She looked intensely uncomfortable, as she always did this time of year, when custom demanded she wear male season-garb and leave her imbued, counterfeit tits at home.

'You have to go now,' I told her.

Thezda nodded. The smell of us must have been intoxicating to her birth-body but there was a draw far greater. She was of us, she wanted to be with us. She turned and ran.

You were beside me.

'Thezda?' you asked me through your veil. 'A girl-born-boy?'

I nodded. 'She follows every year.'

'This season breeds cruel laws,' you said.

I looked at the corpses in the alley, the walls, imagined all Corso beyond them.

'Why blame a season?' I said.

In the gloom of the theatre stalls my anger abated, retreating from the rising dread.

We were sat beside one another, our hoods drawn. I would not look in your eyes, could not get lost in you. I had responsibilities today. All twins had.

'Do you think it was a planned attack?' you said.

'Someone must have let them through the lines.' I shifted in my seat, as if that might lessen my desire. Some ninety women perspiring, their lust-stink tickling the air.

'Touch me,' you pleaded. 'Please. Just my wrist.'

I winced.

'*Please*, Kyra.'

I bit my lip. 'When we get back.'

We purred, picturing what that would be like.

'Do you have the Aghast Play back in Skarrach?' I asked you. Anything to change the subject.

'Of course.' You nearly *aroo-ed*, but suppressed it. 'But there's only a dreadmask. Not a...' You wiped your brow, lips pouting. 'I'm not sure how I'll respond.'

You slapped my shoulder. 'Stop it,' you said.

My groin was jutting back and forth.

I gripped my seat's arms. 'Apologies.' Deep breaths.

'You've seen the city's mask,' you said, looking to the empty stage, a scene before a crime. 'Does... *arooo*... does it get less terrifying? Ever?'

'No.'

A naked stage before a black wall. No place for decoration or prop.

Our seats began to judder.

We turned our necks to see a woman, one of the house servants, directly behind us. Both hands up her long skirts, thighs shaking, eyes screwed.

'*Stop it*,' I hissed.

'Sorry,' she said, ramming her parts convulsively. 'Sorry...'

The women either side of her began to touch their own torsos, watched her with heaving breaths.

'I'll fucking *stab* you,' you told her. 'Do as Cal'Adra commands.'

'*Sorreeerrroooo...*'

Water drenched her, splashed us. The two women beside her shrieked. The self-fucker got dragged backwards out of her seat by two Climacterics, one of whom had poured the bucket.

'More where that came from,' the bucket-pourer – a male asexual, one of a minority in the Climacterics – declaimed to the stalls.

I'd ice cold water on the back of my neck. So had you, more in fact.

The candles were dimming, as were the purrs and moans. Dread rose in their place.

'I always wanted to be an actor,' you whispered from nowhere. 'To wear the mask in the Aghast Play.'

Bemusement cut through my anxiety and my lust.

'The terrormask?' The word made me shiver. 'All who wear it are shunned.'

You teased your red hair. 'I am already.'

You were gazing at the stage. A grin erupted across your face.

'That lone moment,' you said. 'That moment when you are no longer shunned, no longer...' You spat the next word. '*Pitied*. You wear the mask and become its horror. Nightmare of all who watch, both low and high. To bring fear to all equally. *That* would be worth everything.'

The season's heat left me. I wanted you to stop talking like this.

You eyed me, then relaxed in your seat.

'A foolishness,' you said. You shook your head. 'Season's madness. Forget it.'

The drum beat. Loud, slow as a malady.

I began to tremble, like someone who sees the blade above her wrist, poised to swing down.

The theatre fell to silence. The Aghast Play had begun.

Footsteps, stage left. A growl, deep and malevolent. Though we all knew that growl the distorted product of some vocal device, a set of leather pipes inside an actress's throat, primal instincts urged us on to flee. For we were prey.

Someone hyperventilated in the crowd. The guards had left. All lights were extinguished save one, above the stage.

The terrormask of Corso had to be hung up and veiled all year around, save for today. Ancient, touched by generations of our foremost artists, imbued with all their fears, the mask was of Bolgada, the Crawling King, lord of the fomorg, invader of our Isle. The play existed so that our race would never forget.

We saw the wearer's legs first, the shunned actress, walking into light, then her yellow robe.

Her mask.

You grabbed me, Shen. I you. We screamed.

Everyone screamed.

13

I wore my new cloak with the hood up. No point announcing my nature. Not here.

Shortleg and I walked along Becken's north-east quay. A bright morning, citizens and dock workers ambling by, and I felt absurd in a hood. Everything stank of dead fish and ox shit.

I'd avoided Becken city until now. The whole Brintland in fact. My friend Mertha, a sister in good standing on the Orton Road scene, hailed from Becken and the first thing she'd taught me, aside from how to wash clothes, was that Becken had gone persecution-crazy during the war. The most populous city in the entire east never could feed itself and thus intermittently burned anyone different, believing spectacle and persecution turned minds from an empty belly and no work.

'Look at that gigantic bastard,' Shortleg said. He nodded out to sea.

The two-towered, nine-sailed ship plied across Batbay, most likely toward Becken's royal wharf. Biggest thing I'd ever seen on water, three times larger than any commrach technereme, though doubtless far slower. One of Becken's renowned galleons.

Its white sails shone like summer clouds.

'Back from Antardes or the Far West,' Shortleg said. 'Heaving with spice.'

'And clap,' I replied.

'Becken knows how to fill its coffers. I'll say that for this shithole.'

I looked about the wharf at all those passing, their ragged trousers and flapping shoes.

'You wouldn't think so to look.'

Shortleg squinted. 'Daft cow. Rich didn't get rich handing out coin.'

'They'll get lynched eventually if they don't. Call it a chopping-block tax.'

'Shite,' he replied. 'Everyone here's too busy getting by to revolt.'

I looked at him. 'You know, for all my people's faults, not one commrach has starved or been without a roof in sixteen thousand years. And the emphasis there is *sixteen thousand years*. You creatures are lucky to make anything last a hundred.'

We turned a corner around a sagging warehouse and got a wide view of Batbay's eastern side. A small island sat a half-mile off in the waters; a jutting rock peppered with foliage, a black near-featureless tower rising from it. The trade obelisk.

'Kyra,' Shortleg said. 'If you people have been around so long, and are so fucking dazzle-bobbins, how come you ain't conquered the world? Why you only got an island and a handful o' big black hard-ons?' He gestured at the obelisk.

'Shorty, it's exactly that attitude that keeps your race praying to the sky and pissing in the gutter.'

We walked over to the edge of the quay and stood beside a

giant anchor someone had thought worthy of mounting on a plinth. I rested my arm against its shank and gazed out toward the obelisk. Standing eight storeys, the trade obelisk was half as wide as it was tall. An empty port lay before it.

'Not doing much trade,' Shortleg observed.

'They were never really built for trade,' I said, 'despite the name. They were built as a sort of prison, far away from civilisation.'

'There's a city here.'

'A village back then, if that. It was humans who associated obelisks with trade, on account of we'd throw you some trinkets once in a while to keep you happy. To this day an occasional tradesail from home comes here crammed with tat. Selling half-imbued swill to your nobles at absurd prices is the foundation of Rosho power upon the mainland. But it's also why they're mocked back—'

Shortleg had put his arm around me.

I flinched, slapped his hand. 'What the heaving shit are you doing?'

'If we look like we're courting no one'll suspect.'

'I bloody would. As if someone like me would court someone like *you*.'

'Oi,' Shortleg said, 'you could be a right munter under that hood. *I* might be the looker.'

I sighed pointedly. 'Fine. But get any friendlier and you'll be arse-up in the tides.' He put his arm back around me.

I spied gardens all around the obelisk's base. Hedges and pavilions and the like. Places to hide.

'A long copse of trees behind the obelisk,' I said. 'Takes up the sea-facing side of the island…'

'Well, there's our way in,' Shortleg said. 'Go at night.'

'You wouldn't stand a chance you grunting lummox,' I told him. 'Not against commrach ears and eyes. Trouble is… I might not either.'

'Must be agony, confessing that. I'm moved. Truly.'

'I didn't say impossible, Shortdick.'

'Perish the thought.' He gave my shoulder a squeeze. 'Maybe Sister'll rustle summat up.'

The galleon we'd been gawping at wasn't sailing to the royal wharf; I'd spent enough time around Corso and Hoxham's docks to know that. Too sharp a turn.

'It's heading for the obelisk,' I muttered.

Shortleg said nothing, perplexed as I.

It was too large to dock at the obelisk's port. Presumably it would drop anchor nearby and transport its hold via rowing boats, a process that would take more than a day. Which, I should not have to emphasise, was the cause of my shock: the scale. This was no galley of commrach trinkets. This was one of the largest ships ever built, its hold fat with several fortunes in spice and pepper and silks and who-knew-what-else from half a world away. Grandmother had never mentioned this to me. Had she even known? Something told me that the wealth accrued from this operation would not be sitting in a Corso repository any time soon. Indeed, it would not even be used to further the Isle's aims on the Main. The Rosho family, far from miserable in their 'humiliating' mercantile punishment, were avidly rolling in gold like a dog in fox shit. And why ever not? Human money had a way, a lure all its own. I'd only been here a few years and would happily kill anyone you asked, no questions, as long as your purse rattled.

I found myself reassessing the Rosho family. Their resources were titanic. This prey we stalked could bite us in two, crush

Benadetta and all of us. I got the sudden feeling their obelisk was looking right back at me. I shivered.

'You alright?' Shortleg said.

'Yes…' All this commrach stuff had me rattled. Nothing so unsettling as the past. 'Come on, heartthrob. Let's get back.'

'Where are we going?' I asked Sister Benadetta.

'Shopping.'

'I hear dour grey is back in,' I muttered, eyeing her Perfecti's robes.

The street heaved with people. My hood allowed only a forward view, one crammed with loud street traders and gormless citizens, surly town-watchmen and heroically talentless buskers. Every ten steps I had to shoo some beggar away. Worse, every fifty steps some dunce would stop Benadetta and plead for a blessing. She'd do so, happily, and cause our side of the street to halt. Those behind us would moan at me and not her. How marvellous.

Gazing above the throng only made my claustrophobia worse. Becken had all these new buildings, wood and brown daub, whose first and second storeys lurched overhead as if on the verge of collapsing into the street. Rows of them. They shrunk the sky into a ribbon of blue.

The crowds, the houses, the stink of rotting vegetables and dried human waste. I genuinely missed Hoxham.

'Here we are,' Benadetta said over her shoulder. At least I think she did; some prick was yelling about carrots. She turned and entered a shop doorway.

I didn't even see the shop's sign before I entered. The noise outside shrank to a murmur as I closed the door behind me, replaced by an instant stuffiness. I removed my hood.

We were in a tailor's, mainly women's dresses. A young dark-skinned woman sat in one corner of the thin room sewing a skirt's hem. She looked up and beamed at Sister Benadetta.

'Perfecti,' she said. She stood up, placing the skirt on her stool. 'A blessing to see you.' She saw me and her smile flickered. I get that a lot.

'A blessing to see you too, Mistress Vohte,' Benadetta said. 'May I introduce Kyra Cal'Adra.'

I offered my hand. Miss Vohte curtsied.

'Pleasure to meet you,' I said. I offered my best put-them-at-ease smile, only to realise that allow-me-to-ravish-you-atop-a-wine-barrel was the only kind of smile I possessed.

Miss Vohte smiled perfunctorily and turned to Sister Benadetta.

'I'm afraid Father is not here,' she said. 'A client in Westbay.'

'I'm certain your skills will be more than enough,' Benadetta said. 'We need to be measured. We've an en…gagement in nine days' time. With any luck, a dance.'

We have? I thought.

'Nine days lends ample time,' Miss Vohte replied. She didn't seem perplexed as to why a Perfecti would be going to a dance, much less need apparel for one. She stepped out from behind her counter, walking to the door. In a fluid movement she locked it and gestured to us. 'If you'll follow me to the back room.'

This back room was larger and refreshingly cool, if dusty to the nostrils. Male and female clothing hung upon rails that stood in lines upon the blonde wood floor. They ranged from maid uniforms to banquet finery. I spied some real oddities. A priest's vestments hung beside a town-watch uniform, clothing illegal for the average citizen to wear.

'Finery for the pair of you?' Miss Vohte asked.

'A little more com…plex, I'm afraid,' Benadetta said. 'I sh-shall require a handmaid's clothing. It should be of choice material but not brazen in cut.'

'Of course.'

'Cal'Adra requires the finery of her people.'

'Oh,' Miss Vohte said. 'I'm afraid I've no idea what that would look like.'

'Your father will, have no fear.'

'Excuse me,' I said to Benadetta. 'I'm confused.'

Benadetta turned to Miss Vohte. 'Could I ask you to, er…'

'Of course,' the seamstress said, once she saw Benadetta was merely letting a sentence hang and not stammering. 'I'll select some fabrics.' She smiled and walked through some other doorway at the end of the room into a room far larger. This humble tailor's seemed to go on forever.

'Where's this party?' I asked.

'The obelisk of course. Foundation anniversary. All Becken's great and respectable are invited. Though who'll go is another… matter entirely.'

'Hold up, Sister,' I said. 'Slow your fucking wimple. When you said "go in deep", I thought you meant scurry over a hedge and snoop.'

'Originally, yes. But Holy Pilgrim smiles upon our efforts. Your dear compatriot, Mr Nail, has been absent of late. Doubtless you have noticed. He spent some years in Becken in much the same profession as yourself and has made many contacts, perhaps even friends. One of them, he's just discovered, occasionally freelances for House Rosho. Paulus Jaggard, a businessman of sorts. You're to meet him tomorrow so that he might vet you for them.'

'He knows my name?' I had to stop my mouth from gawping. 'The Roshos know my name?'

'They know *a* name. Nileen Sil'Asu of Corso. Runaway and ex-bondswoman to the twelfth tower.'

'That's *my* tower!'

'Which is perfect.' Seeing me stare at her like she was petting a dead seagull she'd found floating in the bay, Benadetta continued: 'You *are* a runaway. It is best to wrap a lie around a greater truth.'

Better to wrap these here tights around your neck, I thought, eyeing the clothes rail nearest to us. But the anger was racing out of me. My legs felt weak. I turned my back to her and rested one palm atop the clothes rail.

'I never volunteered for this,' I said.

'No.' She smiled. 'You were compelled, remember?'

I sighed. I thought to say the Roshos might recognise me. But they wouldn't. They never left their island save their yearly sacrificial offering in the abomination suit, and whoever that was would be more concerned with the broken glass and turds being thrown at them than whoever was throwing it.

I simply did not want to attend that dance or ball or whatever it was, nor talk to any Rosho. The act of standing in a commrach context horrified me. Amid its architecture, its perfumes. Its ways. I had run from all that. I never wanted any of that again.

'You don't understand,' I protested. 'I can't do this.' I had to take a deep breath. 'I cannot.'

'Look at me,' Benadetta said. A hand took my shoulder and, gently, compelled me to turn.

I met her eyes. Wonderful things, seen that close. Bright and auburn, like tiger's eye stones.

'I wouldn't even consider this gambit, Cal'Adra,' she said, 'if you were not part of it. You are a consummate liar, a merciless survivor, possess a flexible wit and – above all – are immoderately brave. And somewhere, somewhere in that sin-ridden soulless, putrid heart of yours is a moral instinct that can never be assuaged.' She nodded. She squeezed my shoulder. 'The Roshos will never know what hit them.'

I paused, stunned. No one ever talked about me like that.

'You… didn't stutter through any of that,' I said. It was all I could think to say.

'That'll be God again.' Benadetta shrugged. 'You need to do this, Cal'Adra.' Her hand remained on my shoulder. 'What… ever your past… you need this.'

I sniffed.

'So,' I said. 'You'll play my handmaiden.'

'Indeed. You'll be able to talk to the Roshos and—'

'You'll be able to explore.'

'Quite.'

She still had not removed her hand from my shoulder. Strange. I reached up and placed my own palm upon it.

'I find these assigned roles…' I gave her my look. The look that never failed. '…compelling.'

'*Desist.*'

Her hand burnt mine. I winced, let go, stepped away. I shook my hand of the pain.

'Your final warning, devil,' she said. Her face was blank but a threatening sort of potential hovered all about her, like she could turn me to cinders with a word.

'A joke,' I said, sneering. I looked her up and down like she was the most absurd object. 'I mean, really, look at yourself.'

She said nothing. She strode toward the doorway Miss Vohte had gone through.

'Miss Vohte,' she called. 'I'm coming through. I've one more request…'

I didn't follow. I rubbed my hand, though the pain had gone.

An involuntary reaction, I told myself, *that's all.* Human women were like braised steak to me. I was just bored.

I had to be bored, simply had to be to do… that. I hated Sister Benadetta. Hated her. Especially when she made me forget to.

The Sister's 'one more request' to Miss Vohte had been for sackcloth. Turns out they had it, and Miss Vohte had been only too happy to assist Benadetta in applying it. Indeed, both human women had been grinning like mooncalves by the time they had me wrapped up.

And so it was, the very next day found me traipsing the streets of North Becken dressed as a rag-arsed fucking beggar. *Me.*

'I don't see the problem, love,' Shortleg said, his compassionless nature revealing itself. 'It's not like you haven't slept in barns and under stars before.'

'But no one would ever guess from my attire,' I said. I pulled at my right arm's hessian sleeve. It kept biting into my armpit. 'My usual attire proclaims rough diamond. Now it mutters—'

'Sack of shit,' Shortleg said, finishing my sentence and laughing.

'Yes, whereas you're the very triumph of the season.' I waved a hand at his own getup, a journeyman's grey gambeson uniform much like that of Sergeant Gilbertia's back at St Waleran's. The Sister had given it to him. We both looked absurd but at least his costume was cutting a path through the crowd.

'Look,' Shortleg tried, 'aside from the humiliation, it's not for ever is it? It's not even 'til noon. Just go up to Nail's pal, have a chat and fuck off again. Easy.'

The passers-by were getting that little bit fancier in their clothing, a little more ignorant to our passing. We were closing in on Grand Gardens.

'Nail,' I said. 'This was his idea, mark my word. He's just blamed it on his friend.'

'It's Beggar's Day,' Shortleg replied. 'You ask me, it's a great ruse, getting you dolled up like that.'

'Beggar's Day my balls. It's Nail,' I said, nodding. 'Or it's Benadetta. Or it's the Roshos ordering Nail's friend. Or it's Nail's friend. I've somehow accrued an entire troupe of bellends obsessed with humiliating me. We should just run, Shortleg.'

He didn't reply. We both knew, one way or another, that that was no longer an option, and hadn't been for some time.

'Hey,' Shortleg exclaimed as we reached the end of the street. 'You said Nail.'

'What?'

'You kept calling him by his name. That's a first, that.'

I was about to snap at the fat prick when a woman in a shawl walked up to me.

'Here you are, petal,' she said, offering an old half-pip coin. 'Get yourself a meal.'

I glared at her. 'Fuck off.'

The Great Gardens were a gift from Becken's royal line to the people of the city, and were completely walled off. That is, aside from three gateways that were locked at night and guarded by day. The two guards at the south gate had their work cut out for them today, we could tell that much as we approached. Some two dozen beggars and urchins loitered around in hope of being allowed in, a few pleading with the guards. Passers-by stepped into the centre of the street in order to avoid the sorry scene.

'Happy now?' Shortleg said.

'What?'

'Rich inside there,' he said, gesturing at the gardens behind the gate, 'giving to the very poorest. Can't be all bad, us humans, eh?'

Idiot. Just then, a beggar came out of the red-brick gateway and the others immediately jostled for the guards' attentions. It looked as if a scuffle might break out but then the taller guard raised a club and bellowed for civility. Next, he grabbed the nearest beggar and pushed him through the gateway, much to the chagrin and protest of all the rest. A one-in-one-out policy, it seemed.

'What *ever* was I thinking?' I said to Shortleg. 'It's clearly a faultless and elegant system.'

'Right,' he said, looking at the guards and ignoring my sarcasm. 'Get behind me.'

Shortleg's brawn forced its way through the crowd of stick-thin bodies and I followed in his wake. His journeyman's uniform soon caught the larger guard's interest.

'Help you, sir?' he asked.

'Got one here,' Shortleg replied, and his meaty forearm drew me to his side. 'Done good work by Church and now Church requests you let her in.'

The guard looked uncertain. 'Hardly regular.'

'You think I wanna be stood here long, pal?'

'Welcome to my world,' the guard said. 'These shitehawks stink like granny's gusset.' He gave the beggars all about him a scowl then looked at me. 'What's up with her eyes?'

I decided to get things over with and pulled down my hood.

'Pilgrim preserve,' the large guard muttered. 'She's Isle spawn.'

'So?' Shortleg said.

'So there's true men of Becken here.' The guard waved at the beggars. 'City folk all their lives. I'm sorry, mate, but I'm not letting some foreign bint take front of queue. This is Becken.'

Many of the beggars muttered support.

'You just threatened to club them all,' I said to the guard. 'Your patriotism's alarmingly flighty.'

Shortleg nudged me. The guard scowled.

'No,' he told Shortleg, ignoring me entirely.

The other, shorter guard glanced over. 'What's she do, eh?' he asked Shortie. 'What's she do to help Church?'

Shortleg paused, frowned. 'Saved a bishop,' he said.

'What from?'

'Peeping toms,' I replied.

I could feel Shortleg's masked irritation. 'Yep,' he told the guards. 'Whole pack of the bastards.'

'Pilgrim's heart,' the smaller guard said. 'What's the bloody world coming to, eh?' Some of the beggars nodded agreement. He looked at his comrade. 'Let her through, Sebast, eh? Church's request, innit? Eh?'

'She's a liar,' the big guard told him. 'We're not letting a she-sprite take front of queue for shitty little lies.'

Shortleg pulled out his piece of vellum with the hook stitched in it: his sign of office. He practically shoved it in the big guard's face. He also, I noticed, placed his fingers atop the pommel of his opponent's sword in its scabbard.

'Listen, pal,' he said. 'What d'yer think "the Church requests" actually fucking means?'

'Oi!'

'Don't think too long neither,' Shortleg continued. 'Else I'll "request" yer knackers up on a spike over Wessel Bridge.'

'Alright, alright,' the big guard said. But he wasn't so big after all. 'Sorry, sir. Bring her here.'

Shortleg did so and quickly made off.

The guard took me by the forearm and into the gatehouse, his grip brutal and shaking. There was a pile of cream-coloured robes in a pile by the inner door. He let go of my arm and pushed me toward them.

'Put one on, devil,' he said. 'Be quick about it.'

I did so. The hooded robe was rough but clean, though it had what looked like painted stains upon it. Freshly made holes too.

'Listen here,' the guard said. 'Keep your hood up; the quality don't need to see those fucking ears. And keep from them 'til they permit you approach.'

'My friend there really shook you, eh?' I said.

He grabbed me by the shoulders. 'I'll be about, you split-arse pixie. And if I see you playing silly bastards I'll break you on the spot. You hear me?'

I tapped my right ear. 'With these? How could I not?'

He opened the rear door and launched me out by my shoulders. I stumbled out into sunshine and gravel.

The air was already fresher, fat with spring's green hum. Chatter and bird song and pipe music carried on the breeze. I was stood upon a gravel-lined path, lawn either side. Violet blooms – I did not know their name – fountained from soil beds and stone vases within and beyond the grass.

This garden was grand alright; it stretched a good half-mile to the tree-lined wall on the opposite side. Beyond that wall rose the crenellated towers of Becken Keep, a vast and brutal-looking citadel designed to intimidate those below its ramparts as much as awe. The garden was a network of snaking paths between green lawns, risen flowerbeds and copses of trees. Here and there around the Great Gardens were the foundations of some long-vanished building: low walls and jutting cornices of red brick festooned with vine and lichen.

I started walking. The caliban and his likely-as-repellent acquaintance – Paulus Jaggard – would be sitting at tables beneath an old arch somewhere at the centre of the gardens, likely behind a copse of oaks I could already see. The gravel crunched rather wonderfully under my boots – it's a sound I've always enjoyed for some reason – and I spied on passing visitors. Many were dressed identically to me, the same cream robes with the painted stains and cut-out holes. It seemed the affluent of Becken-on-Brint liked their vagrants to look a particular way: classically, even romantically, destitute. These uniformed beggars would stop and bow before the rich as they promenaded along the many pathways, sometimes in couples, sometimes carried in palanquins, but always guarded. A coin would be passed, usually via an intermediary, and the beggar would bow and the noble would never look back. Beggar's Day. Strange custom, but I suppose it served as a form of down payment. The rest of the year these same nobles could kick vagrants into the drains free of guilt.

I passed the copse of oaks at the centre of the gardens and immediately saw the arch. A ruined thing, part of the same ruin I'd seen earlier. Indeed, I suspected the red brick of the garden walls had been sourced from these same remains. There were round tables all around and beneath the arch, and people in fine-but-not-too-fine apparel sat about them. Nail was sat at one table near a main pathway, a man in a wide and feathered hat beside him. Nail wore a hat himself, a woollen one to cover his ears.

Nail saw me approach. He pulled a coin out of his jacket and waved the thing at me. Bastard. The other man – Paulus Jaggard, apparently – looked at him and grinned. Jaggard was a barrel-chested man, hearty in bearing. I'd long found that manner of human draining at best.

'A penny for you, urchin,' Nail said just as I reached the table. I was ready to turn around and fuck off.

'Better take it, dear,' Jaggard advised, his voice deep yet rough-edged. 'Appearances and all that.'

I did so, snatching the coin from Nail's fingers and never making eye contact. I noticed three small pewter cups upon the table, each filled with some golden liquid.

Jaggard gestured for me to take the empty seat on the opposite side of the table to himself and at a right angle to Nail. I did so and reached for the pewter cup, because I wasn't a fucking urchin and I did as I pleased.

'Wait,' Jaggard said. 'That's the finest sherris you'll find this side of the Spine Mountains. Which is to say it far surpasses the goat piss that passes for sherris-sack on your side of the mountains.' He laughed. 'No offence.'

'None taken,' I replied. 'The best thing to come out of Hoxham is an army that's just looted it.'

Jaggard slapped the table and guffawed, though he was careful not to topple the cups. He waved a finger at Nail, as if to confirm something Nail had said earlier. I did not like that. Not one bit.

Jaggard controlled himself and said to us both, 'This sherris. We'll drink it as a toast.' I went to reach for mine and he waved a finger at me. 'Once – and only once – I decide you are fit for an audience with my esteemed associates.'

'The Roshos trust your judgement?' I asked.

'They pay for it, do they not?' Nail said, as if I were a fool.

Jaggard slapped Nail's back, an act the caliban found irksome and I delightful.

'Tell me,' Jaggard said, his laughter abating, 'how did you get to the mainland? Not your reasons, Mr Nail has explained your loathing of Cal'Adra well enough. I mean that every commrach tradesail from the Isle to here belongs to Rosho, or near-as-damn. I cannot fathom why you wouldn't make yourself known to the Roshos as soon as your passage docked at any obelisk.'

'We're lied to back home,' I said, which was true generally. 'I assumed any obelisk would be overseen by Corso loyalists and so I jumped—'

He grinned and waved a hand; he'd rather I didn't continue, not while we were having a good time. At least that's how it came across.

I could not figure this Jaggard fellow out. Was his joviality a mask, or was he just taking Rosho money and doing fuck all to earn it save laughing at everything?

'And what of this mongrel?' he said, and he gripped Nail's shoulder and shook. 'This old bullyrook and reprobate! Surely no true commrach approaches a caliban? Why, even I know enough not to tell the Roshos of our go-between. Thank the Pilgrim he's sense to cover his ears.'

'He…' I offered. 'Was a friendly face whereas humans turned me away.' I suddenly remembered my words to your father, Shen. 'Friends in damnation.'

Jaggard stared at me, his eyes wide. Then he smiled.

'I like that,' he said. He went to lift his glass of sherris but recalled he was saving it. He pointed at Nail. 'Has he told you how we met?'

Nail frowned. He sighed.

'He was *singing*,' Jaggard said. 'Can you believe that?'

'What?' I said.

'Yes! A sweet voice, this sombre fellow, and when short of a pennyblade's work he'll sing for coin.'

I laughed. 'Nail, you never told me.' I smiled at him as if we were friends, something I found entirely dreadful. He looked down and checked his fingernails. He would have to suffer this anecdote yet again, it seemed.

'It was in a bawdy a few streets off the bay,' Jaggard explained. 'He sang in a corner while others aled and whored. A wondrous voice, as I say, but, then again, I suppose if he had sung like a privy door in need of oil it wouldn't have mattered much: most drunks will throw a shilling for the sight of such a creature alone I'd imagine.' He grabbed Nail's shoulder again, squeezed and let go. 'He takes no insult,' Jaggard insisted to me. 'Eh, halfbreed?'

Nail half-smiled, more of a grimace really, and shrugged. Smiling was not a talent of his.

I noticed a uniformed figure over Nail's shoulder: the big guard from back at the gatehouse, walking along the gravel path that ran by our table. What had his colleague called him? Sebast.

Sebast stopped a moment and glowered at me, the cocky beggar-sprite who had now helped herself to a chair and table. I took his glowering as a sign he wanted me to get up and fuck off.

I smiled at him.

Sebast squinted at me. He looked at Jaggard in his mercantile finery and opted not to come over. Fine by me. Sebast marched off down the path and I pretended my smile was at Jaggard's continuing anecdote.

'...a terrible fellow and my dearest rival. Well, I took no chances and hired me a pennyblade as guard. Thing was, *he* had hired a pennyblade too! So much for trust! So there's our "conciliatory" meeting: the pair of us facing each other across a table, paid murderers at our command and a bloody man-mongrel singing sweet sonnets in the corner.'

Yes, he was definitely taking Rosho money and doing what he pleased. I had to respect him in a way.

'So what happened?' I asked. I reached for the cup before me.

'Hey, not yet, not yet!' Jaggard said with a grin and wagging finger. I desisted and he continued with his story. 'Well, you know how things get between rivals – I'm sure it's no different on your Isle – we scratched each other's prides and then – quick as rabbits – we're commanding our pennyblades kill. A task they were entirely too good at. The two of them ran each other through and dropped to the floor embracing each other like amorous Mary-boys which—' He looked at Nail. '—the bawdy was fair full of.'

Interesting. I had not known that of the caliban. But I suppose we were all keeping our proclivities from Sister Benadetta. Jaggard's reveal didn't seem to faze Nail. Not like the halfbreed jokes.

'The place emptied quickly enough,' Jaggard said. 'Only my rival and I stood there, neither willing to back down, yet both accustomed to commanding steel rather than wielding it. But Nail here... he kept singing.'

'I did no such thing,' Nail replied. 'I merely watched.'

'Shhh.' Jaggard looked pained at this intrusion of reality. 'You are ruining this tale.'

'Such as it is,' Nail said.

'He... *stops*... singing.' Jaggard looked at Nail pointedly. 'Then he looks at the pair of us, his smile beatific but his glare as black as the badge of hell, and he says, "I happen to be a pennyblade." Then he throws one of his devil-spawned spikes into the tabletop between us and says, "Where shall we start the bidding?" Can you believe that, Nileen? Eh?'

I nodded. Much as I hated to admit it, Nail had style.

'And you won the bid?' I asked Jaggard.

'Neither man had coin upon their person,' Nail said. 'But ultimately Jaggard had the finer hat.'

Jaggard and I laughed, a real belly laugh. I couldn't recall when last that had happened.

Just then a powder-blue box palanquin came to rest on the gravel path some thirty yards away, its four gartered bearers placing it down with care. There seemed room for only one in the palanquin, though a white veil obscured whoever sat within. I was reminded of Grandmother's palanquin, all the fuss around it, though I imagine this one's human bearers were motivated more by coin than the cane.

'Well, well,' Paulus Jaggard said, noticing the palanquin. 'Seems I have to relate my judgement sooner than I thought.' He smiled and winked at me. 'Back soon.' He tapped the table, stood up and walked toward the palanquin.

The Roshos. We hadn't expected one of the Roshos to actually appear. But whatever, we would have met them sooner or later. And Paulus Jaggard seemed primed to give me a warm reference.

'We're in,' I muttered.

'Don't bet on it,' Nail said, brushing his blond hair over his ears. He'd his eye on Jaggard's wide back as the man conferred with the occupant in the gaudy box. 'Perhaps I should leave.'

Someone cuffed me about the head.

'Fuck,' I snapped and looked up.

It was the big guard, Sebast. The stroppy cock-end couldn't leave me alone.

'Beggars don't get to sit in Grand Gardens, you sleek-eared cow,' he said. 'You're leaving. Now.'

I was ready to get up and in his face. But Nail stole both our attentions when he whistled.

'She's with us,' he told Big Sebast. 'It's quite fine.'

'Pilgrim's balls,' Sebast said, taking in Nail's eyes. 'There's a bleeding army of you night-goblins. This city's going to the fucking dogs.' He growled. 'Piss off, the pair of you, back to your fucking obelisk, you godless devils.'

'I couldn't possibly,' Nail said. He pointed at Jaggard and the palanquin. 'I work for that merchant there and, frankly, he could buy you in packs of ten. Stick around a moment longer and you'll be sure to get his attention.' He paused a moment, then looked quizzical and leaned forward. 'You're *still* here, garden man.'

Sebast took a final look at Jaggard and, more importantly, the palanquin containing someone of extreme note. He looked back at us both.

'I'll be watching you scum,' he said. He slapped my shoulder, in the bad way. 'Especially you. Worse than the dirty fucking beggars.'

He snatched the pewter cup that had been set for me and drank it down in a glug. He grinned and did the same with Nail's. He thought about taking the third, but eyed Jaggard again and thought twice. He walked off into the copse behind the arch.

'Prick,' I muttered.

Nail had a blank look on his face, like he knew something. Before I could ask, Paulus Jaggard had returned to us. He sat down.

'Well then,' he announced cheerfully. He lifted his cup. 'I think it's about time for that toast.'

I lifted the cup before he could see it was empty. So did Nail.

'They approved then?' I asked. That had been simple enough.

'I gave them a glowing report,' Jaggard told me, and he knocked back his sherris.

I smiled and winked. I pretended to swallow from an empty cup then gave my best shudder, as did Nail.

'Unfortunately, Rosho are impossible to please.' Jaggard's expression turned blank. 'You've been poisoned.'

I froze. Then I remembered I hadn't been poisoned at all. I decided it best to maintain my look of shock.

Jaggard took a small vial from his doublet's pocket. 'You'll be reassured to know I have the antidote. You have but minutes, Nileen Sil'Asu. No doubt you already feel the symptoms.'

'Which are?' I pretended to look uncomfortable, as if at least some symptom was kicking in, whatever it was.

'It's *lay da lan fay-gay*, an obscure poison I acquired from a Far West trader. Already your extremities are turning numb.' I dropped the cup and let my hands fall on the table. 'Your vision is shrinking to pins.' I didn't really know what he meant but I crossed my eyes somewhat. 'Soon an agony will overtake you the like of which you could not previously imagine.'

The old Paulus Jaggard had vanished. There was no jollity to him now. Perhaps it had been a charade all along.

'Followed by torrid hallucinations,' he continued. 'One man told me it's like being shat out your own eyeballs.'

'What?' Nail said.

Jaggard shrugged. 'People say strange things before they die.' He looked at me. 'Ah, and here come the shakes.'

I did as he asked, but only a little. I was having enough trouble with crossing my eyes. If the next symptom he mentioned was rubbing my tummy and patting my head I swear I'd scream.

'Who *are* you, Nileen?' Jaggard said, studying the antidote in his hand. 'Who sent you?'

'N-no one,' I replied, shaking. 'I ran.'

'The Cal'Adras sent you? Is that it? Played you off as a runaway?'

He knew of my family. The Roshos had filled him in. Of course they had.

'No,' I replied, putting on the shaking a little more.

'You'll be shaking uncontrollably soon,' he mentioned.

Fuck's sake, I thought.

I got a glimpse of the palanquin. Whoever was in there must be loving this. Probably did it to everyone running from the Isle. Probably did it to your father, Shen.

'R-ran,' I said, 'ran from their grandmother.' I feigned a spasm and shook even more. 'Absolute bitch.' I grimaced. 'Please, please, I've nowhere to run, I…'

He smiled. A bleak smile.

So this was how the Roshos played. Arseholes. They were loving this, sat in their palanquin. A taste for humiliating the lost and damned.

Jaggard squinted. 'Wait,' he said. He shook his head. 'You're not poisoned. Not slightly. You should be foaming at the mouth by now.'

I thumped the table. 'Well why didn't you *tell* me that?' I relaxed and sighed with disappointment. 'Honestly now…'

'So you poured it away?' Jaggard asked.

'I swapped your cups,' Nail replied.

Jaggard stared at Nail open-mouthed. Then he fumbled with the stopper in his antidote bottle.

Time for a change of tack, I thought.

I leapt up from my chair and slapped Jaggard across the jowls. Panicked, he half-stood before toppling to one side and falling face first into the grass. At first he searched frantically for the bottle he'd just dropped, but Paulus Jaggard wasn't a fool. He soon realised he'd none of the symptoms he'd mentioned.

I booted him in his arse. He bellyflopped forward and his hat glided from his head. The four palanquin bearers looked on in shock, but none broke from position. The veil covering the palanquin's window didn't flutter.

But the Rosho in the palanquin would be watching. How could they not?

I stood astride Jaggard's hips. 'Look at me!' I bellowed.

He turned over, his eyes wide. Sweat had broken on his brow. He'd a grass stain on his nose.

'I will *not* be treated like this!' I yelled. 'I am Nileen Sil'Asu of Corso! I am commrach and I will *not* be humiliated!' I spat on him. 'You animal! You human animal! I'm your fucking better! How *dare* you!'

I let him get up, but I didn't let him take his hat. I picked it up and doffed it at the palanquin.

The window veil rippled and a hessian package slipped out from beneath it, falling upon the gravel path. The four bearers took this as a sign to lift the palanquin and march off.

Jaggard swiped his hat off my head.

'Congratulations,' he said. 'We really mustn't do this again some time.' He turned and strode away toward the western gate.

I ran over to the package on the path. Wrapped in what looked like several layers of hessian, the thing was the size and shape of a baby, one wrapped up for burial. It was extremely light and likely very fragile.

It made me nervous. What could it even be? I didn't want to open it here, that was for sure.

I turned around and saw Nail searching through the grass. His shoulders slumped when he picked up half of the broken antidote vial.

'Probably too late anyway,' I told him before striding off.

Indeed, it was. As I passed under the shade of the oaks beside the arch I noticed two beggars kneeling over someone. Sebast the guard, limbs juddering, his face a mass of drying foam. The beggars were rifling through his pockets.

'He's ours,' one of them said upon seeing my robes.

'He's yours,' I replied. I gripped the package tighter to my chest and headed for the gateway I'd come from.

I practised my stances as dusk drew in, my feints and guards and strikes. High panther, weeping wall, ripple strike. The standards of Corso. My rapierwork was not rusty, exactly, but the pennyblade life had not sharpened me, not for the graceful feints and sudden lunges of my own kind. I was certain the knowledge was still in my muscles. By the Blood it would have to be.

The small high courtyard of our safe house was empty save for myself. There was an old clothes hook on one wall, for purposes unknown to me, from which I had hung a bag of sand. Perfect for working up a sweat, though hardly a sophisticated opponent. The stone walls echoed with my grunts and the shuffling of my boots.

Faster. I had to be faster, as fast as I used to be back in my tower's gymnasium. Too easy to become lethargic, fighting humans. I was within the gaze of powerful commrach now, with commrach guards in possession of sabres and rapiers. Weapons swift as wasp stings, a world away from the bludgeons and axes of the mainland. A life ago.

The Roshos' package had bothered me.

I stopped and sheathed. I had stripped to vest and trousers, my hair up in a tight bun, like a hull scraped of barnacles. I rolled my shoulders and shook my hands. I stared at the hanging sandbag. I readied to draw.

Sword out, then knife. I lunged and ran the bag through.

I held the stance. Knees bent, blade in the target, my eye-line following its length, knife guarding my head.

'Too slow.' I pulled my blade free, and sand trickled over cobbles. 'Sloppy.'

I pictured myself in the gymnasium ring back in Corso, my peers laughing at me.

I sheathed. Drew, lunged.

Same again: blade on target, knife high.

'Too slow.'

But that was my problem, wasn't it, Shen? Ultimately.

I closed my eyes. 'Too slow…'

I pulled my blade out again, flicked off sand. Sheathed and readied.

I drew.

'Formidable.'

I span to face the speaker before the word was even finished.

Sister Benadetta. Of course.

She was stood on the four steps before the door that led inside. Her left side was illuminated by a lamp shining through a small window. I hadn't realised it had gotten that late.

'You're quite terrifying,' she said, 'with both your blades readied to strike like that.' She took a step down, careful to avoid stepping on the gift the Roshos had given me. I had left it on the step beside my jacket. 'I'm glad you are on our side, Cal'Adra.'

'The knife's not for striking,' I replied.

'I cannot imagine it's for spreading b-butter.'

'Defence.' I flicked my knife wrist. I liked how she found me formidable. Not in the sense of having power over her, though I might have relished that weeks before. It was more the respect, the respect for my art if nothing else. 'I'll be defending us both soon enough.' I eyed the hessian package upon the step. 'I must be at my best.'

'Then you have to eat.' Her face had that spasm of hers, then she said, 'Come inside.' She smiled. 'There's wine.'

'Later,' I said.

'Oh my.' She looked concerned for me.

'I can drink later,' I said with a carefree shrug.

'Oh my,' she repeated. 'They have you… scared, don't they?'

Anger flashed in my chest, but the cooling sweat down my spine won out. My vest was sticking to my back uncomfortably.

'They have me *focused*,' I said eventually. I sheathed my blades.

Benadetta picked up the Roshos' gift from its hessian wrappings and studied it.

'Do I make a good commrach?' she said and with that she placed the mask over her face.

The Final Countenance, with its 'perfect' cheekbones and pouting lips. I'd never wanted to see that visage again. This version wasn't exactly like my old silver copy, however, or like any back in Corso. It was constructed of plaster and gaudy gold leaf. A thing to please mainland tastes, not the Isle.

She stepped closer. She held the mask up by the chin. It fitted less than snugly upon her round face and within the confines of her wimple. In the twilight gloom I couldn't see her irises; the mask's eyes were two black pits.

'Why do you do this?' I snapped.

Benadetta stopped. She didn't reply.

'I do everything you demand,' I said. 'Everything. Why do you keep pushing at me? Why so…' I paused, sighed. 'So cruel?'

She removed the mask. 'I'm sorry,' she answered. 'I was trying to amuse.' Her head tilted to one side. 'Which, in all fairness, is hardly my strong suit.'

I nodded. 'I see.'

'I forever have trouble judging the moment,' she said. 'Judging how people will be. What their faces even mean.' She looked down at the mask in her hand. 'I suppose that's why, like you say, I push at people.'

I was getting cold. I'd either have to continue practice or go in.

'It's fine,' I said.

She kept her eyes on the Roshos' mask. 'I promised not to raise your past.' She paused. I was unsure whether out of kindness, or her affliction. 'And I never will. But if *you* ever wish to raise it, I'd b-be honoured to listen.'

I felt angry. I felt good.

Gently, I took the mask from her hand. 'What was it you just said about judging the moment?'

She looked up. She pointed at my lips.

'A smile,' she said. Almost a whisper. 'Smiles I understand.'

We were too close to one another. I took a step back.

'Well,' Benadetta said, taking a step back herself. 'I'll ensure some food is left for when you come back in.'

I nodded and she turned away. She was halfway up the steps when I spoke.

'Sister.'

She stopped.

'I'm committed,' I told her. 'This mask, it's like a challenge. From my past.' I'd said too much. 'I want you to know that. That I'm committed.'

She turned to look at me. 'I know.' With that, she went back in.

I was left in a cold courtyard with no one but a hollow face in my hand. I tried to read its expression.

No luck.

Becken Bay stinks at dusk. The water around the abandoned wharves of the Hook particularly so. The air was all rotten egg and gnats.

'Check this one,' the caliban said, nodding back at the derelict wharf-house we floated towards. He didn't look at me. Kept his eyes on his rowing.

'You don't get to order me.' The first words I'd said to him since we'd got in the rowing boat.

'You want to row?' he said.

I spat over the edge and cursed Benadetta. A delight to her, no doubt, putting me in a floating wardrobe with the abomination. *Your night vision is superior,* she'd told me. *You both possess Isle blood.*

Some more than others, I'd countered, and she had raised an auburn eyebrow.

The wharf-house sagged over the water on stilts, as broken and obsolete as all the Hook, a promontory on the far east of the bay. We headed between its wooden, salt-caked legs.

I clambered onto my feet, wary of toppling into the putrid tides.

'You're shaking us,' I told him.

He ignored me.

A face peered out of a window above. Wild, bearded.

'Pilgrim sees you!' the face yelled, pallid as a mask. 'Sees you, devil!'

I yelped, fell back on my arse.

'Tramp,' Nail said, never looking over his shoulder at the wild man. 'We'll try the next one.'

My heart was pounding. I took deep breaths. The man was still shouting as we floated beneath him and his home.

'I see you, devil! See you!'

'Fuck this,' I muttered. Rats scurried along a trestle above.

'Have to be one of these,' Nail remarked, gazing over my shoulder toward the bay's middle. 'Good view of the obelisk's rear.'

'No rear's worth this.' We came out of the other side, into the sinking sunlight. Across the bay, the obelisk of the Roshos was a silhouette, a black knife slicing the sea and sky. 'Fucking Benadetta. Lumping me with beggars and halfbreeds…'

Nail stopped rowing. He brought up the oars and rested them. He stared at me.

'I asked her to order you,' he said.

Something had changed in him, his tone. That casual and unearned disregard of his had vanished, replaced by an icy focus.

'Why?'

He said nothing. A bat dived to our right, danced over golden ripples and rose up. Gone.

'Why?' I repeated.

He half-smiled. 'So we'd be alone.'

I drew my rapier and the hilt got caught on an empty rowlock. I fumbled the hilt free and nearly slashed my own shin in my haste to run him through. I braced to lunge.

He had a throwing spike ready.

I froze. A cramped rowing boat. Nowhere to go. We'd kill one another in a blink.

'You're with them,' I said, mouth barely moving. 'A ropeface.'

'Hardly.' His lips were similarly as tight. 'But I'll blame them. Happily.'

The tides. They were going out. He'd drop me overboard, row back. No corpse. He'd planned this. Naturally. His connections, his friendship with Jaggard. The promise of Rosho gold. How had I been so stupid?

'There's no faster blade than mine,' I said, never glancing at it. I wouldn't break from his eyes. Neither of us could risk the slightest action.

'This isn't a blade I'm holding,' he replied.

The problem with a rapier was he'd live long enough to chuck his spike. The problem with his spike was he only had one throw. We were both nimble, nimble as hares. Both of us knew the truth of it.

'Never could fathom you.' I sneered as much as I dared. 'Caliban.'

'I fathom you too well, inbred.'

I squinted. 'What?'

'The Sister,' he said. 'Leave her be.'

I nearly laughed but stopped myself. Too much movement.

'You love her?' I said.

'Quite the opposite.'

The boat rolled on a tide. We both flinched. Stopped ourselves.

The tension in his face must have been the mirror of mine. Somewhere along the wharves a cat howled.

'I'm a year into a five-year penance,' he explained. 'For fucking rent boys.' Matter of fact, no shame. He knew I was hardly one to judge. 'You carry on trying to raise her robes and maybe I'll get more years. With you beside me. Not happening, commrach.'

'I preferred it back when we first met,' I said. 'You hardly spoke.'

'This torc around my neck? She put it on me. She can cause me agony through it. Has done. She'll put one around you.' He half-smiled again. 'It's what she does.'

'I'm not so easy to catch.'

'You think you are seducing her? She's leading you in. I'll wager she's already offered to be a sympathetic ear.' A look of bitter satisfaction crossed his face when he saw the truth of it upon me. The satisfaction shifted to a cruel stillness. 'She hates you quim-lickers. She had two of them whipped, you know that? I saw it all. Middle of a village. Great chunks out of their backs by the time it was over. That's her, inbred. The good…' He was mocking her impediment. 'Sister… B-B-Benadetta.'

I recalled the threat she'd made at the tailor's, her final warning. Then I thought of her hand on my shoulder. Her reassurances. Her eyes.

'I hate the bitch,' I said. 'I should think that obvious. Mongrel.'

He gave me a look, an adult before a lying child. 'Of course the Sister is just like you and me, except her church has mangled her with such self-hate she cannot even see it within herself. The more you trifle with her affections, the more you tempt her to a path she wants deep down, the more self-righteous her sadism will be.'

'You bore me.'

'Keep upsetting her,' he said, 'and the next time we're in a rowing boat you'll be unconscious.'

'I'd have to be.'

He lowered his spike.

I lowered my blade.

Watching each other, we sheathed.

Nail looked toward a little pier we were floating toward.

'Looks perfect. We'll shore the boat here. Then you can walk all the way home. Inbred.'

'Anyone tell you you should have been strangled at birth?'

'Get in line…' He resumed rowing. 'Wait your turn.'

I readied to clamber out. 'You've used that line before.'

'My repertoire is stale,' he muttered. He eyed me. 'My audience is hardly challenging.'

We spoke no more. Across the bay the sun sank behind the Obelisk of Rosho. A vast silhouette, waiting.

14

'Have you seen my slather pot?' you asked.

'Forget that,' I said. I grabbed your bare waist and pulled you back on the bed. 'Hold me a little longer.'

You didn't need persuading. We rolled over each other twice, giggled, flesh smooth and sliding. You were better now, your shaking gone, gaze returning life and love. It had been some hours since the Aghast Play and the terrormask. You sucked my lip, released it.

'You delay the inevitable,' you said. 'Your little reign is near-ended.'

'Ah, a silver age.' I nuzzled your throat.

'Hmm… bronze at best.'

I pulled back and looked at you. 'Traitor.'

I play-slapped your shoulder. You retaliated and, before we knew it, we were wrestling, laughing again.

We stopped, took in the vista of the wide season-chamber.

By the Blood. Forty-one naked and unmarried women, their figures pale in the silver light of hanging moontiles. My pride, in all senses.

Expectation filled the chamber. The males would be here within an hour. Most women were smearing their bodies from hair to toe with the grey slather, throwing empty pots to the sides of the large room and opening fresh ones. Others were a little further ahead, applying black warpaint over the slather, painting symbols of family, blood status and sexual proclivity across their torsos. In the coming masked frenzy these demarcations would be vital.

Aroo-oo… they sang. *Yip, yip.*

There were a few like us, the sluggards, still dallying with each other's flesh in the hour that remained. I had enjoyed the fruits of this chamber for days, had each peach and pear beg for my touch, had known their gratitude. My fun was almost finished. It would be for me to oversee the tumult, prowl this chamber as males jostled to mount my hungry pride-girls, my season-invigorated strength and altered vocal chords subduing the over-eager and discourteous. Along with my brother, I would be the most feared, the most hated creature in the room. A twin.

There would be tumults of every kind across Corso tonight. Some all female, some all male, a few concerning themselves with the outlier sexes. Commrach, in the main, found pleasure in all flesh. But twins presided over the tumults where female and male met. Such was custom. I had no choice in the matter, Shen, but you could have gone almost anywhere, one tumult being as savage as another. But you would be a stranger in this city anywhere else. Nowhere might have you without me.

'Friends,' you called out to the room. 'Has anyone seen my slather pot? Anyone? It has my name upon it.'

No one replied.

I caressed your back. 'Plenty other pots.'

You slapped my stomach. 'I brought it from home. The berries of Skarrach are famously potent.'

I grunted and let my head fall upon the pillow. Male-fuckers were absurdly picky about this-or-that slather cream. As well they might be. Pregnancy outside of wedlock was abomination. Insult to the Blood.

I seized you again. I reached for your grove.

'We've an hour, Shen…' I licked your spine. 'Please.'

'Stop it, longboot,' you said. You *arrooed*. 'Just think of all those men a-cat-mounting me, spurting hot silver.' You *yipped*.

'Ugh.' I let go of you. I'd no wish to see that. But what choice? You were at season's height, Shen. Nature's law. Only I and my brother would hold to civilisation tonight.

Somewhere at the other end of the chamber, cousin Zymo scream-giggled. I winced. She had made the days in this chamber difficult, or as difficult as she might.

You sighed, turned to face me.

'Look for me in the tumult,' you said, stroking my hair. 'You'll see my eyes staring back at you. Wanting you. Thinking of you.'

I sniffed, made coy eyes. 'As wretched males take you.'

You kissed me. 'You're like a human, all jealous. Like in the comic verse.'

'I'm sorry.'

'Listen to me. I love you, Kyra. *Love*. I always will.'

We kissed.

Someone screamed.

A woman, Kalika.

At first I thought she'd made a mistake, daubed warpaint on her face before applying the slather. But this was no paint, this was blood. Dark, flowing from her mouth and nose.

I leaped up.

You stayed me with a hand.

'No one touch her,' you shouted. 'Poison.'

Kalika staggered forward, reaching her arms out for help, for anyone. She'd a patch of slather on her belly, a pot in her hand.

You gripped my wrist. 'Spiteshade. Nothing we can do.'

Kalika heaved and lumpen blood came out like vomit. She fell face forward. She went still.

Silence. Then fear, people checking the slather was not theirs.

'Calm,' I commanded. 'No one touch any fresh pots.'

I gave what I thought was a reassuring silence. In truth I was waiting to see if anyone else would die. But no.

A few people cried. Most looked sad, but I knew they were relieved the tumult would continue. There'd have been rioting otherwise.

'Kyra,' you said. You were pointing at the half-used pot of slather beside Kalika's corpse.

Your name was writ upon it.

'I cannot wait,' Zymo announced to others nearby. 'Watch me fuck this chamber dry tonight!'

Zymo.

I strode toward her. She was at the other end of the great chamber, her hip resting against a mounting-couch. Her body was entirely smeared with drying pale-grey slather, though her ram's-horn hairstyle remained untouched. She noticed me approach.

'What?' she asked me. 'I'm trying to keep morale up.'

'You fucking *killed* her.' I pointed at Kalika upon the floor.

Zymo looked horrified. Her horror seemed a total act but, then again, every expression Zymo ever made seemed a total act. It didn't help her face was smeared and cracking.

'You were trying to kill Shen,' I said.

'Who?'

'Shen!' I barked and I gestured over at you.

'Oh,' Zymo said. She shrugged her shoulders and checked her nails. 'Your ruddy-locked thing…'

I lifted my open palm to strike.

Zymo froze, her eyes wide.

'*Arooo…*' she uttered involuntarily.

My hand faltered. I couldn't help but look her body over. It was her scent of course. Zymo's season scent was infamously formidable.

She grinned, realising her power and knowing the entire chamber watched us both. She drew her finger across one shoulder. 'I think it's time we prepared for the males' arrival.' She looked me up and down and, in a pitying tone, said, 'Eh, little longboot?'

I walked away to the sound of her giggling. Guilty or not, she meant to dominate the season chamber this night. All her deference toward me had vanished since the war ritual. Glory had been denied her and now a new Zymo had emerged, or been revealed, always been there below the insipid fool. As crass and dim as ever but now full of the audacity and focus of any Cal'Adra.

But one capable of outright murder?

I looked at you, Shen. You were staring over at Zymo as she laughed and cavorted with her group of friends. You she might well kill. But so blatantly? While in the same room?

'Kalika,' you said, suddenly disinterested in Zymo. 'We can't just leave her there.'

'I'll get a Climacteric to move her.'

'The poison's on her,' you said. 'Besides… there's no time.'

We looked at one another. Then, as one, we walked over to the bed, lifted a feather mattress and placed it over Kalika's corpse.

'Let's get you out of here,' I said. 'It's not safe.'

'No. I don't think it's her.' You nodded over at Zymo. 'It'll be a Cal'Dain plot. You've real enemies now, my love.'

'Regardless, it's not safe.'

'I can't,' you said. 'I just can't leave now.'

The promise of so much fucking. The itch scratched. Of course.

'I'm sorry, Kyra,' you muttered.

'It's fine.' I put on the best natural smile I could muster. 'Let's get ready.'

You borrowed someone else's slather, despite it being not up to the standards of Skarrach. Then, like every girl in the hall, you strapped on your mask-atavistic, a strip of padded black leather that covered the upper half of your face. The mask was styled after an ancient skull fragment, believed to belong to one of our earliest ancestors. The mask's brow was far more pronounced than a commrach's, the eye sockets almost twice the diameter, and down the right side hung a copy of the fragment's one remaining tooth, a jet-black incisor long as a lynx's fang.

You had smeared slather into your scalp and now, aside from the occasional exposed root of scarlet, you were indistinguishable from almost anyone else in the chamber. Primal figures, all of you, your limbs cracking with dried grey slather, your torsos daubed with black sigils.

I had coated my own body with the same black paint, or at least one side of it: the right side. My own mask was a domino covering the eyes and nose. It was supposed to make me resemble a panther, in an abstract sort of way, that hunter of our ancestors. I thought the whiskers made me look ridiculous. Finally, I picked up my slim club. I was complete.

A knock rang through the chamber and all eyes turned toward the double doors. Many *aroooed* and muffled calls came back from behind the ebony threshold.

I strode forward, passing the eager young women on their couches and rugs. I stopped before the doors and winced unseen. I pulled the doors wide open.

Kyran stood before me, panther-masked and naked as I, black warpaint all down his left side. Behind him stood forty-one young males, their skin grey with dried slather, all wearing the mask-atavistic, hungry at the crotch, their pricks like ranks of spears.

My brother's eyes were as my own: sad, condemned to the task at hand.

'We ask to enter,' he said, ritual words in a ritual moment.

'Enter,' I replied.

The males barged past me before I'd finished, their lust waiting only so long. The women howled their joy. The two armies rushed at one another, equal in strength and desire.

Another hateful tumult night. Hours of breaking up fights, punching men, hissing at their hardness, of being cursed by frenzied women who'd caressed me only hours before.

The first hour passed. Deep breaths. Kohl-ringed eyes watched me from behind an ancient death-mask. A smile broke out beneath the mask's curved fang: Zymo, lolling upon her mounting-couch. Three males caressed her, nuzzled at her, minds lost in her musk, rabid for her consent. She petted each of their wet glans then drew their faces to her own. She whispered to them. She smiled.

The men looked at me. I readied my club.

They launched from the couch and belted across the tiled

floor, their leather masks blank of expression.

The first hurried to reach me before the other two, so much so he'd no plan save grabbing me. I offered my left arm and he took the bait, digging nails into brawn as I swung the club's head at his shoulder.

He dropped on his arse. He seized my thighs, tried toppling me. I whacked his mask and the nose burst beneath. He flopped on his back.

Pain wracked my skull and I stumbled sideways. A foot slammed into my hip and I went over, sliding in something warm, either blood or seed. The club slipped from my grasp.

The two other youths pummelled me, fists flailing and brainless. With the moontile chandelier above them I could not see their eyes. These were animal-men, wild, beating their prey beneath a feral moon.

Blocking with my left arm, I scrabbled for the club with my right. Nothing. The women's pleasure shrieks filled the air, the men they coupled with grunting. A punch to my brow and my skull slapped against tile. My world shivered and sparkled. I heaved for air and another punch stung my collar.

Fuck the club. My spare hand clawed for a cock. My nails met balls and I dug in. I crushed, twisted right then left. It didn't work at first. But I hung on, taking the punches, knowing it soon would.

The male's punches weakened, turned to palms pushing at my biceps then fingers desperately trying to prise my own from his greasy sack.

I should have let go, let him scurry away so that I might focus on his comrade. But no, by the Blood no. Zymo would be watching. Let her see me torture those she sent to break me.

My victim kept his feet, thighs wide and spine bent, fingers grasping my wrist almost tenderly as I continued to squeeze and twist. He hissed, his spittle dappling my chest, dragging me across the floor as his accomplice punched me about the hips and crotch. My season-strength took the hits, and I used my other hand to punch my victim's still engorged prick.

One.

Two.

Three and my punch connected with the base of his shaft. It snapped.

I laughed beneath the silver light, unheard amid the screams.

The broken male dropped to his knees and vomited on my throat and collar, a hot streak of mostly wine. I let go of his ruined treasures just as a black length connected with the side of his head. He flew onto his side.

Kyran with his club. He span and flew at my other assailant, kicking him square in the chest.

I got up. My legs felt barely there. My vision shrunk and expanded with each breath. I touched the back of my head: tender, but not wet.

Just ahead of me six people were fucking atop a lumpen mattress. I recalled moving it only earlier. There was a body beneath that mattress. Kalika. Poor creature.

My club was beside my toes. I picked it up. Somewhere behind me Kyran was calling my name.

I turned to see him sitting astride the chest of a supine youth, the one he'd only just kicked to the floor. Kyran was simultaneously holding him down and masturbating him vigorously. An effective tactic: the male was losing the will to fight with each expert tug.

'Ra-ra,' Kyran said, looking up at me. 'Are you quite fine, dear?' His eyes sparkled within his panther mask.

I nodded, adjusting my own mask.

I remembered Zymo. I looked over to her couch, eager to drink in her horror and regret. She was on her back, thighs wide and haunches raised. One of her hairstyle's ram horns had bent out of shape. It shook with her fumbling.

The fire flew out of me. I felt weak, distant from everything, as if I were borrowing my body from someone else. Cold bile ran down my sternum. I had to sit down.

On the tiles before me lay the broken youth, clutching his genitals, his sobbing drowned out by others' joy. Either an Explainer would fix his cock, or his world was ruined. I didn't care either way and neither did anyone else.

You were just beyond him, Shen, lying atop a mounting couch, your head and arms hanging over. The dry slather in your hair was beginning to powder and your red locks showed. You still wore the black mask, but now silver gleamed across its brow, a lightning streak of jism. You were being pumped, hammered, your rear jutting in the air as a masked male reached climax. He'd no time to relish it, for his shudder was sign to other males to tear him off you and throw him aside. The next closed in too eagerly. Displeased, you hissed him away then enticed another, your back arching as he mounted and entered. *Yip*, you snapped, *aroo*, as other males waited, jumping, jostling, pleasuring each other and themselves. You were so very happy, Shen. Adrift upon a sensual sea.

You never looked at me. We'd both known you wouldn't. You were queen of your carnal realm, beckoning twenty men to take their turn, denying me your eyes. Your eyes.

Aroo-rooo.

Minds dulled, the chamber glittered, glowed with countless secretions. My body ached.

Zymo, I thought. *It must be you. Must.*
You would kill my woman.
I shall make you suffer.
Suffer.
Blackness took me down.

PART THREE

15

Tonight. I had waited for days and this was the night.

I lay on my bed in our safe house, a rickety thing I could never get a full night's rest on. I was sick of the ceiling. Sick of the warped windowsill. I had waited too long. I sink if I stop moving. To the point where I have trouble speaking, even getting up.

They were hanging people who didn't worship God in the proper way. Near-thirty, Shortleg told me, in Becken's main square. Rumours of covens, he said, monstrous noises heard up country. Evidence enough to snap throats.

Shortleg had gone along though not for the hanging. Public executions offered the potential to flirt. True enough – it was the same back on the Isle – but I think Shortleg needed to get out. I know I did. I just couldn't.

I was afraid of tonight.

I thought of Mother. Rather, I thought of Mother in my vision, the one that came to me when the churchwomen, Benadetta's lackeys, strapped me to their iron chair. I thought of the strange words she had cooed to me, a babe in her arms.

'Why be always so, sweet Kyra? Pouring out snakes and digging hearts from the ground.'

I'd still no idea what those words really meant. But I could, well, *feel* them. Feel their meaning rising. Perhaps they'd breach the surface of my awareness soon, the moment I needed to understand. As the Explainers describe.

'I'm still pouring out snakes, Mother,' I whispered. 'Still digging for hearts.'

Ridiculous, of course, talking to someone who'd ceased to exist. Waiting in this place had driven me to madness.

A knock at the door.

I sat up. 'Come.'

'You'll have to open the door,' Benadetta said.

I grumbled, hoping she heard me. I'd kept away from her for days. Since Nail and his rowing boat.

I got up and opened the door.

She stood in the gloom of the landing, a bulging sack between her arms like a dance partner.

'Your apparel for tonight,' she explained.

I let her stand encumbered.

'Thought you'd be at the hangings,' I said. 'It's your friends' festival after all.'

'The Church has never… approved the public act,' she replied. 'That's the decision of temporal powers.'

'But it approves the act.'

'The road to God's—'

'*Boring.*'

'Could you take th-this bag from me?'

I studied the bitch. Had she really had two women whipped, as that halfbreed had claimed? Who was I kidding? Of course she had. The Church's willing tool.

'Drop it on my bed,' I told her.

I let her pass. She did as I said then stood up straight and put her hands on her hips.

'We've but hours,' she said. She gestured at the sack. 'Take a look.'

I sniffed, pouted. I opened the sack and poured the contents onto the bed.

Miss Vohte and her father had done a fine job, I had to concede that much. A black longjacket, one that offered no hint of house loyalty. A shoulder-less trouservest of impeccable damask. And jewellery: jet bracelets, a black choker with a silver pendant.

Then I saw the shoes.

'Idiots,' I said.

'What?'

I picked one up. 'These are shoes.'

'What else would they be?'

'They're not longboots. I'm a *twin*.'

'You're m-making no sense.'

'Fucking humans.' Her clueless face irritated me. 'A girl twin wears tall boots. So women know. So men know.'

'Why?'

I wasn't going to explain that to someone who whipped chunks out of lovers of the same sex.

'I...' I clenched my fists 'I suppose it does not matter.' My alias wasn't necessarily a twin of course but implying so seemed a needless and foolhardy lie.

'Well... why not wear your usual boots?'

'What? These?' I pointed at the boots I already wore. 'At a function? They're for outdoors. It would insult the hosts. And, besides, they simply *cannot* go with that ensemble.'

'Does it really matter if clothes don't "go"?' Benadetta said.

'Not if you wear grain sacks,' I said, eyeing her Perfecti robes.
'The rest of us have pride.' She was looking at me like I was a
child in tantrum. 'Fine. I've already said I'll wear the shoes.'

'Magnanimous of you, Cal'Adra.'

I looked at the jewellery again. 'Oh, now *this* is a complete
disaster.'

'Looks… more like a necklace.'

'I'm twenty-three, yes?' I said. 'My surname in this ruse is
Sil'Asu?'

'Yes?'

'Sil's one below Cal,' I said. 'My family would have married
me off by now. I'd have a chain matrimonial, talon jewellery.
Your tailors have put me on the shelf.'

'A lie works b-better built on truth,' she replied. 'You… have
come down in the world. Inarguably.'

I scowled at her. She smiled and left.

An hour later and I was staring in the mirror above the
fireplace. I had not dressed this way in years. A creature of the
Isle again. None of it felt right without my brother beside me.

I'd put my hair up into two fist-size buns. Much too fancy
for my tastes, but it proffered me distance from myself. I had to
become Nileen Sil'Asu. Whoever that was.

Benadetta entered. She'd brought a lamp with her. The light
dyed the room saffron. I hadn't noticed dusk draw in.

'You look good,' she said. 'Cal'Adra.'

I turned to face her.

She didn't. She resembled a priestess failing to impersonate
a woman. Her handmaiden's dress was lumpen, angled wrong
somehow, like she was humpbacked.

'Could you tighten my straps?' she said, setting the lamp on a
table in the corner of the room. 'I'm n-not used to this apparel.'

I'd never seen her hair before. Thick and auburn, she'd tied it back into a scalp-pulling tail. A wonder she could move her eyebrows. Sister Perfecti Benadetta, adrift in the world of real people. Pitiful.

Or was it? This insane bitch hurt people for who they chose to tup, had had her cronies chain me to a chair. What had Nail said about her leading me in, trapping me? Asking me to tighten her straps, by the Blood.

'You look ridiculous,' I said.

She looked discomforted for the briefest moment. Then she nodded.

I took a moment, breathed in.

'Fine, come here,' I said. 'Let's make you shine.'

'Shine is not required.'

'Come here.'

She did so.

'Turn around,' I said.

She did so.

She waved her hand. 'Don't…' She paused. 'You know.'

'You've never appealed to me, Sister,' I said.

'Good.'

'Rather suck off Shortleg,' I added. She needed reassurance.

'Continue,' she said.

I studied the back of her corset. What she *had* tied of it she'd tied wholly wrong. It explained her misshapen cast. I undid it, a little, and began again.

'Too tight,' she said.

'You can't breathe?'

'No. I m-mean…'

'You've got to convince, Sister.' I tightened her a little more. She had hips, a waist. Who'd have imagined?

'Wait there,' I said.

I took a comb from my bed and came back. She shuddered as I loosened her hair, then relaxed. I began to comb.

'Luxurious,' I whispered into her ear. 'That one should hide such…'

She said nothing. I could smell her skin. Clean. Smooth. I tied her hair once more, but artfully now, locks of it hanging down.

Everything felt foolhardy, dangerous. Alive. Yes, that was it. I teetered on a cliff's edge, blood rushing, infatuated with the threat Sister Benadetta embodied. But not her. Not her.

'We shall paint your lips,' I told her.

'I've never—'

'I have.'

I pulled my rouge from my jacket pocket. I placed my palm on her cheek and turned her face. Her body followed.

Her eyes were closed, like in those moments when she lost control and stammered.

I applied rouge to her full, yielding lips. Her breath blew slow and warm upon my fingers, her shoulders rising and falling with the rhythm. I cast the rouge on the bed.

'Trust me,' I said.

Oh. But she'd a bosom. Full, the sort one could lie on and forget the world's stupidities. I reached up to her collar – she'd been sure to do that up fully – and began to undo it.

Her hand stopped mine. She opened her eyes and looked at me.

'Trust me,' I whispered.

She let go.

I undid it, buttoned the flap to one side. I revealed no cleavage, merely her collarbone. She'd slight freckles there. A pleasing feature.

'Go look at yourself,' I told her.

She turned toward the mirror above the fireplace. I stood behind her, a hand's distance.

Benadetta gazed at her reflection like it was a purported relic of her Pilgrim, a thing either wondrous or heresy.

'Do I...' She faltered. Perhaps her verbal affliction. Perhaps not. 'Convince?'

'I'm persuaded,' I whispered by her ear.

'Tonight...'

'Yes?'

'We'll look... q-quite the—'

A knock at the door.

Benadetta stepped away from me. She faced the door.

'Enter,' she said.

Shortleg came in. In a second he went from animated to stunned. Stunned by us both.

'Yes?' I waited for him to stop staring.

'Your... palanquin's outside,' he said.

I smiled. We'd fill his dreams tonight.

'We're ready,' I told him.

Black night, black waters. Few stars and no moon. The clouds sagged above us.

Perfect.

Benadetta and I sat in a gilded sandolo. I was no mariner, but the boat felt far too low to the bay's tides. The rise and fall was getting to me, so too the salt-caked sharpness in my nose.

Benadetta, my alleged handmaid, was handling this better than I. She looked stately, in charge. No actress, that woman.

'Look into the distance,' she said. 'You'll feel better.'

'I'm fine,' I told her. I looked into the distance.

Ten other sandolos rowed along with us, their prow-lamps transmuting the crest of each wave to gold.

Toward the prow of each sandolo sat the Roshos' invited guests: Becken's merchant class for the main, a few aristocrats. I'd seen these guests on the pier before we had embarked: men with absurd hats and oiled beards and wives with dresses so outlandish a beard might actually restore their dignity. The arc of wealth always bends towards conspicuous impracticality. As yet, none of them had donned their masks. I was the sole commrach in this congenial armada.

Each sandolo's crew toiled unseen toward the stern of the ship, away from the prow's lamps. Our own crew heaved behind us, their oars creaking like boughs in the wind.

The obelisk stood upon its reef. Trade obelisks were short, dumpy things compared to the towers of home. The ground floor was skirted with a tiled roof held up by a score of slender pillars. Lamplight shone from the windows and doorways between them. The floors directly above were not illuminated and barely discernible from the night sky beyond. The highest floors were another matter. Their small windows twinkled silver like stars, moontile light therein. The illumination of home.

'Wondrous,' Benadetta said.

'You're easily impressed, girl.'

She squinted at me. Strands of her hair danced in the bay's breeze. In her right hand she clutched my golden mask. The Final Countenance. I'd no wish to wear the thing. Not until I had to.

The mask felt tight and cold against my face.

'Nileen Sil'Asu of Corso city,' announced the human in the sparkly jacket.

We were stood atop a wide marble staircase that descended into the ceremonial hall and, for a moment, I expected the hundred or more guests below to stare up as one when my name was called.

No one did. They carried on dancing upon the chequered floor, a polite back-and-forth popular in Manca. Others stood about in groups, chatting and taking drinks from passing silver plates. All of them masked in the Final Countenance and each mask painted the most garish colours. An obscenity to my upbringing, an absurdity to my experience. I spied no obvious commrach.

'Mistress,' Benadetta said beside me.

I looked toward her. The man who'd announced me had an uncomfortable expression. I was holding the line up.

I made my way down the stairs. Commrach melodies played on human flutes. Few, if any, masks sat comfortably on the faces of these well-fed merchants and lords. One had even had the chin removed so as to allow his pockmarked jowls.

I'd had dreams like this. Dreams where my current life and previous existence blended. Humans within commrach halls, blithe to their incongruence. My two lives colliding. I never liked those dreams.

'Are you fine?' Benadetta asked as we reached the hall's tiles.

I mustered a smile. 'You're a very considerate handmaid. But don't think you'll get a rise out of me.'

'My sentiments exactly,' she replied. She'd a way of sneering that might pass for compassion to anyone not compelled to know her. 'Mistress.'

She looked up at the dome. I'd been avoiding that.

It was of marble, illuminated by several braziers. They stood along a walkway that ringed the dome's circumference. Below the walkway, dolphins played, wooden carvings full of that near-moving vitality our touch brings. I shivered.

A figure stood up there, loitering in an arched doorway. A scarlet mask. They stepped back into the doorway's blackness.

'Did you see that?' I asked Benadetta.

'See what?'

I kept searching the walkway in the hope the figure might return. But no.

'Sil'Asu,' said a female voice behind us.

We both turned.

A dainty woman in a human's ballgown and tiara, her white hair cascading over the straps of her powder-blue mask. She wore white lace gloves leaving only her forearms exposed, which were the olive tan of commrach, if a little pale.

'*Shoola*,' I said in greeting. 'You must be our gracious host.'

'Sada Cal'Rosho,' she replied. She sniggered.

I bowed. 'Always an honour to meet a Cal.'

She wasn't, of course. No Rosho was. They'd pissed away that title around about the time they got exiled.

'And a delight to finally meet you,' Sada said. She spoke in Commrach. 'I was filled with mirth – and not a little nostalgia – to see a commrach of notable blood—' She paused, as if to suggest she was doing me a kindness. '—set about a skivvy with blows and curses.' She sniggered again and her white-laced fingers touched her throat.

'It was you in the palanquin?' I said. 'Apologies for my behaviour, but I *cannot* be ordered by these…' I gestured toward the humans all about. 'Not for long at any rate.'

'As soon as you kicked Jaggard in the rear I thought, here's someone we simply have to bring into the fold. I told Arlo, my brother, if nothing else she will delight. He dearly wants to meet you.'

'I'm glad,' I replied. Arlo. Your father had mentioned him, Shen, before I'd murdered him. Arlo had shown him the dark king, he'd said. The devil. I tapped the nose of my mask. 'I was rather startled to receive a Final Countenance mask. And in such a challenging colour.'

'It's a sort of twofold thing really,' she said. 'A masque that is in itself a mask, if you see what I mean. Do you see what I mean?'

'Not presently.'

'Oh. Well, for all the humans here tonight – and there's some wonderful specimens; no king, admittedly, but he sent his third queen – the masks are a piece of authentic Isle culture, one that happily fits with their fashion for masked balls.'

It was true that the guests showed no discomfort or awkwardness with their masks. One young woman in a voluminous gown – likely the third queen herself – not only wore a mask edged with rubies, but drew eyes with her bodice made entirely of Final Countenances. I dreaded to think what Grandmother would have made of it all. A mass execution, I suspect.

'Fascinating,' I replied to Sada. 'And behind that mask of a masque?'

She pushed her powder-blue mask over her head and smiled at me. With her dark, sunken eyes and upturned nose she reminded me of a doll. Everything about her seemed fragile.

'A jape,' she said. She watched the dance, nodded a greeting at a passing guest. 'None of these lumbering beasts know the significance of the Final Countenance. To see them cavort and jibber with the visage of the perfect being? I'll be chuckling about this in old age.'

I laughed with her politely, all the while thinking, *Jape? You tried to poison me for a jape only last week, you weird fucking shit. But I guess we're not talking about that are we?*

'Your maidservant?' Sada said, eyeing Benadetta.

'My maidservant,' I replied. One who, unknown to Sada, could talk basic Commrach and had understood every bit of Sada's prattle.

'Oh, you should have said,' Sada replied, ignoring Benadetta. 'We've a room for those.' She gestured to a human servant. 'We've a room for almost everything I dare say.'

'I dare say,' I said. 'This obelisk is magnificent.'

'It's not the same as a tower,' Sada said. Her flicker of sorrow seemed practised, the frown of bitterness that followed real. 'You'll know of our fall, of course.'

'The infamy lies not with you,' I said. I took a drink from a passing tray. 'That's the broad sentiment back on the Isle.'

'You're too kind.'

A servant approached.

'Go along, Beni,' I said to Benadetta. I hid a smile with a sip from my glass.

I watched Benadetta leave, a woman singularly incapable of making a dress work for her when she moved. It was as if she waded through mud. With any luck she'd fare better searching around whatever scullery they'd dump her in.

I looked back at Sada. She most definitely *could* make a dress work. A rarefied skill in a commrach given we didn't typically wear them.

'Ah, here comes my brother,' she said. She waved over my shoulder.

I turned to see two figures striding with that singular commrach grace toward us. The one on the right must have been a foot taller than me, about as tall as our race gets. He wore the fine apparel of a human noble, though sombre in tone. I assumed he was Arlo Rosho, for his mask was the same powder-blue as Sada's.

The figure on the left was more or less my height. He wore all black, and walked a foot behind Arlo with palm on rapier's pommel. A guard then, or more likely a bondsman. His mask was his most striking feature: an Isle original, as silver and gaunt as the one I used to wear on festival nights.

'Greetings,' I said.

'Arlo Cal'Rosho,' the taller one said. He didn't offer his hand. Yes, sombre described him well. His whole bearing was oddly funereal.

'Great patriarch of Cal'Rosho,' I said, and I bowed again. 'Your reputation precedes you.'

Through the holes in his mask, he squinted at me as if I'd veiled an insult.

'And nothing precedes you, Sil'Asu,' he replied. 'You are a mystery to both me and all my wide network.'

'There is little to be said about me,' I replied. 'A bondswoman of Cal'Adra, now self-exiled and seeking patrons.' I pulled my sword out a little way from the scabbard, so that they might see the glyph of Cal'Adra. I sheathed it back again. 'The fact you know nothing about me, if I may say so, sir, means I performed my duties well. A bondswoman's life should remain discreet.'

'A bondswoman's life,' the bondsman said, 'should remain loyal.'

'Loyalty works both ways,' I told him. I looked to the Roshos. 'I think we all know the Cal'Adras possess little of that.'

Neither of them nodded exactly, but I took their silence to be a form of agreement.

'You shouldn't be standing here,' the bondsman said. 'You should be dead.'

Arlo raised a hand gently, waving his bondsman away. The bondsman left, taking pains to do so with dignity and deference so that I might see.

'He seems a traditionalist,' I said.

'You think that so odd here?' Arlo said.

'These masks aren't exactly traditional.' Too harsh a comment. I was meant to be seeking patronage and shelter here. 'An observation, sir. I meant no—'

'A new take on old means,' Arlo replied, cutting me off. He looked about the hall, seemingly wishing to end the conversation.

'Brother has much to say on that theme,' Sada told me. 'It's sort of his whole philosophy.' She nodded emphatically.

'How so?'

Sada looked to Arlo, an odd sort of look, and Arlo, reluctant yet indulgent of his sister, spoke.

'The mainland is brutish, but it has much to teach us, Sil'Asu. There's a vibrancy here that the old Isle needs to drink from.' He lifted his mask off his head and stroked its lacquered surface. He'd the same sunken eyes as Sada, the same upturned nose. His cropped hair was the same silver-white. 'These masks are a metaphor for the Rosho instinct, I suppose: the old ways in new fashions. The root of human vibrancy is coin. Look around you, see the merchants and compare them to their "betters", the aristocrats. It hardly needs saying: the former rise and the latter fade.'

In all honesty, I couldn't tell who was merchant and who aristo. These guests were just a mass of garish velvet drowning in too much perfume.

'You would introduce coins to the Isle?' I said. I was glad I wore a mask now. My smirk would have got me thrown into the bay.

'And abolish the Explainers,' Arlo declared. He was becoming more animated now, relatively speaking. 'Do not misunderstand, I believe in the perfection of blood, naturally. But gold and the market is a better decider of bloodline superiority than some unhinged philosophers with their dusty creeds. With gold, the capable rise and the weak fall. And at a speed of decades, not centuries.'

Sada linked her arm through Arlo's. 'It's a comely theory, isn't it?' she asked me. 'My only problem with it is all the smelly beggars you'd get.' She wrinkled her upturned nose.

'Maybe Corso needs a few beggars,' Arlo practically snapped. 'A reminder to the rest of us not to fall.'

I sipped my wine and nodded. Exile had sent these two insane. What was that absurd human notion again? Ghosts? Yes, that was it. Arlo and Sada reminded me of ghosts. Trapped between realms, full of tortured and incoherent prophecies, unaware that they were fundamentally dead. Unlike ghosts however, they had material power. Wealth too terrifying to laugh at.

'When we return to the Isle,' I said, 'you can suggest these new changes.'

'When we *take* the Isle,' Arlo replied, 'I'll enforce them.' His eyes shone in a way I'd have thought them too dour to achieve.

'Oh, Arlo,' his sister said, 'not here.' She giggled and shrugged at me.

'Show me your face,' Arlo said to me.

'Of course.' Inevitable I suppose, but still I tensed. I took my mask by the chin and pushed until it rested atop my skull.

'Didn't I tell you?' Sada said to Arlo. I prepared to run. 'A most charming face.'

Arlo didn't respond to her.

'You left the Cal'Adras,' he said to me. 'Why?'

'Later, Arlo,' Sada told him.

'Why?' he asked me again.

'Their matriarch,' I replied. 'Her desire for an Isle-wide army. Her boundless need for control.'

Sada looked at me with something like pity.

Arlo smirked joylessly. 'You haven't heard.'

'Heard what?'

'She's crushed the Jades. Executed one in twelve colonists. Cal'Adra are heroes back on the Isle. There's even talk of them being raised up a tower or two.'

I had no idea. I'd grown up on the Jades, had lived among colonists who had now quite possibly been tortured and killed. Mother would never have stood for it. Not ever. A true Lady of the Jades, unlike me. She'd have spat snakes.

Arlo was drinking in my shock. Then he smiled, as if I had passed some test.

'I'd better mingle,' Arlo said to his sister. He strode off.

Sada smiled at me.

'He likes you,' she said. 'Truly.'

'I'm pleased.' I wouldn't have thought Grandmother so crude as direct invasion. Changing times back home.

'I like your clothes,' Sada said.

'Thank you.' What could have driven my family, all Corso, to such extremes?

'Is that what they're wearing now?' Sada asked. 'On the Isle?'

'Probably…' Desperation or supremacy? It could be nothing in between with my family. I'd have to find out more.

'Would you like to have sex with me?' Sada said.

I looked at her.

She sniggered, her nose wrinkling, as if she'd made the lousiest pun.

'You've...' I looked about the party. 'No pressing duties?'

'I was hoping we might press our duties together.' She tapped my collarbone. "Til dawn.'

Why not? All this conspiracy and deception and cold slaughter: it just made me want to fuck. Confusion always did. If you want simplicity seek the body of a stranger.

'It's a sort of diplomacy, I suppose,' Sada explained, her confidence ebbing. 'To celebrate our new alliance. Besides, I rarely have allies to, you know, try diplomacy with.'

'I'll open up a little dialogue.' I moved closer. 'With pleasure. Where exactly?'

'My chambers,' Sada said, her eyes lighting up. 'Go tell your handmaid you're staying tonight, then ask a guard to show you to my chamber.'

'Very well.' I gave Sada a lascivious grin, to which she purred, and then headed toward the stairs at the other end of the hall. I made five strides and then stopped.

'Where will I find my handmaid?' I asked Sada.

Sada looked at me like I'd just asked the exact weight of Becken Keep. She shrugged, her gaze taking in the vast and people-filled interior of her home.

'I imagine someone around here must know,' she said.

Someone did. I was led to a suite on the fourth floor.

The carvings in the suite had faded. Not physically; the wooden dolphins were as fresh as they presumably always had been. Yet they lacked that unique aliveness imbuing brings to a piece of art. There were simply not enough commrach hands to go about every room and corridor, touching things. If we commrach ever vanish, whoever finds our works ages hence will never know their wonder.

The carved patterns around the four-poster bed were similarly drained. Sister Benadetta, still dressed as a handmaid, stood the other side of it. I couldn't see her face for the veils hanging from the bed's upper frame, the poor candlelight.

'They marched me... up here,' she said. 'What is happening?'

'We're staying the night,' I replied. 'Sada Rosho invited us.'

'Good work,' she said. 'Gives us more time. I... tried to reconnoitre downstairs. No luck. Though there's a heavy guard presence outside the door to the cellars. All commrach.'

'Keeping it in the family then,' I said. 'Whatever "it" is.'

I walked around the bed and faced her. Her features seemed like calligraphy in the poor light, almost a drawing of herself, pencilled eyelids black and sharp against vellum skin.

'Return to the ball,' she insisted. 'I'll saunter along the halls again.'

'Hardly worth it.' I hesitated. 'I've an in-road. Sada has granted a private audience.'

Benadetta nodded. 'Excellent. Bring me. I'll observe while you get all you can from her.'

'Erm...'

Benadetta squinted. She frowned. 'Pilgrim's mercy,' she muttered. She rubbed her forehead.

'I saw a chance and I took it,' I said.

'Oh, I've no doubt.' She eyed me with a mannered venom. She took a breath, her expression suddenly blank. 'No. I cannot permit this. The... Church can... not allow this.'

'I'm doing your god's work.'

'No.'

I shrugged. 'His ways *are* mysterious.'

'Yours aren't.' She shook her head. 'How am I supposed to note this in our account, hmm? W-what will my su…periors say?'

'Nothing. They don't know we're doing this, remember?'

She stared at me.

Oops. I only knew that fact because I'd climbed up a tree and listened in on her conversation.

'I might have overheard,' I said. I looked at the ceiling.

She said nothing. She walked away and sat on the side of the bed.

'But that's *all* I heard,' I said too swiftly. 'And I no longer felt coerced once I knew you were lying to your superiors. Then it felt fun. I'm resolved to go the entire way now.' I pursed my lips. 'I meant—'

'Just fun?' she said. 'There's nothing in you that… wishes to root out evil?'

'I leave that to you, Sister.' I headed for the door.

'And if it's a trap?' she said.

I stopped. I chuckled.

'Sada Rosho is deranged with boredom in this obelisk, Sister,' I said. 'Trust me. I know these things as you know scripture. I know when people want me.'

Benadetta looked at her knees. 'What if she's cleverer than you? Better?'

'Sada Rosho?' I grinned. 'That souvenir of vintage incest? She's got nothing in her life save pretty gowns and her brother's rants. When I'm done she'll open like a flower, leak every secret. That's what people do, Sister, when they share each other's bodies. But you'll never know that.'

Benadetta said nothing.

'Anyway, she's waiting,' I said.

I headed to the door. I stopped before it, like when I'd stopped before the door of St Waleran's. I felt suddenly angry.

'You know,' I said. 'There's nothing *wrong* with any of this. Between a woman and a woman. Or anyone. Your storybook sky-king ruins this world. He twists you into a sadist, like with me and your chair, like with those two girls.'

I looked over my shoulder at her.

Her face was placid, faintly quizzical. I abhorred that face.

'It's just a pleasured hour,' I said. 'It hurts no one.'

She pouted at that. I'd never seen her pout. She made her damn holy gesture, absolving me.

I drew my mask – still resting atop my head – down over my face. I said no more and left.

Our masks fell to the floor and soon her bodice was torn wide and my trouservest pulled down to the waist and we were pawing each other's torsos, purring and kissing in the gloom. Sada's private chambers had not been lit for human eyes: a lone moontile glowed on the ceiling. Illumination from my old life, grotesque in its familiarity. Beyond its moonlit cone everything was black, the room's corners unseen.

Sada Rosho smelled good: a perfume from the Isle, rose petal. You had oft worn the same, Shen. It was *your* scent. I ran my nose along her slight neck. I breathed you in.

'Rougher,' she said.

I lifted her by the thighs and carried her across the room, dropping her onto a writing desk and pushing her back against the wall. Ornaments fell to the floor. Sada giggled. I pressed my teeth into her shoulder and her fingernails raked my back. Her thighs squeezed my waist.

'That's it,' she said.

I inhaled your perfume again. I drove my lips into Sada's hair, sucked her ear.

Above her hung a small picture in a gilt frame: kings, peasants, clergy, collapsing in shock. Above them hovered a hairy skeleton with furnace eyes. Goat's legs. No commrach work; a human painting, garish and devoid of depth.

'What's the matter?' Sada whispered in my ear.

I thought to ask her about the painting but stopped myself.

'Nothing,' I said. I seized her chin and kissed her. She received my mouth hungrily.

A knock at the door.

Sada stopped kissing me. She placed her fingers against my lips.

'I'd better answer that,' she said.

I moved her hand away. 'It can wait, my sweet.' In truth I was more unnerved than frustrated by the knock.

She stood up and slid by me, walked over to the carved double doors. Opening one of them slightly she put her head around the door. She whispered to someone then brought her head back and looked at me.

'Brother wants to play,' she said. Her face shone coy in the icy light.

She didn't wait for an answer. Arlo stepped through. He wore a black nightgown. He'd no mask, just the faintest smile.

'Greetings,' he said to me.

His sister took his hand and cupped it around her left breast.

He leaned in and kissed her temple.

Sada looked at me and grinned. 'We've always imagined ourselves twins.'

That's a popular fucking misconception, I almost said, quite repelled. What is it with people thinking twins desire one another? It's a fantasy rooted in their own narcissism, I'm sure.

But I wasn't a twin, not to these deviants. I wore no longboots. I was giving off entirely the wrong message: that I enjoyed both girls *and* boys.

Shit.

Sada prowled forward. She slinked behind me, draped her arms around my bare belly and rested her chin upon my shoulder.

My jaw shivered.

'You've the most sensual lips,' Arlo remarked. He undid his gown and let it drop to the floor. 'Might I beg you to use them, Nileen?'

His snake was minuscule but furiously hard, practically pointing at his nose. It twitched.

'Now *this* I want to see,' Sada said. She purred.

I felt her palms push down on my shoulders, urging me to kneel.

Well, this was awkward. He'd every right to expect me to please him. I was a guest in his house and, more to the point, my last name was supposedly Sil'Asu. Sil being one lower than Cal, lower in blood. If a Sil woman had turned down my overtures in my family's tower I'd have been offended. I now regretted that past attitude.

'Why so shy?' he said, and he stepped closer. He caressed his unimpressive length. 'It doesn't bite.'

'But it'll make *you* bark,' Sada assured me. She sniggered. She pressed her palms harder. 'Go on, silly.'

Options. The options. Draw my sword? Attractive, but then what? Fight my way out? Benadetta: I'd have to fight my way to our room, retrieve her. Not happening. Stupid idea. So was flat-out running.

Tell them I was a twin? He'd demur, embarrassed. Shamed. They'd want to know why I lied. And, yes, why *would* anyone lie? How could I begin to explain?

Fuck it. Suck it. I'd sucked one before, but that had been the cock of a girl-born-boy, not a man. Utterly different. And not to… completion. Penile completion was like cooked rat: I'd witnessed it a surprising amount, but I'd never permit it in my gob.

Arlo's glans glittered wetly.

'Actually…' I said. 'I pleasure men best using my… fingernails.'

'*Fingernails?*' he said.

'Thumb and forefinger?'

'Hmm. Show me.'

'Alright. Alright, I will.'

I inched my fingertips toward the object. It twitched and I jolted away.

'Maybe some gloves.' The words came out high-pitched. 'I'm my best with gloves…'

The Roshos laughed. Guffawed. Sada slapped my head playfully.

'We know who you are, Kyra!' she said. 'You silly!'

'Fuckers!' I barked. I darted to one side. I grasped my sword's hilt, awaited the glint of blades, or the boot shuffle of guards or the poison to take me or, well, something.

But no. They drank in my shock and guffawed even more.

'Shut up,' I said, comfortable now, if naught else, at our equal blood-standing. I pulled the straps of my trouservest back up over my shoulders. 'How do you know me? I've never met you fools.'

'Yes, you have,' Sada said, stepping closer and pressing herself against me. 'Back in Corso. The Shame Parade. And later in your chamber. You doused everyone in honey and spanked my poor bottom scarlet, recall?' She ran a finger down my spine. 'A most obliging host.'

Yes. She was one of the two girls I'd woken beside the morning after. We had all worn masks the night of the festival and, by the time we took them off, I was too far gone to remember anyone's face.

'How?' I said. 'I know your exile is half a show, but just walking around Corso as you please?'

'I was there on a mission of compassion,' Sada said. 'One of our family is permitted to accompany the family member selected to wear the abomination suit.'

'I wore the suit,' Arlo added. 'I've worn the suit every festival for half a decade now.'

I pictured the armoured pear with its repugnant mask carried aloft through the streets of Corso by the condemned. It had been Arlo inside, Arlo I had screamed and thrown glass at. But he was no scion of Rosho, he was its young patriarch.

'You *choose* to,' I said.

'Keeps me sharp as your rapier,' Arlo said. 'To be a people's altar of loathing? There's nothing so enriches a character.'

'He ravishes me like a panther afterward,' Sada said. She drew a finger down my abdomen and sighed. She looked up at me. 'I was startled when I saw you in Grand Gardens, delighted too. The great mystery answered: whatever happened to Kyra Cal'Adra?'

'If it's all the same to you, dear hosts—' I tried to hide my disdain, my fear. '—I'd like to remain overlooked. Disregarded even. Indeed, I aspire to achieve completely forgotten.'

'My,' Sada said, 'you really are out of the circle, aren't you? You're a gripping conversation piece back home. Hushed conversation.' She laid a kiss upon my collarbone. I slid my palm around the small of her back.

'Stories of your fate are multitudinous,' Arlo said as if recounting an epic myth, an effect tarnished by the fact his penis still saluted the ceiling. 'Some say you threw yourself off a cliff, others that you are a mercenary. The colonies claim you are a hidden merchant grown rich on Becken's trade. As for Cal'Adra, they say their fallen daughter births calibans in a whorehouse.' He looked me over. 'I'm guessing hidden merchant.'

'Mercenary,' I said, shrugging. 'Pays my way, good hours, interesting people.'

'You can afford a handmaid,' Arlo noted.

'Her? Oh, she's just some clap-ridden whore I've dolled up.' I smiled. 'Helps the cover story.'

Sada's hand ran through my hair. 'To the youth you've become a symbol, Kyra. A rebel, who fought for the love of a lowblood.'

I removed my hand from her back.

Sada clearly sensed danger in me. She took a half-step back and crossed her arms.

'You're proof life beyond the old ways is possible,' she said.

'And to the Jade colonies you're independence personified,' Arlo said. He checked his fingernails. 'We could use that.'

'Whatever do you mean?' I said.

Sada stepped away from me and over to Arlo. She put her back to him, mercifully hiding his skin-spear, and brought his arms around her belly.

'Tell her, brother,' she said. She closed her eyes and sighed.

'Why have you come to us?' he asked me. He kissed Sada's temple, lifted her skirts and then, with a sudden violence, shoved a finger into her grove.

She shuddered. Eyes screwed, mouth blissful.

He began to work her.

I passed my disgust off as a shameful hesitancy. 'I suppose I'm alone. I need my people. And… despite the differences between both our houses, I imagined Cal'Rosho would understand.'

Sada purred.

'We do,' Arlo said. 'We make a home for all those mistreated, all our disgraced. For the disgraced are too often visionaries. Those who see. What if I told you you could have all Corso, Kyra? Remodel its ways to your liking?'

'Mmm,' Sada said. 'The Jades too.'

What fantasies did this unsound clan entertain?

'Power, Kyra,' Arlo said. He squeaked as Sada threw her hand behind her rear and worked her wrist with vigour. 'Total… power. The commrach Isle and the human Main under one rule. One order.'

'I don't understand,' I replied.

'Our master…' Sada said.

'Our master,' Arlo repeated. He fingered her faster, stabbing with an increasingly audible violence.

'Who?' I said.

They ceased hand-fucking simultaneously. They gazed at me, faces naughty as children.

'Don't be coy,' Arlo chided. 'We all know perfectly well who.'

Sada giggled.

'You must commit yourself,' Arlo told me. 'You must promise. There is a cave on the shore of this reef. It runs under all the Main. He lives there.'

Caves. Like your father had said, Shen. He hadn't been so very mad after all.

'You could meet him tonight,' Sada said, her silliness gone. I sensed hidden intelligence in those eyes, greater than her brother's. Might it be she who truly led? 'Our master would love to meet you. He wants to meet all the fallen.' She licked her lips. Her rose perfume – *your* perfume, Shen – had blended with the sugary scent of her sex. My nostrils twitched.

This fever-madness was real. Someone waiting, in the darkness of a cave. I didn't like the idea. Time to get out of here.

'Well?' Arlo said.

I fluttered my lashes. 'First you have to promise me something.' I ran my hand down my neck, my chest and belly. 'I crave to watch you… "twins" mix thighs.' I reached out and put a finger under Sada's chin. 'Is that acceptable?'

She giggled and bit my finger playfully. 'Thought you'd never ask.'

'Sit there,' Arlo said. He pointed to a high-backed wooden seat in the corner of the room on the other side from the door.

I did so.

Arlo dragged his sister over to the other side of the bed, where I'd get a good view. He threw her face-down on the mattress so that her knees were on the floor.

Sada barked.

Arlo threw her skirts onto her back and then he thrust himself up and into her. He pumped at her with no build-up, no finesse.

'Say it,' Sada barked. 'Say it, slave.'

'Thank you,' Arlo said. He spanked her. 'Oh, great matriarch, thank you.' He yanked her hair back and she moaned.

They both kept looking at me like weekend actors, amateurs with nervous smiles. They'd have gone down laughably at a Corso tumult-orgy, in all senses.

I smiled back, ran a finger along my thigh, feigning lust. I'd slip out of here soon, grab Benadetta, head to the gardens and find Nail's rowing boat. But I couldn't just go; they kept looking up for my approval. A few minutes and they'd reach their last strokes, become insensate to the outside world. I knew the signs. I'd slip out then.

Something flicked my right ear.

I turned to look. Nothing there beside me. No one in the gloom.

Something on the floor by the chair leg: a paper dart.

I looked at the siblings. They smiled back. They couldn't have thrown it. Someone else in here. Some joke of theirs, a servant. I looked about again and still no one.

Could it be Benadetta? Blood, she'd have learned a few fucking things lurking in the shadows in this place.

Checking to make sure the lovers didn't notice, I picked up the dart. Bleached parchment, lines of dried ink upon it.

'Ooooh…' Sada moaned.

Their final act had begun. Time was of the essence.

I unravelled the dart. It was hard to discern the ink in the gloom, but it certainly wasn't writing. A drawing of some kind. I folded it flat and slipped it down my top. Time to leave.

Hot wetness sprayed my face and right forearm. *Damn it, Arlo.* I blinked and saw the fluid on my forearm was dark as wine. I looked over at the bed.

Arlo's torso had no head. Sada's neither. Blood, dark and glittering, was slowing from a jet to a burble from their freshly severed necks.

No jape, this. No jape.

I leapt up and fumbled for my sword's hilt. I almost tumbled. I righted myself, pulled out my sword and ran to the centre of the room, just before the bed.

A scratching sound. Coming from the darkness, the unseen edges of the chamber. I couldn't locate it, the scratching in one corner then the next. Everywhere.

Movement from the bed.

I span to see Arlo judder.

I gasped. I pointed my blade at him.

Just spasms. One, another, his lifeless hips acting out a final order. The force pushed a final tongue of blood from Sada's neck. The blood's glitter lent those unstained parts of the sheets a ghostly hue. Arlo slid sideways, out of Sada, tumbling onto the floor in front of me. His blood bloomed across the wooden floor, splattering my shoes and trousers. I leaped backwards.

I checked the space before the doors. No one.

I wouldn't run out. They'd want that. I retreated, step by step, backwards, toward the doors, sword raised. I could see no one. *Cruel*, I thought, *not to permit the Roshos their climax*. Stupid thought.

A black shape on the ceiling, above where I'd sat. I couldn't make sense of it in such darkness. It had not been there before. Man-size.

The shape stirred. Two thin limbs emerged, dragging the shape across the ceiling toward me.

I ran. Fumbled for the doorknob, threw the door open. Lamplight outside. I belted down the corridor, terrified my head would topple to the floor at any moment.

I turned a corner and collided with another black shape. I screamed and leaped back, fell on my arse.

'Grab her sword.'

Two guards. Commrach. I hadn't seen their like the entire evening. One of them had my rapier out of my hand before I could react. My heart was pounding. My breath swift as sparrows.

'Calm down,' one of them said.

'Blood on her,' the other said. 'All over.'

They held me and I struggled. I checked the ceiling for the black thing.

'What is this?' came another voice. I recognised it.

The bondsman. He still wore his silver mask, his genuine Final Countenance. He'd a rapier and dagger about his belt. I had not noticed them before. Their matching pommels were polished to an immaculate shine, like twin moons against his black jacket.

'Came from Sir Sada's room,' one of the guards told him. 'Sword drawn.'

The bondsman looked at my bloody shoes.

'Hold her,' he ordered, and he marched towards Sada's chamber door.

'Don't go in there!' I yelled. I looked at my two captors. 'We must *run*.'

Moments later the bondsman returned. He closed the double doors behind him, paused, and then screamed furiously through the slit of his mask. He composed himself.

'Dead,' he muttered. 'The pair of them.'

'What?' a guard said.

'She's murdered the archons!' the bondsman shouted.

The rest of us said nothing, all of us stunned for differing reasons.

'Take her belt,' the bondsman said. 'Take her down to the cellars.'

I didn't resist as they removed my sword belt.

'It's not me,' I said. 'Not me.' I was surprised he didn't just run me through.

He strode over and seized my face with a gloved hand. 'I was wrong about you, bondswoman,' he said, his irises green fire in the eyelets of his mask. 'You never betrayed your tower, did you? Cal'Adra sent their most loyal assassin.' He growled behind the mask. 'My respect grows with my rage.'

'I'm not a killer,' I protested. 'The killer is still at large, man.'

'There's an artist down in the cellar,' he said. 'I dare say she will glean the truth from you.'

By the Blood. The obelisk had its own torture artist. Now I wished the bondsman had just run me through.

The two guards gripped my elbows tighter and this time I struggled.

'Lock down?' one of them asked the bondsman.

'The masque continues,' he said after some hesitation. 'Arlo would have wished it that way. Too many of Becken's great down there.'

'Aye, sir.'

The bondsman looked at me. His silver mask seemed to leer. 'I have to see to matters,' he said. 'But I'll be sure to visit you in the agony salon.'

He hand-waved his guards and they dragged me down the corridor. After a little way I ceased struggling. They had me. For now.

'The artist is going to break you,' the guard on my left said. He was trying not to weep. 'Sada was a pure creature, a *perfect* flower.'

I'd never wanted to watch the 'whispered art', let alone be clay for it.

I didn't want Benadetta to be clay either. She'd no context. It would be hell for her. Her made-up hell made real. *No. Not Benadetta.*

We made our way down some stairs. I kept waiting for an opportunity, but none made themselves known. Things were desperate.

'I saw it,' I told them. 'A creature. I think.' I sounded mad. 'Please listen.'

They ignored me.

'Everyone here is in danger,' I said.

'Silence.'

We came out in a long wide corridor. Statues lined either side: marble, obsidian, glass, the subjects mostly human. It dawned on me they were from the chisel of Attawan the Perverse, that artist whose work had stimulated my pubescent fancies. These seven examples rippled with that living quality of a recent imbuing; likely they had been caressed into vibrancy mere hours before the had guests arrived. The oil lamps above twisted on their chains in an unfelt draught, lending each statue four shadows that stretched and interlocked with that of their neighbours'. My captors' boots echoed off the walls as we marched.

'Loooook…'

The air warped and shimmered. A statue stepped out before us.

We stopped. No, not a statue, a—

'Loooook…'

An open hand floated before our eyes. The most fascinating thing. We stared.

Wait. Why so fascinating? It was just someone's hand.

Benadetta's hand.

The two guards were still captivated, gawping at her palm. I broke free of their now limp holds and drew the sabre from the right guard's belt. I jabbed it in his sternum then pulled out and slashed the other guard's throat. Red warmth sprayed my bare shoulder. It raced and glittered down my arm.

The first guard dropped on his back. The second seized his throat, suddenly aware his life was through. He watched as I unhooked my hanging sword belt off his own. He staggered on to his knees then fell face first. Scarlet blossomed around him. It smelled fresh in my nostrils.

'Why kill them?' Benadetta said.

'It's the evening's theme,' I answered, putting on my belt. 'The Roshos are dead.'

'Your lechery breeds murder.'

'I didn't bloody kill them. Another did.' I did not want to think about that.

'Let's go now.'

'Wait.' I pointed at one of Attawan's statues. It was almost the spitting image of Sister Benadetta. That is, Sister Benadetta if she stood akimbo in nothing but a torc.

Benadetta stared aghast.

'I understand,' I told her. 'You were young, you wanted to express yourself, the money was good…'

She slapped the back of my head. 'Come along!'

We ran down three flights of stairs, then a corridor. She'd already tied her skirt up, the hem pulled up between her legs and tied about her hips into a bow, the result looking like a pair of pantaloons. Very proficient too, as if she'd had to run in a skirt several times in the past. Clearly she was no beginner at this kind of thing, not as much as I'd thought. Her calves were muscular beneath her stockings. Like the statue.

The music and chatter of the ball was audible as we reached the bottom of the stairs. We'd entered a hallway somewhere along the hall's edge.

'Which way now?' I said.

Benadetta hesitated. 'We n-n—'

'Yes?'

'Away from the music. Should lead to the back g-gar…'

'Gardens.'

She nodded. She put an arm around my shoulder and forced me to bend forwards.

'Everything fine?' inquired a male voice. A guest.

'Let it out, my lady,' Benadetta said to me. She looked up at him. 'A little worse for wear, my lord.'

Catching on, I pretended to heave.

'My lord,' Benadetta said. 'Might I be so impertinent as to ask you to find a servant?'

'Of course, girl.' I heard him walk away.

We gave it a moment and then we ran down the corridor, away from the ball.

The next hallway had a series of double doors along one side, all of them wide open. Fresh night air poured in.

I motioned to Benadetta to wait and I ran over to the nearest door. I popped my head around. The gardens. Hedges, more statues. A small wood lay beyond. Beyond that, Becken Bay's waters; I could smell sea air.

Nail and his rowing boat would be waiting, if he hadn't been captured. I couldn't imagine what the Roshos' torture artist might do if offered a caliban.

Dark out there – moonless, cloudy – as we'd hoped. The only light was that which poured out from the open doorways onto the patio before us.

'We'll have to run,' Benadetta said.

I checked the blood of various commrach that currently adorned me: it had dried, its luminescent glitter vanished. Good.

We counted to three and then belted across the patio. Fortune smiled: not a shout nor footfall.

Benadetta slowed.

'Come on,' I said.

'It's dark.'

'Fucking human eyes.' I took her hand. 'This way.'

She withdrew it. 'I'll adjust.'

We moved as fast as her eyes allowed us, hunched over, keeping low, moving from statue to statue, ornament to absurdly cut topiary.

Footsteps to our right.

I grabbed Benadetta by the waist and threw us both over a low hedge. She grunted as I fell atop her.

'You see them?' The bondsman's voice.

We lay in the dark. Belly to belly, cheek to cheek. I felt her face muscles tighten beside my own as she tried to silence her breath.

The footsteps began again. For a second they became louder, and then they faded.

I pushed myself up a little with my arms. Benadetta's eyes were like embers in the darkness. I became aware of her body's softness against mine. I grinned. Reassuringly, you understand.

She glanced away from me. She threw me off. I rolled over into wet grass.

'*Burn!*' she hissed.

I looked up to see a guard stood above us, clutching his face.

He hit the floor and rolled around. Blood, Sister Benadetta was useful to know.

Up on my feet, I grabbed her hand and pulled her up. She seemed weakened by her little conjuring, almost stunned. I pulled her along into the darkness of the trees. This tiny wood,

I realised, was a simulacrum of the hinterforest back on the Isle, all black pine and dwarf oak.

'Which way now?' I said. Everything was dark, even for me. I could hear water ahead, the brine on the air ever stronger, but it came from many directions. I didn't fancy skirting along the shore. We'd hardly the blessing of time.

Benadetta did not answer. She was panting. She gestured in a general forwards direction.

'Obliged,' I said.

Feet kicked through the undergrowth to our right: two figures running toward us.

One stopped and lifted their arms.

A crossbow. I dodged to my right and a bolt whistled past my elbow.

The other figure bore down upon me. Silver mask: the bondsman. Rapier drawn left-handed, a dagger in his right. Exquisite poise.

I drew my own blade in time to beat his away.

His dagger jabbed at me and I just parried it.

'Run!' I shouted to Benadetta. I couldn't rely on her mind-addling powers; she'd clearly worn herself out.

The bondsman came at me in a high panther stance, dagger overhead, and I met it willow style, blade held forward at shoulder height. Classic moves. Nostalgic, like I was back in the gymnasium. I eyed the other guard reloading her human-made crossbow. I sashayed left so as to force the bondsman in the way of his crony's aim.

The bondsman used that against me. Blizzard-style, right-hand willow, then low claw: attack, block, surprise. His moves pure textbook, his parry dagger making promises I could barely refuse.

'Surrender,' his festival mask said. He'd got me playing his game. Had dragged me right back to the Isle.

No. Not now. Now I was a pennyblade.

I swirled my rapier, drove it through a hole in his sword's hilt, held it in place.

The dagger in his right hand came at me. I grasped it, felt it slice the ball of my thumb. We struggled. Then I head-butted the prick and his nose crumpled. He fell on his arse.

My sword punctured the Final Countenance and slid into its wearer's mouth, pushing through neck bones and out the other side. His whine melted to a gurgle.

I yanked the sword out and lifted the bondsman up by his collar. A bolt flew into his back. He shuddered, puked gore.

I threw him aside. His accomplice stared at me, her crossbow empty, its bolt in her commander's back.

I grinned.

Thin metal appeared in the side of her neck. She clasped at it, did an embarrassed sort of death-jig, then collapsed.

Some feet away, Nail readied another throwing spike.

'Took your time,' I told him.

He didn't look at me. He looked past me, his face unreadable. I turned around.

Sister Benadetta leant against a tree, gazing down at her stomach. A crossbow bolt jutted out of it. The one I'd managed to dodge.

16

'Do you remember when we fell in this canal?' my brother said.

'You fell in. I jumped after you.'

'Thoughtful that,' he remarked, studying the black waters as if he'd located the actual spot. 'Though having a plan would have been especially so.'

We were arm in arm, walking along a canal tributary at night. Silver clouds lay on the surface, as did the half-moon that dyed them. Corso was silent, as it always was after Tumultsnight. A time for reflection, recuperation. Regret. Above us, the towers were black spears against the stars, their walls peppered with moontile light. Within each tower an archon plotting. And their family eager to act.

'We were laid out for two weeks,' Kyran said. 'Nearly died. Doubtless someone would have carved a verse about your heroism upon our shared tomb.'

'Doubtless.' I squeezed his arm. 'Though you'd have found it mawkish.'

'I'd already composed my eulogy by the time I was eight.'

'Didn't we all know it.' I spoke it with that admixture of venom and affection only Kyran could read. Blood, I'd miss that.

'I'll miss these walks,' he said. He knew my thoughts like his own. We were one, of course; we'd never been apart. 'But we knew these times would come. We're not free like the lowbloods.'

We stopped to watch two men carry a cargo palanquin between them on the other side of the water. They were gone soon enough.

'I'm scared,' I told him. 'For you, Ran-ran.'

I added no more. He knew. His married life would be in Darrad, in the tower of the Cal'Dains. And when he had sired two, perhaps three children, what then? I recalled how Grandmother had said I could kill Urse Cal'Dain after he'd sired a few babes with me. Kyran's life would similarly not matter. Perhaps not even to Grandmother; she had my loyalty now, my significance. His use was close to served.

Kyran faced me, threaded his fingers through mine. He lifted our hands and studied them.

'I can look after myself,' he said.

'You cannot.'

'Then I shall make friends who can. I've a knack.'

True. Almost all my friends were really his.

'Lady of the Jades,' he said. 'My sister.'

'I don't—'

'Nonsense. I can bore everyone shitless at important occasions, lift a glass and say, "Oh, do you know my sister? She's Lady of the Jades." You'd deny me that?'

I smiled. 'No.' It would be several months until I could sail to the Jades and begin my rule, such was the bureaucracy and etiquette of any undertaking overseen by every tower family in Corso and Darrad. None of any of that seemed real, not tonight.

'You love her, don't you?' he said.

'Shen?'

'No, the fucking chamberpot cleaner.'

I studied my right hand and his left. Clasped.

'It scares me, brother.' I swallowed. 'How much.'

'Well. Then I've never known you this brave.' He'd tried to say it matter-of-fact, but he sounded sad.

'You think me absurd,' I said.

'I think you luckier than you know.' He looked up, met my eyes. 'She's a good woman, whatever her birth. She'll look after you.' Guilt tinted his brow. 'I'm sorry. Had to ask. Had to know.'

Too serious, too heartfelt. I didn't want our final night to be like this.

I grinned. I play-growled, my eyes wide. I bit down, softly, upon his shoulder. Our sign, from childhood, that our fight was over for the time being.

He chuckled. He did the same.

We stayed like that for some time, rocking gently. Somewhere in the night a gull called out.

He let go with a suddenness that startled me. He'd a gleam in his eye.

'I've a game. Want to play, Ra-ra?'

I nodded.

'Remember the old wharf house? The one we'd hide in?'

'Yes.'

'Come on.'

He led me by the hand and we ran along the canal. The way was familiar to me still. It lay outside our tower's district, in the border streets between ourselves and Cal'Valtah.

Cal'Valtah. Relations had been strained with them ever since that pack of young males assaulted us on our journey to the

Aghast Play. Their noseless patriarch Ezral claimed the whole matter an accident, but no one in our district believed that true, not from tower's spire to sewer tavern. Lowblood bones had already snapped in border alley brawls. We were on dangerous ground here. But I was with my brother. Together, what did we have to fear?

The wharf-house stood the same as it ever had, its tarred planks skeletal, a broken and hollow fist.

'I can't recall the way in,' I said, stood before it. It stunk of damp, of rats' piss.

He led me around the side. There was a pile of slate, an accidental ramp that led into a slit in the wooden wall. He slipped through.

'Come on,' he whispered.

I faltered a moment, an odd trepidation taking me. I slipped through. The smell of fungus and wet wood filled my nostrils. And… blood. Why could I smell blood?

It was entirely black in there. I'd expected more light, what with the holes in the roof.

'I can't see,' I whispered.

'I thought of that.'

Kyran pulled a wallet from his jacket and opened it, revealing the moontile inside. His face became a silver mask in its light.

'Can I show you something?' he said.

'What could be worth seeing in here?'

'Quiet, Ra-ra. Just follow.'

I followed. I felt cobbles under my soles. I nearly slipped on a half-brick.

Then I saw her. Tied to a rotting pillar. A rag in her mouth.

Cousin Zymo. She stared at me, eyes wide, face bloody. Her stupid ram-horn hairstyle tangled and frayed.

'I had to be certain Shen was no idle game to you, sister,' Kyran said. 'That she was worth this risk.' He placed his palm on my shoulder. 'My parting gift to you. To the only woman I've ever loved.'

I drew a deep breath. But… yes, why not? Why ever not? Shen was my woman and Zymo had tried to kill her. She would never permit Shen to live. My woman. My love.

Kyran unsheathed a blade. He passed it to me.

I took it.

'We're in enemy territory,' Kyran announced, so that Zymo could hear. 'The boon of this is we can blame it on the Cal'Valtahs. The minus: we cannot permit her to scream. Cannot hear her… beg.'

Zymo shook her head. Pleading. Vile worm.

'This'll mean a street war,' I said to Kyran. 'Us and the Cal'Valtahs.'

He nodded. He leaned in, whispered: 'We can stop now if you want. Let her go, call it a loathsome trick. A warning.'

Zymo would only tattle to Grandmother. Bring Shen to attention.

'A street war will give me something to do when you're gone,' I told Kyran. 'Thank you, brother.'

'I'll miss you, Ra-ra.' His face was molten silver in the light of his moontile. A face identical to mine.

'I'll miss you, Ran-ran.'

We stared in each other's eyes. We smiled. Then I stepped toward my cousin, blade glinting in the half-light.

17

'Grab her legs, you fat shit!' I shouted at Shortleg.

He ran along the rickety oak pier toward us, his steps reverberating through my shoes.

Nail had Benadetta by her armpits, while I had his shirt pressed against her wound. Her screams as we'd got her up and out of the rowboat had drawn Shortleg from the old warehouse and into the night.

'Shit,' he said. A fair assessment.

'Stop gawping,' Nail bellowed.

Shortleg grabbed her legs and we carried her. Benadetta moaned as she was lifted, dry-heaved as we carried her.

'Minor wound,' I told her. I realised I'd said it in Commrach and repeated the phrase in Mainer.

Nail gave me a look.

I scowled at him.

I scanned the abandoned wharf for danger, for help. It had seemed a fine waypoint when Nail and I had rowed there, as unremarkable as it was unwatched, but the distance from the obelisk had clearly been an oversight. It had taken us an hour.

The rowboat's planking was veined with blood.

We pushed our way through the door of the warehouse and put her on a nearby table, atop our map of Becken. Stuffy in there: warmth, dust. Benadetta sighed.

'Can't she heal herself?' Shortleg said. He stroked his scalp, looked at her. 'C'mon, love, heal yourself eh?'

Benadetta tried to shake her head.

'Too weak,' I told Shortleg. Had using her powers to save me ensured she could not save herself?

Had I killed yet another?

'Right,' I said. 'We need a physician, or, or a Perfecti…' The church toward the city's centre: Benadetta had reported there only yesterday. 'I'll make a run for the church. Someone hold this.' I nodded at the shirt I was using to staunch her wound, the bolt's feathers sticking out from it.

'No,' Nail said. 'I'll go.'

'You've been rowing,' I said.

He shook his head. 'Still faster than you, inbred.'

The insult did not barb me. Not now.

He made for the door.

'Oi,' Shortleg called to him.

Nail looked back.

Shortleg pulled off his jacket and threw it at him.

Nail caught it, looked down at his own bare bloody torso and nodded thanks at Shortie. He burst out the door.

'Finish this,' Benadetta said. 'Finish…'

I met her eyes.

'We will,' I said. 'All of us. We'll have you fixed.'

'Yeah,' Shortleg added. But he was no actor.

Paler now, like milk. Her make-up, so strange upon her, was smeared. I'd only applied it hours ago.

'Keep awake,' I said.

She nodded and wept. A gut wound. Excruciating. Slow to kill.

My arms were shaking. They ached. Sweat stung my brow.

''Ere,' Shortleg said, 'I'll take that.' He moved beside me, ready to hold the wound.

I growled, shook my head.

'Yer daft slag,' he said, 'yer hands are weak.'

He put his big hands over mine and, slowly, firmly, I removed mine from under his.

My hands were red as roses, their fingers all stuck together like those on a statue. I wiped them on my trouservest. Pulled my fingers till they came apart.

'Cal'Adra,' Benadetta muttered. 'Thank you.'

'Kyra.' I wiped back her hair from her forehead, mucked up the beads of sweat with gore. I stroked her auburn locks.

She smiled, as if to say, *Use your first name? Hardly.*

I giggled at that and a sudden hollowness took me. I didn't want this sky-mad sadistic bitch to die. I didn't want that all-too-familiar moment; the rattle in the breath, eyes fading to dead jelly. Not here. Not her.

Perhaps a half hour passed. Perhaps minutes.

She whined. Her eyes rolled back.

I grabbed her hand, laced my fingers through hers.

'Stay awake,' I said. '*Stay.*'

Her eyes flickered open, as if she'd nearly nodded off before someone had announced lunch.

'Lips tingle,' she said.

'That happens,' I said. 'Nothing to—'

'Sinner,' she murmured.

'Hardly news.'

'Nuh… I'm sinner…'

I squeezed her hand. 'You're the most decent person I know.' Well, she wasn't up against much competition.

'I let them hurt you,' she said. 'Chair. Tried to stop… tried.'

'Doesn't matter now.' It didn't.

The whites of her eyes were darker than her skin.

'Devil in me,' she mumbled.

'Nonsense.'

She fixed me with a stare. 'Very mirror…'

'She alright?' Shortleg said. He sounded scared. A dreadful corroboration to my fears.

'M-mommee,' Benadetta said.

Shortleg sniffed. He'd seen this enough times. Devils, mirrors and mother. Classic babble. The end.

'Mommee…' Benadetta whispered. Her accent had changed. She sounded Ralbridean. 'D'nae let 'em take…'

I squeezed her fingers. I stroked her head. 'I won't.'

Her throat began to rattle. It was happening.

The door banged.

'Get that demon from her,' a woman's voice barked. 'We need purity.'

Hands grabbed my shoulders. I didn't struggle. The fight was gone.

Benadetta stared at the ceiling, her lips an open rouged ring.

A woman stood next to Shortleg. A woman in Benadetta's robes. She'd her hands on Benadetta.

I was stood outside. I must have been outside for some moments. I hadn't noticed. I only noticed now because it had begun to drizzle. Something flat against my stomach too, pressing and clammy. The parchment. The paper dart. I'd forgotten about that.

Nail stood before me. I suppose it was he who'd pulled me out of there. I looked in his eyes.

'I don't know why I'm bothered,' I said. 'Why am I... bothered?'

Nail's face blurred.

'Come here,' I heard him say.

The caliban took my hand and pressed some cloth against the knife wound there.

I let him.

18

'Need help?' I called to you.

'Quite fine,' you said. You ducked a punch.

We were stood in the wrecked square, a gaggle of House Cal'Adras, watching you fight this last Cal'Valtah fool.

You and he darted around one another, seeking weakness. The way of the world.

He fled through our circle and we let him.

'Very wise,' I shouted at him.

He stopped before a collapsed market stall and picked up a table leg.

Oooooh, we all exclaimed.

'You're disqualified,' I told him. 'Go home, piss-a-bed.'

'Cal'Valtah!' he yelled and ran at you.

We moved to overwhelm him.

'He's mine!' you barked.

You barged past the rest of us, ducked his first swing, caught his wrist with his second and booted his guts. You grabbed his throat and head-butted him.

He dropped.

We cheered.

You grinned at me, your forehead daubed a glittering red.

I strode over and kissed you long and hard. The others whooped.

I broke off and shouted, 'Raise the rabbit!'

They were ahead of me. A skinned rabbit with Cal'Valtah's twin dolphin sigil daubed upon it got hauled up on a rope from the third storey of someone's house.

We all cheered. A few gathered to dance beneath the rabbit. Kyran would have loved the scene.

I shook the thought off. I waved a hand to the crowd waiting in the street before the square.

Lowbloods of our district began pushing market stalls forward. The place was ours now, at least for the afternoon.

'Have no fear,' you called to one passing. 'We'll protect you. Kyra will protect.'

The lowblood nodded with vigour, likely performed. He pushed his stall around the broken shells we'd smashed up earlier.

Cal'Valtah's cronies had mainly picked themselves up and ran. The one you'd put down would scarper when he came to his senses. He'd no choice. Not one Cal'Valtah stood within the square; the rabbit had been raised.

'They'll not surrender,' you said. You rested your chin on my sore shoulder. 'They'll fight the last street.'

I watched a gull land on a toppled gooseberry stall. More would follow.

We'd been fighting unarmed these last two days, as city rules demanded. Now Cal'Adra had bruises all over and vengeance in its grasp. The murder of Zymo Cal'Adra, dearest cousin, could not be forgiven. Not until Cal'Valtah offered up one of its own family as reparation. Or, of course, if it voluntarily moved 'down house' to a lower prestige tower, though no one considered that likely.

'There'll be no fight on the last street,' I said, ruffling your already ruffled hair. 'That would mean a hundred daggers either side, not fists. Perhaps a hundred deaths.' I took a deep breath, tried not to imagine. 'No. One of Cal'Valtah will offer themselves for the good of their house.'

'You overestimate,' you asserted. 'Highbloods happily let inferiors perish.'

'You underestimate. If they lose the final street Cal'Valtah will be shamed into falling a tower.' I shook my head. 'There'll be a family good-for-nothing like Zymo they can sacrifice before that.'

'Let's hope so.' You kissed me again.

I certainly did. In fact, I hoped Grandmother would be working something out now, some way of saving face with no one dying. One that did not implicate me, or even our neighbours, as Zymo's killer.

You looked at me, sensing unease. You could always spot that.

I smiled back. Your eyes, Shen. Zymo would have plucked those eyes of life. And where she had failed she would have tried again. If a Cal'Valtah had to die so that you might live, so be it. And if a hundred of our own should perish in the final street, under unearned blades?

It would not happen. And yet... so be it.

The agony was I could confess naught to you, Shen. There'd been no secret between us until now. A barbed wound I hid from you.

For your own good. You had vomited and bloomed to fury over a dead pregnant human, the sort of incident that, at worst, might procure yawns from most of Corso. What, then, if you found yourself implicated in this folly of revenge? In the bloodshed it might soon procure? You would tell Grandmother, offer yourself up. By the Blood. If I hated a single part of you it was your decency.

'I love watching you brawl,' I said. 'Seeing you break someone. When I rule the colonies I'll have you pick a fight every day.'

'Him?' you said, nodding your head toward your fallen opponent. 'I'd broken him before I laid a fist. No truer art than teasing a mind to capitulation.' You wiped his blood from your forehead. 'I simply *adore* that.'

'So that's why you cleave to me, eh?'

'I don't believe you at all breakable.' You pressed in closer. 'That's why you've filled my life entire.'

We kissed. Pipe music echoed off the square.

'Do you think they actually did it?' you said.

I froze. Before I could answer footsteps approached. Slow Thezda, back to her more natural female self.

'Sir,' she said to me. 'I come from the tower.'

I let go of you. 'Yes?'

'A message from your brother. Urgent.'

She handed me a sealed letter.

'No news from the tower?' I asked. 'The Cal'Valtahs?'

Thezda shook her head. The sun flashed in her eye-mirrors.

No news. I didn't like that. I liked Kyran's letter scant better. I'd lost sleep over him. His precarious existence in Cal'Dain's tower in Darrad city, his sheer absence. A severed limb.

I felt as scared for you as I did him. Irrational, of course. And yet…

I opened the letter.

Sister,
Come to Darrad. Urgent. Everything depends.
K

No wit, no verve, none of his floral style. Like he'd barely had time to write.

I passed the letter to you. I watched a group of lowbloods manoeuvre a war drum into the square, a man-high cream disc with my family's glyph freshly painted upon it.

'Thezda,' I said, 'I'm placing you in charge here.'

'Sir.'

'What?' you said.

'You've seen the letter.'

'And he can wait for you,' you said. 'We've war here.'

I nodded to Thezda to be anywhere else. She knew that nod well enough and did as it demanded.

'He's my brother,' I told you.

You stared at me. 'Please, Kyra. Don't do this.'

'That's all there is to it.' I chewed my lip.

'Please. You're being impulsive.'

'I would not expect you to understand.'

'I understand we may face a lethal street fight in these next few days. And now I faintly comprehend that Kyra, beloved Cal'Adra, victor of the hinterforest—' She waved her hand at those dancing under the rabbit. '—hero of everyone here, is about to just vanish.'

'Cal'Valtah will break.'

They would, surely. These things never came down to the final street. But Kyran: his issue was indeterminate. Its mystery terrified me more than my present certainties. Had someone found out about Zymo? Used it against us? Or was it his own life? But, surely, he'd be safe until he sired. Neither would the Cal'Dain family use him as a lure to kill me. The Isle needed me to keep the colonies in check. Cal'Dain would never disobey all Isle.

Blood's mercy. It was about you, Shen. Somehow, I knew that. Kyran's words: minimal, allusive. He was scared someone might intercept and read it. Grandmother.

If only I could tell you. About Zymo. About the danger that surely hung over you. You were the last I could.

I pulled my hair back and tightened the knot. I was going.

'There's responsibility,' you said. 'To those who fight beside you. Who look up to you.'

'My brother fought beside me all my life.'

You took my hands in your own. 'I'm scared, Kyra,' you said. 'Scared to be alone in this city without you.' You squeezed tighter. 'And I'm terrified for you in *that* city. To we of the forests, Darrad is a city of coldest horror. The families there would happily eat your heart off a platter.'

Gently, I tried to break free of your grip. It only tightened.

'But they *cannot* because your heart is *mine*,' you insisted. 'As mine is yours.' Your glass-green stare bore into me. 'Isn't it?'

My lips spoke a silent *yes*. Strip the world away, banish every fool and villain and leave only us. Then plant me with kisses more numerous than our enemies' blades, whisper to me, each second a century in your embrace. A beautiful, simple life. *Yes*.

Our lips drew closer. Your rose perfume, your body's heat.

I stopped. *No truer art than teasing a mind to capitulation.* You had only just admitted as much. Were you working that art now? Ours was a selfish love. You were happy for it to be so.

'He needs me.' I pulled my hands from yours. 'You will see me soon enough, Shen.'

I turned and walked away.

You followed. 'Coward. Fucking coward. What about—'
You hesitated, snarled. 'What about the honour of our tower,
our Cal?'

I laughed, a single bitter, 'Ha!' I span to face you. I looked
around and muttered, 'So much for the great rebel. Easy to wish
the world to crumble when you suffer at the base of it. Different
when it cradles you, eh?'

'Fuck you.'

'You were a toady waiting to happen,' I said, suddenly furious.
'Like everyone el—'

You slapped me. People looked.

'Highblood fool,' you said, lip trembling. 'I'm thinking of our
future. If we're to be free we need to make *legend* of you.'

'You sound like my grandmother.' I winced. 'You all
sound like…'

Fuck her. I walked away. Fuck them all. Me and Kyran, that's
what mattered.

'My father's coming to Corso,' you called after me. 'We've made
amends now I'm a bondswoman. I wanted him to meet you.'

I didn't answer.

'You're a fucking idiot!' you yelled.

I did not reply. I kept walking.

I'm sorry I hurt you, Shen. I only ever meant to protect.

19

Shortleg smiled down at me as I climbed the tight staircase. He was stood upon the landing before the bedroom door, face plastered with one of his knowing smiles, though I'd no clue what he knew.

I passed him, said nothing, opened the door and entered.

A small attic bedroom, its ceiling a fierce triangle. Afternoon's light upon cream walls and black timber. The smell of soup.

'You're paid to take the bolt for me, pennyblade,' Benadetta said.

I had expected her to croak her words, yet she spoke them well enough. Still, her face was sickly pale and framed with lank and knotted auburn.

'A popular misconception of our trade,' I told her. I felt an odd sort of excitement in my bones, one I elected not to analyse. 'As you discovered.'

'Where is this place?' Benadetta asked.

My excitement lessened to a smoulder.

'Above an inn near the wharf,' I said. 'The Perfecti who saved you didn't want you moved too far.'

She frowned at that. For a moment I thought she'd sensed my lie. But no. And, indeed, it was no lie. We hadn't moved her *too* far. And we were near *a* wharf.

She looked uncomfortable. 'Who's been... seeing to me?'

I sat down on the end corner of her bed. 'Have no fear, Sister. The deeply devout barmaid took care of you.'

'I sup...pose you tested that devotion, Cal'Adra.'

'Oh no, Sister.' I hadn't. Hadn't seemed right somehow. Anyone will tell you I am a very thoughtful person. 'Shortleg and I have been away these last few days.'

He must have heard his name for he took that opportunity to walk in.

'Looking well, Sister,' he said. He leaned against the wall facing her.

She didn't reply.

'Where?' she asked me.

'Around,' I replied. I made a shrug that came off more flamboyant than I'd intended. I reached into my jacket pocket and produced the paper dart. 'I was given this, sort of, in Sada Rosho's chambers.' I passed it to her. 'Open it.'

Benadetta looked at me, then did so.

The ink lines I'd seen in the gloom of Sada's chambers had transpired to be a sketch: a cliff by a sea at night. The cliff was pockmarked with caves, all near-perfectly round, perhaps artificial. Lines jutted out from the cave mouths' circumferences, carvings in the grey rock. Like spikes. Spikes wreathing a circle. Identical to the symbol smeared on the ropefaces' foreheads, or on Kyran's old shirt.

'No fancy,' I told her. 'Drawn from life. By someone in a fishing boat most like. Sailing the coast.'

'This place exists?' she said.

'The locals reckon so,' Shortleg replied.

'What locals?' Benadetta said.

'Damn it, Shortleg,' I said.

'You'd have to tell her sooner or later,' he replied.

'We're not in Becken,' Benadetta stated flatly.

'No,' I said.

'Where are we?'

'Bargetown.'

'But that's… t-ten miles from…' She let a spasm pass. 'Send word to the Church. I'm—'

'I'd rather not,' I interrupted.

She stared at me with that… Benadetta stare, somehow startled but underwhelmed. I was surprised to find I'd missed it.

'As your second,' I said. 'I made—'

'You're not second anything,' Benadetta said.

'As your *de facto* second I made a command decision.'

'You d-did what?'

'The Perfecti who healed you said she'd send journeymen to carry you from the wharfhouse come the crack of dawn. That the mission was over, that we scum should scarper and that you would be removed from your current duties. That we had all brought the Church into disrepute. So, given this information, I thought about what your decision would be. It was imperative we acted upon your likely wishes, Sister, and, after much reflection and a group vote we elected to—'

'Kidnap you,' Nail said, entering the room.

Benadetta stared at him. Then she glared at me.

I tutted. 'Pennyblades, eh?'

'Pilgrim give me strength…' the Sister muttered.

'You mustn't strain yourself,' I said.

'Why bother? I've hired the very best for that.' She glared at me again. 'Patently.'

Shortleg stepped forward. 'Sister please—'

'Silence.'

He obeyed. I was in no rush to speak either.

'You've ru…ined any chance we possessed to root out this conspiracy,' she told us all. 'Without the blessing of the Church we are but rabble. We stand out…side the Pilgrim's light. Indeed, a Perfecti without the Church is merely a witch.'

'You're still a Perfecti,' I remarked. 'We're kidnapping you, remember? I've even got Nail writing an extortion note. He's surprisingly eloquent.'

'Extortion without it is mere blackmail,' Nail said.

I waved a finger at Benadetta. 'You've a choice, Sister: return to the Church and spend the rest of your days frightening children about that underworld of fire and turds and what-have-you or… or do some actual *good*. End this rope-faced madness, this plot or whatever it is.' Her frown maddened me. 'Sometimes you have to throw it all away, Sister. Cast off your trappings and stand *free*.'

She gave me a look both acidic and pitiful. 'Look where it's got *you*.'

I stood up. I clenched my fists. Insufferable woman.

'Ladies, ladies,' Shortleg said. 'I won't see you fight.'

'You've pictured it enough,' I muttered.

'Sister,' Shortleg said to Benadetta. 'You know I don't know shit. But the holy books and that, they've always said no one knows how God works. Dun't they? We wouldn't have come this far if God hadn't wished it.' He gulped. 'We gonna let him down now?'

'Presumption, you fool,' Benadetta said.

'Yeah, a fool.' He snapped the words. 'Bastard too. Killed men who'd done me no wrong for coin. Betrayed every twat, left me wife.' He shook his head. 'And, yes, now I'm bloody presuming. Bet on it. Presuming to avenge Ned and Illsa, presuming to meet the devil eye to eye.' He'd a look I'd never seen before, perhaps one that had perished alongside his comrades a decade past. 'Presuming to do some *good*. Shitting hell, how did I end up doing your job?'

Benadetta seemed to shrink. For a moment I thought she'd pass out.

Instead, she looked at me. 'And you?'

I turned my face to the small window above. Closed my eyes and felt the sun upon my skin.

'I thought I saw a monster crawling upon the ceiling of the Roshos,' I said. 'I ran, terrified. Now… I rather think that monster a man, one using trickery and fear of the unknown to break my will. No devil. A man. With no doubt paltry aims.' I chuckled. 'You know I think you both idiots, yes?' I nodded at both her and Shortleg. 'What you deem ineffable I call our own ignorance. For this world is explicable from sky to sea's chasm. Even that magic in your bones, Sister. Thank no god for it; it rises from your species like the imbuing rises from mine, ever-sharpening from nature's pressure as a blade on the whetstone. No. A man, this fiend. A mere man. When this is over, you'll see I'm right.'

'There's your reason?' Benadetta said. 'Intellectual vanity?'

'Oh, I don't expect you to ever understand, sky-fool.' I turned from the window and looked at her. 'As I will never understand you. But I've no interest in highlighting your delusions. I'm not cruel. This "devil" presumes to know me. To control me.' I shook my head, never breaking contact from her eyes. 'Kyra Cal'Adra is no pawn.'

Benadetta leaned back into her pillow.

Nail scratched his chin. 'For what it's worth, I just find you idiots diverting.'

Benadetta gave Nail a look. Then she gave us all a look.

'I cannot condone any of this,' she pronounced.

We three pennyblades looked at one another. It was easier than meeting her stare.

'You wretches are a compost heap of lies, arrogance, rapaciousness and vanity. So much so…' She sighed. 'It would be a sin if I did not keep an eye on you.'

20

The southern winds carry one swiftly upriver to ancient Darrad, the rivers back home swifter. I arrived in Darrad at dawn, two nights after leaving you, Shen. A night more and our street fight would be decided, one way or another.

I kept my eyes low as I paced the dry and shadowed streets, calves straining with the constant incline. Darrad city sits on a hill surrounded by five mountains. Its thirty-two towers are twelve of malachite, ten of marble, then ten pewter: the 'Shining Ten', wonder of all Isle. On a bright day, as upon my arrival, the city's silver heart can blind you. *Eyes low, steady pace,* I kept reminding myself. My nerves wanted me to break into a full-tilt dash all the way to the sixth tower.

But to run would be to break the peace, to draw even more attention than I was already getting. I wore the black attire of my city amid so many thousands in white and cream. The only reason I had not been arraigned or set upon was the fact I'd a rapier and other trappings of the higher castes. I found myself wishing I'd taken an honour guard. But not you, Shen, no matter how much that would have buoyed me. My brother was in danger here, I knew it, and I would not endanger the only other person I loved along with him.

Street after street, curling and rising toward the Shining Ten. Where Corso had damp, here was dust. Already a crust of it rimmed my nostrils and collected at the edges of my mouth. I had to keep spitting it out on to the sand. I passed a lowblood with no nose or lips: a common punishment. Minutes earlier I had seen two women chained to a glass pillar with their eyelids and mouths stitched. Darrad was not as progressive as Corso.

In Corso the streets and buildings surrounding the towers were built in a similar style and of the same materials, whether they were a public amenity or a low family's tenement. Even the humblest building was of a fair quality. Here things were different. I passed wattle and daub constructions that were practically huts, sagging rows of cracked brick and dribbling mortar. As I crossed from the marble tower enclaves into the gleaming pewter heart of the city, the common streets only became worse. I'd visited Darrad twice before, but I'd never really noticed the phenomenon. The difference was that I had been carried back then. Now I strode. Fast as I might.

I was approaching the sixth tower, home of Cal'Dain. I looked up and had to squint: the tower's silver skin reflected the blue of the sky, the dazzle of the sun. Another square and then another street and I would be there. *Wait for me, brother,* I thought. *I'm coming.*

'Hey there,' a female voice called.

I kept walking.

'Corso,' she called. 'Hoy there, Corso.'

I kept walking but glanced over. A young highblood, leaning against a giant sculpture of the Final Countenance with a fountain for a mouth.

I pretended not to hear, blatantly so, given the situation. Everyone else in the square was almost entirely silent. But I couldn't stop. Couldn't dally.

'I wanted to congratulate you on Corso's victory,' she shouted. 'You rude shit.' Pause. 'Come here, you rude shit!'

An apple flew past my head. When I heard a sabre unsheathe and footsteps belting across sand I took off across the square. I saw an alley to my left, all pigeon shit and trash, and darted down it. I hoped she would not lower herself to follow me.

I was right. 'Coward!' she shouted. 'Corso piss-a-bed!'

It vexed me she thought herself the winner. I had met her bragging type before, many times, and had always proved the better sword. I promised myself I'd fume later. Nothing mattered but getting to my Ran-ran.

I turned a corner then burst from the cool of the alley into the hot and dusty street.

At the gates of the sixth tower the guards saw me through. I needed little explanation. My clothes were Corso-black, travel-worn, my face my brother's.

The entrance hall was cool and dark, circular and as vast as that of my family's tower. No statues though. Perhaps the Cal'Dains considered themselves too tasteful. A lone figure, clad in white, stood upon the chequered floor.

'Welcome,' she said. Ousile, Kyran's new wife. Dead Urse's sister.

I stepped closer. I had to stroke my hair back from my eyes; I'd let it grow longer these last few months.

'Where's my brother?'

'He's fine,' Ousile said. 'He'll be here.'

She wore the chain matrimonial. I'd seen it put on her at the wedding back in Corso. Condemned to desire a man who would never want her. And desire him alone.

'Wine?' she said. She appeared neither sad nor angry with her fate. Did the chain take away even the dignity of those emotions toward it? So blissfully blithe. It unnerved me, for I, in killing Urse, had arguably put it on her. I shook the thought away. I had to focus on Kyran.

'Where is he?' I looked about, aware of how exposed I was. The hall was too empty, too minimal. 'He demanded I come.'

She pouted. 'There's no rush.'

'I'm compelled to disagree.'

She looked at me like I'd raised my fist.

'I've had to leave some vital matters,' I said. 'Tell me what's happening here.'

'Oh.' She looked to the great stairs at the end of the hall. 'Here's my beloved.'

Kyran wore a white summersuit, the colours of Darrad. He stood, quite relaxed, upon the stairs. He beckoned me to him.

I looked back at Ousile and she smiled. *Beloved.* I almost believed her.

I met him on the stairs. There was a sanity in Kyran's smile I did not realise I had missed. He held his arms wide. We embraced. I could smell his scent beneath Darrad's perfumes.

'Ran-ran,' I whispered.

'Ra-ra...'

I pulled my head back from him.

'Why am I here?'

He took a deep breath, then he smiled. 'The oldest question, that.'

I gave him a look.

'Yes,' he said. 'The matter.' He looked about the hall behind me. 'There's a pleasant balcony a floor or so above. Let us discuss it there.'

'Very well.'

He paused again, put a hand on my shoulder. 'So good to see you.'

I followed him up the stairs. The frescoes lining the walls were the negative of our tower's: white line figures upon black. For the first time I felt in danger, that my brother might have planned something. Awful, that I might think that.

The balcony was pleasant, I suppose. All pewter and opal and a view of the mountains. The air was fresh up there, rarer than jewels in any city.

'They quite spoil me,' Kyran said. He leant his back against the balcony rail. 'You needn't worry; I've settled in.'

'I'm pleased.'

'And I love her.' He snorted. 'I really think I do. I didn't think it would be possible to love someone I didn't desire. And when season comes, we should both be piqued enough to, well…' He wiped his chin. 'Perhaps some wine? Hmm? Like old—'

'Kyran,' I said. 'You're prevaricating.'

'I've barely started,' he muttered.

'What's going on? What's wrong with you? I've travelled two nights, I've…' I trailed off, but my eyes were fixed upon him.

He looked down. 'I'm meant to soothe you, you see. Grandmother says I'm good at that.'

Fear shook me. 'I don't understand.'

'I've no reason to invite you here. Save… inviting you here.'

'What?'

'The vital thing is you're not in Corso,' he said.

Realisation. A dread shadow crossing the sun of all I held true. 'Shen?'

He nodded. 'Best you were here. Best… She said I'd console you.' He began to sob. 'Blood, I'm so fucking *scared* of her…'

Grandmother. Shen. By the Blood.

'How *could* you?' I hissed. The sound didn't seem to come from me, but some snake inside. The balcony should have cracked beneath my feet, crumbled like my trust, my life. I stood on nothing.

'Because you cheated me,' he hissed. He scowled with wet and reddening eyes. 'You know you did. I was her *favourite*. As favourite as that old beast would permit. Now you're Lady of the Jades and I'm put out to stud.' He wiped away tears with his Darrad-white sleeve.

'You can't lie to me,' he said. He was right. 'I try to crawl back up, but she only gets me to push and polish you. She had me end cousin Zymo because she threw poison your way, but it was me who gave you the pleasure of doing it.' He winced. 'Because I still love you, Kyra. I always will.'

I remembered Zymo's eyes that night in the ruined wharfhouse. Wide, pleading with me. Kyran had gagged her. To stop her calling for help, he claimed. But doubtless Grandmother wouldn't have missed the chance to lecture Zymo before sending her to her death. Doubtless it had been her idea to leave Zymo's bloody corpse on Cal'Valtah land too, make the idiot useful for once.

'Shen is to be dealt with,' Kyran said, and I shuddered. 'You'll be perfect then. Your final weakness gone.'

I seized his head and shook it. 'You fucking—'

'Me?' he said, cutting me off. 'I never asked for it to happen. My only fucking duty is to soften the blow. To make you "see sense".'

You betrayed me, I tried to say. I couldn't form the words.

'Nothing matters,' he said, almost snarling. He pushed me away. 'We're all just conduits, remember? The Blood just passes

through us like piss through the sewer and none of us matter.'
He sank down onto his rear, his back still against the railing.
'I'm *tired*, Ra-ra. Tired of these games upon games.' He closed
his eyes. 'And sick of every mask.'

He tore open his collar, exposed his throat and heart.

I drew my rapier. The rage, Blood, the rage. I could see Kyran
now, truly see him. Spoiled. Weak. A pretence, even to himself.
He had done nothing, *nothing*, to protect you, Shen.

He flinched to hear me step forward. His eyelids twitched
but kept screwed tight.

I slashed his left cheek.

He seized his face and looked up at me.

'Let a slice be the last word,' I told him. He had told Urse
Cal'Dain as much back in the hunting gardens. That summer
morning a lifetime ago.

I wiped my eyes but not my blade. I sheathed and, turning
away, left a dead man sobbing on his pewter balcony.

21

I pointed my rapier in the innkeep's mottled face.

'Forgive my candour,' I said.

He stood in the noiseless highway inn's doorway, the light from inside making a half-silhouette of his figure. He stared at the rapier's point.

'What's that?' he asked.

'*What?*' I said. 'A bloody sword.'

Trepidation caught flame in his wet eyes. 'Where's its edge?'

'Dun't have an edge,' Shortleg said beside me. 'All about the point. Like a big needle, right?'

'Right,' the innkeep said. He gulped.

'It *does* have an edge,' I said to them both. 'Eight inches' worth either side of the point, see?' I indicated. 'The *emphasis* is on the point, granted, but it's not without edge. Common misconception.'

'Yer couldn't slice an arm off or owt,' Shortleg countered.

'Maybe I don't *want* to slice arms off. You humans and your fucking dismemberment.'

'Nowt wrong with a big chopper,' Shortleg said. He chuckled and grabbed his crotch.

'Oh, yes, very mature.'

The innkeep gulped again. 'You're an *elf*?'

'Fuck's sake,' I muttered.

'Commrach,' Shortleg corrected him.

'Look,' I said, 'could we all agree that this is a sword? If only in principle?'

'Yeah,' the innkeep said. He held his blotchy hands up. He took a deep breath. 'So… you, er, you want letting in?'

'Ah, there's no rush,' I said. 'Our colleague's right behind you.'

The innkeep looked over his shoulder to see Nail levelling a throwing spike at him.

'Anyone back there?' Shortleg said to Nail.

'Silent as the grave,' Nail said.

'Business shit then?' Shortleg said to the innkeep.

'I guess,' he replied.

'C'mon, let's all have a pint, eh?' Shortleg said and he smiled.

The men made their way to the bar.

I looked back and motioned to Benadetta. She was stood by the road, thirty feet away, a grey ghost in the twilight. Desolate moorland stretched behind her.

She nodded and began to walk forward, almost hobbling. Not for the first time I felt uneasy about her wound.

The innkeep, already behind the bar and pouring ale for Shortleg, looked at Benadetta's vestments with surprise.

'She'll have whisky,' I told him.

'A joke,' Benadetta said. 'I apologise for our behaviour, sir. We've h-had to take extreme measures. But, as you see, we are of the Church. You're quite… safe.'

Aside from his inability to recognise offensive weapons, I thought. Unbelievable.

Nail closed the window at the end of the lounge. The one he'd just climbed through.

'Pour yourself one, pal,' Shortleg told the innkeep. 'Join us over there.' He pointed at a nearby table.

'Furry muff,' the innkeep said.

'What?' Shortleg's brow wrinkled. 'Oh, I get it. Nice one, pal. Like it.'

We were all sat down. The innkeep brought our drinks over and sat beside us.

'You here about the caves, Sister?' he said.

'Yes,' she replied.

'And the devils?'

'If devils there be.'

'There are.'

He frowned, his skin ailment rendering it ghastly in the half-light.

'They look through the windows. One time anyway. S'why I sent my wife and kids to Becken.' He twisted his tankard around in thought. 'Why I answered the door. You're the first people I've seen in weeks.'

'What did they look like?' Benadetta asked.

'Rope for faces.'

'Masks,' I said.

'Still devils,' the innkeep said. 'Devils wear masks.'

I sighed. I sipped. Quality ale. Knew it had to exist somewhere.

'Did they speak to you?' Benadetta said to him.

'No, Sister. Didn't try to break in either. Just… wanted to scare us. So far.' He took a big gulp of his beer. 'Fiends have been scaring folk all along the coastal highway. No one travels along here now.'

'Mr Nail,' Benadetta said. 'Let us pay this man for his beverages and board tonight.'

Nail pulled out a purse and poured out ten pips onto the table. Enough for a week.

The innkeep took them. 'Obliged.'

'We shall stay here tonight before visiting the caves,' Benadetta declared. 'We'll take it in turns to watch.'

'Just you four?' the innkeep said. 'Sister, I—'

Benadetta held up her hand. 'Mere reconnaissance. When we've enough information the Church shall—'

'Sister,' the innkeep said, interrupting her, 'even if you do make it back, it's me who has to sit here and wait for you to bring help. They'll have seen me letting you in. They see everything. I—'

He stopped. He winced. He covered his face.

A dull sound, far off, coming under the sea's wind. Soft booming, slow and repetitive.

'What the fuck's that?' Shortleg said. He fingered his dagger's pommel.

'The caves,' the innkeep said. 'Comes from there. Has for months.'

'That's two miles away,' Benadetta said.

'Aye.' He finished his ale in one go.

No one said anything. The booming sound continued. Benadetta made the sign of the Pilgrim. The innkeep rested his face in blotchy hands. Shortleg looked toward the window as if something might climb through.

I placed my hand on the finger ring of my hilt. A thought crossed my mind.

'The hilt,' I said.

'Yer what?' Shortleg replied.

'You'd think people'd know it was a sword from the hilt.'
I shook it. 'See?'

'Give over, yer daft moo.' He sipped his ale.

22

I ran.

    I belted through the streets of Corso, fearful as a hare. I knocked over vendors, shoppers, nobles. I ignored their curses and threats. I didn't stop. I'd hair in my eyes, sweat. My world was a blur, my temples pounding. I had not slept. So filthy.

    But nothing mattered. I couldn't even allow myself to think of you, Shen. Because then I'd think how long I'd been gone, how running was mere folly, how I always, *always*, should have listened to you, how by now...

    I ran.

23

We were stood upon the clifftops, two miles from the inn. The morning was bright and snake-clouded, as we say on the Isle. Stretched and patchy, driven on by the Bound Sea's winds. The sun baked my hair, but the heat was cut through by the breeze's salty cold. Its sharpness filled my nostrils, my chest.

'Dun't look scary,' Shortleg said, looking at the grassy rise before the cliff's drop.

'The scary stuff is below,' I said. 'This is… the roof of the scary.'

'According to the innkeep there should be a way down from here,' Benadetta mentioned. 'Who shall look?'

Only the breeze spoke.

Slowly, Nail lifted a hand.

Seeing that, I did likewise.

'Good,' Benadetta said. 'You two are the nimb…lest after all. Find a way in then signal to us.'

'Of course,' I said.

Nail looked at me. Bemused. Suspicious.

We made our way to the cliff's edge. He stopped a few feet short of it and let me go ahead. I looked over the edge.

A grassy path, of sorts, led down to what seemed to be a cave opening. We were too at a slant with it to truly tell. The path was narrow, of rough grey rock, yet safe enough.

I nodded to Nail. 'You first.'

He looked at me a moment. 'Fine.'

We made our way down, faces to the cliff wall, holding on to tufts of dry, sharp grass.

'You should not have hit her,' I said.

Nail stopped.

'Esme,' I said. 'You shouldn't have hit Esme.'

'The whore back in Hoxham?' He paused. I could see his muscles tense, his poise become ready. 'She's your lover?'

I let the question hang.

He stared at the grass before him, dancing in the wind.

'What happens now?' he said. His long coat had opened in the wind a little and his belt of sharpened nails was visible to me.

'I'm not going to kill you and make it look an accident,' I said. 'However tempting. Esme's an acquaintance, not a lover.' I leaned my head toward him. 'But you should not have hit her.'

'You finally moralise,' he observed. 'Over a precipice.'

'I'll do more than that, halfbreed.' I chewed my lip. 'Listen. There's a burnt barn, two miles west of Tettleby. You cannot miss it.'

He looked at me.

'In the west corner is buried six hundred pip,' I said. 'If only you make it out of here, it's yours. And if only you and Shortleg make it out of here, get there before he does.'

Nail nodded. He returned to the task of edging along and down the path. Then he stopped again.

'You give me enough reason to throw you off the cliff, inbred,' he said. 'You know that right?'

'Will you?'

He thought about this. 'You'll know when I know.'

We carried on. The waves lashed the rocks far below. We'd considered approaching by boat but those ropeface bastards would surely see us coming. They expected us, after all, had invited us with their sketch of this place. Four fools, drawn here inexorably by our separate and singular pasts.

'Caliban,' I said. 'I don't think I believe the excuse you gave for coming here.'

'Do people ever stop speaking back on your isle?' he said back to me. 'Or is there some kind of dignity tax? I'm genuinely interested.'

'You said you're along merely to laugh at us,' I persevered. 'I say bollocks.'

'You'll be screaming it when I push you over,' he said. 'Leave me be.'

'Nail.'

'I don't like bullies,' he said, the words flying faster than his throwing spikes. 'People should be decent. Happy now?'

I left it at that. I was surprised I had gleaned so much.

Far ahead, the cliff face curved. I spied distant cave mouths, carved spikes around their edges. The symbol of our enemy. By the Blood.

Nail reached the edge of the cave's mouth. He pulled out a throwing spike then leaned to his right, looking directly into it. He stayed like that a while and I half-expected him to fall backwards over the cliff with an arrow in his chest.

He withdrew, placed his spike back in his belt. He turned his head to me and nodded. In the sea's winds his blond hair flickered like a hearth.

We entered the cave's mouth. Its grey stone was smooth as a riverbed from floor to ceiling.

A tunnel leaning downward. I looked about the walls. The triangular spikes that we'd seen on the other caves, upon the parchment sketch and, abstractly, upon the ringed symbol on the ropefaces' foreheads, transpired to be linear grooves that led on down the tunnel and out of our vision. There were six: one on the ceiling, one on the floor, two on either of the walls. All equidistant to one another. They showed no sign of erosion, were sharply cut in contrast to the smoothness of the walls. No dirt had collected in the bottom of the floor's groove.

'Strange,' Nail said.

'What?'

'No gulls. No nests. No shit.' He drew a long breath. 'No life.'

He was right. The cave had accrued nothing; no detritus, no marks, no erosion. As if it lay outside this world's flow of time.

'I'll get the others,' I said. I turned.

'Inbred,' Nail said behind me. 'I lied.'

I span around, drew my parry dagger.

He'd no spike in hand. Instead, he chuckled. The first time I'd heard him.

'Those two quim-lickers,' he said. 'They never existed. No one was whipped. It's not in Sister Benadetta to do that.'

'Why… tell me now?'

He nodded up at the cliff top. 'You two negate one another.' He half-smiled. 'It's rather sweet.'

'Absurd.'

I turned away once more, wishing I'd pushed him off the cliff.

24

The guards saluted when they saw me. I belted up the stairs into Cal'Adra tower's great hall.

Busy in there, as usual. Folk of every caste intent upon bureaucracy, petitioning and all things unctuous. I thought to shout, demand the whole hall answer, but that would call down confusion, alarm, people who might stop me. I stepped behind one of the many pewter statues and looked around.

Slow Thezda. She was talking to some lowblood plaintiff, softly denying their pleading gestures. She'd left her monocles on in the gloom. An oversight, that; her vision would be poor.

I seized Thezda by the back of her neck, grabbed her hilt before she could reach for it.

'Too slow,' I said. I drew her parry knife and held it to her throat.

The lowblood she'd been speaking to looked at me in horror. I ignored him.

'Where is she?' I hissed in Thezda's ear. 'Where's Shen?'

Thezda shook her head. I could hear onlookers gasp, mutter. None called out. They knew who I was.

'Grandmother,' I said.

'Her chambers,' Thezda said. 'She has… guests.'

She'd have one more. I threw Thezda and her knife across the floor and made a dead run for the stairs.

Twenty fucking flights. There was a basket lift, of course, but too slow, too likely to be stopped. I bounded past frescoes of my ancestors' great deeds, my heart pounding, my lungs on fire. Hair stuck to my sweating face. I didn't stop when I reached the top, wouldn't allow myself. Two guards stood in the corridor before Grandmother's door.

'Let me through,' I wheezed. I drew my rapier.

'Sir, please,' said the first. She drew her own blade, as did the second.

I yelled, lunged. The guards did not return attack but gave defence their all. I beat my blade against theirs, artless and full of fury.

'Enough.' Grandmother's voice.

I stopped, turned to see her leaning through the doorway, one brass-taloned hand upon the half-opened door.

'Where is she?' I said. I didn't shout. I wouldn't give Grandmother the satisfaction.

'Sheathe your blade.'

I held, deliberated.

'Sheathe, girl. Or you'll never see her again.'

I acquiesced, my arms shaking.

'You look dreadful,' Grandmother said. 'Come.'

I nodded at the two guards. Instinct that; one always did after a show duel. I followed Grandmother into her guest chamber.

The same as always: stuffed panther heads on the walls, dancing carvings, the balcony with its view of the next tower. The two guest chairs with their backs to me.

Someone was sat in the right one, the one I had sat in the day we first talked, Shen. Their hair was a silhouette before the balcony's sunlight, but it was high, in a stately bun.

They stood up.

You, Shen. Alive…

A glint of silver. A chain about your neck.

The chain matrimonial.

My hand grasped my mouth. I fell back against the door.

Robes of matrimony, hair high and styled. Your face so calm, so unreadable.

'Peace has been brokered,' Grandmother said. 'In exchange for not sacrificing a family member, Cal'Valtah pledge to support our call for an Isle army. To this end, a number of loyal bondsfolk from both towers have been bound by marriage.'

I looked to you, but everything about you save youth resembled Grandmother.

'Why her?' I winced. 'Why *her*?'

'Urse Cal'Dain,' Grandmother said. 'You both killed him, or so your brother admits. Self-defence, arguably, but the legality on either side is murky and against all current interests. The Cal'Valtahs – as I told you – are the Cal'Dains' henchmen in this city. Now we three families are bound into a single faction of common interest.' She paused, a serenity of sorts crossing her expression, the tranquillity of someone completing a vast labour. There were armies in her eyes, and battle standards and alliances and always, always the next move up. How much had Grandmother planned? How much improvised? Did she even know? Her composure returned. 'But Urse's death could not be forgiven. He was Cal'Dain's beloved child. You put pain in them, girl. They demanded pain in you.' She shrugged. 'An eccentric clause, but I suppose that's Darrad for you.'

Ousile Cal'Dain. How innocent she had seemed when I had strode into her tower, how pleasant and smiling. Yet she had already known me her brother's killer, had known my own brother already broken and traitorous. She was sharper and crueller and better than me. So was Kyran. So was Ezral Cal'Valtah, so was Grandmother. They all were. Everyone.

'Kyra,' you said. 'What I have done has saved many lives. How many now breathe because I wear this—'

I shrieked, an animal's shriek to keep you at bay. I slapped myself across the temple. I growled.

'Kyra,' you tried again after an insufferable pause. 'I'm sorry for how you must feel. And, yes, I feel nothing for you here and now, nothing romantic. But we're friends, yes? We were always that. It is an honour to be so.'

'She's of our faction now,' Grandmother remarked, filling your silence. 'A faction that shall ever rise. Rejoice, child. Shen has bettered herself and her family in one stroke.'

'Please,' you said. You stepped toward me and raised your hands. They wore brass talons.

I scuttled back and my shoulder blades hit the door.

'Stay away from me,' I said, almost wailing. 'Stay…'

Nothing in your eyes. Nothing that was mine. Not one secret.

'I didn't want to,' you said. 'But the peace's logic was unassailable. The matriarch explained it to me.' You nodded. 'And when Father heard the plan he *embraced* me, *encouraged* me. I never thought Father would love me again, Kyra. Not ever.' Your eyes examined my face for the slightest softening. They found none. 'And I want a child, Kyra.' You looked down. 'You always knew I did.'

'You didn't…' I felt weak, dizzy. 'Didn't even *struggle*?'

'I had to strip down my heart before I allowed this chain around my neck. I thought about us, our impossible future.

Remember our talk on the walls of the observatory? You wanted the Jades more than you wanted me. Don't deny that.' You smiled. 'And, Blood, who would blame you?'

'Shen…'

'Please, Kyra, do you really think you'd love me till we died? Do you? I loved you but, in truth, you never really began.' Something like anger rippled across your face. 'You're Kyra Cal'Adra. Too free for such. You were already bored.'

'No. *No.*'

A hand on my shoulder. Grandmother.

'The agony passes soon enough,' she said. 'Trust me. Drink, child. Pluck every woman you wish; none unmarried will deny you. It's what you're good at, Kyra. It's what you are.'

I reached for my sword, but it flew from its sheath before I even touched it.

It hung from Grandmother's longdagger, caught by the finger ring in its swept hilt. It swung gently as she held her blade high and away from me.

I didn't know Grandmother could be so quick. I didn't even know what I would have done if she wasn't. I just wanted to be listened to, to matter.

I was going to cry. Blood, I was going to cry.

I span and pulled the doors open.

Four guards awaited me, Slow Thezda behind them. They seized me as I tried to pass.

I struggled, turned tears to rage, my eyes stinging. Cursing existence with a wordless scream.

'Let her go,' I heard Grandmother say. 'Let her burn it off.'

My sword was suddenly in a guard's hand and he passed it to me.

I took it. Held the hilt to my face. My legs shook.

'She will not hurt herself,' Grandmother assured everybody. Something gilded her tone then, an amused honesty. 'We selfish never do.'

I fell to my knees. I sobbed till I dribbled and shook. I hugged my lonely blade.

I think you said my name, Shen. But then you were gone.

25

'Should have left breadcrumbs or summat,' Shortleg said. 'We could get lost in here.'

'Wind's still behind us,' I whispered to him. 'We'll follow that back.'

We were four floating faces in the black, Benadetta's lamp the only illumination. We had to be careful not to lose our footing in the groove on the floor. We were still descending, though our way was shallower now. I wondered if we were below sea level.

'Stop,' Benadetta said.

We all froze.

Benadetta took a step forward and raised her lantern.

The tunnel split into three.

'Bollocks,' Shortleg said. 'C'mon, fuck this palaver, let's go back.'

'We need more evidence,' Benadetta countered. 'Thus far we've an empty cave.'

'We'll get lost.'

'Trust in the Pilgrim, Mr Shortleg.'

He almost replied but shut his lamplit mouth.

'Strange, these grooves,' Benadetta noted. She pointed at the unbroken lines along the floor, walls and ceiling.

'How so?' I asked.

'There were six when we entered. There's currently seven where we stand.' She pointed at the left tunnel ahead of us. 'Nine.' Then the middle one. 'Twelve.' The right. 'Four.'

'Well, what could it mean?' I said.

'Perhaps nothing,' Benadetta said. 'Perhaps the number is irrelevant. Perhaps the symbolism of the groove itself is the answer.'

She wasn't stammering any longer. Likely she thought her god was in her again.

'So what do these grooves symbolise?' I said.

'Absolutely no idea.'

I gave her a look.

'Propulsion,' Nail said behind us.

We all looked at him.

'They say devils—' He nodded at Benadetta. '—and fomorg—' He nodded at me. '—take any shape they desire. But in their own lair, why bother? They would build hallways not for man, but for their own bodies.' He gestured a hand around the tunnel. 'We look upon paths that suit their form best.'

All of us took the scene in. What would something that needed grooves fifteen feet up the walls and twenty on the ceiling look like?

'The one time you speechify,' Shortleg said to Nail, 'and you use it to turn our undercrackers brown.'

'Which tunnel?' Benadetta asked Nail.

'The right one,' Nail suggested. 'Only four grooves.' He pulled out his spear. 'Slower propulsion.'

He walked ahead. Benadetta followed. Shortleg and I looked at one another, then did likewise before darkness consumed us.

'My lamp,' Benadetta said. 'It's… brightening.'

She was right. It shone paler, whiter. The walls of the tunnel were discernible ahead as it descended and dipped.

'The air perhaps?' I suggested.

'Perhaps.'

'Why in't we choking?' Shortleg said. 'Wyrd air'd choke us.'

'Stop,' I said.

Everyone did.

The light cast upon the walls did not flicker. A static light, like day only far greyer.

'It's not the lamp,' I said. 'Put it out.'

Benadetta looked at me and licked her fingers, an action I found awkwardly captivating. She placed her fingers within the skin of the lamp and snuffed its wick.

The grey light remained. Like nothing I'd ever seen.

'Evidence,' Shortleg said, nodding. 'Let's go back, eh?'

'But evidence of what?' I said.

'Who cares? Summat fucking evil.'

Nail shrugged. He walked ahead, spear in hand.

'A valiant soul, Nail,' Benadetta said. She glanced at Shortleg.

'Fucking alright then,' Shortleg mumbled. He pulled out his axe from the sash it hung from and followed Nail.

'Cal'Adra,' Benadetta said.

I looked at her.

Her brown eyes were black in the strange light, her skin pale as milk. Her full mouth parted, ready to speak. She was taking me in, my face, my eyes.

'Cal'Adra,' she repeated. 'I—'

'You should come see this,' Shortleg said, simultaneously trying to call to us and whisper.

Benadetta nodded to him and walked over. I followed.

The four grooves glowed white. That is to say, a thin line of pure white lay at the bottom of each groove. Above our heads, at our feet, to either side, the white stretched on down the tunnel, painting everything with a mute and even luminescence.

'No colour,' Nail said.

He was right. His trousers were black as oil, his scarlet jacket iron grey. His hair white.

I gazed down upon myself. My hands were grey marble. Everything, everything here: black and white and greys between. This light leeched colour from the air.

'What is this stuff?' I asked. 'For Blood's sake, no one touch it.'

'A lichen,' Nail said, studying the white in the groove before his feet. 'A moss.'

'The light in a darkness,' Shortleg said. He looked at me.

Shortleg's devil had said he'd meet me in such a place. But we all knew that.

Benadetta made the sign of the Pilgrim. 'I'll lead from here on in.'

As I followed her a sort of spite arose in me. Whoever meant to mock me, whoever hatched these puerile insidious games, must have pictured Kyra Cal'Adra here all along, as terrified as any sky-deluded human. I spat on the floor. Just lichen. I wasn't scared. No more scared than I would be against blades, at any rate. All here would be explicable. Explicable and banal and no doubt fat with self-interest. Fuck their japery.

The tunnel levelled out and the way got brighter.

We came out into a giant cavern, one that seemed neither worn nor hewn but moulded. Almost a sphere, a hundred feet high, a hundred wide, its grey surface pocked with perhaps three-score tunnel mouths. Each tunnel disgorged its grooves, each carrying the luminous lichen, down toward the cavern's shallow concave floor. The grooves swirled downwards, together forming a pattern like a whirlpool, all winding their way, widdershins, toward a pit at the very centre, some ten feet wide. The glow of the lichen vanished into its blackness.

I gazed upwards, craning my neck.

A hole above, at the very apex of the cavern's roof, ten feet in diameter, like its opposite below. It let in daylight, a spray of gold that soon dissolved amid the colourless grey of the lichen-light. Ringing the roof's hole was a familiar sight: the circle with its spikes.

'Wondrous,' Benadetta muttered.

'Explicable,' I replied. I chewed my lip.

Nail pointed to something at the other side of the cavern.

A pale disc, upright on wooden legs.

'A drum,' I said. One of the great war drums of home. A familiar black glyph upon its skin.

'Explains that booming sound we heard,' Shortleg said.

'More besides.' I chuckled ruefully. 'The symbol upon it is my family's sigil. This is all Grandmother's plan.' Of course. Why hadn't I thought of that? I shook my head. 'Her or my brother.' Damn it. Couldn't they just let me rot? 'You'd all better leave quickly. I'll handle this.'

The cavern screamed.

Ropefaces. Lurching from the tunnel mouths, their robes and masks like iron in the lichen-light. Scores of them.

'Retreat,' Benadetta said.

More screams. Running footfalls. From behind us.

Stupid, stupid. Surrounded. This had been no plan. Awful. Just awful.

Ten ropefaces ran out of the tunnel whence we came.

We braced.

They stopped ten feet before us. They waved their blades and cudgels, screamed and gnashed. Tongues poured from their tattered mouths.

'Well?' Shortleg bellowed at them. 'Come on, yer pricks. Come onnnn!'

The ropefaces screamed back. They swung their weapons in the air, unconcerned for those around them. But their legs kept still as statues.

'Listen to me,' Benadetta tried saying to them, but their screeching and Shortleg's bellows drowned her out.

I looked behind me, at the other ropes. They remained at the mouths of the tunnels along the cavern's hemisphere. Screeching, weapons aloft.

A shadow passed behind them, crossing from one tunnel mouth to the next, left to right, using unseen passageways. After all, it couldn't be passing through walls. It couldn't.

The shadow was a figure striding at leisure, twice the height of a man. Crowned, or maybe horned…

'Twats!' Shortleg was yelling at the ropefaces. He stepped forward, clanked his axehead against their blades.

'Shortleg,' Benadetta said. 'Quiet, I've—'

'Ropey shits! I'll fucking 'av yer! Come-here-get-banged, yer arseholes!'

Damn death wish, Shortleg. Always had.

The shadow figure passed more tunnel mouths, closer to us now, as if heading toward the tunnel we'd come from. Which was impossible because there were no passageways into our tunnel. Its stride was *wrong*. Joints backward, like a goat.

I turned. Benadetta and Nail were trying to pull Shortleg back, Benadetta telling him to be quiet, like it still mattered.

'People,' I barked. No one heard.

The shadow loomed. A silhouette, it strode toward the backs of the ropefaces from our tunnel, its cloaked torso towering over its minions' heads. It stretched its arms wide as it approached. Arms too short for its body, hands too long. Two thumbs either side of either hand.

Light fell upon its face.

Shortleg screamed. I screamed. My muscles froze. I dropped.

My entire body lay paralysed. But a sliver of me, deep inside, was most tickled.

For I suddenly understood.

I awoke atop a wide bed, dazed and without my blades. Deep, inhuman laughter rattled behind me.

Blinking, I realised there was colour in here. No more lichen-light, but sunshine pouring down from some hole above. This was another cave, small, yet simply furnished. A bedroom. Clothes hung from a row of hooks embedded into the rock wall. A wide-brimmed hat and a fake ginger beard hung from one, a green dress from another.

The dress was familiar. Outside Esme's boudoir, the lady who had covered her face had worn that dress.

And the hat? The beard?

Yes, the timber yard. The drunkard in the shed who Rossley had told to fuck off. I hadn't seen his face. I hadn't bothered.

Disguises.

A dark hand fell onto the bed before me. Not a hand; a glove.

Long, with two thumbs, the one beside the little finger stuffed.

More laughter. I tried to rise. My muscles were coming back to life, slowly. I knew this manner of paralysis. I knew it would pass.

Something flew over me. It hit the wall and fell, taking the beard and hat down with it. A hoofed foreleg, carved of dark-oak from the Isle. I'd seen such stilts long ago beneath the woven tree-walls of the observatory, used by lowbloods to collect berries from high branches. Another leg followed. Its loose straps rattled as it hit the wall.

The dark laughter choked off, became a brief vomiting sound. Then returned, but lighter. Female. A laughter that echoed in the caverns of my dreams.

'Shen,' I mumbled.

'Hello, Kyra,' you said.

I screwed my eyes. 'No.'

'Kyra.'

As soon as I'd seen the devil's 'face' I'd truly, finally known a commrach was behind this conspiracy. But I never…

'You can look at me, Kyra. I've removed the terrormask. I've wrapped it in cloth, put it away.'

I wished you still wore it. I wished I believed. I wished you the humans' devil. The fomorg, their Crawling King. Not you, Shen. Please. Not you.

A weight settled behind me on the mattress. I wanted to say *don't touch me*, but I couldn't. Blood, I could not.

You didn't touch. You still knew me. So painfully well.

'You were never in danger,' you said. 'Not really. Nothing you could not cope with. This has all been for you.'

'I don't care,' I muttered. 'I want to go.'

'Go.'

I could hear the soft murmur of waves crashing on cliffs. I didn't move, though my limbs were mine again.

'Curious thing, life,' you said. 'Once, I believed the fomorg would arise again whilst you mocked the notion. Now you spend your time hunting them all over the Main and I...' You paused. 'We are in their very halls, Kyra. And they are empty. The fomorg are long vanished from this world. Only their terror remains. Quite a legacy.'

'Monsters still yet breathe.'

'Kyra—'

'Why do it?' *If I could muster the strength to look at you*, I thought, *I would punch you*. 'You broke me a life ago. Why torment the broken?'

'That's not what I meant at all,' you said.

I faced you. All anger ran from me.

You were the same. I'd wanted you aged, scarred, but you were untouched by the passing years. Your scarlet hair was wild again, no longer in the high style I had last seen you wear. Thick black kohl covered your eyelids, framed your eyes like emeralds in jet. By the Blood. You may as well have run me through.

Those eyes studied me. 'You're my life entire, Kyra Cal'Adra.' You smiled. 'Or should be.'

I looked at your neck. The chain matrimonial still hung there. How could it not? You would have had to cut your own head off to remove the thing.

Red marks about your throat: old and tiny. Attempts to remove it. The chain itself was shiny and fresh.

'Regrets?' I nodded at your neck.

'I do not love you, Kyra.'

'Well that's prologue, bitch.' I frowned.

'But the memory gnaws. A problem with the chain I had never considered. I look at you now and feel no love, not the slightest glimmer, yet the *memory* of love haunts. The shape of it, its hollow borders, worse than a missing limb. You cannot imagine. To know passion inch by inch, own its map, but never feel it. Blood… it is an agony to look at you.'

I nodded. 'Each second a century.'

Fuck, I wanted to hold you. To comfort you. But it would mean nothing. Nothing. Cold marble reaching for a mirror.

My eyes felt sore. I looked at the sliver of mattress between us, a cubit of linen that may as well have been a desert.

'What is all this?' I said. 'Why?'

'Power, of course. That's what birthed it at least. The Roshos wanted to be respected again. To be feared. One night, Arlo Rosho wore a family dreadmask for a jape. He scared some human servants. He never revealed himself to them. At dawn they came to him and his sister, screaming of the devil. Delighted, Arlo appeared to them again in the mask, except this time he told them he had taken their souls. The result?'

'Ropefaces,' I muttered.

'Not quite. But the essence was there. The rope masks were my invention. You think the Roshos had imagination for that?' You paused; I only watched the mattress. Upon it lay a thin bundle of leather pipes wet with your saliva. A vocal device used by actors to create Bolgada's voice in our Isle's most monstrous play. 'Sada Rosho, always the brighter one, could see a greater canvas. The humans have no context for a dreadmask and scant rationality: their church has long seen to that. Sada knew that a dreadmask would terrify a congregation, but a true mask could rape the Main entire. The very existence of the mask upon these shores guaranteed it, like rats fresh to some remote island of dull beasts. A terrormask, handled with cunning, would be as an infection turning the body against itself, hollowing the humans' religion out with its own nightmare logic, its own rules. The Roshos looked beyond returning home. They would seize a continent.'

I looked up a little, at your thighs, tight in their leather trews. 'Sada had you steal one?'

'The city mask of Corso, that had terrified us both so that day. Ah, but how could you forget?'

'You said then how you wished to wear it,' I said.

'The Roshos didn't know how easy to persuade I'd be. I'd been lent greater access to the mask thanks to your family, but in truth I did not need it. No one on the Isle would have considered stealing the thing. And Sada knew about me and you. Ironically, I was easier for her agents to find, despite being on a different landmass. The dutiful wife, slowly dying inside the tower of Cal'Valtah and taking every secret precaution never to conceive. I embarked on a Rosho tradesail the very night the offer came.' You shrugged. 'Sada knew you to be my weakness.'

'She did?' I'd been more naked to Sada than I'd thought. I recalled her twee smile, her mock fragility.

'She wanted to bring you in. You've still power on the Isle, though wrapped in whispers.'

'So she and her brother said. You're all fools.'

'You've never really known yourself, Kyra. That's your perpetual weakness.'

'I killed your father, I know that much.'

I glared at you. I wanted pain to break out across your face like a pox.

'But I *wanted* you to,' you said, another smile. 'Father encouraged me to take the chain. He was our love's enemy.'

'An accessory to her, at best.' I tried to pierce you with my stare. I tried. 'So you were the drunk in the shed? The lady outside Esme's?' I waved at the costumes hanging on the wall behind me. 'The shadow on Sada's ceiling too, I'll wager, swift with your kai-bolg's blade. Fun was it? Watching me frightened, the fool?'

'I had to make sure you were on the right track.'

I scowled.

'Alright,' you said. 'It *was* amusing. Occasionally. But more often it was practical. The taxman you killed, Rossley, helped convert that village to our heresy. He knew. The Roshos wanted him removed, and I wanted his money so that I might act freely from the Roshos. I dug up the money you and your pets buried. Spent it.'

Well, you were one step ahead of Shortleg. I had to give you that much.

'As for dressing as the lady,' you continued, 'I've been visiting your whore Esme for a while. I'd hoped to get information about you out of her, surreptitiously of course, but she's oddly loyal. And each time I paid her to fuck me with her remarkable collection—' You paused, tugging at your chain matrimonial. '—I had to close my eyes, think of my miserable Cal'Valtah husband.' You looked at me. 'You almost caught me out that day. I should have known you were in season.'

I thought of the overpowering perfume the 'Lady' had worn. A veil for your body's scent. 'As were you.'

'Just so.'

'I've a question.'

'Yes?'

'Why do you keep trying to kill me?'

You laughed, covered your mouth. 'I've been bringing you back to *life*, my sweet. I've placed nothing in your way the old

Kyra would not have been quick to handle.' Slowly, you placed your hand on the mattress between us, ready for my touch. You were wise enough not to touch me yourself. Because you knew me, Shen. You knew. 'When I heard tales of you on the mainland, when I saw for myself how you lived, I could have wept. Would have, if not for this chain. You've been rotting, Kyra, don't pretend that's a lie. Your new life, its filth, its emptiness. Your little human "friends".' You giggled, shook your head. 'The Roshos had me using you to achieve their ends and I'd have killed them for that alone, along with their banalities and their incest. But I've only ever tried to restore you through adversity.'

'And if I'd died? If your cultists had killed me at the redoubt? Or the Roshos' guards? Or, or Rossley! If he had—'

'It would have been a mercy.' You sighed. 'Though, sometimes, I wonder if I do all this because it's the only way I can touch you.'

'Ludicrous…' But, Blood, you were right. I'd been a shadow, a shade trying to convince myself I thrived. Filling myself with drink and killing and whores. Trying to never stop, to never sink.

'But you've survived, Kyra,' you said. 'You're better than you ever were. I know I'll love you again. I can see that day.'

Too much. The need, the hate, the…

'You sold all that for a silver chain.' I near-snarled the words. I moved to slap your hand. But I feared touching you. What it might bring.

'Wake up, Kyra. Arise from that pennyblade mire. Can't you see?'

'Aside from a traitor before me?'

'I've eaten the Roshos' plan from the inside as they would

have done to the humans. The terrormask. My own father believed me the fomorg king when I wore it. He was aware of terrormasks, had *seen* dreadmasks. Yet, outside of the theatre, its ancient context, even he fell for the lie. Do *not* underestimate the power it has. Over humans and their sky-mad ignorance. You've seen the fury of my congregation. I've a hundred who'd kill themselves on my command and I have done near-nothing to earn it. Nothing. Imagine if we infected nobles with our devil-love. Imagine kings and bishops and armies. A mere flourish of our hands. It's in humanity's nature, Kyra. They thirst for their own damnation.'

'We?' I barked. 'There's no *we*.'

'Listen, you fool. A mainland united could swarm the Isle, and we know the Isle's weaknesses. I've damned myself taking on this chain, I know that. But do you think I have wallowed? I've *learned*. The Explainers know how to make a chain to cauterise our desires.' You paused, pushed back your wild locks. 'But they also know how to remove it.'

Ice in my belly. Sharp as winter.

'You lie.'

You shook your head. 'It's why I still live. It's my reason for all this.'

I rose to leave. You seized my shoulders and held me. I didn't fight. I gasped at your touch.

'We'll burn the Isle's greatest secret out of itself,' you said. 'We'll break this fucking chain. I know I'll love you more than I ever did, than is even sensible. And I *know* you feel the same. Right here. Right now.' Your grip lessened to an awkward caress. 'Is there even a choice?'

No. My eyes were moist. No. Nothing mattered. Not compared to this. And even if we failed, if you were wrong, deluded, we would have meaning. Meaning was all. Shen and Kyra. Kyra and Shen.

I grabbed your head. 'I hate you.'

'You've every reason.'

'But I've love enough to free you.' Saltwater sliced my cheeks.

'Love enough to burn the world?' you said.

'Is there any other kind?'

We walked arm in arm, as in old days, as on the Isle. Your shoulder felt warm against mine, Shen, a lone heat in the lichen-lit tunnel. But only a literal warmth, not that of comfort, not of affection. I felt only the ghost of those, as how a man who has lost an arm feels it still, years later. A ghost, yes, but also a promise. I would have you again, you me. Through wile and willpower we would restore our tiny world. You and me.

'They fear you even without the mask?' I asked. Two ropefaces bowing, almost cringing, as we passed, their rags and masks grey in the colour-drained air.

'I have it with me,' you said, shaking the robed mask that hung from your other arm like a shield. 'And even without it, they obey.' She spoke loudly: 'Their souls are mine. They know who our master is.'

The two ropefaces shuffled away, clearly nervous. You gave me a look, Shen. The same as when cousin Zymo had acted an idiot. And yet I recalled how you had once set upon Zymo, had turned furious at her disdain toward humans. You had developed a little of that disdain now. It was difficult to reconcile. Perhaps it was the price of your survival. If so, who was I to judge?

But your power was undeniable. You had these human fools. We had them. By the Blood! We had the mainland by the throat.

'Grandmother,' I said as we approached the tunnel's threshold into the great cavern. 'We'll burn your towers.'

You stopped and smiled at me. 'We'll show her what power truly is.'

'And take back our love.'

I leaned in to kiss you, but you were already stepping ahead. Your arm compelled mine to follow.

But only so far as the threshold. I stopped there when I saw those gathered in the cavern's floor below.

Shortleg and Nail knelt upon the smooth rock floor in a space between two of the glowing lichen grooves that comprised the swirl pattern. They'd blades at their throats. Neither saw me. They were still dazed from the terrormask. I knew the look.

Benadetta did. She could not have missed me. She was bound to a heavy wooden chair facing the threshold we had walked through. Her mouth was gagged with rope. To the left of her chair, some six feet away, lay the great hole to who-knew-where at the cavern's very centre. Daylight from the hole above – the only colour in the cavern – shone into the bottomless pit, yet the hole swallowed it utterly.

'Her power lies in her mouth,' you said to me. 'As ours lies in our touch. Stop a Perfecti's mouth and she is nothing. She cannot hurt people then, nor mesmerise them.' You threaded your fingers through mine. 'Speech is a weak thing next to touch.'

You smiled at me. Your green eyes were grey flame ringed with black in the cavern's toneless light, your skin as milk. Your hair dark clouds before a storm.

I looked away from you. Ropefaces were gathering, scores of them in the caves along the cavern's diameter. The beginnings of a vast army, the self-convinced damned. Their very devotion to their god making them thralls to his enemy.

'What is this?' I mumbled.

Your hand in mine, you led me down the decline and onto the cavern's floor.

'I think you know.'

You gestured to the other side of the cavern and a ropeface approached. A woman in a rotting dress, she carried a dark cushion with a sword in a scabbard upon it.

My rapier.

Benadetta's eyes went wide. She struggled against the ropes that held her.

'Fear is the enemy of all great endeavours,' you said. 'And mercy is a mannered fear. I'm not cruel, Kyra. The two men I am happy to convert if they wish it. But these people need to see a Perfecti die. They believe her powers their god's. It must be you who kills her. Only then will they hold you my equal.' You looked up, presented me to the tattered throng. 'We are brides of the Shadow! Queens of the fall!'

I drew my rapier from its scabbard. I held it upwards, between you and I.

'You trust me with this?' I said.

Gently, you pushed the end of the blade against your own neck.

'You could never kill me, Kyra,' you said. 'We both know that.'

By the Blood. You were right.

'She tortured me, Shen,' I admitted. 'She compelled me these last months.'

'Kyra should never be compelled,' you said. 'Not even our Isle could do that.'

'No.' I chuckled, despite myself. I – we – were the freest creatures in existence.

But…

A dark thing to let in the light: that's all this was. I thought of young Ned, his leg in the trap. A kiss and my blade in his throat. If I had waited I would be dead, or so I had thought. A dark thing to let in the light. I…

'She had me tied to a chair just like that.' I turned and pointed my blade at Benadetta. 'Bound me in my season.'

You gripped my shoulder tighter.

'For her god,' I said.

'An excuse.' Your palm slid down my back. 'You need this.'

I stepped forward and you followed, hand still upon me. Strengthening me.

'Kyra.' Shortleg's voice.

'Shut up.' I almost hissed it.

The point hovered above Benadetta's heart. A sharpness that could slip through steel. Magic, touch-imbued, mirror of my being.

Benadetta closed her eyes. She prayed, an awful gurgle within the gag.

'You're not *good*,' I told her. 'Stop thinking you're good. The things you've done to me, and you think yourself one of your martyrs. Well, fuck you, Sister Benadetta. Fuck you!'

Benadetta jolted at my shout. She kept praying as its echo abated. Tears welled.

That praying. That fucking praying.

One tiny push and all these wasted years would vanish. You and me, Shen, on the road to our love. And more. Burning it all, all of it. Everyone and everything that ever hurt us: Grandmother and her tower game; brother and his treasonous weakness; the city. The Blood. And the mainland. The fucking humans, their money, their sky-madness, their wars and their witch-hangings and their pennyblades.

All of it. The waste years. The emptiness.

The emptiness.

And me. Me. Still broken.

Still pouring out snakes. Like Mother had said in my vision. Yes. Here I was, pouring out snakes.

'Shen?'

'Yes?' you whispered.

'I'm tired of digging your heart from the ground.'

I drove my sword point at Benadetta's face, and made the most careful slice.

She spat the gag from her mouth.

'In the name of God and the Pilgrim!' she shouted. No magic: her ordinary voice. 'Begone dark spirits! In the name of God and the Pilgrim! In the name of the Holy Church! Begone!'

You seized my sword hand. Your fingers slipped through the holes in my swept hilt, but you could not take it from me.

We struggled as Benadetta continued to shout.

'In the name of the Pilgrim you are free! In the name of God! By His name!'

'Kill them!' you shouted to your throng.

The ropefaces, every single one of them, merely stood. The two hovering above Shortleg and Nail lowered their blades. Others clutched their heads, some kneeled.

This river of your making flowed both ways, my love.

You let go of me and stepped back. Clawed at the material covering the terrormask in your left hand.

I drove my rapier into it, through the outer cloth and silver and wood and bone inside. I pulled my sword up and the mask left your grip, slid halfway down the blade.

'Kyra!' you squealed.

Benadetta had stopped shouting. The cavern echoed to silence.

'Shortleg,' I said. With a flick of my wrist, I sent the mask over my shoulder and through the air. 'Do what you do best.'

I watched your eyes gape, Shen. Heard a hobnailed boot smash a ten-millennia-old trinket.

Your scream filled the cavern.

I placed my blade on the floor. I stepped toward you.

You were staring. Folk were removing the masks you had given them. They saw you. You, Shen.

Your pretty jaw shook.

'You're a ghost behind a mask, Shen Asu,' I said. 'And now your mask is broken.'

You span toward me. You put your hands through your hair, dead and grey in the lichen-light.

'I did this for *you*,' you pleaded, voice cracking. 'All of this.'

'You really shouldn't have bothered.'

'You *love* me.'

'I lost you. Shen died when she put on that necklace.' I gestured at your throat. 'She put it on because she was weak. Fallible, not the perfection I've conjured in these exiled years. I see that now.' I shivered. 'Ghost.'

You bent double. Tears dripped through your fingers.

Benadetta called on everyone not to approach.

I reached out. I held your face. 'You have to answer for your crimes, ghost. To these humans. Their law.'

You squirmed. You pulled your head from me. 'It cannot end like this. Love ending in – in such hate.'

'Love never ends in hate, Shen. It ends in indifference.'

You winced.

'Well then,' you said. 'Well.'

You stepped over to the hole at the cavern's centre, to its edge, then turned your back to it. You looked serene, calm as the canals of home.

'Kyra? We were… good… yes?'

'We were the world.'

You smiled. You leaned back.

I blinked away a threatening tear. And when my eyes opened you were gone.

26

I shook in the cramped darkness. People shouting outside. I lay on my back amongst ropes and such, maritime things, my legs drawn up to my belly. My sword rattled in its scabbard. Only one ship in port going where I intended. A fucking Rosho vessel.

Like a rat. A fucking rat. How had I been so stupid? How had I thought I could ever escape? They were *here*.

Boots shuffled on the decking. They'd find me. Find me skulking in this… whatever it was, this horizontal cupboard.

'Look this ship over!' Grandmother's voice. Blood. 'Every inch!'

There was no escaping the Isle. Grandmother. My fate. They would drag me out of this box full of rope and walk me back home.

I wasn't what I had been. Everyone would see me: a broken thing, mindless. They'd had to feed me these last weeks, kept me in a locked chamber away from sharp things. All things.

Our family's bondsmen checking each and every nook, the ship's crew mute and scared. What had I done? How was this even a—

Sunlight shone in. I froze.

A silhouette above me, holding open the cupboard-thing's double doors. Two tiny discs shone silver in the morning sunlight.

Slow Thezda. The bondswoman stared at me, her face blank.

She looked up, toward the harbour wall. She shook her head.

The doors closed.

Much later, when darkness had settled, I opened one of the doors a little and stared at the moon. As pale as your face, Shen. I felt seasick.

'Thank you, Thezda.' My voice sounded strange to me.

Two nights till the mainland. I'd leap off in sight of land, the crew, avoid commrach. Then no more Isle, no more rules.

Blood, I was free, whatever that meant.

I supposed I'd soon find out.

27

The four of us walked into the busy quayside in silence, as we had done much of the way. Indeed, little had been said during our whole night's stay at the inn with its repulsive, sword-ignorant owner. Still, he'd let the hitherto ropefaces sleep in his barn while they waited for the Church's investigation. Kind that, considering they'd terrorised his entire family and bollocksed his trade. Humans never cease to confound my expectations.

Benadetta and the rest had questions about you, but not as many as I'd expected.

I was glad. I had no stomach for answers.

The sun was sharp as the brine in our noses. I fucking hate sea air. Trouble is the docks are always where the fun is, at least for pennyblades. Like me.

'My ship,' Benadetta said, coming to a stop. It seemed an arbitrary place, deep amid the passing crowds, a hundred feet from the white unfurled sails. I suppose she didn't want her fellow passengers to see a Perfecti alongside the likes of us.

She turned and faced us. Her robes were as white as the sails.

'Onwards,' she said, smiling perfunctorily. 'Up the coast to Ribot, then old Manca and the Holy P-Palace.' Her eyebrows rose. 'I've... quite the... tale.'

'Sister B,' Shortleg said. 'I don't suppose—'

'Payment? Well, there's the recompense of knowing evil is vanquished.'

'Fuck,' Shortleg muttered.

'And eighty gold pipistrell each, waiting for you in Hoxham,' Benadetta said. 'Present yourselves at St Waleran's in th-thirty days' time.'

Shortleg grumbled, but that was the best he'd get.

Nail looked taken aback. 'Sister?' he said.

'You're free,' she told him. She repeated the word and I shivered with its power.

He swayed on his feet. He pulled the torc from around his neck and stared at it in surprise.

'Keep it,' Benadetta told him. 'Might fetch a price.'

Nail nodded and put it in his jacket's pocket. 'About time.'

For an awkward moment none of us said anything, the passing chatter of the quayside belying our silence. Benadetta looked at me. Her eyes darted to the two men.

'Well,' she said to us all. 'The Church thanks you. Good day.'

She turned and walked away. Some dockers carrying boxes passed between us and then she had vanished in the crowd without so much as a look back.

I had the strangest sensation, as if my veins were emptying.

Now what? I looked up at the sails of Benadetta's ship, as if they might tell me what I felt.

'Oi.'

I turned to Shortleg.

'Go on,' he said. He pointed his chin toward the ship. 'We'll wait for yer here.'

I squinted at him.

He grinned. 'Go *on*, yer daft sprite twat.'

I belted into the throng. I pushed past shoulder blades, slipped between torsos. People swore. A crate might have toppled. I didn't care.

Where was she? Where—

I pushed forward.

There. Her white robes, just before the gangplank.

'Perfecti!'

She didn't hear me.

'Sister!'

A beggar stopped her, asked for a blessing.

I near-tripped over someone's foot. On I pressed.

'Beni!' I said.

She turned and saw me. She looked bemused, as if I were some stranger.

She gave her beggar the quickest benediction and he melted into the throng.

'Cal'Adra?'

I opened my mouth. Shit. I'd no idea what to say. I didn't even know what I was doing.

I chuckled at myself. A false chuckle, scared. I looked at her imploringly. *Tell me what to say, you idiot. Please.*

Benadetta looked down. Her jaw twitched. *Do not do this. You should not have done this.*

By the Blood. What had I been thinking? I looked away toward the dank hull of her ship. She'd be back to her own world soon, I to mine. The sword and the penny and the road.

Our eyes met.

'I can track you, remember?' she said.

'I'll see you? We…' I faltered.

'I keep telling you, you soulless scum.' She grinned. 'I'm in your blood.'

Her little finger enclosed mine, unseen by the multitude. Exquisite.

She let go and made her way up the gangplank. She did not look back.

I almost staggered away. Compelled this way, then that, by the tides of the crowd.

I saw Nail.

'Still here?' I said.

'For now,' he replied.

'Where's Shortleg?'

Nail frowned. He looked over his shoulder. 'He was just behind me.'

'What?'

Realisation hit. The six hundred pips we'd buried under the barn back in Tettleby. I hadn't told him they had already been stolen and spent. He'd sent me after Benadetta so he could get a head start. Bastard. Greedy pennyblade bastard!

I laughed out loud.

Nail looked at me. 'What's so funny?'

'Come on,' I said, slapping his shoulder. 'I'll need you, freak.' Then I ran the way we had come.

The crowds thinned out further up the quay. My run turned to a sprint. I took in great scoops of sea air. I grinned insanely.

'Why are we running?' Nail called behind my shoulder.

I laughed again.

For the first time, Nail did too.

I could see it all now. I'd get my money from St Waleran's. I'd put it towards Esme's dream of a place for women who enjoyed women, men who enjoyed men. Because it felt good to help friends who dreamed large, even if I could not. And I'd persuade Nail and stupid fat Shortleg to chip in too. And Poppi, poor Poppi with her comb and her toy rabbit? We'd get her out of St Waleran's, make her our barmaid. Yes! Why ever not? I could see it all! The world was a fine place, or fine enough, and for the first time in my life I would give back to it. Genuinely.

Seriously.

Oh, come now. Would I lie to you?

ACKNOWLEDGEMENTS

Thank you for reading this book.

I've had so much help from so many people along the way it's frankly embarrassing. Foremost on my list of thank-yous is surely George Sandison, managing editor at Titan Books, who took a risk on Kyra and her gang despite them rocking up at his door in a right old state.

Thanks to Max Edwards, agent extraordinaire. Writing can be a dark and scary alley to wander down and I wouldn't want anyone else watching my back. Max is a genuine marvel.

Thanks to all at Titan, especially marketing director Katharine Carroll, press and marketing officers Sarah Mather and Polly Grice and assistant editors Tasha Qureshi and Michael Beale. I've been as delighted with their enthusiasm as I've been dazzled with their professionalism. I've been utterly spoiled.

You'll have seen the cover of this book by now and thus know I am in utter, utter awe of Julia Lloyd.

All praise to those classiest of cats, my early draft readers. To Matthew Tope, Tim Susman, Farah Mendelsohn, Meg MacDonald and Chris Stabback. They put up with a lot and gave back so much more.

I'm unreasonably lucky to live in the same town as The Speculators, an incredible writers' group. My cap is doffed to each and every member, particularly Phillip Irving, Lucy Mack, Daniel Ribot, Jay Eales, Dennis Foxon, Selina Lock, Will Ellwood, Stephen Payne and Jenny Walklate.

Thank you to Mark Bakowski for all his belief in me and his support. Thanks to Daniel Gilbert, Rhys Davies, Aanant and Attual Chand and Catherine Digman. Thanks to Beg To Differ. Thanks to everyone at Premier Inn Leicester North West. Thanks to all the staff and regulars at The Loaded Dog. Thanks to anyone who I've neglected to mention; I'm a damnable fool and I hope you can forgive me.

A super-duper family-sized thanks to Joel, Tom, Nikki, Lucy, Florence, Jake, Kitty and Ruben. Finally, here's to Patrick and Carol Worrad without whom, dear reader, you would be reading something else entirely right now.

ABOUT THE AUTHOR

J. L. Worrad lives in Leicester, England, and has for almost all his life. He has a degree in Classical Studies from Lampeter University, Wales. He has found this invaluable to his growth as a science-fiction and fantasy writer in that he soon discovered how varied and peculiar human cultures can be. In 2011 Worrad attended Clarion, the prestigious six-week SF workshop held at the University of California, San Diego. There, he studied under some of the genre's leading professionals and also got to see a lot of wild hummingbirds. 2018 saw the publication of his first and second novel, the space opera duology 'Feral Space'. He's had short stories published by *Daily Science Fiction*, *Flurb*, *NewCon Press* and *Obverse Books*. He also writes screenplays for short films, one of which, *Flawless*, was selected for both the Cannes and NYC independent film festivals.

BIRDS OF PARADISE
OLIVER K. LANGMEAD

Many millennia after the fall of Eden, Adam, the first man in creation, still walks the Earth – exhausted by the endless death and destruction, he is a shadow of his former hope and glory. And he is not the only one. The Garden was deconstructed, its pieces scattered across the world and its inhabitants condemned to live out immortal lives, hiding in plain sight from generations of mankind.

But now pieces of the Garden are turning up on the Earth. After centuries of loneliness, Adam, haunted by the golden time at the beginning of Creation, is determined to save the pieces of his long lost home. With the help of Eden's undying exiles, he must stop Eden becoming the plaything of mankind.

Adam journeys across America and the British Isles with Magpie, Owl, and other animals, gathering the scattered pieces of Paradise. As the country floods once more, Adam must risk it all to rescue his friends and his home – because rebuilding the Garden might be the key to rebuilding his life.

"Fresh, fast-paced and wholly immersive. Love it!"
– Joanne Harris, author of *Chocolat*

"Astonishing. Riveting. Powerful mythic fiction."
– Ellen Kushner, author of *Swordspoint*

"*Birds of Paradise* sits in a place between Plato and John Wick, a place which frankly I didn't know existed. And it is profoundly human too: whoever has ever known loss will resonate with it."
– Francesco Dimitri, author of *The Book of Hidden Things*

For more fantastic fiction, author events,
exclusive excerpts, competitions, limited editions and more